BULLETS IN THE SAND

BULLETS IN THE SAND

AJ ABERFORD

This edition produced in Great Britain in 2022

by Hobeck Books Limited, Unit 14, Sugnall Business Centre, Sugnall, Stafford, Staffordshire, ST21 6NF

www.hobeck.net

Copyright © AJ Aberford 2022

This book is entirely a work of fiction. The names, characters and incidents portrayed in this novel are the work of the author's imagination. Any resemblance to actual persons (living or dead), events or localities is entirely coincidental.

AJ Aberford has asserted his right under the Copyright, Design and Patents Act X-Bo88 to be identified as the author of this work.

All rights reserved. No parts of this book may be used or reproduced by any means, graphic, electronic, or mechanical, including photocopying, recording, taping or by any information storage retrieval system without the written permission of the copyright holder.

A CIP catalogue for this book is available from the British Library.

ISBN 978-1-913-793-85-2

Cover design by Spiffing Covers

www.spiffingcovers.com

Printed and bound in Great Britain by Clays Ltd, Elcograf S.p.A.

PRAISE FOR THE GEORGE ZAMMIT CRIME SERIES

BODIES IN THE WATER – BOOK ONE IN THE GEORGE ZAMMIT CRIME SERIES

'I thought I knew everything about murders in the Med – not so – this series is a fantastic read!'
Robert Daws, bestselling author of the *Rock* crime series

'What a fantastic debut thriller from AJ Abeford! *Bodies in the Water* gives the real lowdown about crime and corruption in the Mediterranean, in an adventure that ranges from the tourist enclaves of Malta to the war-torn deserts of Libya and weaves together an intricate tale of murder, human trafficking, money laundering, terrorism and organised crime. In the centre of it all is Detective George Zammit, an intriguing new character on the crime thriller scene who is sure to become an instant fan favourite. Meticulously researched by someone who clearly has a deep understanding of the subject matter, *Bodies in the Water* rattles on at a supercharged pace, leaving the reader waiting expectantly for the next novel in what is destined to be a hugely popular new series.'
J.T. Brannan, bestselling thriller and mystery author

'I am definitely a fan of George and 100% will look forward to reading the next in the series.' Alex Jones

'… a cracker. Organised crime, people smuggling, run ins with ISAL and the hapless Detective George Zammit. Tricksy as a Zen novel.' Pete Fleming

'Highly emotive and gripping.' Louise Cannon

'I really enjoyed it. The writing was crisp and flowed well. The characters were strong and it was interesting how their paths crossed. The pace was excellent.' ThrillerMan

'I enjoyed this book immensely … very exciting and unpredictable.' Sarah Leck

'What started as a cross between *The Godfather* and *Midsomer Mysteries* soon developed into a twisty thriller, full of humour and coincidence where you can't help but root for unlikely hero, Inspector George Zammit.' Angela Paull

AUTHOR'S NOTE

Although the plot points are inspired by the political circumstances and certain events at the time of writing, the story is the product of my imagination and not intended to be an accurate account of any such real-life events or a comment on any of the people who may have been involved in them.

Malta is a small island and three-quarters of the population share the same one hundred most common surnames. As a result, there's a chance I have inadvertently given a character the same name as someone alive or maybe dead. If that is the case, I apologise. The events, dialogue and characters in this book were created for the purposes of fictionalisation. Any resemblance of any character or corporation to any entity, or to a person, alive or dead, is purely coincidental.

ARE YOU A THRILLER SEEKER?

Hobeck Books is an independent publisher of crime, thrillers and suspense fiction and we have one aim – to bring you the books you want to read.

For more details about our books, our authors and our plans, plus the chance to download free novellas, sign up for our newsletter at **www.hobeck.net**.

You can also find us on Twitter **@hobeckbooks** or on Facebook **www.facebook.com/hobeckbooks10**.

To my family and my wife's family, who stuck close and tight during the pandemic, helping us to bear our losses and keep our hope.

PROLOGUE
SANT'AGATA PRISON, AVELLINO, ITALY

THE CORRECTIONAL FACILITY of Sant'Agata was hidden away in a wooded area of Avellino province, in the Campania region of Southern Italy. As it accommodated a good number of senior organised-crime figures, and other wealthy white-collar prisoners, its governor and his crew provided a menu of special privileges, on a pay-to-stay basis, to help their guests pass the time more comfortably.

Over the previous four years Sergio Rossi had enjoyed the full range of these concessions, from specially prepared meals to, initially at least, fortnightly visits from his girlfriend, Carlita. His wife, when she was inclined, only visited on his name day and religious holidays. He received an ample supply of cigarettes, DVDs, and even had access to a sports streaming package, direct to the TV in his cell. It was true, he had it better than most, but other more important promises had been broken and that had gradually eaten away his trust in his former associates, to such a point that he now harboured feelings of profound illwill towards them.

He had been sentenced over four years ago. This morning, his term was up. At 08:00, he was free to go. He had paid the price, and anger at his treatment by those he had trusted had helped him survive the physical confinement. During that time there had been plenty of opportunity for him to plan how to avenge himself on those associates who had persuaded him to take the fall for their criminal enterprise, only to abandon him once he was inside.

The buzzer sounded and the steel gate swung open – he was free. Before he crossed the threshold to freedom, he spat on the floor in front of him. Unless a person had survived confinement, they could never understand that no revenge would ever be sweet enough to compensate for the loss of four years of normal life. No revenge would ever be harsh enough to redress the humiliation and insult of standing trial, displayed in a glass box. All because of what had turned out to be a misplaced sense of loyalty. Sergio had agreed to accept sole responsibility for an oil-smuggling conspiracy so that others could remain free.

The prison was set in open countryside. A double wire fence separated the inmates from the fields and forests beyond. Sergio walked out into the sunlit car park and paused to view the facility from an outsider's perspective. It was a stylish three-storey building, with tasteful grey and brown cladding on its lower faces. Only the undersized windows spoke of its true purpose. It looked more like a heavily protected junior school than a prison. Turning his back on Sant'Agata, he immediately spotted the immaculately clean black saloon with heavily tinted windows, parked at the edge of the car park.

Sergio was short, with a barrel chest and long grey hair that he wore swept back behind his ears. The time inside had taken its toll, but he still looked good for a man in his mid-fifties. The occupants of the car recognised him and the doors swung open. Two men got out. Both were wearing black suits, white open-necked shirts and sunglasses. One was holding a silver tray, with a glass and a bottle of champagne on it. Sergio walked towards them, pinning a big Sicilian smile to his sallow face.

"Signor Rossi, Salvatore Randazzo sends his regards and is looking forward to meeting you." The man held out a brimming glass as he spoke and gestured to the back seat while his companion, smiling broadly, bowed slightly and held the door open for Sergio.

He hesitated, one hand on the door, the other around the stem of the glass. He drank some and felt the entire four-year experience begin to recede. He allowed himself to smile, as some of the accumulated anger and hurt started to subside, but his words were still pointed.

"So, he couldn't be bothered to come himself? A big man now, *si*?"

"Please, Signor Rossi." The driver bobbed his head and waved him into the back of the car.

When it had become apparent that someone would need to go to jail and Sergio had been informed that he should be that person, Salvatore Randazzo had replaced him as head of operations within the Family. Though the Wise Men of their organisation favoured Randazzo, who was clever, good looking and hungry for success, Sergio had found him arrogant and disrespectful. Salvatore had never visited him once in the four years he had been inside, preferring to send messages through intermediaries and grudgingly conduct the occasional brief conversation with Sergio by mobile phone, until it seemed he started to find even these irksome and left further calls unanswered. It had been agreed that Sergio would be *distanced* during his time inside. Nevertheless, it still hurt his pride and he thought the behaviour of the younger man at best, discourteous, at worst, insolent and short-sighted.

The rear passenger door shut behind him, with a solid clunk; the driver and his partner got into the front seats. He sank back into the comfortable leather upholstery, taking another long swallow from his glass. As he refilled it from the bottle left in a wine cooler beside him, he noticed a glass screen between the front and rear seats and rapped on it.

"Where're we going – what's the plan?"

To his surprise, the men did not drop the screen, but

continued to look straight ahead, while the one in the passenger seat replied through an intercom.

"We're going to Naples, Signore. It'll take an hour, so relax, drink champagne and enjoy the journey. There, we'll meet Signor Randazzo."

Sergio realised his phone was in his bag, which the guys had put into the boot of the car. He banged on the screen again.

"Hey!"

"Signore?"

"I need my phone, it's in the boot. Pull over."

There was no reply from the men in front, who continued to stare at the road ahead. The intercom went dead. The car rolled on, with no change of pace. Sergio banged on the window again.

"Hey, pull over, I want my phone!"

The silence from the front started to unnerve him. He tried once more, banging frantically on the glass.

"I'm telling you, *stronzi*, pull over – now!"

He put his hand on the door handle and was not entirely surprised to find it locked. Starting to feel uneasy, he sank back in the soft leather seat.

"Listen, you dickheads – let me out now. You don't know who you're messing with."

The intercom crackled.

"Signor Rossi, we know exactly who you are and we've got our instructions. Please, sit back. Everything is fine. There's nothing to be concerned about."

There was nothing dignified Sergio could do in response, other than set his jaw and stay silent. His body tensed, his heart rate began to race. He acknowledged to himself that he was afraid. The only weapon to hand was the champagne bottle. He put it to his mouth, half-full, and took a long draught.

The single carriageway road from the prison ran through countryside for a while, before it joined the state highway to Naples. After only ten minutes, however, the car slowed. To Sergio's increasing alarm, it pulled off onto a rough, unmade track, leading up a gentle slope bordered by a thick scrub of willows and poplars. Beyond this, they found themselves in an area of reforested pines and cypresses. Not that Sergio noticed the details clearly – his mounting sense of unease was now verging on panic. His breath was coming in short sharp bursts, sweat beading on his brow and upper lip.

He shouted and swung at the glass screen with the base of the champagne bottle. It bounced back at him each time he lashed out until, with a gasp of despair, he realised the screen was not glass, but a thick sheet of acrylic – probably designed to be bullet-proof. The car turned off the track and slowly edged its way towards a small clearing amongst the trees. He could not believe what was happening. This was it. The Family wanted him dead. The intercom came on. The man in the passenger seat turned to look at Sergio. His face was completely calm and relaxed, no sign of tension.

"Signore, they told us you'd be a fighter, so we can do this in one of two ways. We're professionals. It can be handled quickly, with respect and without pain. Please, consider that option. It's the best way. Or you can fight and we'll keep you in the car, with the doors locked. We have ten litres of petrol stored behind those bushes and we'll use it to burn you alive. That won't be so quick and there'll be much pain. It's up to you. Either way, the end will be the same."

These chilling words put the matter beyond any doubt. Sergio slumped back in the seat and took a very deep breath. Despite his efforts to appear calm, his voice was shaky and his words garbled.

"I've got money. More money than you can ever imagine. I'll pay you both and then I'll disappear. Tell them it's done and there'll be no trouble. You'll be rich. We're all businessmen, *yes*?"

"I'm sorry, Signore. I have to deliver proof of death, otherwise it'll be me in the back of the car next time. Now, which way is it going to be?"

Sergio was not going down without a fight. There was no

way he was going to sit there and allow the Family to arrange his disappearance. He had one last play left and nothing to lose.

"Do what you have to do."

The men got out of the car and stood well back. With a remote, the driver unlocked the rear doors. After a second, the one behind the driver's seat flew open and Sergio leaped out, head lowered, and charged like a bull towards the men in black suits, champagne bottle in hand. Anticipating exactly that response, the assassins were ready. One raised his Russian PSS silent pistol.

CHAPTER 1
SUPERINTENDENT GEORGE ZAMMIT

ST JULIAN'S POLICE STATION, SPINOLA, MALTA

IT WAS 11 a.m. on a Wednesday morning in early May and Spinola Bay was looking its best: bright sunshine, good-humoured people circulating around the bars and restaurants, the traffic moving smoothly. Superintendent George Zammit, of the Malta Pulizija, was being jostled in a queue by a group of over-excited students from a nearby language school, all clamouring to buy ice cream or soft drinks.

He tried to impose some order.

"Hey, hey! *Mela*, get in line. Come on now!"

A tall Eastern European boy, with blond hair and good teeth, smiled at him and squeezed his shoulder firmly in front of George, blocking his way.

"No time, sir. Only ten minutes for break. I am sorry."

The boy turned away to chat to the two girls he had ushered in ahead of him.

George sighed.

Hands thrust money towards the high counter of the shop front, where a server called Roberto dispensed cones and cans of drink to the crowd of youngsters. He spotted the policeman's reproachful face in the throng below him and shrugged his shoulders.

"Be with you in a minute, George! What can you do?"

He stood his ground, but somehow seemed to move backwards in the queue. He had known Roberto for years; they might even have been at school together, though George could not quite remember. Malta was like that – small enough for everybody to know everybody else.

Feeling the heat of the spring morning sun on his neck, the superintendent put on his sunglasses and loosened his tie. Spring was his favourite time of year. A gentle heat warmed both him and the early-season tourists. Sunlight lit up the brightly coloured fishing boats that rocked on the water, gently stirred by the onshore breeze. At the head of the bay, hotels, apartment blocks and restaurants pressed close to the road that hugged the promenade. It was a colourful and vibrant scene. It was also congested, over-developed and noisy.

Valletta was the island's old-town capital, home to politicians and public officials, but the commercial world revolved around St Julian's. It was here, and in the seedy neighbouring area of Paceville, that the gaming companies and small banks proliferated. It was also in St Julian's that the businessmen and women of the island congregated, meeting in the international hotels and better restaurants, extorting favours, moving money, greasing palms and slowly cementing Malta's reputation as the EU's dirty little sister.

George had been visiting the local police station, where a Latvian croupier was being held. He said he had information about a money-laundering ring operating at a large casino. It transpired the Latvian had a grudge against his manager, who had fired him for signalling hit-or-stand instructions to a long-standing accomplice in blackjack games. George had taken him to one side to tell him his work permit had been revoked. If he did not want to be re-arrested and prosecuted, he must stay away from the casino and leave the island before the weekend.

The Economic Crime Command was already aware of money laundering at the casino, but the time was not quite right for them to act against those involved. A group of Albanians was buying one thousand euro casino cheques from the tellers for one thousand-two hundred euros in cash. He did not want the dealer returning to the casino and upsetting the police surveillance operation before they had finished covertly filming the scam.

George had only just made the front of the icecream queue when the explosion happened. It was a loud, dull crump, unlike any sound he had heard since a trip to Libya four years earlier, when he had encountered hostile militia groups. After his experiences there, he was familiar with the sound of gunfire, grenade and mortar rounds. He instantly knew this sound was no daytime firework, chasing away evil spirits before a religious festival, or noise from a construction site. When he saw a plume of black smoke rising from a residential area a few streets behind him, he knew at once something bad had happened.

He hurried to his car, parked outside the police station, and drove around the corner into The Gardens, an upmarket residential district. It did not take him long to find the source of the trouble.

Along one of the streets of expensive whitewashed villas, smoke billowed high into the clear blue sky. Several agitated people stood outside a house, trying to peer over its high boundary wall. A white metal garage door, that opened onto the street, had been blown off and lay on the road, buckled and twisted. Flames and black oily fumes came gushing across the pavement from the burning vehicle inside the garage.

George drove as near as he could to the house, while phoning the Civil Protection Department HQ in Siġġiewi, telling them to send a fire tender and an ambulance. Then he jumped out of the car and shouted at the bystanders: "Pulizija, stand back, stand back!"

Once the onlookers had retreated, he went up close to the three-metre-high frontage and realised he would have to get over this to see what was happening inside the house. The wall was high and his short, corpulent stature was not made for feats of athleticism such as this. But by using the next-door neighbour's wrought-iron gate as an improvised ladder, he managed to get himself to the top of the wall and look down at the scene of the explosion.

The front of the house had been partially blasted away and was now a pile of stone blocks and rubble. Lying still, on a pile of loose dirt was a small girl, probably six or seven years old. Her arms and legs were in unnatural positions and she was covered in white dust from the blast.

George turned and shouted at the nearest spectator: "There's a child inside. When Civil Protection arrive, tell them I'll get that gate open and bring a medic. I'm going in!"

He swung a leg over and tried to lower himself gently down. The girl was wearing a torn school uniform and her bag lay on the ground nearby. There was a gash on her forehead, presumably from flying debris, but no other visible injuries although one pigtail was bloodstained. George went to kneel down beside her and gently touched her shoulder. She stirred and coughed and looked at him blankly. Then an expression of utter terror took over.

"Thank God! Are you OK? Where does it hurt? Don't be afraid, I'm a policeman."

The girl appeared not to hear and George realised she was deafened by the noise of the explosion. She muttered a few words but they didn't make much sense although he did catch the words 'Mum' and 'Dad'.

"It's OK, help is coming."

Still no response, just a blank look. She stared around her, then seemed to smell the burning rubber and acrid smoke. She visibly tensed, realising something awful had happened. George gently put a hand on her chest to stop her getting to her feet.

"Stay still, don't move. Let's wait for the doctor."

He turned his head back towards the wall and shouted as loudly as he could.

"I need a blanket in here! Please, quickly!"

George had done his first aid course and knew he had to keep her still, awake and warm.

He said, as gently as he could: "You shouldn't really move but you're safe now – is there anybody else inside the house? Who was with you? Do you remember?"

There was no point asking her questions, the girl was dazed and shocked. He saw her looking over towards the blazing vehicle in the shell of the garage. George noticed the side door to the street. He reassured the girl he wasn't leaving and went and opened it. A woman was waiting with a brightly patterned cover from a sofa, that they laid gently over the child. The neighbour stayed with the girl and George went out into the street to be greeted by a silent crowd that had now swollen in numbers. Suddenly, a large black SUV, with American diplomatic plates, came speeding around the corner and screeched to a halt in front of the burning house. Three men jumped out of the vehicle. Two of them ran past George, and through the open side door, into the burning house while the third approached George, waving his arms and shouting.

"Hey, you, come here!"

This man was older than the others, black, with short wiry grey hair and a carefully trimmed beard.

"You!" The man had an American accent and a very bad attitude. He pointed at George and snarled, "Who the fuck are you and what's happened here?"

Feeling all eyes on him, George fronted up to the challenge. He did not like pulling rank, but it seemed it was all this man understood.

"Excuse me, I'm a superintendent of police here and there is no need to talk to me like that. My name is George Zammit and, as you can see, we've got a hell of a problem here. First, let me get some of my men to secure this site. Then you can tell me who you are and what the hell is going on."

"Yeah, OK, OK, sounds good. Sorry, I'm just freaked out by this. Name's Mike Lloyd, Head of Security at the Embassy. The

US Charges d'Affaires lives here, with his wife and daughter. Didn't mean to come across like that." He clenched his teeth and quickly surveyed the scene. "Where's your fire tender? There'll be nothing left in there if it doesn't show up soon!"

George took a deep breath.

"It's on its way. I think there is a body in the car, in the driver's seat and there is a child, who seems shocked, only minor injuries. She's with a neighbour, inside. We're waiting for an ambulance."

"Holy shit! Annie. The girl's called Annie. Poor kid."

George did not reply, he was puzzled by something.

"How d'you get here so quickly? You did it in minutes."

"Look, we know what's happening on this island before it even happens. It's our business after all."

On cue, the fire tender appeared around the corner and Lloyd turned his attention to barking instructions at the bemused fire chief. An ambulance was close behind. The crew took some extinguisher cylinders from the tender and set about spraying the flames, covering the car in a thick layer of foam. Then, unfurling a polyester fire hose, they doused the buildings with water, steam and smoke mingling and drifting in a thick, noxious cloud down the street. Water ran into the gutter, carrying dirt from the explosion and black ash from the fire. The smell of burning rubber and acrid soot hung in the air.

George and Mike Lloyd led the paramedics through the side door and the men in green knelt beside Annie and started to unpack their large medical bags. The American left them to it and began picking around the scene, showing particular interest in the smouldering car, now covered with foam. George, happy Annie was in safe hands. went back out into the street to make a call to Pulizija HQ in Floriana, to let his superiors know what had happened.

In fact, Mike Lloyd had a paygrade well above Head of Security at the Embassy, but the title provided him with the cover he needed for the duration of his stay on Malta. It was twenty minutes before the American came back from inside the wrecked garage and announced: "What d'you know – it's a freakin' car bomb? I thought you guys saved those for your journalists?"

George was surprised by the certainty in his voice.

"How d'you know that – you can't be sure?"

"Three tours in Afghanistan, four years in Iraq – I know a car bomb when I see one, possibly triggered by a motion sensor, don't know yet. Big explosion. No local hoodlum put this together."

"Who was in the car?"

"Definitely Annie's dad, Jim Baxter, our Chargé d'Affaires – number one at the US Embassy. State Department's going to be very pissed. Better tell your guys."

"Who would do this?"

George looked around incredulously.

"Well, there's one helluva question, Superintendent. At the moment, I've got no idea and, even if I had, I wouldn't say. We're gonna crawl all over this. When we're done, we'll let you know what we've found. This ain't a pissing competition, we're going to lead the scene-of-crime stuff. Interfere and I'll have you down at the docks, documenting migrants. Sound fair?"

George pulled himself up to his full height of one and three-quarter metres.

"Have it your way, Mr Lloyd, but you'll need us on the streets to follow through on what you find, so don't get high-handed with me."

"George, come on! This is a diplomatic incident. It's my job to be all over it. And, please, call me Mike – we're all friends here, right?"

He looked at George closely, face breaking into a knowing smile.

"OK, now I've sussed you out. Made a call while I was inside – it pays to know who you're dealing with on this island. You're the Libya hero guy, who machine-gunned those Islamic State dudes and swam back to Malta! All this is pretty weird, 'cos we've been meaning to talk to you."

Four years earlier, George had found himself embroiled in a major criminal conspiracy with its centre of operations in Malta. He had discovered that his superior officer, Assistant Commissioner Gerald Camilleri, had become involved with a shady organised-crime group, known as the Family, who were planning a complex oil-smuggling deal out of war-torn Libya. Camilleri had blackmailed George to go to Tripoli, ostensibly to attend a crime-fighting conference, in reality to smuggle in a briefcase of gold. It was meant as a pay-off to a militia leader, Abdullah Belkacem, who was at the centre of the Libyan end of the arrangements.

George had made contact with Abdullah, but both men nearly lost their lives when they were double-crossed by the Family and ambushed by an extremist Islamic militia, keen to move in on the spoils of the deal.

George and Abdullah escaped and, during their journey to Malta, across desert and sea, forged an unlikely partnership: policeman and people smuggler. It had grown into a friendship that continued to this day. Finding courage, he never knew he had, George had confronted his boss and negotiated a deal. He had used his knowledge of Camilleri's own criminal activities to get Abdullah into the country without being locked up in a camp like the other migrants who ended up on the island. The deal had also secured George's future security. As a newly promoted superintendent in Camilleri's Economic Crime Command, he enjoyed an uneasy peace with his boss, but was aware that he and Abdullah were never far from Camilleri's thoughts and watchful eyes.

"Oh, yes? What do you want to talk to me about?" George asked the American, warily.

"Not about this." Lloyd waved his arm at the car smouldering behind him. "About something else entirely. That Libyan militia guy you brought back in tow, he still around?"

George said nothing, but smiled politely. The conversation went no further. Mike's wife Daisy turned into the street and came running up, bursting through the yellow scene-of-crime tape, like a winning marathon runner.

"Mike – where's Annie?"

"Safe – don't worry, the medics are checking her out. You find Suzanne?"

Daisy drew in her breath sharply and nodded her head.

"Yeah, she's at a gym class. We've sent someone to get her. Where's Jim?"

Mike Lloyd glanced over his shoulder at the blackened wreck of the car, then back at his wife to make sure she understood.

Daisy put her hands over her mouth and her knees buckled slightly. Quickly, she pulled herself together and took a deep breath, saying only: "Oh, sweet Jesus!"

"Will you be here for them? I'm going to be working late. I need to get on top of this."

"Sure, I'll take them home with me, once the medics are done. They'll probably take her over to Mater Dei for a check-up."

Mike nodded grimly in thanks to his wife, who turned away to go and comfort the shell-shocked child while Lloyd stared into the middle distance for a moment, deep in thought.

George stood still, looking on, as Mike Lloyd's private grief almost overwhelmed him. The American allowed himself a pause for private reflection before he spoke again.

"This is a bad day for the Baxter family." He paused before adding menacingly, "And for whichever bastard did this to them."

CHAPTER 2
ARTICLE IN MALTA TELEGRAPH

Reporter: Amy Halliday

22 May 2019

ISIL Kill Ten in Attack on Libyan Gas Plant

The Libyan-Italian joint venture running the VertWay gas pipeline took another blow last week when its facility in Marsabar, western Libya, was taken over for five days by a militia affiliated to Islamic State.

Italian oil company Italbenzina confirmed six Italian engineers and four Libyan workers were killed in an execution-style shooting. There was substantial damage to the gas-compressor facility and also a stretch of the pipeline.

The 540-kilometre VertWay pipeline was inaugurated in 2004 by Silvio Berlusconi and Muammar Gaddafi, and delivered gas from Marsabar to Gela, Sicily. Gas supplies from the Bouri and Wafa fields on the

Algerian border are frequently interrupted by terrorist activity, but this is the first attack on the oil and gas complex itself.

It is believed to have been made by an extreme Islamist militia, led by Abu Muhammad al-Najafi, which has been active in the area for some years. Attacks and kidnapping of industry personnel as well as blackmail are common and hamper the exploitation of Libya's extensive oil and gas resources.

The Libyan Resources Corporation (LRC) in Tripoli say Italbenzina, who operated the gas facility, has terminated its contract and withdrawn its personnel, due to the deterioration in the security situation.

This ends the supply of gas from Libya to Europe and is a blow to the Government of National Accord in Tripoli (GNA), which is engaged in a long-running civil war against the rebel strongman, General Boutros, based in Tobruk in eastern Libya.

The LRC has said that VertWay, which at its peak carried eleven billion cubic metres of gas per annum, has become unviable due to the threat of terrorist attacks. The facility and the pipeline have been sold to Euromasio, a Russian energy company, and the pipeline is to be salvaged for reuse in a carbon-capture project in the Black Sea. The sale includes a provision prohibiting the Russian company from using VertWay to bring gas ashore in Italy, so as to prevent future sales into the protected European market.

CHAPTER 3
YAROSLAV BUKOV
MARSABAR OIL AND GAS INDUSTRIAL COMPLEX, EASTERN LIBYA

Yaroslav Bukov knew all about oil and gas. He was born thirty-five years before in a small village on the Russian side of the Northern Caucasus, a few hundred kilometres across the border from Baku, Azerbaijan, where there was always talk of the money to be made in oil and gas on the shores of the Caspian Sea.

Yaroslav's father had set him to work in the family business when he was a young boy, repairing and maintaining cars and trucks. As a teenager, he graduated to maintaining the massive Kirovet tractors used in the local logging industry, as well as gaining notoriety for the speed of his fists and his willingness to use them.

Although there was a living to be made from his father's garage, it was always clear to Yaroslav that this was not the life for him. Ever since he had seen pictures of the brightly coloured domes of St Basil's, he had wanted to venture north and try his luck in Moscow.

He had no fear of hard work and made the most of the limited education available to him at the under-resourced local school. Afterwards, persuading his father to part with his hard-earned savings, Yaroslav had finally managed to secure a coveted place at the Gubkin Russian State University of Oil and Gas, in Moscow, where he had studied for another five years.

During that time, his keen intelligence and prowess in the mixed martial arts clubs, and underground street fighting scene, brought the well-built and formidable young man to the attention of the security services, who scouted the universities for talent. He was introduced to an officer in the KGB, later known as the FSB, where he was eventually employed looking at the new oil and gas technologies in the West, surreptitiously bringing useful knowledge, or sometimes people, back home, bypassing the problems of sanctions and embargos.

Yaroslav had developed his twin-track career in security and engineering, being placed into large infrastructure projects such as the Druzhba pipeline, which took crude oil 5,000 kilometres from Tatarstan to refineries in Eastern Europe. There, he had learned what was involved in moving huge volumes of oil and gas over enormous distances, in terrain that was hostile, both physically and politically.

Over the years, the FSB developed his practical skills in exploiting the Republic's resources, usually for those citizens most favoured by the higher echelons of the party. He became a wellknown and trusted operator in Russia's highly valued energy sector. His technical abilities were matched by his absence of scruples and willingness to adopt the more ruthless practices of the FSB.

He reported to a high-placed official within the energy department of Russia's Duma, Valentin Petrov. Like Yaroslav, Petrov operated between the spheres of state and so-called private enterprise. He made sure all the money flowed in the right direction – and that was not always towards the Federal Treasury.

That was how Yaroslav Bukov found himself stepping out of an armoured transport helicopter onto the car park of the Marsabar Oil and Gas Industrial Complex, in western Libya, the first Russian to visit their newly acquired gas distribution facility.

As the helicopter engines fell silent and the dust storm cleared, six heavily armed Volunteers, private contractors from the Russkaya Volonterskaya Gruppa, jumped out of the machine and formed a perimeter, their automatic weapons sweeping the car park.

Yaroslav saw the complex had sustained physical damage from the recent terrorist attack. Twisted pipework and scorch marks on some of the plant spoke of RPGs and mortar explosions. He was making a mental note of the damage when he noticed a portly figure, in black trousers and a white short-sleeved shirt, walking across the car park towards him.

Adel Abu Khader ran the complex. His political bosses had asked him to give Yaroslav a tour of the site and walk him around the gas facility Euromasio had acquired from the Italians. Yaroslav wanted his visit to be as brief as possible. He did not trust Abu Muhammad's militia, nor anyone else in Libya. The fact that it was he himself who had arranged for the Islamist militia to attack the refinery did not necessarily guarantee his safety.

He had commissioned a show of force as the last act in a campaign to frighten the Italians out of their deal with the LRC to operate the pipeline. The death of the Italbenzina engineers and the locals had not been part of the arrangement and Yaroslav saw their execution as gratuitous and unnecessary, but it had taught him that Abu Muhammad was not afraid to follow his own agenda. At least the murders had been effective in hastening the sale of the facility to the Russian state-owned company Euromasio.

The men introduced themselves and shook hands. Yaroslav looked around the massive complex, with its towering stacks and tank farms. Kilometres of stainless-steel pipework looped and stretched through manifolds and pump systems, spreading their tendrils to every corner of the plant.

"How big?"

"The site is four hundred hectares; three hundred for refinery and storage, and the rest, your gas facility."

Yaroslav looked towards some fire-damaged tanks, on the edge of the car park.

"Was there much damage to the refinery?"

"Not too much, but with gas plant any damage is bad news …" Khader shrugged. "They don't usually come into the refinery. They must have wanted the Italians and the VertWay pipeline for some reason."

"How many dead?"

"The militia were here five days. They killed six Italians and four local workers, destroyed the stabilisation and compression facility and pumped concrete down the pipeline. They took a barge and ripped up more pipe – how far out, I don't know. The VertWay pipeline is fucked and the Italians have gone. Too dangerous for them."

"Five days? Why did no one come and stop them?"

"If there was a firefight, Tripoli was worried they might do more damage to the oil refinery. That's more important, both to Tripoli and Abu Muhammad. Gas is no use to the militias; they can't easily move it or sell it, but they can move oil, in road and sea tankers. Gas is not so easy for them."

"So why did ISIS kill the Italians?"

Khader smiled and raised his eyebrows.

"Well, first, it wasn't ISIS, it was the ISIL break-off group, Islamic State-in-Libya. Still ISIS, but they make their own agenda. Secondly, militias usually attack the pipelines in the desert. It's safer for them and just as bad for us. This time, they hit the gas facility itself. They scared off the Italians – and then you arrive and buy the place for a few dinars. Forgive me, but I find that a big coincidence."

Yaroslav looked the man straight in the eye and did not comment.

"OK, let me see the damage," was all he said.

Khader was still curious.

"Why have you bought a wrecked gas terminal, a damaged pipeline, and also agreed not to send gas to Europe? It makes no sense."

"We need pipes for carbon-capture project in Black Sea. Simple."

Khader looked at Yaroslav and caught the slight smile at the corners of his mouth. He did not believe a word of it.

The Russian spent the next two hours filming and exploring the wrecked gas plant, making a careful inventory of the damage. When he had finished, he took a walk down the two-kilometre-long finger of jetty, extending into the gentian waters of the Mediterranean, where the tankers came to load the refined oil. Once satisfied he was beyond earshot, Yaroslav took out a satellite phone from his rucksack and rang Petrov in Moscow.

"It's a mess, but we can do something with it. I'll send you the report and photos once I get back to Malta."

"OK, so now we start the next part of the project? Finding some friends there to help us."

"Yes, I've been asking around. There're a few people I can talk to. You won't remember, but a few years ago there was a high-profile oil-smuggling racket, broken up by the Italian Guardia di Finanza. A group of big European players was behind it. This could be right up their street."

CHAPTER 4
ABDULLAH BELKACEM

ABDULLAH'S HARDWARE STORE,
BIRKIRKARA, MALTA

BIRKIRKARA HARDWARE STORE was a successful little enterprise. It opened at 06:30 in the morning and did not close until 20:00 in the evening. It was a Mecca for the many local builders and tradesmen, who were busy making money from the Malta property boom. When Abdullah had originally bought the business, he knew nothing about ironmongery and, to make a sale, had to get the customers to point to what they needed and then tell him, in English and Maltese, the name of each item. It greatly amused the buyers who, in exchange for helping him learn his trade, blatantly cheated him on the prices.

He had bought the shop soon after he had arrived in Malta, after his and George's escape from Libya. Abdullah's migrant-trafficking and oil-smuggling days were over and his brother Tareq lay buried in a field, not far from the scene of their gunfight with the same Islamic State militia that had recently attacked the Marsabar Industrial Complex. To Abdullah's relief, his remaining family lived hidden deep in the Nafusa Hills on the border with Tunisia.

Once it was clear he would gain the protection of the Maltese state and, in time, a red EU passport, thanks to Camilleri's intervention, he had to find a way to house and feed himself. He was determined not to end up marooned in one of the open camps to the south of the island, along with hundreds of other exploited maritime migrants, begging for day work. A small shop, with a flat above, seemed the perfect arrangement.

Despite his humble shopkeeper status, Abdullah had arrived in Malta with the fortune in gold that George had been forced by Assistant Commissioner Camilleri to deliver to him in Libya. This was downpayment for Abdullah's part in an oil-smuggling operation. Fortunately, he had managed to hang onto it when the smuggling ring decided to double-cross him and George and he had been forced to flee Libya, pursued by Abu Muhammad and his Islamic State-in-Libya militia.

Hard work took Abdullah's mind off the enforced separation from his family, distracting him from brooding on the revenge he had promised to take on Abu Muhammad. As time passed, he had come to accept the loss of his home, brother and a large part of his wealth, doubtless looted from his stronghold by the enemy, but the estrangement from his wife and sons still chewed him up inside.

His eldest boy, Jamal, was sixteen already – nearly a man. Abdullah had not seen him for four years. But until he could find a way to return to Libya, strong enough to challenge Abu Muhammad and make things right, he had to bide his time in Malta, selling lengths of guttering, tap fittings and brushes, while learning to laugh along with his thieving customers.

Abdullah had been busy ordering stock when he received a call from George.

"Abdullah, I'm confused. Why would the Head of Security for the American Embassy be asking about you? I'm sure it's not for home improvements. Is there something I should know? Something you haven't been telling me?"

"My friend, you worry me by asking this question! I do not know any Americans and I have upset no Americans. That does not mean they will not poke their noses into my business. All I know about Americans is that they cause much trouble, wherever they go."

"*Mela*, that's true, but it bothers me there's this big explosion in St Julian's and, straight afterwards, they want to talk to you."

"*Wallah*, I swear to God, it will be a short conversation. I know nothing of that."

"OK, I believe you, but keep your eyes open. I suspect you'll have visitors very soon."

That very night, Abdullah was closing his shop, taking the display of hardware in from the pavement, when a large black car with tinted windows drove slowly down the road and parked opposite the shop. He was nervous after the conversation with George and did not want to risk being dragged off to Cuba or somewhere, so quickly went inside, locked the door and pulled the shutters down. He was upstairs in his flat, checking out the vehicle through the window, when his phone rang in his pocket.

It was George.

"Abdullah, it's me. I can see you peering through the upstairs blinds! Come down and open the door. We need to talk to you."

"Who are you with in that big black car? I do not know why I ask ... I know the answer already!"

"Don't worry, come down. All will become clear."

Abdullah went down, raised the shutters and cracked open the door. George was there, together with the tall policeman Camilleri, immaculate, as always in a navy double-breasted pinstripe suit. Abdullah could also see a medium-built black man, with grey hair and a close-cropped beard. He wore tan chinos, with a thick brown belt and a white polo shirt. The casual look was completed with a pair of bright blue trainers. Flanking the door, facing the street, were two heavy-set men in black suits, their earpieces visible.

"Hah!" Abdullah said, smiling and pushing the door wide open. "The mysterious Americans have arrived. Tell those two to sit in the car. The neighbours will think I am being arrested. It is hard enough being a Muslim in a Catholic country, without security people outside my door!"

The older American called to the men.

"Go sit in the car, guys. You're scaring the locals."

Abdullah turned and gave a nod to George, then tentatively shook Camilleri's long smooth fingers. He remembered the senior policeman preferred to avoid firm handshakes.

"So, Mr Chief Policeman, this is my shop. It is good, is it not? You see, I am a Berber, we know what it is to work. I have made much money. *Inshallah!*"

Assistant Commissioner Camilleri could hardly get into the shop for the piles of stock. Lengths of guttering were racked from the ceiling, lowering its height, so that he had to stoop to avoid causing an avalanche of grey plastic. The floors were littered with ladders, plastic boxes and buckets, which were usually stacked outside on the pavement when the shop was open. Although it appeared to be chaos, Abdullah now boasted he could find any item requested within seconds.

"Yes, a great success obviously." The Assistant Commissioner faked a smile.

Abdullah knew Camilleri was a manipulative, two-faced viper. His arrival with the American was interesting, but also unsettling.

"So, gentlemen, have you come to buy a coil of wire? Some tubs of silicone maybe? There is always a good discount for my policemen friends."

George stopped him with a wave of his hand.

"There's no room to talk, can we go up to the flat? I'll make tea and the Assistant Commissioner will explain why we're here."

The party climbed the narrow stone staircase, the American looking around to make a full assessment of his surroundings. George had been there many times and expertly weaved his way around the piles of stock that had been stashed to one side of the staircase. He went to the kitchen unit in the corner of the living room, put the kettle on and got out the small glasses they used for mint tea. Abdullah shuffled the three chairs around. George leaned against the sink and raised his hand, letting his friend know he was happy to stand.

Camilleri sat and watched. When the three of them were seated with a glass of tea in their hand, he closed his eyes and started to speak.

"Abdullah Belkacem, let me tell you a story. Let us see if you recognise the person I speak of. There is a man who has been badly wronged and who yearns for revenge. He has not seen his family for over four years; his children have forgotten what he looks like. His brother lies unavenged in a grave in the desert. All that he once had – money, respect, power, a good family life – is now gone. Once, he had a vision for the future of his town, his district, maybe even his country. But now he is just an Arab ... sorry, a Berber, selling brushes and bags of plaster to ungrateful Maltese. They show him none of the respect he deserves; they laugh at his accent and his religion; they cheat and steal from him, when his back is turned. Do you recognise this man?"

Abdullah said nothing, but glanced at the American sitting across the table from him, whose name he still did not know. He had sunk back into his chair and the tightness of his frown had bunched his features together.

Camilleri continued talking, unperturbed.

"This can all be fixed. How would you like to go back to Libya, with weapons, intelligence support, protection, enough money to buy yourself an army? You can fight the Islamic State barbarians on your own soil and Boutros's militia from the east. You can restore your prosperity and become the man you once were – and more besides. If the years in Malta have not softened you, and if you can still raise men to support you, my friend here can organise that and give you all the help you need."

He nodded at the grey-haired American, who frowned and flared his nostrils, considering his words before he spoke.

"Maybe I can," the American said, running his hand across

his beard. "I'm Mike Lloyd. I fix things. I have everything the Assistant Commissioner mentioned – and some. I have drones, satellite imagery, special forces, artillery. All that you need to wage a war.

"We want the Russian advisers and mercenaries out of western Libya – and with bloody noses. We want the IS jackals to back off the western oil fields, and we want Khalifa Boutros back in Tobruk, or, better still, dead with his army in the dust.

"And another thing – we believe the Russians working out of Libya, busy killing your people by the hundreds, came over to Malta and, for some reason, blew up a good friend of mine. If they wanted to provoke me, they've succeeded.

"It can't be done in a weekend, but we'd like to make a start now before it gets too late. They tell me you're our man."

Abdullah looked at George, still leaning against the sink, keeping a poker face. Abdullah relaxed and sat forward, on the edge of his chair, a half-smile on his face.

He turned to George and said: "What exactly have you been saying to your friends? I do not know who they think I am! Is there more of that tea? This could be thirsty work. I have some questions I would like to ask."

On the way out, two hours later, Camilleri lingered to commandeer Mike Lloyd, taking him aside so they could speak discreetly.

"I hope you have authority for this project and all those promises you made, because a mere Embassy Head of Security would certainly not."

"Well, same, same, Assistant Commissioner. One day you gotta tell me where your authority to act in this venture comes from – 'cos I'm willing to bet the Police Department knows diddly squat about it!"

CHAPTER 5
ARTICLE IN MALTA TELEGRAPH

Reporter: Amy Halliday

27 May 2019

Fight for Tripoli Enters New Phase

Reports of rocket attacks on the outskirts of Tripoli have spread alarm, as General Boutros's Libyan National Army (LNA) advances towards the capital. The Government of National Accord (GNA)in Tripoli has appealed to the UN to intervene and negotiate a ceasefire, as civilian casualties mount.

The LNA is supported by the United Arab Emirates and Egypt, who see Boutros as a trusted partner, capable of curbing the spread of political Islam in Libya. The GNA in Tripoli have strong ties to the Muslim Brotherhood, who believe the Islamic Sharia should be the basis for organising the affairs of state and society.

The UAE has supplied the LNA with air support, Chinese-made Wing Loong II drones and weapon systems for the advance. They also have funding from Saudi Arabia, the support of at least 1,000 Sudanese troops and the presence of a similar number of Russian mercenaries from Russkaya Volonterskaya Gruppa. Russia is bidding to become a power-broker in the oil-rich North African country.

The incumbent GNA in Tripoli, on the other hand, has the backing of Turkey, who say they have sent drones and troops, 'not to fight, but to support the legitimate government and avoid a humanitarian tragedy'. Qatar, which is more tolerant of the Islamist elements in Tripoli's government, has also provided funds and military resources to the GNA.

So far, the United States has refused to become involved, but recent comments from the White House suggest that some form of intervention may be necessary if Libya is not to become another Syria.

Meanwhile, the UN's efforts to achieve a ceasefire continue, General Boutros's advance on Tripoli progresses and casualties mount.

CHAPTER 6
YAROSLAV BUKOV
PHARAOH'S CASINO, MALTA

On first arriving in Malta, Yaroslav had taken stock of the island. As a former British colony, 300 kilometres off the North African coast, things looked to be in decent shape. The roads were in serviceable condition, health care was good, tourism was booming and Malta had established itself as a financial services centre. Just as the Caymans, Jersey and Mauritius operated as a back door for money to creep in and out of the US, UK and India, so Malta did for the EU.

He found there were a good many Russians already on the island. Specialist shops sold food from home and quality vodka; tall blonde Slavic-faced beauties, with hard, tanned bodies, jogged up and down the Sliema promenade; and over a thousand Russian 'entrepreneurs' had bought Maltese passports, allowing them easy access, in and out of the EU.

Yaroslav was aware of the recent case of attempted oil smuggling from Libya. While, as an oil man, he found such activities irritating, he felt a grudging admiration for the scale of the operation and the ambition of those who had organised it. He thought, if he could meet them in person, he would be able to judge at once whether they would be of use to him.

After a few false starts, a Russian banker told him he had

found those Yaroslav needed to speak to. The banker described an old and respected Maltese family, with extensive connections across the island and Europe. It had international business interests, deep pockets, was highly secretive and, if so inclined, could get any deal here completed. It had been rumoured they had been involved in the ill-fated oil-smuggling venture a few years previously, but following its collapse, had withdrawn from the commercial life of the island. The banker thought, if the deal was attractive enough, the time might be right to lure them back into the open.

Making contact with them had proved difficult – Yaroslav had needed a middle man to meet a middle man! The person who finally agreed to see if a meeting could be arranged was an Assistant Commissioner in Malta's police force, one Gerald Camilleri.

It had taken several days of talks to confirm his credentials, but eventually Yaroslav had met with a member of the Family. She turned out to be a striking, tall woman with long dark hair, who spoke English with a faint Italian accent. She was in her early-thirties, olive-skinned, with the indefinable air of a person who had always had everything they wanted as by right. When they met in the casino, she looked stunning, in a long, sparkling, high-necked black evening dress that hugged her figure. She introduced herself as Natasha Bonnici.

After the introductions, she casually played a few spins of the roulette wheel, taking low-denomination chips from a small black clutch bag. After a few minutes, she took her modest winnings, pushed a chip towards the croupier as a tip and they went to a secluded table at the back of the gaming floor. Her security sat at the bar, a discreet distance away, but not so far that Yaroslav did not notice. The woman did not indulge in small talk.

"Let me tell you, we don't do business with Russians because it always ends badly," she began. "That's been our experience over the course of the last two hundred years."

Yaroslav laughed briefly.

"As a Russian businessman, what can I say? But, believe me, I work very hard to find you. Finally, I understand – if there is big pan-European project, with need of patience, resources, connections and vision, your organisation is one of few who can do it. What my project is? I tell you more about it."

She said: "You understand, I'm just a messenger. Tell me what you can. You've got my full attention and an hour of my time. I can't promise you anything in advance. Unless you persuade me there's something of interest to us here, I'll tell you nothing about us. It's not meant to be discourteous, just how we prefer to operate."

What Yaroslav had subsequently learned was that Natasha Bonnici not only had a day job as CEO of a major i-Gaming business, but was also part of a very old organisation, which she referred to simply as the Family, based in Milan. Historically, they had traded across Europe as a financial guild, but the collapse of the Hapsburg Empire and two world wars had taken their toll on the wealth so far accumulated. These days, the Family had interests in commercial property, construction, banking and insurance. More recently, their focus had shifted to energy.

That was how it had started.

CHAPTER 7
NATASHA BONNICI
PIPO'S BAR, ST PAUL'S, MALTA

ON THE SURFACE, BetHi was a hugely successful company, raking in cash and Bitcoin through its virtual casino, sports betting and live gaming lounges. What was not apparent was that it was also one of the most successful money-laundering operations in Europe, washing the ill-gotten gains from the Family's many international enterprises. It had previously traded under the name BetSlick, but Camilleri advised the company to close and reappear under a different name, so he could protect the business from further police enquiries, following the collapse of the oil-smuggling plan.

That afternoon, Natasha hurried out of her office, well before her normal departure time, shouting over her shoulder that she had a meeting and would not be back. She drove her two-seater sports car out of the underground garage and took the coast road north, towards the resort town of St Paul's, but instead of heading inland towards the family home in the hills, she drove down to the sea front and parked alongside Pipo's Bar, a small place with dated illuminated plastic signage, more frequented by locals than the tourists.

She watched the door for a few moments and then looked up and down the promenade. Seeing nothing amiss, she quickly slipped off her heels and took some flipflops from her gym bag. She grabbed her hair, twisted it into a rough ponytail and pushed it through the back of a Yankees baseball cap. A baggy, light-grey hooded top covered her Italian silk blouse, which completed the deconstruction of her classy and glamorous work persona. Natasha covered the upper part of her face with some large, cheap sunglasses, hunched her shoulders, plunged her hands deep into the pockets of the hoody and, deliberately altering her gait, slouched into the bar. Over the last four years, magazine articles and TV appearances had brought the young, good-looking female CEO of one of the island's biggest leisure industries into the public eye. Now, she doubted she would be recognised.

Il-Barri, or The Bull, sat at one end of the bar, his dead eyes staring vacantly into space. The nickname perfectly suited the middle-aged, short, flat-faced barrel of a man, who was a small-time fisherman by day but, when ashore, would use his strength to break fingers and arms for a few euros – or, for a few more, necks. Few would join *Il-Barri* on his brightly painted open boat as it was known the catch was always poor. They said his mere presence was enough to send the shoals diving for deep waters.

He did not move or cast a sideways glance as Natasha sat beside him and reached into her gym bag. She noticed the faint smell of the sea about him and recoiled slightly from the sight of a smattering of fish scales that glistened on his temple. She slipped him an A4 envelope with six photographs inside, given to her by Camilleri. These were the brashly dressed young Albanian blades who had had the cheek, stupidity or ignorance to use the Family-owned casino for their own amateur, unauthorised money-laundering operation.

A second envelope was stuffed with fifty-euro notes. *Il-Barri* reached out, sensing the money, pulled it across the bar top and weighed it in his meaty fist. He said nothing, but turned his head to look at her for the first time. Natasha said: "For that amount of money, you know what I want."

He remained silent, continuing his study of the middle distance ahead.

She knew she should not get personally involved in this sort of thing; she had a host of security people who could take care of business. But she enjoyed it! On the way home, she entertained herself by thinking what misery *Il-Barri* would inflict on the hapless Albanians. When the stupid girls at the cashdesk, who had facilitated the scheme realised what had happened to their clients, she would let them fret and panic for a week or so. Then, just when they thought they had avoided any punishment, she would give *Il-Barri* another envelope of fifty-euro notes. The casino could not afford to get a reputation for being a soft touch.

'Albanians,' she thought, 'always trouble.' She wondered if her father had forgotten, or forgiven her, for the incident with Elbasan, another Albanian. She had used him to set up Nick Walker, her predecessor as CEO at BetSlick, as the business had then been called, and her boyfriend at the time. Nick had held the position she coveted, so Natasha had worked with Elbasan to frame him for the theft of several hundred thousand euros.

All things considered, it had worked out well, given she had been able to step into the job she had wanted so badly. What had not gone so well was the violent quarrel that had blown up between her and Nick. It had resulted in her being injured with a blow from a heavy Murano glass vase, when Nick believed she was about to fire a gun at him. Her lover had left her lying on the floor of his villa, in a pool of blood, and fled the country, with her father, Marco Bonnici, and her Uncle Sergio in hot pursuit.

It had not gone so well for Elbasan, either. He had known too much about Natasha's part in framing Nick and, soon afterwards, had been found dead in the car park of Malta's Aquarium, killed by a vehicle that had repeatedly driven back and forth over his body. Her father had made the connection and been horrified.

Once the business in St Paul's was finished, Natasha turned out of town and up towards the small hilltop hamlet of Il-

Wardija. She felt a keen sense of anticipation as she drove down the narrow, stone-walled lanes on the approach to the family *castello*. Today was special. Her father was coming home!

Whether Marco Bonnici was quite as thrilled to be reunited with his daughter again remained to be seen. Following the unravelling of their oil-smuggling scheme, and the winding up of BetSlick's original money-laundering operation, Marco had felt it best to drop out of the commercial and social life of the island for a few years.

Assistant Commissioner Camilleri had told him he had nothing to fear. The Family's sacrifice and the subsequent conviction of his cousin and best friend, Sergio Rossi, would be sufficient to satisfy the Maltese and Italian authorities that justice had been done. Nevertheless, Marco was tired, stressed and troubled. So he had taken a sabbatical on a secluded estate he owned in western Serbia.

Before Marco had left Malta, he had confessed to Natasha that he was actually fearful of what she had become. For that reason, he felt he had to put some distance between them. Time had helped to soothe his concern and disappointment in her, but he still approached their reunion with a degree of wariness.

Natasha had no such reservations about his return. As far as she was concerned, the past was the past and she had long since set those unpleasant incidents aside. In fact, she rarely thought about them at all.

Her father's return now was a matter of expediency; she needed his help. The conversation with Yaroslav had been more than interesting – it had been exciting. It was many years since an opportunity with such potential had presented itself to the Family, let alone to the Bonnicis.

Petrov, Yaroslav's boss, had planned all along to find a way to bring the Libyan gas through VertFlow and then, via a short spur, into Malta. There was then nothing to stop a Maltese-owned company from piping the gas the hundred kilometres or so to

Sicily, so as to achieve wider European distribution. After all, Malta was in the EU and had access to all its markets.

In the great game of exploiting global energy resources, Russia had made a play to get cheap African gas into Europe, picking up a major pipeline for a few kopeks, and Natasha had managed to win the Bonnicis a seat at the table. This opportunity could help her advance her ultimate personal ambition to occupy an even more prominent seat, heading the *Familia con pane*, or Family for short.

But, for all this to work, she knew she needed her father's connections, wisdom, reputation and support. The Libya deal was potentially massive for a small island like Malta – or 'transformational', as Salvatore would say.

Then there was Salvatore Randazzo himself, the new broom who had replaced Uncle Sergio, following his imprisonment and then shocking murder shortly after leaving Sant'Agata. Salvatore had stepped into his shoes, as the link between the Bonnicis and the Family's Wise Men in Milan. Things between Natasha and Salvatore had soon become difficult.

Salvatore's charm, his crystal blue eyes and dark good looks, were self-evident; he was an attractive man. More out of curiosity than any real affection for him, Natasha had succumbed to a brief affair. She had quickly discovered it had been a mistake. Salvatore Randazzo was an individual with an iron will and a highly developed need for control. For all his easy manners, he was, at heart, as cold as ice, and just as hard. She had continued with the relationship for as long as she had dared, to see how it would play out. He was one of the Family's foremost protégés, a favoured son, so Natasha had been keen to take his measure. If her long-term plans were successful, they would find themselves in competition for power within the Family one day. What better way to prepare for this eventuality than to stay close to him, while she had the chance?

His violent temper had showed itself on several occasions and Natasha had mentally stood back and studied him when he tried to threaten and even physically intimidate her. She was not frightened, but found it interesting to see there was violence in him.

During their last argument, when Natasha had had enough of his behaviour, she had told him that, if his manners continued to be a problem, she would ask the Wise Men to intervene – a scenario she knew he would find deeply humiliating.

It was a low blow, but one she had not been able to resist. She had stood in front of him, smiling, and threatened to tell the Wise Men he had been abusive and about his 'unnatural inclinations'. 'No smoke without fire, Salvatore!' She could tell he was mortified and had secretly rejoiced while she needled his pride and revealed herself to him as a dangerous adversary.

Natasha knew that, one day, the rift between them would have to be allowed to reach its natural conclusion. But, in the meantime, an uneasy truce prevailed, each of them watching the other closely. Natasha was always prepared to play the long game.

CHAPTER 8
SUPERINTENDENT GEORGE ZAMMIT
POLICE HEADQUARTERS, FLORIANA, MALTA

OVER THE LAST FEW YEARS, George had found working for Assistant Commissioner Camilleri quite tolerable. He had never crossed his boss, did exactly what was asked of him and looked the other way when required. Camilleri had also got to know George well enough to be confident he would not knowingly disrupt the smooth running of the AC's lucrative sidelines and that, whenever there was a choice, his superintendent would always opt for a quiet life.

Camilleri acted as a one-man regulator. As with much of the southern Mediterranean, crime and corruption were a fact of life in Malta and, rather than try to fight this, he worked with it, curbing excess and limiting the damage to uninvolved civilians. An upper class of politically connected businessmen plundered government revenues, while a cadre of East European and Asian immigrants based themselves on the island, to enjoy the benefits of an EU passport and Malta's flexible financial regulation. Camilleri knew most of the prominent players and, as long as their activities remained within limits and they observed certain proprieties, he allowed them to operate.

George had managed to avoid becoming involved in anything too distasteful. As he had suspected, his accelerated promotion to superintendent had been mainly so that Camilleri could keep a close eye on him and make sure he continued to appreciate the benefits of remaining silent about the Assistant Commissioner's role as facilitator for the Family, as well as Malta's wider commercial and political fraternity. That did not mean George had stopped mistrusting him, or that he was not still a little afraid of his superior.

The day after meeting Abdullah in his shop, George was summoned to Camilleri's office. Although this no longer filled him with dread, he was always suspicious of what Camilleri might be up to and whether it would upset the equilibrium of his superintendent's uneventful life. That day, he guessed the AC merely wanted to follow up on the meeting with Abdullah and there seemed no undue reason to be concerned.

As George was walking out of the shop the previous evening, his friend had looked at him with his eyebrows raised, making a telephone sign with his thumb and little finger. Later that evening, they had spoken.

"So, my friend, you are now a spy, as well as a policeman! Indeed, you have many talents."

"*Mela*, what do you think? Do you really want to do this?"

"I have been waiting four years. The old policeman is right – he knows who I am and I must trust in Allah and follow his plan, *Inshallah*. I will go back with the Americans."

"Do you trust him?"

"You brought him to me, my friend. If you trust him, who am I to doubt you?"

"Don't put this on me! It's your neck on the line, not mine. You could just stay here, bring your family over, educate your sons and have a good life – safe and free. Think carefully, Abdullah.

"You're not as young as you were. You haven't held a gun for four years. The Americans have big plans. They want war in your country. It mightn't be what you expect."

"You are right. I would lie if I said I did not feel this in my stomach. But there is work to be done, my friend. I would be a coward if I did not take this chance. Allah has smiled on me and brought me good friends who will help me. I will go back."

George did not think too hard about who those *good friends* were. With hindsight, he should have paid more attention.

So, today he approached Camilleri's lair cautiously, but with few real misgivings. The Assistant Commissioner's office was an austere, uncluttered corner room in the stone-built Victorian police headquarters. There was a single pile of papers on the desk before him, no family photographs or career trophies, and no potted plants. Instead, the large office benefited from spectacular views down onto the Msida Marina and over to the high rises of Sliema. George could picture Camilleri sitting at the huge oval rosewood conference table that occupied half the room, deep in thought, like a chess-playing spider, mapping the moves ahead and setting traps for the unwary.

His boss had already taken a seat at the head of the table and George sat to one side of him, at a strategic distance. Camilleri placed his elbows on the shining wood. George could smell the lemon-scented polish on it. He also noticed Camilleri had his palms together, fingers steepled, as if in prayer. It was always a sure sign he was about to embark on a difficult conversation. George went onto full alert.

"Well, your friend Abdullah is happy to exchange his life as an ironmonger for a return to being a warlord – this time, a very powerful warlord indeed. Chances are, he will be dead in a matter of months, of course. There is no guarantee of longevity, doing what he is going to do." Camilleri paused, his creepy, trademark mirthless smile spreading across his face. "I really hope you last longer than he does."

In the past, George would have spluttered and claimed he did not understand, but he had learned such a reaction only played into the Assistant Commissioner's hands. He was obviously intent on following a script he had prepared before they had even sat down. George remained silent.

"You must be a very loyal friend to Mr Belkacem. I do not know the full details of what you got up to on your last adventure, but he sees you as a very different person from the one I have come to know."

Abdullah held to a mistaken notion that George was a soldier, a born warrior. Circumstances had cast him in a heroic light while he was in Libya. They had twice been forced to fight the Islamic State–in-Libya militia and Abdullah had seen George kill several of their fighters; some in reaction to the desperate situation, some by accident and some out of blind panic. However, it was also true that George had, in the past, been a champion huntsman and a medallist in both the bullseye and rapid-fire competitions, on the police range at Pembroke. His marksmanship had undoubtedly saved Abdullah's life when they had been ambushed; his friend's brother, Tareq, had been less fortunate.

It was something Abdullah never forgot and never stopped alluding to. He would point to himself and say: '*I saw it with my own eyes. These eyes do not lie.*'

"Anyway," said Camilleri, "you know how keen we are to develop our people, and nowhere more so than in the Economic Crime Command. So, a development opportunity has arisen and I expect you to grasp it with both hands."

George's eyes widened and his mouth went dry. Last time a *development opportunity* had presented itself, it had led to George's nearly being murdered in Libya. All he could do was stare blankly at Camilleri and wait for him to continue.

"Not surprisingly, your friend Abdullah has accepted the Americans' offer of a return to Libya, in order to embark on a suicide mission against Islamic State-in-Libya, while also trying to prevent the militias in the east from gaining Tripoli. I hope Marianna can afford to do without you for a few weeks … well, months, possibly … because your friend wants you to accompany him to Libya, as his special adviser. How is that for a show of trust, George? You should be flattered."

George's mind started racing but words were beyond him.

After a few speechless seconds, he stammered: "M-m-mela, I can't. It's my daughter's engagement p-party in two weeks!"

It was true. Gina was getting engaged to Giorgio, a presentable local boy who worked at Mifsud's, the butcher on Birkirkara High Street. George's wife, Marianna, was delighted by the whole affair and the engagement party, to be held in their house, had been her only topic of conversation for the last month. Her husband's absence was unthinkable – but, looking at Camilleri, George realised such an excuse would not be good enough to get him out of whatever had been arranged.

The last time Abdullah and George had been thrown together in Libya it had been a nightmare from which George had only just managed to escape with his life. He did not want to repeat the experience.

"Assistant Commissioner, what use would I be in Libya? I'm a policeman, not a soldier. I haven't fired a gun in months. I've got duties here. I'm needed at home. Please, you can't ask me to do this, especially not there!"

He realised he was whining, and it was unbecoming of a senior officer in the Pulizija to behave like that, but he could not help himself. A feeling of desperation engulfed him. It was all starting again. Camilleri was sitting back in his chair, face inscrutable. It seemed to George that his boss was actually enjoying watching him squirm.

"Well, George, I do not think Abdullah wants you there for your military prowess or your leadership capabilities. I agree, you need to develop your skills in these departments. He obviously wants you there as a guarantor, so that he is not abandoned should things go wrong. If you like, I see your role as that of willing hostage. He saw how you secured his safety, and his asylum case, on the last occasion you decided to meddle in affairs well above your rank. So, I can see why he is keen for you to accompany him this time.

"Anyway, there is not a lot I can do about it as our American friends are insisting that all his conditions are met. They feel he and, by association, you, are crucial to their venture. Geopolitics, George – you are playing in the big league now! If only I were a few years younger …"

George was beyond words. He could barely stand to listen to what Camilleri had to say next. The Assistant Commissioner dropped the faintly mocking tone and switched back to business.

"You fly out next week, to the American Al-Udeid Air Base in Qatar. Apparently, it is the biggest in the Middle East and home to their Special Operations Command. It is a very impressive set-up, I am told. They run an induction course for desert warfare. I believe it is run by the Green Berets, or Commandos, something like that, very competent people. You will be perfectly safe! Anyway, that is where the whole thing is being managed from. So do your best, fly the flag for the Pulizija. I know you will not let us down. I will try to arrange a hardship allowance for you. Something to cheer you up if things get uncomfortable at home. Marianna will be pleased about that, at least."

CHAPTER 9
MARCO BONNICI
CASTELLO BONNICI

It was late afternoon when Marco heard Natasha's car crunching on the gravel, under the portico that sheltered the double front doors. He rose from his easy chair in the library to go and meet her. Despite his reservations about returning to Malta, Natasha was his only child and he could not help but smile as he watched her step out of the car into the bright afternoon sunlight. He jogged down the short flight of entrance stairs to hug her tightly.

"Welcome home, Natasha!"

"You're the one who's been away," she replied. "How's everything here? I hope it's to your satisfaction. I broke all my nails for you yesterday, cleaning this place!"

"I noticed the smell of polish – but I did not think it would be you, down on your hands and knees, scrubbing floors. Things have changed!"

"OK, you're right, I got some contractors in."

The *castello* was a large, fortified limestone building with crenellated towers to each corner. It stood inside a substantial estate, with olive groves and vineyards planted in narrow terraces that stepped down the valley sides, towards the coast.

As a home, the *castello* had a somewhat gloomy atmosphere with its heavy, dark antique furniture, long stone corridors, hallways hung with tapestries, and suits of armour standing to attention. But, to Natasha, it was what she knew and she had spent many happy times here while being brought up by her father. Her mother had died in a freak accident, falling on the main staircase, to which Natasha had been the only witness when she was just five years old.

Marco looked around the cavernous hallway, breathing in deeply, taking in the ancient, musty aromas of smoke, leather and tobacco.

"The house is the house, I am sure it has not changed from one century to the next, but the garden is a bloody mess!" he said.

"That's down to you, Dad. Nobody dares mess with your garden."

They went through the house and outside onto the rear terrace. Natasha sat in one of the wicker armchairs and took in the view over the resort of St Paul's. To the north, across the channel, she could clearly see the grey limestone cliffs of the island of Gozo, whose bells, when the wind was right, could be heard here even though they were ten kilometres away. The familiarity of the view comforted her. Marco appeared with a bottle of their own wine, from the fridge in the breakfast room, and pulled the cork. He poured two glasses, then dipped his nose to take in the aroma.

"This is last year's; young, probably a little sweet, but quite palatable. Well, to Sergio." He raised the glass. "He always hated our wine. Maintained it bore no comparison to the Sicilian stuff. Stubborn to the end."

It was the first time they had been together and able to speak properly since his death.

"I'm sorry about Sergio, Dad. I know how close you were to him. What happened? Tell me what you heard."

Marco sighed deeply.

"I rang Salvatore as soon as I could and he told me very little. Later, he conceded Sergio had become a loose cannon, forever making a nuisance of himself. It seems, rather than acting contrite for the mess in Libya and doing his time quietly, he developed a sense of entitlement. Started to make demands for the future, which others found unreasonable." Marco paused, rolling the wine around his mouth, savouring the developing citrus flavours.

"Apparently, he wanted the Family to give him a sizeable stake and set him up in Argentina. Imagine how that went down!"

Marco smiled at the thought.

"Sergio was always headstrong – it got him into trouble all the time. He never cared or watched what he said. Apparently, he made some threats about what he might do if he did not get his way, which was the last straw. He threatened Signor Bruno directly. Well, even Sergio should have known you cannot go around threatening the Wise Men. Prison brought out his Sicilian side and Signor Bruno, in particular, did not like that. The Milanese have firm views about good breeding and manners. Ever since he was young, Sergio was always a bit of an outsider. That is what I liked about him."

"But then they murdered him, Natasha. Shot him down, in cold blood, and burned his body. They have never done that to one of our own before. I will never forgive them for it."

They both sat in silence for a few seconds.

"Are we tainted by association?" Natasha asked.

Marco laughed.

"No, they will not bother us. Malta is regarded as an outpost. I make sure I do not get too involved in the Family's internal politics. But do not underestimate the importance of this gas deal. It has certainly raised your profile. It is massive, even by the standards of the Family. How is Signor Bruno, by the way? He must be getting on these days."

Natasha had done a post-graduate business degree in California and then worked for an American bank in London, before returning to Malta. Then, she had caught the eye of Signor

Bruno, a former assistant governor of the Banca d'Italia and now the most senior of the Family's Wise Men, or governing body. She currently worked for him two days a week, helping him to look after the trusts and corporate structures that the Family used to conceal its less legitimate business affairs, as well as managing its complex banking and accounting operations. It was tricky to combine her job at BetHi with the work for Signor Bruno, but Natasha was not afraid of hard work and long hours. Nor would she have missed the opportunity to learn as much as she could about the internal affairs of the Family.

"Signor Bruno's much the same. I keep watching and learning. I do exactly what he asks and still make the fortnightly trip to Milan, to report direct to him. I'm not sure how much he trusts me; he seems to be closer to Salvatore. Maybe he doesn't like women?" She shrugged. "When I mentioned the approach from the Russians, the first thing he asked me was whether I had told Salvatore."

"Had you?"

"No way! He would probably have spun it as his idea all along."

Marco smiled. He knew Natasha had a plan to ingratiate herself with the old man and, for the time being, was being outplayed by Salvatore.

"Well, do not let Salvatore Randazzo get under your skin. If you can bring this deal home, you will be well thought of for years to come and this generation of the Family will feel it has acquitted itself well. Legacy is important to old men, remember."

Marco cradled the cold glass between his hands.

"We have to be careful, Natasha ... or rather, you have to be careful. I am yesterday's man; they will not bother about me. But you? You are pushing yourself forward and that gets noticed. People will be watching you closely."

He looked over the valley at the olive groves below. It was early evening and the cicadas were rattling away, like high-speed maracas. Years ago, his father had planted a small orchard of orange trees, just below the terrace, so the fragrant smell of the blossom and fruit would be caught by the onshore breeze that blew up the hill. He inhaled the scent and confessed to himself he had missed it all: a glass of wine, the company of his daughter, the warmth and scents of a Maltese afternoon. He turned his attention back to Natasha.

"Speaking of which, Salvatore telephoned me in Serbia, you know, before all this business. I got the feeling you and he were getting on much better then than you are now. It set my antennae twitching. Is there something I should know?"

He smiled and sat back in his chair. She lowered her eyes to show him there was nothing she could keep secret from her father – except everything of real importance, she reflected.

"Hmmm ... you guessed! Well, OK, we'd a thing going at the end of last year. It was lovely, but not long-lived. We went on trips to Venice and Scotland, but I realised he's a strange man – and not for me. He needs a nice Milanese wife who will shut up, do what she's told and not ask too many questions. I told him things wouldn't work out between us and he didn't take it well. He's been in a sulk ever since."

Marco understood and nodded along with her words.

He looked at his daughter, sitting there in front of him, smiling, relaxed, beautiful. He hated the way he always doubted her, but could think of no good reason why she should involve herself with a duplicitous snake like Salvatore, other than to further some agenda of her own.

"Well, the best thing we can do is keep pressing forward and get this gas deal finalised."

"Well, yeah," said Natasha, "but I've got some concerns about it. We've got a lot of work to do. Signor Bruno has split the deal in two. At the Malta end, we've got to work with the Russians, get the gas onshore and organise all the construction, as well as lay a new underwater pipeline from Malta to Sicily. Salvatore is then going to buy the gas from us in Sicily and organise its onward sale into the wider European transmission network. Oh, and I nearly forgot – we also need a programme of works to pipe the gas to every house on the island. Sounds simple, doesn't it? Well, it's not!"

Marco pondered and said: "It seems everything hangs on the cheaper gas from Libya that the Russians have promised. But when all is said and done, this *is* the Russians and the Libyans we are talking about …"

"True, but they've never reneged on a deal like this. It would send a terrible signal to the markets if they did. The Libyans need the money and the Russians claim they and their allies can manage security."

"OK, maybe you are right. I hope so. What about our friends in Castille – are they on board?"

The Auberge de Castille housed the office of the Maltese Prime Minister, from which his advisers and favoured ministers ran the country in the traditional southern Mediterranean way.

"That's one of the reasons I need you back. They smell money. The conversion of the island to natural gas is a huge political deal. Brussels is talking about a fortune in grants to support the idea. You can imagine the opportunities in construction!"

"But the Russians aren't in control of western Libya yet. Or am I wrong? We are gambling, what, two hundred million?"

"There are considerable financial risks, yes."

"Have you met these Russians? What are they like?"

"The lead is an oil and gas guy, in his late-thirties, Yaroslav Bukov. He's worked pipelines all over Europe and knows the technical stuff backwards. He's nobody's fool – smiles a lot, but is as arrogant as hell! I suspect he's tied in with Russian security services. He's on the island now. I thought we could meet him tomorrow and I will introduce you. Let you get a feel for him."

"OK, sounds sensible."

Marco heaved himself out of the chair and pushed his glasses up onto his greying, wiry hair. He looked tired already and he had only been back a couple of hours.

CHAPTER 10
SUPERINTENDENT GEORGE ZAMMIT'S HOUSE

SUPERINTENDENT GEORGE ZAMMIT'S HOUSE

GEORGE NEEDED to tell Marianna about his conversation with Camilleri. There seemed no right time to approach the subject, as party planning was all she and Gina talked about. Excitement crackled through the house like a charge of static. When things were going her way, Marianna was a delight to be around but, when they were not, there was usually trouble.

At the end of dinner, two nights after his meeting with Camilleri, he thought he had caught her in an exceptionally good mood. Responses to their invitation to celebrate the engagement were flooding in and she had just got him to agree to hire a traditional accordion player to entertain the guests while the buffet was being served.

George decided to seize the moment.

"*Mela*, I've got some news of my own. I had a meeting with Camilleri and he's got a job for me, outside the country. I'm not sure how long I'll be gone. It's all a bit hush-hush."

"Well, that's exciting. How many shirts will you need?"

"It's not exactly like that."

"Well, what exactly is it like?"

"The dates are, sort of, flexible. I mean … I don't really know when I'll be back."

"How can you not know when you'll be back? How long is this going to be for? One or two days ... a week?"

"*Mela*, as I said, Camilleri wasn't sure – he said it could be up to a month."

George clenched his teeth and tensed his body. That was it, the touchpaper had been lit. It took a while for her to realise the enormity of what had just been said. She was humming a tune while wiping the dinner dishes. The humming suddenly stopped and her whole body went rigid. Marianna turned to look at him, her face twisted with disbelief.

"A month? No, that's impossible."

"I'm afraid it isn't. I've tried everything I can to get out it – but I just can't."

"You know what that means?"

"Yes, I'm sorry."

He saw the tears welling up in her eyes. Marianna threw down the tea towel and started to cry – not out of sorrow, but pure frustration. Within moments, this turned to rage and she was shaking with it. Gina came rushing into the kitchen to see what the commotion was about, and her mother told her, through sobs: "Your father has said he doesn't want to come to your party and would rather work!"

"Gina love, that's not true. I've been told I have to go away for work. I can't help it."

His daughter looked at him in disbelief.

"No, Dad, no! That can't be true! Let someone else go."

"I'm sorry, I've tried, but it has to be me."

Her wailing soon joined that of her mother, which brought Denzel, George's eldest child, rushing into the kitchen. He had graduated from the Police Cadets and was now working as a constable in the Immigration section of the Pulizija, George's old department. He looked at the wailing women and his hapless father, cowering by the sink.

"What the hell's going on?"

Marianna rounded on her son.

"I suppose you've got some lame excuse not to come to the party as well? You men – you just please yourselves and don't care about all the effort we put into things. Neither of you cares about anything!" She turned to George. "How can I invite the Assistant Commissioner, if you're not going to be here?"

Denzel was confused.

"What's this got to do with anything? Is Assistant Commissioner Camilleri coming to the engagement party?"

"No," George shouted, "he's not!" The thought of his conniving boss here in their home, patronising George's friends and family, made him shudder. Then it dawned on him – he should have paid more attention to the guest list. "Who else have you invited that I need to know about?"

The tears abruptly stopped and his wife looked at him sheepishly, with a sideways glance, her head held low. George knew immediately there was more to come.

"*Mela*, tell me who else. Tell me!"

Marianna had an incredible ability to infuriate him. He knew there was something she was hiding behind the tears and swollen eyes. She often got carried away, over-excitable even, and, when that happened, was capable of extraordinary errors of judgement. He feared this was one such occasion. What he heard next beggared belief.

"I wrote to the President to tell her it was Gina's engagement. I know she'll probably be too busy, but I thought she'd like to know, seeing as we all met her when you got your medal."

On his return from Libya, four years before, he had received the Police Medal for Bravery, from the President of the Republic, in the Grandmaster's Palace. After the presentation, they had been served refreshments and the President had briefly spoken to the family. How this gave Marianna licence to ask her to an engagement party at their house, George had no idea! The thought of Camilleri turning up made his blood run cold as it was, but this was off-the-scale lunacy.

"Are you completely insane? How can you make a fool of me

like this?"

His wife gulped and the sobbing started again.

"I thought she might like to know. She has met Gina, after all. I just wanted the party to be a success. It doesn't matter now, it's all ruined."

At this, the sobbing stopped and the wailing resumed. Denzel looked askance at his father.

"Has everyone gone mad? Where're you going anyway?"

"I can't say. Abdullah and I have been asked to sort out some police business."

Marianna leaped off the chair she had slumped into. Reinvigorated by the mention of this name, she launched back onto the attack.

"Abdullah? Where're you going with that awful man? You're never away from him. You two should just move in together! You're missing Gina's party to go gallivanting around with him? You're going to Libya again, aren't you? Oh my God, I don't believe it! Libya, with that Arab! What will Father Borg say?"

George was confused as to what any of this had to do with Father Borg. The views attributed to the Catholic priest by Marianna were often her own, introduced into their arguments as the ultimate authority on whatever was being discussed.

"He says we shouldn't spend too much time with them – you know, the migrants. It's not good for our faith."

Denzel spun on his heel.

"I can't listen to this anymore. I'm going out." He flicked Gina's hair and said: "Text me when things are back to normal."

His sister screeched after him: "Things'll never be back to normal now. My whole marriage is doomed!"

That had been just the start of it. The atmosphere in the house immediately turned ice cold. Preparations for the party continued, with Gina and Marianna ignoring George and talking about him in the third person, as if he was not even in the room. Denzel became even more elusive, missing meals and drifting in and out as he pleased. He often worked odd shifts, for the overtime.

When not at work, he played top-level amateur football and was active in the local Labour Party. George felt he might as well be living alone.

Marianna loved the status conferred on her by being the wife of a Pulizija superintendent. She loved the senior officers' garden party, the civic receptions she was invited to attend and the more glamorous social invitations that came to an officer of George's rank. She had been a poor fit at first, unpolished and lacking not just in her wardrobe, but also in the social graces of the middle-class wives. In time, her sense of humour, and propensity to say the first thing that come into her head, had gained her access to a group of the less snobby wives whom she now counted as her friends. Still, George tried to keep an eye on her as much as possible at such events, to save her from herself more than anything else.

At home, in the unpretentious suburb of Birkirkara, he feared she had turned into a shameless snob and serial namedropper. He heard her talking to neighbours in the shops and on the local high street, and often wondered what people really thought of her. Underneath the gossip and posturing, George knew Marianna was a good wife and a good person, but she had the capacity to drive him to distraction.

The day after his argument with her, he went to see Abdullah at his shop. He needed to have it out with his friend, understand why he had dragged George into this fool's errand. When he arrived, Abdullah was in a state of high excitement while in the process of handing over the care of the shop to Abeao and Mobo.

Abdullah and George had made the crossing from Libya, after their encounter with Abu Muhammad's militia, with these two Nigerian brothers. They were formerly desperate migrants who had paid to make the crossing to Malta in one of Abdullah's inflatable rafts. Abdullah had never expected to need to escape his own country in the same way, but had been glad of the former fishermen's expertise once he and George were at sea. Afterwards, the brothers had kept the secret of Abdullah's history as a trafficker and he had repaid them by giving them jobs in the shop and setting them up as small-time builders.

There were lists of suppliers, invoices, bills, orders and piles of paper all over the countertop. George looked at them. He was not sure whether the brothers could even read, let alone manage business accounts.

It was pointless mentioning it, as Abdullah was not thinking straight these days. He was too excited by the prospect of returning to Marsabar, armed with the hellfire of American weaponry. There, he would unleash his vengeance on his enemy, Abu Muhammad, who, in one cruel afternoon, had effectively ruined Abdullah's life.

The brothers stood looking at him, nodding sagely as he rambled from one aspect of the ironmongery business to the next. They paid no attention to the mounting pile of papers on the counter to which Abdullah enthusiastically pointed and waved.

Suddenly, with a loud "Hah!", he threw a pile of them up into the air.

"Papers! What good are they, eh? They will learn from day to day. These men are honest and good workers. We have more important things to do. We must go training, no?"

George scowled at his friend.

"No! No training."

Abdullah had been watching the Green Beret boot camp films on YouTube and had texted George that they needed to start a fitness campaign before meeting the American Special Forces people.

"First, I'm very pissed off that you told Camilleri I have to come with you to Libya. Why me? What business is this of mine? I have a family and Gina's engagement party is only a couple of weeks away. Marianna's furious. She's not even talking to me," George said bitterly.

"Ah, the lady wife is not pleased." Abdullah pulled a mock-despondent expression, before realising George was genuinely angry. "That is not good, I am sorry. And you will miss your daughter's party – that also is not good. But you will soon be back and she can chide you all the more then, no? I say we buy her and the beautiful Gina a big present and make them happy again!"

He beamed at George and opened his arms in an expansive gesture. Abeao and Mobo beamed too, nodding enthusiastically.

"Abdullah, you're selfish and think of no one but yourself. Fighting Abu Muhammad and retaking Marasbar has nothing to do with me. I don't want to be involved. You're going to tell Camilleri you've changed your mind and don't need me."

George made to reach for his phone. Abdullah's sinewy hand swiftly grasped his wrist. There was strength and resolution in that grip.

"Look, my brother Tareq is dead. He was my help in all things. My general. I need someone to take his place. I cannot do this alone, do you not see that? Who else can I trust with my life? Allah has given me you. What can I do? This is the will of Allah – not Abdullah!"

"*Mela*, I'm not Tareq! I'm not a soldier. I'm a pen-pushing policeman. I don't want to fight IS, radicals, extremists, jihadis or anybody else! Can't you understand? This is not my fight and I don't want to go to the desert – I hate it!"

George slapped his hand down on the counter, more loudly than he had intended. He was upset. Abeao and Mobo looked on, confused.

Mobo suddenly said: "If you want good soldiers, take us. We hate Boko Haram and all Islamic State people. They kill our parents and burn our village. We happy to kill them."

"Oh, for God's sake," George exclaimed, shaking his fists in front of him with frustration. "I think I'm going insane!"

The three of them looked at him, then at each other, confused and concerned, wondering what could possibly be wrong. At that moment George realised he would definitely be going to Libya, like it or not.

CHAPTER 11
ARTICLE IN MALTA TELEGRAPH

*REPORTER: **Amy Halliday***

28 June 2019

Malta on Verge of Libyan Gas Deal

Sources close to Castille have confirmed that Malta could soon become reliant on gas from war-torn Libya!

In a secret deal, they say a new Maltese energy company, part- owned by the Department of Energy, has agreed terms with the Russian company Euromasio, to import billions of cubic metres of Libyan gas a year.

The deal would involve a huge project to supply gas to every home on the country's islands, significantly reducing domestic energy costs. The Russian company recently purchased the VertWay pipeline, which formerly ran from Libya to Sicily, but the terms of that agreement prohibited them from exporting gas via Italy.

Sources suggest the new deal creates a loophole by which surplus gas can then be exported to Europe, via a second pipeline to be laid between Malta and Sicily.

MEP Gianluca Borg said: "We are most concerned about a state-owned Russian energy company taking a dominant position in the supply of energy to Malta."

Mariella Gera of the Malta Green Party said: "The last thing Malta needs is to increase its consumption of fossil fuels. As a Mediterranean island, we have access to abundant wind and solar power that is chronically underdeveloped. I am also alarmed that Malta is being used as a back door, through which the Russians can undermine the EU's energy market."

The Department of Energy has not replied to our request for comment.

In related news, a Russian security company has sent over 1,000 'security advisers' to assist General Boutros's Libyan National Army, which is advancing towards Tripoli in a bid to wrest control away from the UN-backed Government of National Accord.

Unconfirmed security sources claim US-led investigations into the car bomb, that killed the US Chargé d'Affaires in St Julian's, have discovered evidence of Russian involvement. An apartment with a line of sight to the scene of the bombing was leased by a company fronted by two Russian 'businessmen', and materials found abandoned inside suggest it was from there that the bomb was triggered. It is believed the men left the island shortly after the explosion. A Pulizija spokesman declined to comment.

CHAPTER 12
YAROSLAV BUKOV
ST GEORGE'S BAY, MALTA

THE NEXT MORNING, Natasha and Marco drove the short distance to one of the large five-star hotels on St George's Bay, where they were meeting Yaroslav Bukov. They found him already seated at a shaded table on one of the wide terraces that overlooked the narrow inlet. The late-June sunshine could be intense, even by midmorning. At the head of the bay, the faint beat of music could be heard from the many outdoor bars and cafés. The narrow patch of sand that served as the only local beach was already thronged with a colourful crowd of clubbers and partygoers, relaxing and sleeping off the previous night's excesses in Paceville's club land.

Yaroslav had made an effort for the meeting, discarding his usual designer leisure wear for a blue-and-white-striped business shirt and light grey suit. He took off his sunglasses and rose politely to greet Natasha and Marco.

She had decided to take a back seat during the meeting, to let her father and Yaroslav try to establish some sort of relationship.

The Russian was speaking.

"Now, we replace a large section of the VertWay pipeline from Libya, and we survey route for new spur to Malta. So, we're ready for starting to lay pipe. Moscow tells me assault on

Tripoli is beginning and our advisers and Volunteers say the city will soon be ours. Then, we have access to gas plant and oil fields!"

Marco nodded and said: "Still, that is a big concern. You are promising something that is not yet yours."

He remembered Natasha's description of the man's arrogance as the Russian dismissed this fundamental problem with a wave of his hand.

"Not to worry about that. Big problem is here, in Malta. You need to build many things and it is complicated work."

Yaroslav sat back in his chair, pausing the conversation, while he appraised Marco.

"So, who is this 'Family'? One person tell me the Family is masonic lodge, with Pope for boss; another, he say Family is worldwide Mafia!" Yaroslav rolled his eyes dramatically. "Then, a very intelligent man say to me, no, none of these. You are state within state, like Putin, but better, as very private! So, yes, my question to you is, 'Who is Family?'"

Marco studied Yaroslav, his expression unchanging.

"You are right – and, if it helps, over the centuries we have been all of those things. Today we are just a private consortium of old families who jointly do business."

Marco smiled serenely.

"I can say no more."

Yaroslav sat back in his chair.

"I like to know who we do business with."

"Would you like to see a bank statement?"

There was silence for several seconds as the men scrutinised each other. Finally, Yaroslav shook his head and said: "No. It's OK you don't tell me. All is OK as long as the money is good and ready, and I can trust your word. If that is not how it is, then I get on plane for Moscow – no questions."

"I would expect nothing less."

"So, Miss Natasha tells me Salvatore speaks with Italian operators who own pipelines in Italy, taking our gas all over Europe.

That is going good. But I worry there's not good progress in Malta. How do you make all this happen?"

Marco looked at him with the patience of an understanding father, indulging a misbehaving teenager.

"Yaroslav, this is my territory. I am not a technical man, but I know my countrymen. At heart, they are small-island people in a big bad world. If you bully them, they will back away and close themselves off. Then you will get nowhere.

"If you do it my way, the deal will happen because everybody wants it to happen – because there is money to be made. Lots of money. There is a man who helps me with this sort of thing very close to the seat of power, but not hampered by it. He is a practical man who sees the big picture, a businessman in a politician's suit. He will work with me. Not us – me. I prefer to stay one step back. It is better that way."

Yaroslav smiled. He liked Marco. He was a different proposition altogether from his nose-in-the-air daughter.

"Ah, now we have it. I can tell that is good. You see, Natasha, your father knows how to make things happen. But you need to start the works. We will be old men soon! So, I am going away – for maybe one month – I have work to do abroad. Always work. *Yaroslav, go here; Yaroslav, go there*! You do your work, with your politician who is not politician, on buildings, tariffs and the concessions. If there is not good progress when I come back, well, people will not be happy. OK?"

Natasha listened to Yaroslav, with his bad manners and loud mouth, his voice carrying indiscreetly around the terrace. She started to think there had to be a better way of doing this deal than committing themselves to a partnership with these people. Her own words came back to haunt her. *'We don't do business with Russians because it always ends badly. That's been our experience over the course of the last two hundred years.'*

Then she thought about the bomb in St Julian's. The island was awash with rumours about who was behind that but, thinking about it, there could only be one answer. The Americans were very pissed off and she wondered who would dare twist their tail. She smiled to herself – there was something in that line of thought …

Marco's voice broke in.

"So, your partners in the LNA – I suppose with sanctions and Tripoli controlling the oil money, the eastern militias must have funding problems. Who are the biggest supporters? It costs money to wage a war, even a civil war. If we are going into business with you, we need to know your commitment to their cause."

"Ah! You don't answer my question about who is Family, yet you ask me about our money. Not a fair question, is it?"

"It is. It is directly related to your ability to do the deal. We do not want it to fail because the LNA run out of money and Tripoli kick you out of the Marsabar refinery and gas plant."

Yaroslav smiled broadly and wagged a finger at Marco.

"No, very good thinking. So, the Saudis, Egyptians and French all give money to the General Boutros. But we also give much cash, to pay for government, soldiers, fuel, weapons and so on. Big bundles of Libyan dinars, printed in Moscow."

Marco leaned forward, obviously interested.

"You have been supplying cash?" He was more than surprised. "So how much are we talking about?"

Yaroslav was a shameless show off, a dangerous trait for a man in his position.

"Well, last shipment filled two shipping containers. It was one billion Libyan dinars. And that was not first shipment."

Marco was doing the mental arithmetic. He looked at Natasha.

"That is about three-quarters of a billion US dollars! In cash!"

"A lot of money, no? Russian Mint prints the money. We move it by train from Moscow to Novorossiysk, a container port on Black Sea, and then to main shipping hub in Istanbul, then into Benghazi. We expect next shipment to leave last week of next month. I go to Libya myself to organise handover and try to stop too much stealing by LNA. You put cash in warzone – what happens?"

"What, you just send it though standard shipping channels? That much money?"

"Yes, it's OK. It's tracked every mile of journey, but really it's worth nothing, only its weight in blended cotton and linen. Who wants Libyan dinars except for Libyans? General Boutros wants payment in cash, so every time he can be first to steal some, yes? It is always the same, all over the world."

With a smile, Yaroslav gathered his cigarettes and threw a fifty-euro note on the table.

"Good meeting. It is nice to talk to you, Marco, and to see you again, Natasha."

They stood and he shook Marco's hand, then turned to leer at Natasha and gently press her fingers with his. She fought an urge to physically recoil.

She had been sitting back and listening carefully. She was now certain this was her chance to do something that would have a real impact on the Family in Milan, but could not see it happening with this uncultured lech and his fellow Russians.

The gas project was a golden opportunity, and the idea of billions of dinars floating down the Bosphorus a fascinating prospect. If they were to deliver this project without the Russians, they would need to snare another partner with the money, muscle, technical capabilities and motivation to step into their shoes. Realistically speaking, there was only one option.

CHAPTER 13
YAROSLAV BUKOV
SIRTE BASIN, LIBYA

BAYDA LIES ON A HIGH RIDGE, thirty kilometres from the Mediterranean and 600 metres above it. They call it the White City, not because of its white-plastered buildings but because, uniquely in Libya, it occasionally gets snowfall in winter.

In 1960 it was a new town, built by the recently installed monarchy as the future capital city of an emerging, independent, oil-rich Libya. However, things did not turn out that way. Following Gaddafi's coup in 1969, the business of state remained in Tripoli.

That left Bayda with its glossy white Parliament building and a newly built central bank that was supposed to run the finances of the upstart government in the east. All well and good but, if you went inside the bank, you would not see any desks, computers or people. Tripoli kept the oil, so Tripoli kept the money.

Yaroslav had arrived in Libya a week ago, leaving Malta the day after his meeting with Marco and Natasha. He had flown from Malta to Cairo and then driven west for thirteen hours, to Benghazi, where he met Lev Artamonov. He led a group of approximately one hundred volunteers, part of Russkaya Volonterskaya Gruppa – a well-funded security company that had furthered Russian interests in the Ukraine, Syria, the Congo and elsewhere around the globe. The Kremlin was frequently called upon to deny any association with this well-equipped, private army of ex-special forces soldiers.

While Marco politicked in Malta, Yaroslav had been asked by Valentin Petrov to check out their plan to increase output from the oil fields in the Sirte Basin, a place rich in hydrocarbons, some 200 miles inland from the 'Oil Crescent' on the Libyan Coast. He could do the surveys and be back in time to meet the container of cash due to be off-loaded in Benghazi at the end of the month.

The desktop work on the oil fields all spoke of impressive and accessible reserves, but nobody really knew what the situation was like on the ground, at the sites and plants. In the late-1960s, the Sirte Basin had produced more oil than Saudi Arabia, but nationalisation, the war with Chad, embargos, Gaddafi and now the civil war had all reduced output to a fraction of what it had been and what it could be again.

The biggest problem was security – production was frequently halted due to strikes over safety concerns and the difficulty of recruiting skilled workers into an area where kidnaps, shootings and harassment were commonplace.

Yaroslav filled in Lev on the purpose of his visit.

"So, a trip south should be a welcome change for you. I've got a list of seven sites I want to visit, mainly in the Sirte Basin. Security OK down there?"

"It depends. IS-in-Libya come up from Chad and Western Sudan, drive around, make trouble, upset everybody, then disappear. They want us to give up trying to run the fields, so they can just walk in. If they did, they wouldn't have a clue what to do. Ignorant bastards!"

Yaroslav knew differently. Islamic State groups in Iraq did have the knowhow and the logistics, but whether those capabilities had survived the defeats in that country and Syria was anyone's guess.

Lev continued: "At the moment, recon says a handful of technicals have been seen in the area, but nothing we can't handle. They look like they run with the Islamist group led by Abu Muhammad al-Najafi. He's mostly been active in the west but now he's showed up down here."

'Technicals' was army slang for the thousands of Toyota flatbed trucks and other pickups that sped around the deserts and plains of Africa and the Middle East, fitted out with machine guns, rocket launchers or cannons. Compared to armoured military equipment, they were cheap to buy, run and repair, and agile enough to outsmart most heavy motorised weaponry. They were the ideal weapon for hit-and-run militias.

Yaroslav said nothing to Lev, but he was surprised to hear the name Abu Muhammad. It was his militia that had been paid to make the attack on the Marsabar oil and gas complex in the west of the country, to scare off the Italians. Yaroslav thought it strange Abu Muhammad was now operating as far east as the Sirte Basin.

Their trip was uneventful. After two days, the convoy reached Jalu, about 200 kilometres south of the coast, the area where the Islamic State-in-Libya militia had last been sighted. Lev had ordered a stop just outside the town, so he could send some pickups to find fuel, before hitting the desert further south.

Yaroslav had climbed onto the roof of the Land Cruiser and spread his jacket over the white-hot metal, flopping down onto it to enjoy the sun, but still catch such breeze as there was. He was in that far-away state that came from hours of driving down long, straight, hypnotic desert roads, with nothing to see but endless, colourless scrub, set against clear blue skies. All conversation had long since dried up and the group in the vehicle had become locked into the torpor of the journey. Yaroslav had just shut his eyes when he became aware of one of Lev's officers running across the scrub towards them. He was shouting as he sprinted away from the command truck.

"We've got two militia vehicles, six kilometres south but coming north on the desert road, moving fast. They're heading towards one of the Waha oil fields. If we're quick, we can intercept them – or we can radio in and let the drone take them."

"Let's not waste drone missiles! The boys could do with some action. It'll wake them up. Take two personnel carriers, the ones with autocannons. Ask for a grid reference for the intercept and get to it. Can we get a visual on this?"

Yaroslav listened to the orders being shouted and watched the men spring into action. He had instantly become fully alert and could sense excitement rising around him as the Volunteers organised themselves, strapping on body armour and tactical belts, then throwing ammunition and supplies between the vehicles.

Within minutes, the two armoured personnel carriers revved their engines and trundled off, amidst a cloud of dust. After twenty minutes of anxious waiting, Lev shouted at Yaroslav and he joined Lev and two others around the laptop on a bench in the back of the command truck. Yaroslav felt his heart beating fast. It had been a while since he had been involved in any combat action, so he had forgotten the thrill of an attack and the energy radiating from pumped-up professional soldiers.

They watched the lead armoured personnel carrier drive out of a side gully straight into the path of the first IS pick-up truck. The IS technicals slid to a halt, throwing a cloud of dust and gravel into the air. From their silent drone feed, they saw a fighter jump out of the rear door and leap behind, onto the deck of the truck, to start readying the twin-barrelled machine gun.

Before the fighter could fire a shot, the personnel carrier opened up with its twin-barrelled autocannon. It fired explosive shells into both pickups at an alarming rate. On the screen, it looked like jets of flame were spurting between the two vehicles. The first IS truck was pushed around the road by the impact of the shells and was soon in flames. The doors had been flung open and two bodies were lying on the road.

There were shouts and yells of excitement from the Russians watching inside the truck. Yaroslav found himself joining them and excitedly banging his fist on the roof above him.

The grainy picture on the laptop screen showed the second vehicle trying to turn away from the clash, but its engine seemed to be running out of power. Its machine gun was manned and flickers of light and a jolting movement told them it was returning fire.

The second personnel carrier drove through the burning wreckage of the first pickup and blasted the fleeing vehicle from behind. Bullets from the mounted machine gun bounced off the carrier's thick armour plating. The hydraulic ramps at the rear of the personnel carriers were lowered and a team of Volunteers quickly jumped out of each vehicle.

There were more cheers and shouts from inside the truck as they watched aerial footage of the Russians finishing off lightly armed militia fighters who tried to flee across the rough scrubland. The Volunteers in the truck were cheering on their comrades in pursuit of the fleeing men and no one was shouting more loudly than Yaroslav.

Lev was watching intently. Yaroslav heard him say to the sergeant on the radio: "Don't kill them all. We need at least one of them to get back and tell them we're onto them!"

Just then, they heard what sounded like an explosion outside. At first, Yaroslav thought it had come from the drone feed, but then he felt the blast waves and everyone inside the comms vehicle instantly fell silent. They stood looking at each other, registering the shock of what they feared had happened. Before anybody could say a word, the rear door was swung open by the tip of an automatic weapon.

A voice speaking perfect English said: "Gentlemen, please put down any weapons. It would be a shame to have to clear you out with a grenade."

Yaroslav, who was probably the most fluent English speaker present, felt his stomach sink as the excitement of the attack was suddenly replaced by hard-biting fear. The voice belonged to a young, heavily built man with a bushy black beard, wearing a brown shirt buttoned to the neck and a green and brown camouflage jacket, a stained pakol beret perched on his head. Sweat was running down his face and he was breathing heavily. Outside, the chatter of automatic weapons and shouts of guttural Arabic voices could be heard.

The Englishman kept smiling, observing the drone feed they had been watching.

"When you charge out of the front door, always make sure the back door's locked. You never know who might come in! Who's the oil man?"

Lev involuntarily glanced towards Yaroslav. It was enough.

"Good," said the bearded man, "now we're getting somewhere. You! Out, now!"

He pointed his gun at Yaroslav and motioned for him to move. Yaroslav looked to Lev for help, but he just stared back blankly, keeping his hands raised in front of him. Yaroslav jumped out of the shaded rear of the truck into the desert light. There were four Volunteers lying on the ground, brown blood soaking into the dirt around them. The fighters were stripping them of weapons, ammunition and other gear.

They herded the remaining dozen Volunteers, as well as some LNA militia who had accompanied them, against a low rocky outcrop on the side of the road. The other personnel carrier was lying idle, black smoke pouring from the windows. It had been hit by armour-piercing shells from the cannons on one of the five IS technicals that had surrounded them.

It had been a carefully executed trap. The IS militia had seen the drone over the desert road and come out to tempt them to split their forces. The decoy had worked. They had correctly guessed expensive missiles would not be wasted on a couple of technicals. Once they knew the Volunteers were distracted, watching the action in the next valley, they had struck. It was typical of the ruthlessness of Abu Muhammad that he was prepared to sacrifice his own men in the ambush, to win the bigger prize.

The Englishman walked towards Yaroslav, gun loosely held but pointing directly at him. The Russian desperately tried to control the fit of shaking that had taken hold of him. He knew he could be minutes away from death.

"Get in the truck. Put your hands on the dash."

The inside of the truck was filthy, every surface thick with desert grit, and cigarette packets and plastic bottles in the footwells. The windscreen was caked in dust and insects, apart from two scallop shell shapes made by the windscreen wipers. The Englishman got into the driver's side of the truck, kicking the litter to one side, took a cable tie from the glove compartment and slipped it around Yaroslav's wrists, pulling it tight, making him wince as the nylon strap dug into his flesh. The fighter then fastened Yaroslav's arms above the level of his shoulders with a second tie attached to the grab bar over the door. Satisfied that the prisoner was secured inside the vehicle, the Englishman got out of the truck and shouted in Arabic towards the rest of the fighters who were making their way back to the pickups.

Yaroslav allowed himself to breathe out. It sounded like a whimper. They were not going to kill him just yet. Then he saw one of the fighters peel off and walk back towards the Comms truck. He took something from a cloth bag that was slung across one shoulder. He fiddled with it and threw it into the back of the truck. There was some shouting, followed by a dull blast. The truck bounced up into the air and smoke streamed out of the rear of the vehicle.

Yaroslav could not believe what he had just seen. There were cries and screams. Lev tumbled out and fell flat onto the scrubby ground. He rolled once, his arms around his head, then lay still, smoke slowly rising from his body. Yaroslav twisted against the tie to see half a dozen fighters start to fire their automatic weapons at the dozen Volunteers and LNA militia fighters standing against the rocks. Some fell and some ran, but the result was the same in every case. The Englishman stood by the open driver's door, calmly smoking a cigarette and watching. He glanced down to see how Yaroslav was taking it all.

"This is war, Russian. I thought you would've known that."

Yaroslav was numb with shock and the shaking made him incapable of speech. He could only look at the Englishman, wide-eyed in disbelief.

Many were not killed outright but died as the IS fighters wandered around between the prone bodies, despatching them with head shots and bursts of automatic fire. Yaroslav felt the bile rise from deep in his stomach and, to find relief, had to bend, as best he could, and retch.

With that, the fighters lit more cigarettes, laughed and chatted between themselves, before making ready to leave. One came and slipped onto the back deck of their vehicle and the Englishman fired the engine. They headed south at speed, the third man sitting out on the bed of the truck, using binoculars to scour the sky for the returning drone. Yaroslav figured the plume of dust from the speeding vehicles would be visible for miles. He shuddered at the irony of being killed by a missile from their own aerial spy.

After thirty minutes of being bounced around inside the speeding truck, they came to the junction of two dirt tracks and the Englishman peeled off to the left, while the main convoy raced south towards the border with Chad. Some hundred yards later, they bumped into a rough camp and drove under a roof of camouflage netting, held up with scaffold poles embedded in concrete blocks. The nets concealed the makeshift camp from drones and satellites, but also provided some shade from the intense afternoon sun. The Englishman killed the engine.

"So, we wait here till dark. Your drone can chase the others, if they think it's worth it."

With that, he got out of the Toyota and went to a small shipping container, hidden under more nets, in a low gully. From there he fetched two small bottles of water. He threw one to the fighter who had been on the back of the truck and returned to the vehicle. He leaned on the roof and pushed his head through the window, looking at Yaroslav. He drank the water, beads of moisture spilling down his thick black beard. His dark brown eyes never left Yaroslav's. Putting the top back on, he grinned and threw the half-full bottle onto the driver's seat.

"Go on, oil man. Have a drink! It's five hours till sundown. There's some shade, but I think it'll get warm in there!" With that, he laughed and turned away.

With his hands bound to the grab bar, there was no way Yaroslav could get to the water. He slumped against the door and rested his head against the window. Fear and shock finally found release in the tears that ran down his cheeks, leaving streaks through the film of fine desert dust that had covered his face.

CHAPTER 14
ARTICLE IN MALTA TELEGRAPH

Reporter: Amy Halliday

17 July 2019

EU Cautions Against Gas Deal with Russia

The Department of Energy has confirmed that negotiations are progressing well to allow Euromasio, a Russian state-owned company, to become the supplier of Libyan gas to Malta. The department is set to grant concessions to MalTech Energy, the mysterious new energy company that will have a monopoly on the gas supply to Maltese homes, as well as exporting Libyan gas into Europe.

EU officials have voiced concern over the lack of transparency of MalTech Energy, owned by a British Virgin Island trust. This arrangement hides the true beneficial ownership of the company and its sources of funding. Representatives from the Department of Energy said they have completed their due diligence into these matters and are satisfied with the explanations they have received, but refused to answer further questions.

Opposition MP Carmelo Gauci said: "It is bad enough allowing the Russians to hold the country hostage, but now we are handing over the profits to a group of shareholders who hide in the shadows of a complex offshore trust. The Panama Papers showed us how they work! It is not only we Maltese who will be the losers, we are also giving these people a back door to sell gas into Europe."

There have been objections from Brussels to MalTech Energy's plans to build a pipeline to Pozzallo, Sicily, giving access to Europe's independent energy transmission networks. These networks had previously been national assets of individual member states, until the EU ordered their privatisation to boost competition. There are fears that cheap Libyan gas will destabilise existing supply arrangements, as well as increasing dependence on the capricious Russian government and a politically unstable regime in Libya.

Sources inside the Prime Minister's Office in Castille said there was growing concern that the project was proceeding so quickly, despite the fact it relied on General Boutros Boutros's rival Libyan National Army deposing the Government of National Accord in Tripoli. The Tripoli government is recognised as the legitimate authority in Libya by the UN, the EU, and has many friends in Malta.

CHAPTER 15
NATASHA BONNICI
CASTELLO BONNICI, MALTA

CASTELLO BONNICI SAT on top of a long ridge that bisected the island at its narrowest part. From here you could look both east and west and see twin flashes of deep blue as the Mediterranean Sea lapped against the two coastlines. Like most Maltese buildings, the *castello* was constructed from local limestone which, in the flat winter light, could look drab and uninviting. It came alive in the summer sunshine when the stone took on the warm hue of Gozitan honey.

The *castello*'s extensive flagged terrace overlooked Marco's formal gardens and stretched the length of the house, on the north-eastern side. For most of the year, this was where the Bonnicis spent their time. Weather permitting, breakfast was always taken in the gentle morning sunshine, and it was their custom also to meet there for pre-dinner drinks. This evening they had turned their table to face west and were watching the sun going down behind the Marfa escarpment, together with their guest, Assistant Commissioner Gerald Camilleri.

It had come as a surprise to receive Camilleri's call. Strictly speaking, he was not a friend of theirs, but was retained by the Family to look after their interests on his territory. He knew everybody and everything that happened on the island so, when he said he had some urgent business to discuss, the Bonnicis were intrigued.

Although Camilleri seemed at ease, lounging back in his high-backed wicker chair, his long spider-like legs were crossing and uncrossing like those of an agitated marionette. Natasha could tell he was nervous. As always, his formality made no concessions to the beautiful spring evening. He was wearing his usual garb – a grey double-breasted pinstripe suit, with a white shirt and unassuming navy tie.

Marco poured him some sparkling water and topped up Natasha's wine. Camilleri took a pack of cigarettes and a lighter from his jacket pocket and started smoking. Then they got down to business.

"So, Gerald, we are curious. To what do we owe this pleasure?"

Camilleri clasped his hands together, narrowing his eyes as he stared at them. His speech was measured and, most likely, carefully rehearsed.

"I hope I can speak both as an old friend of yours and a servant of Malta? I know that sounds pompous, but I am worried by the current turn of events concerning the gas supply arrangements with Libya."

Marco nodded. "Go on, Gerald. Anybody who fails to listen when you express concern is a fool. You have our attention."

"I fear the current direction of travel may not be in your long-term best interests. I might be wrong and, please, if I speak out of turn, just raise a hand and I will stop immediately. We can forget this conversation ever took place.

"I am aware of your arrangements with the Russians – who is not? Also, that you have commissioned Edward Refalo to help you negotiate with Castille."

Refalo was an old acquaintance of Marco's and a former minister whose connections with the current administration ran deep. He was an operator in the private sector now because, while in public office, he had seemed incapable of recognising a conflict of interest if it bit him on the nose.

Marco and Refalo were currently busy all over the island, negotiating concessions, construction permits, distribution agreements and more. They were establishing the physical and commercial arrangements necessary to bring the gas ashore and construct the new pipeline to Sicily.

Camilleri continued speaking.

"There can be no doubt that Libyan gas is a good thing for the island. It is an excellent opportunity to become a player in the European energy markets and, make no mistake, I am fully supportive of the Family's efforts to acquire an interest in it.

"But I am also worried about the articles in the *Malta Telegraph*. They seem to be very accurate and the journalist, Amy Halliday, must have an inside source who keeps on giving. People are becoming concerned and that will be a problem for you, Marco. You understand me?"

"I have read the pieces – some are true and some are wide of the mark."

"Marco, it does not matter what is true and what is not. People believe what she says and there is certainly no love felt for the Russians on this island. You know that. The idea that we should tie the country's energy supply to them is unacceptable in many quarters, especially when there is an alternative. It cannot be good for the project and we do not wish this opportunity to slip through your fingers."

Marco was intrigued.

"An alternative?"

"Yes."

"Go on."

Camilleri shifted in his chair, crossing and uncrossing his spindly shins.

"My investigators tell me the bombing of the American Chargé d'Affaires' residence was the work of the Russians. The Americans have been watching the disruptive Russian involvement in Libya closely and they do not like what they see. In fact, I am told they are on the verge of entering the conflict themselves, and soon. I do not know any details, but you can see how this reflects on your arrangements. In short, I am worried you may be backing the wrong horse."

Marco was shocked. He picked up his glass of wine and glanced at Natasha as he took a sip. After a few moments, he sighed and said: "Hmmm ... well, Gerald, that is worrying news indeed."

Marco looked again at his daughter, sitting perfectly still, with a neutral expression on her face.

The Assistant Commissioner continued speaking.

"Once the Americans enter the Libyan theatre, political and commercial pressure will be exerted by the EU to support US efforts, in both the commercial and military spheres, you know that. Western powers have always used Malta in their military and commercial operations in North Africa."

Marco replied, "But we are not even a member of NATO and, technically, non-aligned to it. We refuel the Russian Navy, for God's sake!"

"Come on, Marco, you have to agree, the EU, the US and NATO itself would not countenance Malta becoming an ally of the Russian Federation, even in the most notional sense. This is bigger than a few cubic metres of gas.

"I do not wish to interfere in your business affairs, but there is certainly a feeling you are helping the Russians into Europe by stealth, which is going to make it difficult to get the support you need to deliver the project. Or, at least, that is what I am hearing on the ground."

Marco stood up and paced across the terrace, taking up position next to one of the *castello*'s life-size Neoclassical marble statues.

He looked at Camilleri.

"May I ask how close you are to those who think this way?"

"Since the murder of the Chargé d'Affaires, I have been

working with American security and have been brought into their circle. The Russians organised the St Julian's bomb, to mark their turf and deter the US from getting involved in Libya. I am afraid it has backfired badly on them. Also, I like my friends to be winners, not losers."

Natasha put down her glass and, with a nod to Camilleri, said: "Dad, I hear what Gerald's saying and I think he's right. Amy Halliday's articles have certainly had an impact. Maybe that's why it's proving such a struggle to get the agreements we need here. But if it's not the Russians we partner with, then who?"

Camilleri said, "I think the Americans have one or two ideas about who might step into those big boots. The US administration and their international energy companies have strong ties."

"You are suggesting that the Americans will offer themselves as an alternative partner?" Marco asked.

Camilleri nodded his head very slightly in confirmation.

"Well, we cannot do anything until I have spoken to the Wise Men. And I will also have to find a way of stalling our friend Yaroslav Bukov when he gets back."

Camilleri smiled and said: "I think you may find your Mr Bukov has other things on his mind at the moment. My American friends tell me he is being held by an Islamic State militia in southern Libya."

It was Natasha's turn to express shock.

"Really? What was he doing there?"

"Apparently, he went to survey some oil fields needed to provide the gas and crude for the project, and got himself captured in the southern desert. An Islamic State militia is trailing him round the oil fields, using him as a consultant. When they have finished with him, they will either ransom or kill him."

Natasha tried to suppress a short laugh that turned into a snort.

Her father glared at her.

"I'm sorry, but he isn't one of my favourite people, although I wouldn't wish that fate on anyone. Poor Yaroslav!"

Camilleri looked at her mirthlessly, thinking her remark in poor taste.

"Well, Gerald, as always, our meeting has been illuminating and thought provoking," her father said.

"One last thing, Marco: an ironic twist that may amuse you. The Americans are building a militia around Abdullah Belkacem – you recall, the warlord from Marsabar who caused so much trouble with our oil deal a few years ago? Mr Belkacem has insisted on taking my very own Superintendent George Zammit with him, as a special adviser. Small world, is it not?"

Marco nearly choked on his wine.

"What! Gerald, nothing about that time amuses me, although maybe sending Belkacem back is not such a bad idea ... I hear he was quite somebody back in his day. But what on earth is your officer going for?"

"Good question, Marco. A very good question."

With that, Camilleri stood, shook hands, politely kissed Natasha on both cheeks and left.

Marco returned from walking the Assistant Commissioner to his car and slumped into a chair. He grabbed his glass and leaned back, legs extended in front of him. A thought had occurred to him while he walked back onto the terrace.

"You have never liked our Russian involvement, have you?"

"I've made no secret of it, I suppose."

"But you are happier now the Americans might step up?"

"Yes, I definitely am."

"I suppose we should be grateful for Amy Halliday's articles, then?"

There was a pause.

"Yep," Natasha admitted. "I mean, we would've realised it ourselves at some point. It's true, I never liked dealing with the Russians, and especially not Bukov. He was a bully and a thug and too used to getting his own way. He was also a lech. The thought of doing business with him for years to come … Well, it wasn't a pleasant prospect."

Marco looked carefully at this daughter. Something here did not feel quite right. She had taken the proposed change of tack in her stride and seemed unnaturally calm and composed. He could not put his finger on it, but it was almost as though she had expected it …

Marco dismissed such a thought from his mind.

"Well, setting personal antipathies aside, we do not have to worry about him now. I am not sure Salvatore will be supportive of a change of plan at this stage. I doubt he is particularly sensitive to geopolitical considerations. Only the Family's views count for him."

"So, you're going to tell him?"

"Well, yes. And the sooner the better. I will play the 'what is best for Malta, is best for the Family' card. We will see what happens."

CHAPTER 16
SUPERINTENDENT GEORGE ZAMMIT

SUPERINTENDENT GEORGE ZAMMIT

GEORGE WAS MISERABLE. Even his departure from home had not gone well. He had decided to play it cool, given that Marianna and Gina were still not talking to him. On the day itself, he had taken his pick from a pile of newly ironed clothes and quietly packed his suitcase. Then he had gone to see his daughter, who stood stony-faced, peeling vegetables in the kitchen.

"I have to go, Gina. Official business. I'm sorry I can't be at the party but I don't have any choice in the matter. I've got to work. One day you'll understand. Have a lovely time and I'll make it up to you once I'm back and we're all talking to each other again. OK?"

No reply.

"Where's your mother?"

Her bottom lip had protruded, but her stare remained fixed on the courgette she was destroying. She had said nothing but pointed towards the corridor leading to the bedrooms. Marianna was nowhere to be seen.

George had shouted: "I'm off then. See you in a couple of weeks."

Then he paused. Still no reply. Denzel had been waiting in the hall, in uniform, jangling his car keys.

"Come on, Dad. You know what they're like. They'll both be in tears as soon as you close the door."

George had checked his pockets to make sure he had his passport and tickets, slid into Denzel's Subaru and they had set off for the airport.

To George, that all seemed such a long time ago, even though they had only been on the base for ten days. It was a six-hour direct flight from Malta to Doha and the Americans had booked them into business class. Abdullah had never enjoyed such luxury, although he looked disapproving as George accepted a gin and tonic, followed by an endless supply of red wine.

"Enjoy it, my friend. Where we go now, it is water, tea or fruit juice only!"

George did not normally drink a lot, but had become more and more nervous as the flight progressed. He had no idea what they were heading into. He was also slightly unnerved by the change in Abdullah's behaviour. He had pulled back, no longer his chatty and friendly self, and become withdrawn; he, too, seemed anxious. His expression had hardened and his smile was more tense. George understood. Much was expected of him and he expected much of himself. Happily, George was not burdened with such high expectations.

It was only later that Abdullah confided he had never been in an aeroplane before and the experience had terrified him.

On arrival, they had been met and taken by a military SUV on the thirty-minute drive from Hamad International Airport to the Al-Udeid US Air Base. Once inside, they had both been amazed by the sheer scale of it.

The buildings were all camouflaged against the desert sand and rock. They were largely prefabricated units, with rusted air-conditioning systems protruding like ugly tumours. The planes, dozens of them in all shapes and sizes, nestled under large tented structures, to protect them from the scorching sun. Where the fabric was torn or frayed, the canopies fluttered in a stiff breeze, heavy with dust. Even the cheerful branding of the Pizza

Hut and Coffee Beanery could not lift the desolate mood of the place.

Abdullah had given George a grim nod before he was directed to his room, up a short, galvanised-steel staircase and into a grimy building, carrying his personal possessions in a red and yellow Birkirkara FC sports bag. George's accommodation was no better. It was dark and at the end of a corridor. It held a bed, a desk and a wardrobe. The window was shuttered and there was a sign saying it was to remain closed at all times. The air conditioner rattled and clattered incessantly, as if a refrigerated truck had been reversed into the wall.

The driver had given him a map of the site, a security pass on a lanyard, and directions for where and when to show up for an orientation meeting. He had also passed over a thick envelope addressed to 'Superintendent George Zammit – Recruit 008/9765'. It had contained a set of instructions headed: 'The Basics of Desert Warfare – Induction Course'. It told George where to collect his equipment, where to attend for a haircut and a description of what was to come. A handwritten amendment then instructed him he was not after all required to attend the barber's as he was 'assuming an Arab identity'.

The advance materials had been blunt and to the point. The focus of the course was to teach the skills necessary to survive in the 'blistering hot sun and frigid nights of desert climates', as well as training in 'direct action combat skills at team and squad levels'.

George had tried to imagine what that might involve. He had not liked the sound of it at all.

Outside the airfield perimeter, the US Army had access to one million acres of desert, where the battlefield training took place. 'This involves a live-fire exercise and hand to hand combat skills,' he read on.

They were to be dumped in the middle of this nothingness, with a compass and a protractor, no GPS or support, and would then be required to find their way back. All George had been able to think was that a person could die out there.

After that, the document said they would spend two days on 'desert survival training: building shelters; starting fires; finding, collecting and filtering water; and setting snares and traps to catch food'. Then, they were expected to put this all into practice with a 72–hour field exercise, where trainees would be divided into squads for 'clashes' with an opposing force of troops, selected from the Green Berets stationed on the base!

By the time he had finished reading the file, he had been panic-stricken. He had to find Abdullah straightway and get him to explain there had been some terrible misunderstanding. This was not what George had signed up for. But he never seemed to get to see his friend, who was busy with the senior Ranger officers, planning strategy and logistics.

George was placed in the care of Sergeant Mario Barrasso, a small squat man with a shaved head and no eyebrows. He was a veteran of the Iraq Wars and had been training what he considered to be 'idiots like you' for too long to stay sane. He ran with the troops, carrying a full twenty-kilo pack, trained with the troops and shouted at the troops. The young guys loved him. George was terrified of him and he did not think much of George, either.

Barrasso and the other trainers soon realised George's limitations, after he collapsed during a twenty-kilometre forced march around the base perimeter. George thought it was barbaric to force people to walk that distance in late July, when it was nearly 40 degrees outside. To his relief, Barrasso told him that, given he was not a genuine recruit to the Army Rangers or the Green Berets, he could sit out some of the rough stuff. He was appointed squad medic and for two days attended a hands-on class in basic battlefield medical techniques, using the US Army's latest *Tactical Combat Casualty Care* protocols.

He was fascinated to learn how to stop traumatic bleeding from gunshot and knife wounds, using the latest pressure bandages and tourniquets. He studied field-fracture immobilisation, clearing airways, wound-cleaning and disinfection, the injection of local anaesthesia and wound closures. When he returned from the course, George actually felt a sense of achievement. He was quickly called into action, to tend a broken arm after a soldier fell out of the back of a moving truck.

He had always had a good eye on the police range so, when it came to marksmanship and the live firing exercises, he excelled. He enjoyed handling the military-grade weapons and could keep a steady aim, despite their weight and powerful recoil. He fired battle rifles, automatic weapons and even a fully automatic SAM machine gun. Sergeant Barrasso looked twice at him when George told him he had already used a mounted Browning machine gun, fighting Islamic State militia in Libya.

"Well, hear that, soldiers. Stay close to Zammit, he's the man. He shot up the ISILs!"

At the end of the day on the range, Sergeant Barrasso even complimented him when he addressed the squad, saying: "In this team, everyone has a role – you may not believe it, but even Special Agent Zammit has his uses!"

By the end of the ten days, George was starting to enjoy himself. He could light fires, catch and skin small mammals, and filter dirty water. He was always a good sleeper and a night in the desert, in a military sleeping system bag, did not prevent him from enjoying hours of solid sleep. He only woke up when Barrasso shook him and told him there were complaints about his snoring from downtown Doha.

All that changed the next day, during the seventy-two-hour field training exercise, when twenty Green Berets rushed the recruits' camp in the middle of the night, hitting them with batons and tearing down their rough shelters. George was so shocked at the screaming, shouting and fighting that he leaped out of his sleeping bag, only to be lashed across the back of the head with a wooden truncheon. Dazed and bleeding, he fell semi-conscious into a gully.

His squad scattered and, conceding defeat, some made their way back to the Al-Udeid base, whilst others were held 'captive' by the Green Berets. As a result, a full head count was never taken. It was only when the two groups were reconciled in the morning that they realised they were a man down.

As the freezing night turned into the blazing heat of day, George awoke from a deep sleep in the wrecked camp, miles away from the airfield, nursing the cut on the back of his head and feeling sorry for himself. He restored one of the shelters they had built, to protect himself from the sun, and started a fire, as instructed, making as much smoke as possible, in the hope someone would eventually come looking for him. Smoke from the dried sticks and bits of leaf rose vertically in a thin thread into the sky of a perfect desert morning.

After thirty minutes or so his head was really hurting, so he decided to lie down on his bag, in the shade of his shelter, as the night's excitement began to catch up with him.

What seemed like an age later, he woke with a start and saw there were two soldiers kneeling over him, in full combat gear, staring at him intently.

"OK, buddy, where're you hurt? We've got a head injury here," one of them observed.

The other had a small laminated sheet in his hand and was reading from it.

"I think he's a Priority 3 casualty. There's no imminent risk to life, so we progress to examine the patient's wounds."

"Yeah, I can go with that."

They were both peering at George's head.

"Any immediate treatment necessary?"

George saw Sergeant Barrasso, standing a little apart, arms folded, staring down at him.

George was a little dazed and still half asleep.

"He's catching some Zs, you dummies!" the sergeant roared. "Zammit, get up, it's nearly lunchtime!"

George raised himself on one elbow and smiled at the sergeant in recognition.

"Good timing, sir. I could do with a bite to eat!"

Sitting in the back of the personnel carrier, a bandage wrapped around his head, avoiding poisonous looks from the sergeant, George was feeling pretty pleased with himself. He had completed the course – it was over – but now that he was officially ready for desert warfare, he began to worry about what Abdullah might expect of him.

CHAPTER 17
ARTICLE IN MALTA TELEGRAPH

*REPORTER: **Amy Halliday***

27 July 2019

US Ultimatum to Russia on Libya

The US Secretary of State, Mike Phelps, today told the Russian Ambassador in Washington that the US was no longer prepared to tolerate Russia's blatant intervention in the Libyan conflict.

The Secretary of State accused Russia of deploying a dozen fourth-generation warplanes to Libya in support of private military contractors known as the Russkaya Volonterskaya Gruppa. Such a deployment must have been made with the full knowledge of the Kremlin.

In a statement to the press, he said: "For too long, Russia has denied the full extent of its involvement in the ongoing Libyan conflict. This week, we watched every step of the way as Russia flew jet fighters to Libya."

The American response has so far been confined to a war of words with the Kremlin, but there are growing signs that an American intervention is now a real possibility.

What this means for the gas supply deal with MalTech is unknown. Sources in the Department of Energy said the company will find few friends in Castille, or Brussels, if it aligns itself with Russian interests in Libya, when the West is falling into line behind the US.

Sources in Castille went further, saying that, given the level of investment required from the government, it might be unwise to proceed further with the project just when Libya could be plunged into deeper turmoil, thereby increasing the associated risks.

The situation in Tripoli remains tense, with gunfire and shelling now reaching the outskirts of the city. Turkish efforts to broker a ceasefire are making slow progress, with General Boutros not prepared to make concessions from what he perceives to be a position of strength.

CHAPTER 18
MARCO BONNICI
NEAR THE SAN SIRO, MILAN

NATASHA AND MARCO had flown into Milan together. At the request of the Wise Men, Marco was reluctantly meeting with Salvatore to talk about bringing the Americans into the gas deal, while Natasha had her regular meeting with Signor Bruno. The taxi had cruised down the toll road from Malpensa Airport, hitting the outskirts of north-west Milan when, for old times' sake, Marco asked the driver to go past the San Siro stadium.

"Slow down," he shouted, "let me get a look at it! You see, Natasha, don't you think the spiralling ramps look like giant bed springs?" Her father laughed. "You know, when Sergio and I were at university, we came here as often as we could. It was a three-hour drive from Bologna, in Sergio's beat-up Alfa. He was mad about Inter and, just to wind him up, I supported Juventus. They were good days, we had passion to burn."

She smiled at him.

"I wish I could've seen the pair of you then!"

"When we both first came to Milan, before term started, we stayed with Zio Nico, my father's cousin. I had not seen Sergio since he was a young boy, but we were thrown together in Milan when his mother died. Uncle Nico arranged for members of the Family, including your Signor Bruno, to meet us individually, at their grand Croce Bianca club. They set us tasks, sort of an assessment. We were told to go away, earn some money and do something that would impress them. That was all they said. Hilarious when you think about it."

Natasha laughed.

"What did you do?"

"Ah! That is another story. I will tell you some other time, we are nearly there now, but ask Signor Bruno if he remembers the tasks!"

"He doesn't really go in for small talk."

"No, I don't think he ever did."

The taxi slowed down outside a nondescript parade of shops.

Marco said: "Yes, yes, this is the place."

He paid and then asked the driver to wait for a moment at the curbside. He grabbed Natasha's arm and pointed out of the window.

"You see the office up there, on the first floor, above the dry cleaner's? It has no broadband or WiFi, no telephone, and we sweep it for bugs monthly. I use it whenever I am in Milan, for meetings. I took the lease when I was twenty years old so as to have somewhere to work on my VAT scam – my response to Signor Bruno's challenge. More importantly, it has a parking space round the back, so Sergio and I could park the Alfa there before going to the San Siro. Happier days, Natasha. Anyway, I cannot keep Salvatore waiting. Self-important prig! Good luck with Signor Bruno."

"And you, Dad. Give him what for!"

Marco got out and the taxi pulled away. He waved and walked towards the door to the stairs that led up to the office. He punched in the code for the lock, twice, before realising it had been changed. He took out his phone and sent a text to Salvatore.

Outside.

With a loud buzz, the door lock was released and Marco climbed the stairs. As usual, there was coffee waiting on the table, from the café down the street.

"Salvatore, you have changed the entry code?"

They did not bother with the charade of a formal embrace or handshake. It was just the two of them.

"A lot has changed, Marco. You've been gone four years. Things don't stand still."

"Indeed they do not."

Marco looked around the office, noting nothing much had changed in the furnishings.

Salvatore watched him closely.

"Does his ghost still haunt you, Marco?"

He was surprised by the younger man opening the conversation in this way.

"Whose – Sergio's? No. Why would it? I did not kill him. But if you are interested in hearing whether I miss him, the answer is yes. I do not want you to explain why things had to happen like that, because I will never understand. The best I can do is try to put it behind me and forget that people I trusted and liked could do such a thing."

"I see."

They sat down and then spoke at length about Camilleri's briefing. Marco had already discussed it in outline over the phone with Salvatore and it soon became clear that he had been busy sounding out the Wise Men in the interim. Marco let Salvatore talk and work his way towards presenting their conclusion.

"The feeling is, the Russians are more flexible in their approach. I mean, like it or not, we've more in common with them than we do with the Americans.

"You've got to agree, as partners, the Russians will be more willing to let us seize opportunities, as they arise. The Americans will be all red-tape and they'll want to run the show. Also, the big 'if' is whether they have the commitment to get the job done, scare off the LNA, the Russian Volunteers and the rest?"

Marco exhaled loudly.

"Salvatore, the decision here is whether the Family wants to align itself with a volatile and provocative partner that only wants to be a disruptive influence in North Africa. This is why we never do business with the Russians. You cannot trust them."

"Well, Marco, if you put it like that, you've obviously made up your mind! The Wise Men see it differently, and that's what counts. They're keen on the Russian deal. There're too many unknowns in changing now."

"OK, I hear you, but I do not agree with you. Listen, I have one final thought. What is good for Malta, is good for the Family. It is easier for me to make things happen, at a government level, if what is good for us, is also good for the country. Once the American option is understood, and gets EU backing – which it will – the Russian deal will become toxic. When that happens, our plans for European distribution go out of the window. Just remember that. I am warning you – when the Americans go into Libya, I cannot promise to get the Russian deal through."

"Marco, look, the Wise Men have asked me to ask you to have faith. We push on with the Russians. That's the end of it."

Marco shook his head in frustration. Salvatore went on: "And before we finish, if you know who's leaking information to the *Malta Telegraph* and stirring things up, I urge you to stop them, now."

There it was again, the question of who was leaking to the journalist. Marco was shocked by the insinuation that it might be him.

"How dare you suggest that I might know? Here I am, telling you what I think is in the Family's long-term interests. I do *not* go leaking to the press. You should know me better than that! So, is that it then? Your final word? Push on with the Russians?"

Salvatore looked at him in silence.

Marco decided to bite his tongue and moved to end the conversation.

"OK then, I disagree with you. I reserve my right to have my own conversation with the Wise Men on this one. I think they are making a big mistake and I am not certain you have tried your best to represent my point of view."

He could see he had riled Salvatore, who had clenched his jaw. Anger was reflected in every part of him and Marco wondered if Natasha had ever seen that side of him.

"It's not for you to second guess the Wise Men, Marco. Like me, you follow instructions, whether you like them or not. I thought you would've understood that by now? Be careful. People are aware you were close to Sergio and, for you, what happened to him remains a problem. They're watching you and expect you to toe the line."

Marco had held himself in check for long enough; he could not stop the words spilling out of him. As he spoke, tears of anger welled in his eyes.

"Do not threaten me, you upstart! I am proud to say Sergio was my friend. And you, you little shit, had him imprisoned and killed. Do you know what? You will never be a fraction of the man he was. While people might go along with you for now, there are others in the Family who know what you have done and consider it a black stain on your character. They will never trust you again. You have screwed up your own future, you arrogant young prick, and it is *you* who had better be careful!"

With that, Marco turned his back on Salvatore, staggered down the stairs and out into the street. The world had certainly changed and he was no longer sure of his place in it.

Meanwhile, in central Milan, in Signor Bruno's *palazzo* just off via Brera, Natasha was working her way through a pile of papers involving the purchase of some mining leases in South Africa. The palazzo was a small Neoclassical masterpiece, originally built as a Jesuit college in the seventeenth century, with wide galleries around a quiet central courtyard. It had been in Signor Bruno's family for centuries. He had been born here and declared he would probably die here too.

They worked in his book-lined study and Natasha had to concentrate to be sure she did not test his limited reserves of patience. Although Signor Bruno must have been in his late seventies, and seemed the embodiment of a courtly, elderly gentleman, Natasha knew there was a steel core behind his mild retiring manner. She had already experienced the merciless grip of those heavily veined, liver-spotted hands, when he had once grasped her arm while uttering the warning *'never underestimate me'*.

Natasha always focused on her work, but was also trying to get a sense of the old man, to understand his motivations, to find an angle to latch onto – or a weakness. As far as she could make out, the only family he had, or at least ever mentioned, was his mother, with whom he had shared the *palazzo* until her death, some years before.

He was Natasha's sole direct connection with the Wise Men and, so far, was proving totally inscrutable. At the end of their session, when he had declared himself satisfied with her work, she dared to initiate a conversation.

"My father was meeting Salvatore today at his old office, near the San Siro. He told me he took the lease thirty years or so ago, while he worked on a project to try and impress you. That's all he would say. I was wondering what it was?"

"Well, if he will not tell you, then he must have his reasons. But I remember that time well. He was introduced to me at the club, the Croce Bianca, by your great-uncle Nicodemo – as was Sergio." Signor Bruno paused for a moment while his mind travelled back to that time. "Both such fine boys." Suddenly, he snapped out of his reverie. "Anyway, if that is all?"

Natasha took her leave, frustrated as always by her failure to make progress with him, when usually any man to whom she paid attention was instantly won over. But there had been something there today, something she had noticed for the first time about this man who had lived with his mother, never married and whose only non-work-related comment to her, ever, was: 'Both such fine boys.'

It was not much, but it was a start. On the way to the airport, Natasha placed a call to an ultra-discreet private investigator who occasionally did jobs for her.

CHAPTER 19
ABDULLAH BELKACEM
AL-UDEID US AIR BASE, QATAR

ABDULLAH FOUND WORKING with the Americans difficult. He did not have the patience for it. The preparations were extensive and Abdullah understood little of what they were talking about. Like all soldiers, they spoke in acronyms and military slang, which left him feeling confused and excluded. Whatever was being planned was codenamed 'Operation Establish Freedom', which would involve an initial force of 'contractors', followed by a company of 130 Rangers, organised into four platoons.

They told him the aim was 'joint forcible entry' into Marsabar, and then on into Tripoli. The Rangers involved were an elite light infantry force, whose proud history went from the D-Day landings, to fighting Iranian-backed Shi'ite militias in Syria, as well as clearing out ISIL units near the Turkish border.

They planned to land the company at a secure airfield in the southern desert, where vehicles and supplies would be brought in later, by helicopter and larger C130 cargo planes, from the Bizerte-Sidi Ahmed Air Base in north-west Tunisia.

Abdullah was to go into Libya some weeks ahead and prepare the ground. He had to establish a local militia of at least one hundred fighters, loyal to him and ready to execute the plan.

He had also to find an area where they could set up a preliminary base, which meant he had to identify a village where they would be welcome or which they could take by force. They were going to give him one hundred thousand Libyan dinars, about seventy thousand dollars, to help him buy the support of the people and prepare a camp.

No one had asked him, but Abdullah had a plan of his own. Regardless of what was said to him, he was going to return to the Nafusa Hills, a ridge some fifty miles south of Tripoli, reaching six hundred and fifty metres high and stretching all the way west into Tunisia. If George and he were going to reach Tunisia, which he thought likely, he would be able to find his way through the concealed, twisting valleys into western Libya. There he would find his family. He had not seen his wife and sons for four years. It was long enough. The Americans could strategise and plan all they liked, but this was what he was going to do.

Abdullah was from a Berber tribe and his family had lived in those hills for generations. When he had moved to the coast, with his wife Rania and his brother Tareq, his wife's family had stayed behind in the hills. They continued living in the traditional way, raising goats and sheep, and cultivating small fields of wheat and barley for bread. Once Abdullah had seen his family, he would go to Marsabar and contact those he thought might still be loyal to him. Four years was a long absence, though, and he was worried that he might not be as well remembered as he was hoping.

The soldiers never asked him for his thoughts as they continued on their steady route, oblivious to the fact that he had already decided on his plan of action. After many hours and days, they suddenly seemed satisfied. They piled several large binders of papers onto a line of desks and stood to attention when a group of older senior officers arrived to review their work.

The senior officers listened, looked at maps and read papers. One, older than the rest, with sunken cheeks, walnut skin and white spiked hair, asked Abdullah if he agreed with the plan and if he had anything to add.

Abdullah said: "Sir, thank you for your help. This is your plan and I am sure it is a very good one. All I ask is that you take me to western Libya and give me a month, then we can speak again and I will tell you what can be done. This is my country and these are my people; they will tell me. Until I speak to them and see the way it is, all this writing on paper makes no sense to me."

The colonel laughed.

"Well said! When do we deploy him?"

A lieutenant, who had been doing all the writing, replied: "Well, it's him and a Maltese adviser. They're good to go any time. He's as ready as he'll ever be. The adviser is a disaster. He flunked basic desert warfare training in the first week."

"Really? Mr Belkacem, did you hear that? Your friend is a disaster. You still want to take him?"

"Hah! Sir, the most important thing is, he is my friend and," Abdullah wagged a finger, "he is more dangerous than you think. He has fought alongside me before. I know this man. I am happy with him."

The white-haired old man laughed again.

"How do we infiltrate them?"

"We fly them into Tunis on a commercial flight. We've got an agent who'll take them to the border and give them ID, transport, cash, basic weapons. Then he'll set them off and we'll see what happens."

"Hmm." The colonel did not seem too impressed. "Sounds kinda vague to me."

The lieutenant looked at Abdullah and shrugged.

"We work with what we've got, sir."

The colonel turned back to Abdullah and said: "So, what do you say? You think this will all work out?"

Again, Abdullah smiled broadly. Then he dropped the smile

and hardened his expression. He had to show he was a serious man.

"Colonel, I said put me on the ground in western Libya and give me a month." He swept his hand contemptuously towards the piles of printouts, maps and flip-chart pages. "All this is useless.

"Four years ago, nothing happened in north-west Libya without my knowledge and permission. I had a militia of over one hundred men, full-time fighters, loyal to me alone. If we needed to go into action, I could rely on five hundred more. We had vehicles, arms, communication systems, all bought and paid for by me. I fought Gaddafi's soldiers three times, and won; I fought militias and jihadis from Iraq and Syria, and won. Your lieutenant says he does not know what he has got. But he will soon find out, eh?"

"I've read your file. I know who you are."

"No, sir. This is not true. You do not know who I am. You see, four years ago I had a brother, a family home, gold, a place in a good community, respect ... I even had an oil tanker. I was robbed of all this, and the chance to see my sons become men. They grew up without me. My wife tells me her hair has become grey. All the while, I sold hardware in another country. I am the man who has waited four years to put all this right. That is who I am."

"Mr Belkacem, I hope you do put all that right, but listen to me carefully."

The colonel walked over to Abdullah and held his face very close. He talked softly but there was menace in his words and fire in his eyes. He was an experienced soldier and had seen it all before.

"You are going back to Libya to help fix your mess of a country and your mess of a life. I get that. Shortly, there will be American lives at stake and I will *not* be fucked about. We will kick back Boutros, destroy the Islamic State-in-fucking-Libya and watch the Russians take their shit back home. *That* is what we are going to do.

"I hope you get your revenge, find your family and recover what you lost. But if I ever think my priorities and yours are in conflict, I will pull the support so fast you will not see it go. If I think you are using us for your own ends, then I will send a message to Abu Muhammad, with your last known coordinates. No warnings. Can I be any clearer?"

Abdullah understood the colonel. He bowed his head.

"You are most clear, sir."

"OK." He offered his hand. "Good luck to you – and remember this conversation."

"It is all in the hands of Allah now, *Inshallah*."

"Not if we have anything to do with it, it isn't!"

They shook hands.

"Lieutenant, send them on their way."

Abdullah watched the officers climb into a large SUV. The heat was searing, but he knew the desert awaited and he had better get used to it again. So he walked the kilometre to George's building. He wound between the low, drab prefabricated buildings and did not see a single other person on foot.

He looked around him at the coffee shops, the runways and the billions of dollars' worth of airplanes. All of it could vanish in a matter of weeks. Once the people and the planes had gone, the desert would strip back the fencing, the sand would cover the runway, the buildings and canvas canopies would be burned up by the sun and blasted by the wind. In a short time, it would be as if they had never been there.

He asked himself what the Americans were really doing? They did not like the country, they did not like the people and they certainly did not understand Islam. Why did they not just go home?

Cars and SUVs rolled past him and, in the distance, he heard the engine pitch of an F-22 Raptor turn into a scream as it blazed down the runway, filling the air with the aroma of its light, sweet exhaust. Off it flew to do harm to some unsuspecting Syrians, Iranians or Kurds. But, all things considered, Abdullah was in an upbeat mood. He wanted to tell George the good news that they were finally leaving for Libya the day after next. He was going home.

When he reached George's room, the noise from the TV was deafening. The policeman was lying on the bed, in baggy white shorts and a vest. Dirty clothes were piled on the bed and there were fast-food takeaway boxes all over the floor. He was watching a baseball game and eating icecream. The room smelled of stale food and unwashed bodies.

"I see military life is suiting you well, my friend. I must tell your lady wife that, without her to look after you, you turn into a goat. And smell like one also."

George got off the bed and used the remote to turn down the sound on the television. He was listening out for something.

"Thank God that rap music has stopped! Fourteen days of it. It's been hell! *Mela*, I can tell you all the words."

"Be quiet, do not make chatter. I bring good news! We leave for Libya in thirty-six hours!"

"What?" George stood, icecream spoon in hand and the residue thickening on his moustache and beard. "Is that all the training we get? I'm not sure I'm ready yet."

"You are ready, my friend. An M-16 in your arms, the sand beneath your boots and the sound of a Toyota engine. It will all come back to you soon."

"That's exactly what I'm afraid of!"

"We meet at Building 34-12, sixteen hundred hours, for equipment checks and final briefing. We fly from Doha, direct to Tunis. It is only six hours in the plane and then we cross the border. Maybe we fly over Malta and you can wave to your lady wife?"

George turned away from him, head down. Abdullah realised why he looked a little sad.

"Tonight is the party night, yes? Do not be sad, my friend.

Think, when you return, you will be a hero again! Maybe there will be more medals?"

George looked at him with raised eyebrows. The thought did not seem to cheer him up.

"You must telephone them before the party – wish them a happy time."

Abdullah was worried. His friend had not phoned his wife or daughter since he had arrived at the camp. He had spoken to his son at work, who had said he tried to spend as little time as possible at the house, due to all the crying. But it seemed nobody wanted to be the first to end the quarrel. Indeed, George was becoming a true Berber.

CHAPTER 20
ASSISTANT COMMISSIONER GERALD CAMILLERI

PRESIDENTIAL GARDENS, ATTARD, MALTA

Mike Lloyd had telephoned Assistant Commissioner Camilleri and suggested it might be an idea if they met up to chew the fat. Camilleri had suggested they take a walk in the San Anton Gardens, part of the Presidential Palace, in central Malta. Although the palace's architecture was unremarkable, its public gardens, with graceful shaded walkways, sculptures and ornamental ponds, made for a good place to relax and hold private conversations.

It was a midweek morning and the gardens were not busy. A mother with a pushchair bumped her child towards the play park, and one or two people with time to spare found cool spots under the palms, jacarandas and cypress trees, to read or study their phones. A man in a cream cardigan and English brogues sat on a bench, reading the *Malta Telegraph*. In front of him, a fountain splashed water, playing games with the reflections on a pond, vivid green with lily pads and aqueous growth.

Mike Lloyd came bustling into the gardens with two security types. They were all dressed in plain white shirts, grey trousers and dark sunglasses, walking at top speed, three abreast, the ripples of their haste immediately disturbing the calm of the gardens. Gerald Camilleri wondered why he had bothered to choose such a discreet and tranquil venue. He should have known better – Americans!

Camilleri sighed. The three of them came thundering towards him. The two security men peeled off, turned their backs and started a visual sweep of the gardens.

"Mike, good of you to meet me here. Lovely day, is it not? I thought we could enjoy some of the morning, while we talked."

"Gerald, yeah, I suppose so. What gives?"

"What gives? You asked me to meet you. I have no idea *'what gives'*."

"OK. In plain English – is Marco Bonnici onside? Are they with us or against us? That's what gives."

"Ah! Well, it is complicated."

Camilleri had already spoken to Mike and told him that the Bonnicis might be prepared to review their arrangements with Euromasio.

"I would say they could be persuaded. Whether their larger organisation can, I am not so sure," the policeman added.

"Hmm, I see. Do we need the larger organisation or can we get what we want from the Bonnicis acting alone?"

"Again, it is complicated. Splitting the Bonnicis from the Family is not something to be undertaken lightly. The Family dynasty, I use the word advisedly, goes back hundreds of years. Although the Bonnicis' links to them run deep, they have good standing in their own right. Marco's father, Franco, was a cousin of Nico Rossi. The pair of them salvaged the Family fortunes after World War Two by rebuilding the infrastructure of Italy and Malta, and by constructing half the hotels on the Mediterranean coast."

"Look, Gerald, I don't want a history lesson. Are they with us or not? You know how pissed we are right now. The Russians at best connived to kill our Chargé d'Affaires, at worst actually did it. It's tantamount to a declaration of war! We're not going to take it lying down. I am asking you to use your famous charm to get the Bonnicis to play ball. So, how's it going to go down?"

"Goodness, we are in a hurry this morning. You will have to learn to employ a little patience, Mike, especially in Malta. It works wonders."

"Gerald, don't fuck with me! I'm not in the mood."

"Well, I am trying to help you and some better manners on your part would go a long way. I have spoken to the Bonnicis and I believe they have some sympathy with your point of view. It might take time to bring them round, but I think it can be done. What exactly do you want them to do?"

"Cancel their deals with the Russians. Sign new deals with us or our proxies. Get the permits and finish all the other stuff they're doing so that, when our militia kick the Libyan National Army of General Boutros all the way back to Egypt and we bring in Exxon and Total to finish the job, it's all good to go."

"And they will want to know, what is in it for them? If they go breaking their very lucrative prior arrangements, there had better be adequate compensation. It is a reasonable position to take, is it not?"

"I don't know about the money and I don't give a rat's ass. I'm security, not finance. Ask them what they want. We do deals. I'll find someone who can make them happy."

"Good. Have you ever met Marco Bonnici? He is a very agreeable chap."

Mike Lloyd shook his head.

"Can't say I've had the pleasure."

"Well, we can put that right. He is sitting over there by the fountain. Would you like to go across and say hello?"

Mike Lloyd was taken aback. After a few seconds, he looked over at his security guys and nodded in Marco's direction. He let Camilleri lead the way to the bench, where Marco sat in his cream cardigan and oxblood English brogues.

Camilleri made the introductions. Mike Lloyd was tense and unsmiling, whilst Marco was relaxed and his usual charming self.

"Beautiful gardens are they not, Mr Lloyd? We do not have

many such places in Malta. Not enough spare land and the climate is too intense. It's such a shame. I always think you can judge a country by the quality of its parks and public spaces. That being so, we in Malta have a lot of work to do."

Marco paused for a moment.

"Did you know, it is customary for every visiting head of state to plant a tree in these gardens, as a symbol of the long and mutually beneficial relationship they hope both countries will enjoy?"

"No, Marco, if I may call you that, I didn't know, but the symbolism of the story doesn't escape me. I don't believe in signs or omens. I'm more the pragmatic type. I'm all for mutually beneficial relationships, but I ain't planting any trees. Is a 'mutually beneficial relationship' something you're interested in?"

"That is a good start to the conversation. To get to the point, we Bonnicis are happy to talk to you. But my associates are cautious people and I am still trying to persuade them to review their arrangements. I hope I will be successful in bringing them round to my point of view.

"You must know, that cannot and will not come cheaply. We believe, if the Americans can secure gas from North Africa through VertWay and feed it into the European transmission system, at the expense of the current Russian supplies, you could transform the economic landscape of Europe by reducing its reliance on Russian gas.

"I do not need to tell you, Russia's GDP, including its energy revenues, is smaller than Italy's. Without its energy revenues, it falls to below that of the Netherlands. It would be interesting to see how it would maintain its defence spending, if that came about."

Mike Lloyd grunted. Marco smiled at him and continued.

"So, you could say there is much to play for? We are prepared to let you into the game, but we want a reasonable share of the upside."

"I hear you, Marco, but seriously, a lot of this I've got to take back home. I'm sure it can all be arranged. We know what's at stake here, but I can't make you any promises, here and now. Gerald, thank you for arranging this, it was a good idea."

Mike Lloyd took off his sunglasses and met Marco's eyes as he spoke.

Marco was folding his paper, ready to leave. He paused.

"Oh, Mike, as a gesture of our goodwill, how would you like to get hold of three-quarters of a billion dollars, cash, in Libyan dinars, to help fund your efforts on the ground? Currently, it is due to be put into a shipping container and moved by standard freight to Istanbul. From there, it goes on to Benghazi and ends up in the clutches of General Boutros, and his Libyan National Army. I can provide more information, if you think it would be helpful."

Marco smiled and slid his newspaper under his arm. He clapped Camilleri on the shoulder, nodded at Mike Lloyd and slowly wandered away through the gardens, stopping to inspect a bed of roses, a variety that was unfamiliar to him.

Mike Lloyd sat in the back of the black SUV as it drove the three kilometres from the San Anton Gardens to the embassy buildings. It was an interesting conversation. Maybe there was something in it or maybe it was what the Russians wanted him to think. Either way, if the money did exist, he did not want it finding its way to Boutros's rebels. Not if he could help it.

CHAPTER 21
SUPERINTENDENT GEORGE ZAMMIT
TOZEUR, TUNISIA

Leaving the debris of the business-class flight littered around their seats, George and Abdullah collected their small sports bags, then transferred from the luxury of the international carrier to the local, one-hour flight to Tozeur.

Stepping out into the searing white light of the desert, George realised they were on the edge of the Sahara. Tozeur lies due south of Tunis and is as near to the Libyan border as can be reached by a commercial flight. It was in that crumbling, desert oasis town that they were due to meet the fixer who would take them across the border. Like many travellers before them, who had assembled for the camel-train journeys to Mali, Niger and beyond, George felt that he was standing at the end of the world.

South of this point was dangerous country. Not only were there a thousand kilometres of inhospitable desert, but across the sand was the Sahel. If the Sahara was a sea, then the Sahel was the beach. The strip of scrub that ran from the Atlantic Coast, south of Morocco, through Mali, Niger, Chad and the Sudan, all the way to the Red Sea. Not only was it home to violent tribes, such as the Tuareg and the Fulani, but also to a large number of Islamic State splinter groups, who followed their own agenda, stealing, murdering and kidnapping, on a daily basis. Meanwhile, coming north were the waves of refugees, heading for the coasts of Tunisia and Libya, trying to escape the chaos brought about by the incessant violence in their home countries and the hunger caused by drought and climate change. In their desperation, they could be equally dangerous.

Tozeur was once a classic oasis, the 'go to' location for any desert movie, from *Star Wars* to *The English Patient*. The thousands of palm trees still marked the town out as having an abundant water supply but, over the years, mismanagement and increasing population had led to a general air of poverty and decay. Not even the highly decorated yellow and orange, clay and sand-brick buildings could hide the fact that the town was losing its charm.

Abdullah was in high spirits, however. He was back in North Africa and heading home.

"It is a beautiful place, yes, my friend? Look, try one of these – they are the best! Tozeur is famous for them."

He had insisted on buying dates, a local speciality, farmed in the palmeries on the outskirts of the town. Afterwards, they had made their way to the centre, eventually sitting down at the roadside, their battered sports bags beside them, to eat the fruit. Abdullah draped a newspaper over his head to shield him from the worst of the sun. In Al-Udeid, they had been supplied with locally made clothing and the sports bags, which contained their carefully curated possessions. They would collect more equipment when they met their contact but, for the time being, had only what they carried.

Over the last three weeks, George had let his beard grow and acquired an acceptable moustache. It was now turning from a thick stubble into something recognisable as a full set of whiskers. His hair was getting long at the back and the wisps across his brow were wild and untamed. The time spent in the desert in Qatar had tanned his skin and, with his sandals, cheap baggy jeans, worn T-shirt and unkempt appearance, he fitted comfortably into the street scene of the North African town.

He squatted on the kerbside, his feet in the gutter, kicking the plastic and litter to one side. Rivulets of sweat ran from his hairline, down past his ears. He did not bother to wipe them away.

He thought about what might be happening at home. Before he had left Al-Udeid, he had phoned Camilleri and told him the whole thing was all taking much longer than expected and that he wanted to come home. Camilleri acknowledged that it was 'a difficult and onerous' assignment but said George's commitment to his duty would not be forgotten and would serve him well in the future.

George had mustered as much sarcasm as he had dared and asked him: "How, exactly?"

He was told to stop whining, but Camilleri promised to visit Marianna and make sure she was aware that her sacrifice was being appreciated at the highest levels. The family would start receiving hardship payments, in recognition of their contribution to the wellbeing and security of the state of Malta.

George acknowledged that would help – his wife would no doubt be happy about the increase in the household income. However, it did nothing to lift his own failing spirits.

George kept in touch with Denzel, who told him the crying had stopped and Marianna was now telling neighbours that her husband was on a secret mission, at the request of the President herself! The President had, in fact, sent Gina a card congratulating her on her engagement – something that George could scarcely believe, but which no doubt had thrilled Marianna, who had framed it and had Denzel hang it opposite the photograph of the Holy Father.

While he was pondering affairs back in Malta, he noticed Abdullah was talking to a young teenager wearing a Barcelona football shirt and a Star Wars-branded baseball cap. Abdullah pulled George to his feet.

"Let's go! The boy will take us on the first stage of our journey!"

"*Mela*, how did he recognise us?"

Abdullah pointed behind him to a high stone arch that bridged the street, with tiling across the top, adorned with Arabic script.

"The western gate of the Medina! It was arranged we meet at this time and place."

"Thanks for telling me!" George was miffed. "I hope it's not going to be like this all the rest of the way?"

"My friend, I will tell you what you need to know. Why tell you more? It will only make you worry. You must be happy – it is my job to keep you happy, eh!"

With a laugh, Abdullah set off after the youth.

After winding through the narrow streets, dodging and weaving past the teeming life of the old town, they turned down a lane an arm's-reach wide and ended up in front of a traditional orange-coloured, brick-built house, deep in the Medina. Inside, the rooms were beautifully tiled with patterned ceramics and the inner courtyard was calm, quiet and deep in shade. The only sound was the cooling water that flowed through terracotta channels, which irrigated an array of palms, flourishing in large earthenware pots.

They sat on a low sofa and were served tea in small green glasses while traditional Arabic-Andalusian music played from a radio in another room. After half an hour, just as Abdullah was getting impatient, a bespectacled, white-haired man in his sixties appeared, dressed in a long pastel *jebba*, with baggy pants and an embroidered waistcoat.

"Sorry, sorry, I am Edal Essa, I have been to a wedding!" he announced, holding out his arms to indicate his costume. "Please, five minutes for me to change. Then we go. We will be on the road for some time, so be sure now to be clean and comfortable."

His pickup was in a garage, under a nearby shop, with locked steel boxes bolted to the floor of the flatbed. They set off, driving up the steep concrete ramp, working their way past the narrow streets of the old town and out onto the state highway. They drove south, through the night, across the huge dry salt lake of Chott el-Djerid, until they reached the Jebil National Park, where the scrub gave way to rolling mounds of sand and tracts of exposed rock. They were on the most eastern side of Tunisia, on the north-eastern edges of the Grand Erg Oriental, the vast sea of sand dunes.

Edal drove his 4x4 twin-cabbed Toyota with skill and ease. The route he had chosen was longer, he had said, but safer – fewer smugglers, militants and less security. George slept for long parts of the journey, feet stretched across the back seat, head bouncing back and forth against the window pillar, while Abdullah talked endlessly with Edal, sitting alongside him in the front.

Looking at the map, George knew they were heading south, away from the coastline and from the Nafusa Hills, behind them. They would have to turn east, to cross from Tunisia into Libya. Edal told them he was heading for a crossing point near the Libyan town of al-Nalut. Officially, all the borders were closed, to prevent the passage of smugglers and the Islamic militias, and many of the roads had checkpoints manned by government soldiers. The crossing was a danger point so Abdullah decided they would wait for nightfall the next day. He knew the old smuggler roads well and, once inside Libya, he boasted he would not need a map or GPS, he could find his way home by sense of smell alone!

Edal was a relaxed companion and, although George could not follow all of the conversation, he could tell Abdullah and he were engaged in long and earnest discussions about tribal politics, the strength of the militias and the appetite for change. From time to time, Abdullah would pull a small notebook from his sports bag and make notes, or copy phone numbers from the directory on Edal's phone. George did not want to interrupt; he could sense this was serious business.

After about twenty hours of continuous driving, they arrived at an isolated, single-storey, concrete-block building, with a boundary marked by old tyres, once painted white, now half-buried in the sand. It was dusk. Edal explained this was an abandoned checkpoint, scene of a massacre of Tunisian soldiers by the Islamic extremists who came north from Chad, shortly after the Arab Spring uprising in 2011. The rear wall had mostly collapsed and he drove the truck into what was once a room, to conceal it from view.

Edal jumped out, stretched, urinated and announced that now he needed to sleep. He pulled some filthy foam mats from the back room of the building, shook off some of the straw and dust, checked for scorpions and promptly lay down, closing his eyes.

Abdullah took George to one side to tell him what he had learned. Edal was a Tuareg, from Ubari in the south-west of Libya. He had been helping the Americans for the past two years. The Tuaregs were looking for allies in the north and he believed they would give men and support, in exchange for a promise of autonomy in the south. Abdullah knew they were good and committed fighters who hated Islamic State as much as he did. They had been betrayed by Gaddafi and everyone who came after him. Edal had promised to speak to the leaders, to explain they had Americans behind them and that change was coming.

"This is a good start. And there is better news! Tomorrow is a happy day. We will find my family – I will enjoy a little time with them; then we will decide where fortune takes us next. The Americans have served us well so far."

Early the next morning, a battered, ancient lorry pulled up. The sun and the wind had stripped most of the colour from its paintwork and a thick coating of dust gave a near-perfect camouflage effect. Edal told Abdullah to relax. He lowered the Uzi machine pistol he had taken from the truck's lockbox. Edal chatted with the driver, then went to the rear of the truck and took out a box of food and a dozen bottles of water, which he gave to Abdullah.

"I leave you now but we meet again soon. From now on, it is your country. Travel at night. There are checkpoints, smugglers and the roads are not safe."

"May the road be kind to you, my friend. I do not worry about bandits and terrorists. I have George to defend me!" Abdullah said.

George shook his head.

They all embraced and then Edal climbed into the lorry and, with a brief wave, left them alone in the desolation of the desert.

Abdullah seemed happier by the hour.

"He is right, we must wait till dark. I have not got so close to my family only to stumble into a nest of Muhammad's killers or greedy militia. We leave at dusk and arrive late in the village. It is not far away now."

The daylight hours were interminable. They lay in the shade of the ruined building, to avoid the scorching sun. In the early afternoon, the heat made it difficult to breathe. The flies soon found them and attacked their exposed skin, desperate in their search for drops of perspiration. If they swatted them from their arms and faces, the insects made for their eyes, trying to steal minuscule drops of moisture. A wind had started to blow and the sand soon found its way into their hair, their pants, their mouths, so that every movement became an abrasive torture.

Abdullah lay still and stared at the ceiling. George could not tell whether he was awake or asleep. He tried talking, sleeping, scratching, pacing around the building. He longed to be in Edal's truck, where the air rushing in through the open windows provided some relief at least. By mid afternoon, Abdullah gave in and let George sit in the pickup for thirty minutes, with the air-con running. As his core temperature reduced, he found he could breathe more easily again.

"The desert is a cruel place, no? I have been away too long and grown soft."

"How much time will we spend in it?" George asked, fearful

of the answer. He found the environment taxing and longed to be back home, swimming in the fresh blue waters of Balluta Bay.

"I fear Allah's will means we will return this way before too long." Abdullah pulled at his black beard, straightening it. "We must go south, to Ubari. It is a long journey but we must meet Edal again and talk to the Tuareg leaders about what must be done."

The thought of another long journey, crossing the Grand Erg in the truck, made George feel ill.

"I don't know why you need me here – I'm doing nothing to help!"

Abdullah pondered.

"You have seen *Top Gun*? It is my favourite film. I know they are Americans – for that we must forgive them. So, I am 'Maverick' and you are 'Goose' – my wingman. See? That is how it is."

"*Mela*, I've seen that film; it's good. But doesn't Goose die in *Top Gun*?"

"Well – ummm, yes, that is true and it is very sad. But it is the fault of Iceman, no? And," Abdullah glanced around the shimmering flat lands surrounding them, "there is no Iceman here. It is too hot, eh?"

He laughed, very amused by his own joke, as usual. George shook his head with resignation.

"We must rest, for tonight we do the final part of the first journey."

They set off a little before seven, just as the sun was fast disappearing below the bright orange horizon. Abdullah drove with confidence. After a couple of hours, the moon was nearly full and they could drive without headlights. Once, when he saw another vehicle's lights approaching in the distance, Abdullah pulled off the road. He got out of the truck and waited for the vehicle to pass, hidden from sight, on the opposite side of the road. He cradled the Uzi.

Soon they were in the winding valley roads of the Nafusa Hills, the dunes of the Erg behind them. They could make out enclosed fields, and the straggling bushes on the roadside had become taller and more imposing. They slowed down through the small isolated ribbons of housing that occasionally abutted the roads, even though all the villages were in darkness.

"Here, they sleep when it becomes dark and rise with the sun. It is a sin to waste Allah's sunlight!"

Eventually, they stopped at the head of a long valley, where rocky bluffs rose to each side of them. There were a few isolated farmhouses and the small fields of wheat or barley were bordered by outcrops of rock on the valley sides. From what George could see in the moonlight, the village centre comprised a dusty square with two petrol pumps, a small green and white mosque and a single minimarket. There was blue fluorescent light coming from inside the shop. Abdullah left the truck, ignoring the barking dogs that had gathered outside the shop's front door, and banged on the window.

The door opened a fraction and an elderly man peered out. They spoke briefly and then suddenly the man rushed out, threw himself to his knees and grabbed Abdullah around the ankles. George found it hard to swallow when Abdullah raised the man and they put their arms around each other. Abdullah was home.

With that, the men went inside the shop, leaving George in the lorry. After ten minutes, he noticed car lights coming over the ridge at the head of the valley. The vehicle snaked down the side of the incline, making its way towards the village. As it approached the square, George crouched low in the footwell, unsure whether this was friend or foe. He had his answer soon enough, when the doors flew open and a tall youth in a white singlet and jeans jumped out, closely followed by a plump middle-aged woman in a blue *jilbāb* that covered her head and fell all the way to her feet.

The shop door flew open and Abdullah strode out towards them, arms outstretched. In the moonlight, with tears in his eyes, George watched Abdullah's reunion with Rania, his wife, and their eldest son, Jamal. After embraces and some short but earnest conversations, where no one let go of anybody else, Abdullah turned towards the lorry and beckoned George to join them. As he approached, Abdullah came towards him and pulled him into the family huddle. George's tears joined those already flowing freely.

That night, he insisted on staying with the shopkeeper, who was only too honoured to show him hospitality. Abdullah was able to return to Rania's brother's farm for a full reunion. He was beside himself with excitement at the prospect and the three of them rushed off to exchange news and for Abdullah to see the younger children, who had been told to wait until it was confirmed that the unimaginable had actually happened!

George lay on the low cot in the rear of the shop. The large chest freezer shook and rattled, the mosquitoes buzzed around his head and a mangy shop dog snuffled and farted at his feet, but he was the happiest he had been in many weeks, until he started thinking about his own family back in Malta. He missed them and cursed himself for the manner of his departure.

CHAPTER 22
ARTICLE IN THE MALTA TELEGRAPH

Reporter: Amy Halliday

31 July 2019

US Calls for Ceasefire in Libya

The US Ambassador to the UN, Sally Di Canio, today called for an immediate ceasefire in Libya and urged those involved to respect calls from the UN-backed Government of National Accord (GNA) in Tripoli to lay down arms.

The Ambassador regretted that recent Turkish efforts to agree a ceasefire had failed and said the situation in Libya was becoming increasingly unstable, with the country at risk of deteriorating into a full-scale civil war.

This instability has given rise to increased activity by ISIS-affiliated terrorist groups while production from the once fruitful oil fields has reduced alarmingly.

The Ambassador was critical of Russia, the United Arab Emirates and Egypt, who are all actively supporting General Boutros's Libya National Army with the supply of weapons, advisers and money.

The Government of National Accord was formed under the terms of a United Nations–led initiative in 2015, unanimously endorsed by the United Nations Security Council and recognised as the sole legitimate executive authority in Libya. It was unconscionable, the Ambassador said, that UN members were actively involved in operations to undermine the lawful government.

The Ambassador urged the Security Council to condemn the fighting and redouble its efforts to negotiate a ceasefire and send peacekeepers to enforce it. She said the lessons of Syria had been learned and the point had been reached when the US could no longer stand by and watch one of Europe's near neighbours descend into chaos.

The Russians continue to deny any involvement in the conflict in Libya and are on the verge of signing a strategic energy agreement to use Malta as a staging post to bring Libyan gas into Europe.

CHAPTER 23
NATASHA BONNICI
CASTELLO BONNICI, MALTA

NATASHA WAS SITTING on the terrace, browsing the Al-Jazeera website on her phone, feeling the spring breeze coming in off the sea. It was getting warm in the evenings and outdoor dining was only a few weeks away.

Marco had told her about his meeting in Milan and what had happened with the American in the San Anton Gardens. Natasha was careful to conceal her satisfaction that her father had reached the conclusion he had and that the Americans had taken the bait, as she had planned all along.

She had not planted the stories with Amy Halliday herself, but fed them through an old friend with whom she had gradually reconnected over the past few months. When she had first rung Nick Walker, he had understandably been reticent to engage with her, suspicious of her motives. Before making the call, she had had to work hard to convince herself that she had no underlying reason for it, other than an innocent curiosity about how he was doing and what he was up to.

Natasha had few, if any, close friends and, in those rare moments when she thought about such things, Nick was the only person, outside of her immediate family, with whom she had ever had a proper relationship. However, her feelings towards him were not exclusively sympathetic in nature. There were times when she also deeply resented the fact that he had assaulted her, nearly killed her, in fact, then fled, leaving her behind without a word. She had never taken rejection well; it ate away at her. The feeling that there was unfinished business between them fortified her resolve not to let him slip away from her again.

Nick was no fool and set a high value on the fact he had escaped from Natasha's orbit and extricated himself from the clutches of the Family, with his life intact and no criminal prosecution for his time spent running BetSlick's money-laundering operation. However, he remained fascinated by Natasha and knew he would never again meet anyone quite like her.

The memory of their relationship lingered for both of them and, while there were many sound reasons for them never to speak to each other again, they found their guarded conversations edged them ever closer together. They circled each other like boxers, each nervous about making the first move. In Nick's mind, another impediment to the relationship going any further than the occasional telephone call, was the fact that he owed Marco a million euros in recompense for the boat he'd stolen, and later sold, to make his escape from Malta. Natasha had promised him that problem would go away if Nick helped her on a small project with which she was having difficulties.

She had asked if he would contact a Maltese journalist with the *Malta Telegraph* and periodically, and anonymously, pass on some information. There seemed no harm in it, although Nick knew he could never be certain whether this was the real reason Natasha had got back in touch with him in the first place. Nevertheless, he went along with the request. A million euros was a million euros and he would be glad to be out of Marco's debt.

Natasha placed her phone down on the table as her father wandered onto the terrace, filthy in corduroy garden pants and an old checked shirt. He plonked himself down in one of the chairs and reached for the wine bottle in the ceramic cooler.

"You always look happiest when you're covered in filth and rooting around in the garden."

Marco smiled at her.

He was a gardener – or rather, a horticulturist – of some renown. During his stay in Serbia, he had used the time to write a couple of well-received books on the succulents of the Mediterranean. They would never be bestsellers, but were the sort of reference books that would stay on specialists' bookshelves for years.

"Give me another year or so and I will have this place looking as it was before I went away. Anyway, I have good news. I've just spoken to Signor Bruno and he says the Wise Men are now convinced we should do business with the Americans. So, they are prepared to let us tell the Russians the deal is off and see what we can put together with Mike Lloyd. I knew they would see sense in the end."

"Really?"

"Yes, it is great news and one in the eye for Salvatore! The only proviso is that the Americans have to prove they can get control of VertWay by buying it from Euromasio. That is for them to sort out, we stay out of it."

"OK. So far, so good. What happened with Salvatore? I can't imagine he took that decision well?"

"I do not care about Salvatore. I told Signor Bruno what I thought of him about what had happened to Sergio. I said I had to get it off my chest. I said I could not, would not, forgive Salvatore, but I would try to be civil towards him in future, in the interests of the Family as a whole."

"Wow!"

"Yes, wow! The phone went very quiet. Signor Bruno thanked me for my candour and said he totally understood my position, wished me a good morning, and that was that!"

"My God, those people …"

"I know, unbelievable." Marco paused for a moment and took a swig of his wine. "So, while I am clearing the air, I want to ask you about those articles in the *Telegraph*. On the one hand, they really helped. They changed the mood in Castille. But, on the other, I would like to know who the source was."

Marco watched her face carefully, but Natasha gave nothing away. He sighed. His tone hardened.

"Tell me, please. Do you know who was behind them? Because I have my suspicions. I have had for a while."

Natasha pondered while studying her glass of wine. It was pointless lying.

"It worked, didn't it? I'm really sorry. I wanted to tell you, but I couldn't before now."

Marco's eyes flashed at her, but he kept his anger under control.

"Of course you could not. You could not tell me because it was a despicable and deceitful thing to do. You could not tell me, because you were playing games with Yaroslav and Salvatore, probably two of the most dangerous men you are ever likely to meet. Because you knew it would scare me to death. There are a million reasons why you chose not to tell me."

"Doesn't the result count for something?"

"When it comes to matters of trust between us, no, it does not. I have known for weeks, but I could not bring myself to believe it. So, you were the source and no one else?"

"There was someone else, who was the actual source, but I'd rather not say. It's not important. It'll just annoy you even more."

"Really? Is that even possible? Spill it."

She had no choice.

"OK, it was Nick Walker."

Marco sat quietly and tried to absorb what Natasha was telling him.

"That man again? But he nearly killed you! He is a loathsome individual. He still owes me a million euros for stealing the *Blue Cascade*, which he has not paid yet, by the way. My God, I do not believe it!"

And there was one more thing that Natasha needed to say.

"Now we're getting it all out on the table, there's something else you should know."

"Oh, fantastic! You have been busy. I had no idea – what now?"

"Well, I needed some leverage to persuade Nick to be the source, so I told him if he helped us, you'd forgive him the debt he owes you for stealing the boat. I mean, you never really expected him to repay it, did you?"

Conveniently, at that moment, Natasha's phone rang and she glanced at the screen, excused herself and left her father sitting on the terrace, quietly fuming.

It was her contact in Milan who had being making some enquiries on her behalf. She held the phone close to her ear.

"Well, there's definitely life in our elderly gent yet! He lunches punctually at 13:20 …"

"I know that. Tell me something I don't know."

"Well, after lunch he goes to Orto Botanico di Brera for a constitutional, then home for a nap and then …"

"Yes?"

"Then, on a Monday and a Thursday, his trusted servant, Toni the Sicilian, opens the side door to the palazzo and admits a young *raggazo* for the Signore to enjoy."

Natasha let out a low whistle.

"Oh, dear, Signor Bruno. Shame on you! And how old are these boys?"

"Varies, from fifteen through to late teens. The younger, the better, I suspect."

"Is it always the same boy or do his tastes vary?"

"Signor Bruno seems to like variety. I get the feeling he loses interest quickly and feels the need to … regularly refresh his appetite. "

"How very interesting."

CHAPTER 24
MIKE LLOYD
FREEPORT, MALTA

THE SOUTH of Malta was one of Mike's least-favourite parts of the island. He was not a fan of the island generally, but he thought the south, with its broken roads, quarries, small dusty fields and dry-stone walls, was underdeveloped and backward.

If anyone flying into Malta kept an eye out, just before the wheels touched down at Malta's international airport, they would see a rough track, running east to west, leading to a remote farmhouse two hundred metres from the end of the runway. It belonged to one of Mike's 'informal' contractors, a young man called Saviour Azzopardi.

Saviour's father had farmed the small sandy fields that lay to the south of the main runway until his death, a few years before. His son, Savi, declined to follow the family farming tradition and, after a period doing IT for a small startup bank, decided to make a career out of farming people's personal data from the internet instead, selling lists to unscrupulous buyers in eastern Europe and Asia. It was not as backbreaking as scraping a living from the small plots of land his father had once worked and it certainly paid better.

Mike Lloyd had been tipped off by a colleague that when he needed some off the books work doing, this guy could be useful.

Savi had unwisely tried to hack the embassy systems for information about the arrival of an American movie star who was due to start filming on the island. He had nearly succeeded, a fact that impressed those in the embassy's cyber-security team. From that point on, the embassy's Head of Security had Savi's name in his contacts.

For certain projects Mike would rather not have to seek clearance. Planning to steal a billion Libyan dinars from the Russians was one of them. The other benefit of using Savi was that he had connections at Freeport Malta and understood the systems that moved containers through the dock there every month.

One of the downsides of visiting Savi was that his house was a health risk. His kitchen was a source of all manner of infections, waiting to leap right at you. His living room stank of stale dog and sweet rotting food. Despite the smell, which stuck in his throat and threatened to make bile rise, Mike Lloyd was pressing on with the conversation. He was talking in general terms, trying to avoid telling Savi what they were up to. Unfortunately, he was failing miserably.

"So, say I wanted a container to leave a cargo ship at a certain place – how would I do that?"

"You'd just change the EDIFACT message features. You've got access to an EDI terminal, yeah?"

"Maybe."

"There's no room for 'maybe'. Without EDIFACT messages, nothing moves. But that's easy enough.

"You send a COSTOR message, asking a for a packing facility to stuff a shipping container with goods; a COPARN message to make it available; a COREOR message to …"

"OK, OK, I get it. Say I don't have access to the EDI stuff, but I still want to get the container from A, not to B, but say to C?"

"And you don't want whoever is waiting for the cargo at B to know it has gone to C?"

"Hell, you're sharp. Now we're getting somewhere."

"OK, so you want me to hack the EDIFACT system and divert

a container?"

"I do."

"Where's this container coming from and where's it going to?"

"I don't know but, for instance, let's say it's leaving from Novorossiysk, on Russia's Black Sea, and it arrives in Istanbul for transhipment to Benghazi."

"Right!" Savi paused, wondering what he was getting himself into. "All nice places, I'm sure. So, where d'you want to heist it? Istanbul or Benghazi?"

"Probably Istanbul."

"What's the cargo?"

"Stuff, Savi! Stuff! It doesn't matter."

"Russian stuff. That's great. How pissed off will the shippers be when it goes missing?"

"Oh, I'd say pretty pissed."

"Good to know! I'm assuming this 'stuff' is an ambient load, not refrigerated or anything?"

"Yeah, yeah, it's just normal stuff."

"Normal stuff? It's not weapons, toxics or nuclear stuff, is it?"

"I said, normal stuff!"

"Not drugs or human cargo, or anything really nasty – because, I'm telling you, that's not my thing."

"Don't worry – it's just stuff! So, can you heist it or not?"

"Well, sure. I don't want to end up being the fall guy here."

"Not a chance. We look after those who look after us."

"OK, you better promise me that. I'm just a civilian."

"Uncle Sam promises."

"Well, you could send a COPRAR message to have the container offloaded at a different port and, if you want to do the business at Istanbul, send a COPINO message to alert the container terminal that a land-based carrier, your truck, will be arriving at a certain time to collect the container. All you have to do is get there ahead of the owner's haulier."

Savi was lost in thought.

"The other thing is, at most larger ports they operate a system of PIN authorisations, which the driver will need to get the cargo released. He enters the PIN at the gate, then the port automatically releases the container.

"You can usually get access to the EDI stuff, if you can identify the agent who does the shipping. A bit of phishing and you'd be surprised what people give you."

Mike was getting impatient.

"Yeah, yeah, whatever – can you do it?"

"Well, the PIN to get the haulier into the port and trigger the movement of the container, is given by the carrier to the haulier and he gets it from the person receiving the goods. It operates as the release authority under the bill of lading. That's a bit trickier. Do you know who's going to receive the goods?"

Mike smiled. He certainly did, but there was no need to give the boy all the information in one go.

"So, am I right that you can do all this shit?"

Mike looked at Savi with his most innocent expression.

Savi clicked this was not a hypothetical conversation.

"Whoa – steady, tiger! If we're really going to do this, I need to know a lot more about what the fuck's going on here and who's involved."

"Trust me, the last thing you need to know is what's going on here! You do me a list of all the details you need and we'll see what we can do. I've got no timescale for this yet. But when I say move, you've got to be ready. It could all kick off tomorrow, for all I know. So get doing your homework."

"How much are you paying for this operation? And, if I get involved, I don't want any blowback to me!"

"You'll be happy. Just get on with it. By the way, did you ever get to see Angelina Jolie in *By the Sea*?"

Savi had a thing for Angelina and it was details of her arrival on Malta that he had tried to hack.

The geek looked at him with a furrowed brow. Mike grinned.

"No? It was a really shit film."

CHAPTER 25
ABDULLAH BELKACEM
GHAT, SOUTH-WESTERN LIBYA

ABDULLAH SPENT four days in the village, talking to an endless stream of relatives, friends and well-wishers, who had come from near and far to welcome him home. They sat in the main room of Rania's brother's large stone-built farmhouse, which nestled below a ridge some way above the valley floor. This allowed a cool, clean breeze to sweep through the open windows. A wide loggia ran along the front of the house. This not only provided deep shade, but also gave a great view of the winding valley road, down which any traffic from the north would have to approach.

Abdullah listened wearily to the same stories he had heard before the fall of Gaddafi. Nothing here had changed. The oil revenues in Tripoli were much reduced due to civil war and sanctions but, even so, Libya should have been one of the wealthiest countries in Africa and it rankled with him that it was not.

All the visitors pledged their allegiance to a fight for a new Libya and Abdullah gave his thanks, although he knew these were not the people he needed to win over. There was a family from Marsabar who had heard of his return and travelled for several hours to meet with him. Razan was a carpenter and had made the journey with his brother and their two cousins. All had served with Abdullah previously and they had fought together to push Gaddafi's troops out of Marsabar, down the Coastal Road back to Tripoli, in 2011. He charged them with contacting as many of his former comrades as still lived and breathed, to prepare for his return.

He was shocked by how fast news of his arrival had travelled. It made him realise he needed to leave the village quickly, before he put his family in danger. He knew not everybody would welcome him back. He spoke to George, who had been idling away the days on a low sofa at the back of the room eating, sleeping and watching Abdullah's earnest discussions. At the end of the fourth day, when the farmhouse was quiet, Abdullah told him of his plans.

"Well, my friend, the time of rest is over. Now the hard part begins. Tomorrow morning, I must say goodbye to my family again, and then I will meet you at the shop in the village. You must be ready for a long journey south."

"Are we going to meet Edal Essa?"

"Yes. Can you speak like a Frenchman?"

"No."

"A pity. We go through Algeria for maybe ten hours of driving. In Algeria, they speak the French. I understand only a little. Then we go across the Tassili Mountains. Very high. I have been, it is like driving on the moon! All rocks, no shrubs or sand. The wind has blown them into shapes, so they look like trees! I do not lie, you will see. Rocks shaped like trees. It is a fine sight."

"It sounds like a long way. Can't the Americans help – fly us or something?"

"Hmm. No! These early days, we must be as clever and sly as the fox. Nobody will expect us to go to the south! I told Razan I was coming back north to Marsabar; that is as good as having the Imam announce it at Friday prayers. The man's heart is big, but his mouth is bigger!"

Early the next morning, Abdullah collected George and they set off for the drive south. Abdullah was in a sombre mood and not inclined to talk. George guessed his departure had been painful. The Toyota held additional fuel in twenty-litre plastic jerry cans and two cool boxes of food and water, all concealed under a blue plastic sheet tied down with old nylon rope. Rakes, hoes and other pieces of farming equipment were thrown on top of the sheeting to make the truck look like a local farm vehicle.

Abdullah had wrapped George's head in a long, deep blue turban or *cheche*, in the Tuareg style, with the loose ends wrapped round his neck. The cloth was about three metres in length and Abdullah showed him how to tie the ends around the lower half of his face, so just his sunglasses showed, to protect him from the dust and from suspicion, should they be stopped. It was said that the Tuareg often had a blue tinge to the skin on their faces. The reason lay in the indigo they used to roughly dye the cloth, which combined with the action of sweat and the desert wind.

Rania's brother had given George some battered and torn khaki cargo pants, which were tied with a length of rope, in place of a belt. He offered one of his own long, well-worn cotton tunics, which nearly reached to George's knees, to complete the look.

Abdullah had laughed at the overall effect.

"Mr Policeman, if the lady wife could see you now, I think she would scream! If we are stopped, all you have to do is be quiet and it will be fine. We have the American papers and passports. I have looked at them and they are not so good. The Americans are not good with Arabic script. There are mistakes. But no worries, because I have this. Now we are at war!"

With relish, Abdullah produced a pistol that he had taped to the underside of the driver's sun visor.

"You look under your dashboard, my friend."

George felt the cool butt of a hand gun.

"Is it loaded?"

"Oh, yes! Allah will understand, if you need to use it, eh?"

George looked at his friend to see if he was joking. The set of Abdullah's jaw gave him his answer.

The drive was unremarkable, other than that it took twenty hours and the monotony of the long flat desert roads was only surpassed by the anxiety George felt at the two border crossings. As Abdullah had promised, the road across the Tassili plateau was spectacular and they forgot their weariness as they marvelled at the two thousand metre peaks and the weirdly eroded sandstone boulders, blasted over time into strangely shaped mounds and hollows. The area had not always been a desert. A mere 8,000 years ago it bore the name Plateau of the Rivers. The last echo of those fertile times was in the scattered groves of cypress trees.

Soon, the mountains fell away. After driving east and re-entering Libya, on an unmarked track, they arrived at the town of Ghat, where they were to meet Edal.

It was an old walled frontier town of 22,000 inhabitants, some 700 kilometres south of Marsabar. Inside its walls, the narrow alleys and tightly clustered, irregular white housing made it look like an attractive oasis in the arid sandstone landscape. On getting out of the truck, they found a cruel hot wind was blowing, thick with dust, making its inhabitants draw their scarves across their faces and hurry about their business, heads down to protect their eyes.

Ghat lay on the border with Algeria and on the route north from Niger and Chad. Originally a Tuareg slave-trading town, it was still a transit point, with dozens of migrants sitting listlessly on the roadside. It was clear from the numbers of people making their way north that the borders were wide open. Resources and the will to stem the tide were in short supply.

On a hill high above the town stood a large red sandstone fortress, originally built by the Italians in the 1930s, at the height of their imperial ambitions. Just as the French had waged war against the Tuareg across the border in Algeria, so the Italians in Libya had tried to protect their colonial borders. However, lines on a map in Rome went largely unrecognised by the nomadic

Tuareg and those who used the age-old migratory routes from Mali and Niger to the northern coast.

After many stops and requests for directions, Abdullah found the address Edal had given him and they parked at a distance from a small, flat-roofed house. It had a metal gate over the front door and heavy bars protecting the windows. A number of well-worn old cars were scattered in front of it. Abdullah and George eased their stiff limbs out of the truck. George stretched his arms above his head, yawning wearily.

"So, my friend, today we meet Edal Essa and the elders of the Tuareg. There will be much talking," Abdullah announced.

George sighed wearily.

"Fantastic. I could do with a sleep."

"You should try to listen, there is much for you to learn, my friend. I am hoping that they will help us. For many years, the Tuareg have fought the Tebu, another tribe, for control of the trade routes in the south. There was peace for some years, but Boutros stirred the pot and there was war over control of Ubari, a desert town four hours away."

"Why would anyone want to fight over a place like that?"

"Ah! I tell you! Ubari is at the south of the Sharara oil field, so it is very important. He who has Ubari, is in a good place to make the security. There is money to guard the oil from the Islamist gangs who come up from Mali and Niger. That is worth many dinars.

"Also, all the good, sweet water we drink in the north, in the coastal towns, comes from wells in Ubari! And that is not all. In the middle of town is something even more important."

Here, Abdullah allowed himself a dramatic pause and looked at George to make sure he had his attention.

"*Mela*, what's so very important?"

"In the centre of town is a three thousand metre runway, long enough for very big aeroplanes." Abdulla nodded his head enthusiastically and smiled broadly. "This is what the Americans like."

"Right, I see. And who controls Ubari now?"

"Nobody can tell me that. But we will help the Tuareg take it, yes?"

As Abdullah's eyes flashed with excitement, the door and security gate creaked open and the heavily lined, smiling face of Edal Essa emerged, looking up and down the empty street, before then hastily beckoning them inside.

The US PR machine had started to plant stories that the Sharara oil field was at risk from Islamic State terrorists from the Sahel and Boutros in the east, which was partly true. They claimed US and EU interests were being threatened. The message was that patience had run out with Egypt, the UAE and Russia, whose covert actions were destabilising the fragile UN-supported Government of National Accord in Tripoli. Ominously, they argued that steps needed to be taken to establish some order in the country. Those stories had not gone unnoticed in Libya.

Inside the house, the front room held a fug of cigarette smoke as twenty men crammed around the table to hear Abdullah outline his plan. He moved glasses, sugar bowls and ornaments, positioning them around the table, to illustrate his points.

"... then the drones fly in from US Incirlik airbase in Turkey." A salad spoon swooped in from the sky to land alongside the folded headscarf that was acting as the runway. "And, to destroy Boutros's aircraft, the Americans send Reaper drones from Kuwait and ... booom!" A salt cellar dived up and down, the elders' heads bobbing along with the action.

Before this, Abdullah had placed two candle holders, together representing several hundred Tuareg militia, alongside a small group of US contractors, who would be first to arrive at Ubari. They would set up the desert base within easy reach of the strategic oil facilities. It would then be safe for the main body of US Rangers to fly in and train the militia on American-supplied weaponry.

The elders craned over each other's shoulders to see the battlefield before them. Abdullah continued.

"Then, an army of Tuareg, US Rangers and contractors move north, to Marsabar, to meet my militia. We will be even more magnificent!" His hand slapped the table; the cutlery rattled and one of the candlesticks fell over. "With American drones and planes above us, we go down the Coastal Road towards the Az-Zawiyah refinery, west of Tripoli, leaving the Sharara oil fields safely protected."

Abdullah lit a cigarette and stood back.

"Boutros will run back to Egypt and the IS dogs will be at our mercy. We will make sure the oil flows and there will be jobs, money for schools, health ... and a place for the Tuareg to live freely.

"It is a good plan, no?"

There were enthusiastic murmurs around the table

"So, I hear you ask me, if you do help us, what does the Tuareg get, eh? What is in it for them from the Americans?"

The elders all fell silent. The only thing that moved were the columns of cigarette smoke that unfurled and spiralled upwards, towards the ochre-stained ceiling.

"The Tuareg will have their own lands, as it was before. Azawad lands, in northern Mali, the Azger confederacy land in Libya and Algeria. All the Tuareg tribes will be recognised."

The was an outburst of excited murmuring around the table.

"The Americans say Tuareg are 'indigenous people' and will go to UN to get proper status and, also, the Americans and French will make it that Tamezgda and Tkerekrit Sultanates in Niger are also autonomous. Tuareg will rule Tuareg. There can be peace in the Sahel. It is good, no?"

A voice spoke from the back.

"All this is good, certainly, but will there be money also?"

"Ah! Yes, there is also money. To get all this, you must be police for national borders. Tuareg will have vehicles and weapons and you will stop the migration into Libya and Algeria from Niger, Mali, Chad and Sudan. You close borders except for proper trade. You keep these people off your land. If IS come, you fight them and the Americans will help. It will be known that to come north is to meet the Tuareg, a thing nobody wants."

Abdullah paused. He had saved the best bit until last. He raised one finger and wagged it in the air to quell the chatter.

"Also, you will provide the security to Wada and Sharara oil fields and for this you will be paid well!"

Many cigarettes were smoked and copious amounts of tea drunk. An atmosphere of excitement built up as it dawned on the elders that they could be on the cusp of reversing the post-colonial losses of the nineteen sixties.

Abdullah was especially pleased as he had achieved all this without touching the one hundred thousand dinars in the lockbox of the truck. He now considered that money his fee for making such excellent arrangements.

Outside, guarding the 'fee', was George, who had left the room, after listening bemused to the first two hours of the debate, and retreated to the truck for a nap, his feet sticking out of a rear window as the wind gradually filled the interior with fine desert dust.

CHAPTER 26
NATASHA BONNICI
CASTELLO BONNICI, MALTA

NATASHA WAS SITTING in her favourite wicker chair on the terrace of the *castello*, feeling energised and excited. She was sipping iced coffee in the company of her father and Assistant Commissioner Camilleri. They had been discussing Maltese politics and the progress being made by Marco and Refalo in getting the permits and concessions they needed to bring the gas ashore. All was going well, but there was another matter that Natasha was interested in, which had yet to be raised.

"So, Gerald, what's happening with the Americans and the cash? Are they planning to heist it or not? D'you know?

Camilleri was a little put out by the bluntness of the question, but could not find a reason to avoid answering her.

"I think they are planning something. I confess, I do not know any details – but it is not our business really. I heard they have some freelance hacker type who lives on a farm in the south of the island. He is putting together a scheme that allows the Americans to walk in and lift the container once it reaches Istanbul. How, I really do not know."

Marco said: "Yes, the Americans' intentions are important. At a local level, in Libya, that amount of cash can accomplish a great deal. We would like to be kept in the loop, if that is possible."

Camilleri replied, "I do not think the Americans are short of money. They are only intercepting it to stop it from getting into the hands of the LNA rebels in the east of the country. They were talking about destroying the cash."

"D'you know the name of this hacker?" Natasha enquired. "Maybe we could try and get some information from him? Spare you having to go and make enquiries."

"No, not his full name. They referred to him as Savi – short for Saviour. I am afraid that is all I know. I have seen him, though, in the back of Mike Lloyd's car. I think I would recognise him again."

Marco and Gerald continued talking while Natasha was engrossed with her phone. After a few minutes, she held the screen in front of Camilleri.

"Is this him?"

They both looked at her.

"How on earth did you do that?" Camilleri asked.

Natasha winked at him.

"Tinder. Look it up, Gerald! His name is Savi Azzopardi. He likes pizza, conspiracy theories and computer games. Just my type!"

At that moment her phone pinged.

"Well, I'd better decide what to wear, I've got myself a date!"

Later that evening, Natasha appeared, dressed for her date, and Marco was surprised to see her wearing a pair of jeans, some white trainers and a T-shirt. Her gold Omega watch had been replaced by a large pink affair, with a plastic wrist strap.

"Where on earth are you going, dressed like that?"

She looked in the hallway mirror to check her lipstick.

"I don't want to scare him, do I? We're going to Pretty Bay promenade, for an ice cream. He doesn't like travelling to the north of the island, says he gets lost easily."

"Jesus! Tell me, why exactly are you meeting him?"

"We want to know what the Americans are up to, don't we? He'll tell me."

"We could just ask them, can't we?"

"We could, but it's better to hear it from the horse's mouth. Oh, one more thing. You needn't worry, Simon is coming with me, just in case there's any funny business. See you later."

She smiled, ran her tongue over her teeth to clear any lipstick marks and left through the huge double doors studded with ancient iron nails.

Marco watched her go and wondered why Simon, his head of security, was going with her on the date. By the look of the lad, Natasha could eat him alive. Then, it belatedly occurred to him what she might have meant about hearing it from the horse's mouth.

CHAPTER 27
GEORGE ZAMMIT AND ABDULLAH BELKACEM

UBARI, LIBYA

EDAL ESSA HAD BEEN as good as his word. The Tuareg elders had agreed that the proposal was a rare opportunity to remedy some historic wrongs, be granted the right to manage their own affairs in the traditional ways – and receive a consignment of free weaponry from the United States into the bargain!

George, however, was bored and feeling useless. He had had little to do since arriving in Ghat and did not see why he could not just go home.

He had raised the issue again with Abdullah, the previous day, when they had taken a break from their discussions, sitting on the roof of the Toyota in the car park of the Old Fortress, high above the town. Abdullah had been in high spirits.

"It is going well, my friend. I could not have wished for a better start. These are good men and I hear that all of Marsabar is ready for me to return and give that dog Abu Muhammad a kicking! Now, we need the Americans to come and deliver what they have promised."

"*Mela*, Abdullah, all this is good, I agree. But I don't understand why I'm here. I wish you well and hope you give Abu Muhammad a good kicking, but do you really need me here?"

"Ah! Of course, yes! Maverick needs his Goose! Where would he be without Goose?"

"Problem is, Goose wants to fly off home, Abdullah. Goose is fed up."

"Hah, Goose wants to get into action, eh? War is like this. Much waiting and little fighting. You must be patient. There will be fighting soon and then you will be happy. I cannot wait to see you again with a gun in your hands and a smile on your face!"

George moaned quietly. The last thing he was looking forward to was actual fighting. In fact, he had no intention of being involved in any at all.

A week later, they were standing at Ghat's small airport, twenty kilometres to the north of the town, in the gathering dusk. Abdullah was excited, talking to Essa and some of the Tuareg elders on a small viewing platform on the flat roof of the one-storey air terminal. George was loitering at a distance. Eventually, his attention was caught by a wave of excitement that spread across the deck as a speck appeared in the distant sky, flying low over the black-silhouetted hills.

"Is this it?" George shouted to Abdullah.

"Yes, I have kept my word to them and the Americans have kept their word to me!" He shook his fist in the air.

They watched the speck form into a massive plane that seemed to hang in the sky, barely moving. Abdullah's eyes were wide in amazement.

"It is a wonder it can fly at all! It is a bigger plane than I thought and it looks heavy."

Abdullah stroked his beard, a look of concern spreading across his face. He put his hand to his mouth and whispered to George.

"I told them the runway was a little longer than is the truth! That will not make problems, eh?"

"You didn't, surely?"

Abdullah looked sheepish.

"We will rely on Allah; he will provide. *Inshallah!*"

They watched spellbound as the giant plane seemed to make a sudden dive for the runway and fall towards the earth.

"Look!" Abdullah grabbed George's arm hard. "The propellers have stopped and are going backwards!"

The plane skimmed the boundary fence and actually touched down on a concrete pad before the runway proper, plumes of smoke blazing from its wheels. The engines screamed as the reverse thrust from the counter-clockwise motion of the props rapidly slowed the plane. At one point, it seemed it would burst through the boundary fence at the far end of the runway but, just in time, it slowed and the pilot forced the turn, dipping the wings as the plane swung off the runway to make its way back towards the apron.

Abdullah looked at George, who puffed out his cheeks and blew a sigh of relief.

"I told you, unbeliever, it is the will of Allah!"

With that, they all ran down the stairs and out onto the apron, forming a small crowd to greet the whale of a machine. George hung back a little, unwilling to be swept up in all the excitement.

An airport worker waved his jacket in the air to guide the plane forwards. When its nose was nearly in the building, he jumped up and down frantically and the plane came to rest. The props stopped turning, the strobes stopped flashing and the rear of the fuselage dropped open. A loadmaster appeared at the head of the ramp, shouting instructions to the waiting crowd, who approached with two forklifts and six flatbed trucks.

The loadmaster quickly winched off ten pallets of assorted weaponry and an armoured personnel carrier, which was to be the transport for a team of six private military contractors. They would give the Tuareg instructions on how to use the new weaponry and then travel to join the fifty other special forces soldiers already on their way to Ubari by road, to establish a perimeter around the airfield.

Within thirty minutes, it was all over and the giant plane, several thousand kilos lighter, trundled to the very end of the runway, spun round, gunned the engines and crawled off, finally inching up into the air, its retracting wheels clearing the boundary fence by a matter of centimetres.

The next day, Abdullah asked George to help unpack the weapons and assist in training the Tuareg. He happily went to the homemade range, in a disused quarry outside of town, glad to make himself useful. He was competent around firearms and his time on the range at the Al-Udeid Air Base in Doha had made him familiar with the M-16 rifle and basic US Army small arms.

The American contractors were a rough bunch, who postured, spat, swore and generally strutted about, wearing wraparound sunglasses, their tactical vests stuffed with more equipment than they could ever have need for. They treated the Tuareg with contempt, speaking to them as though they were a squad of grunts who had never set foot in the desert before.

It took the Tuareg a while to learn how to set up the M-16, zeroing the sights, adjusting the windage drum and elevation settings, but eventually they all became confident and the range rang with the crack of rifle shots. Tuareg learn to fire rifles when they are still children. Soon, they were shredding the paper targets with volleys of measured, accurate shots, impressing their tutors, who started to realise this militia had potential as a powerful fighting force.

When George arrived on the range, he had made himself known to Sam, the platoon leader. The contractors had not known what to make of Abdullah's adviser. George's stubble had now grown out into a proper beard and his indigo *cheche*, expertly tied over his ragged hair, revealed only the upper half of his desert-tanned face. His dusty, worn clothing was being washed, so he had been given a light *bubus*, a traditional long gown worn by many of the older men. He had swapped his heavy, scuffed boots for a pair of sandals and looked every inch a desert nomad.

Sam, the heavily tattooed Texan platoon commander, had

watched him handling the M-16 and sidled over to him afterwards, thumbs tucked into the shoulder pads of his tactical vest.

"So, what's the fucking deal with you?"

George was wary of these hired mercenaries, masquerading under corporate branding.

"No deal. I'm with the Maltese Police, here as an adviser."

"Maltese Police? Dude, you're totally lost!"

"I know. It's not my idea of a great assignment."

"I don't usually ask questions but – how d'you know how to handle the M-16? You ex-military?"

"No, but I've had some experience of desert warfare. I've trained with the Green Berets and the Rangers at Al-Udeid."

"No fucking shit?"

George knew this boast was a mistake, as soon as he'd broadcast it, but there was no way of taking it back.

"Tell you what, have you ever fired an SAW? An M249 squad machine gun?"

"Er, yes, a few rounds on the range at Al-Udeid. I've also fired twin Brownings mounted on a technical."

George could not stop himself from bragging to the big, well-muscled Texan about the time he had closed his eyes, pulled the twin triggers on the Brownings and unleashed mayhem onto Abu Muhammad's men at Abdullah's compound in Marsabar.

"OK! Well, you're the man! We'll fire some bursts this afternoon, but once we get to Ubari, if we get hit, we'll need someone who can handle a squad machine gun, to help in one of the crews. We need four crews covering the perimeter, but we're a bit short of hands. So great, you've got the job! What's your name?"

"George."

Sam looked puzzled.

"George? That's not an Arab name?"

"I'm not an Arab. I told you, I'm Maltese."

"Yeah, cool. I thought you spoke OK English for an Arab."

The night after, Abdullah and George were sitting in their Toyota pickup, their flatbed loaded with boxes of automatic rifles, mortars, ammunition, military ration packs and spare wheels for the technicals. The convoy of nearly twenty vehicles had left Ghat around midnight, to try and cover the 370 kilometres to Ubari before sunrise, so they could arrive in the town undetected.

They drove on at speed through the night, luckily without incident, and reached the town in the half light of early morning. The convoy roared through the streets, causing lights to turn on and citizens to go to their windows, to see what new evil had arrived.

They drove straight into the airport dropoff area. There two contractors, in the by now familiar black personal body armour, waved torches to guide them through a security fence and onto the airside apron. The larger unit of contractors had arrived the day before, from Tunisia, in their own fleet of technicals and trucks.

They had told the few Libyan Air Force personnel stationed at the airport they had an hour to clear the two antique government MiG fighters off the apron, otherwise they would be destroyed. As it turned out, there was only one pilot in the area capable of flying a MiG and the second jet was not in service. So the solitary pilot had quickly got the first plane airborne and headed off to Tripoli, while the second aircraft lay smouldering on the concrete, after the contractors had fired a few grenade rounds into it.

The government in Tripoli had received twenty-four hours' advance warning of US intentions, but knew they could only raise token objections. They had told Libyan Air, the sole commercial operator at the airport, to cancel all forthcoming commercial flights.

A giant C17 Globemaster had landed shortly afterwards, depositing its cargo of bobcat diggers, personnel carriers and a tracked battlefield air-defence system.

The bobcat diggers were scooping buckets of loose rubble and sand from the edges of the runway to fill several lines of Hesco gabions that were to form a defensive perimeter around the entrance to the airport terminal. The Hescos were square, wire-mesh containers, with heavy-duty fabric liners that were filled with dirt and rubble to form instant defensive walls. They littered the warzones of the Middle East, evidence of past conflicts, often piled one on top of another, forming flat-topped modern-day pyramids, in memory of failed ventures and fruitless conflicts.

CHAPTER 28
YAROSLAV BUKOV
ABU MUHAMMAD'S CAMP, NORTHERN CHAD

Yaroslav had already survived several weeks as a prisoner of Abu Muhammad's Islamic State-in-Libya. Abu Muhammad had been in Libya since 2014, when ISIS leader Abu Bakr al-Baghdadi dispatched a group of jihadis from Syria to Libya to establish a new branch of the terrorist group. They had set up a base in Darnah, in the east of the country, and soon after announcing they would accept oaths of allegiance from fighters in Libya, had mustered a force of several hundred men.

The Russian was shackled to a hasp, set firmly in the stone floor of what was basically a concrete box. During the first few days, he had chafed, cut and eventually rubbed the skin off his wrist, trying to work the steel hasp from the floor. The design of the restraint was simple and effective, so he was forced to concede defeat, not something that came easily to him.

There was a small, high-level window that indicated the passing of night and day. Occasionally, there was the sound of a voice, or the revving of a motor vehicle outside, but mainly all he could hear was the rasping of the wind as it blew sand and dust against the structures of the camp. He sensed he was still somewhere deep in the southern desert of Libya, or Chad, or Sudan – who knew where? There was nothing he could do except wait.

Food and water were brought daily, but the extremes of hot and cold were a torture in themselves. For a few hours in the early morning and early evening, his body achieved some measure of equilibrium. Other than that, he spent the sweltering July days in his concrete shed, bathed in sweat, the air around him thick and cloying, praying for the cool of the night. The hours of darkness he spent shivering, curled into a ball and dreaming of the heat to come.

He had a thin, soiled mattress to sit or lie on and a bucket, for his toilet. He had been given so little to eat and drink, eventually he had no use for it.

The bulky young Englishman, who called himself Raheem Green, was the only person Yaroslav saw in the first two weeks of his captivity. Raheem spoke to him sparingly. He told Yaroslav he had taken his first name after the footballer and his second from the colour associated with paradise, as foretold in the Quran. Raheem was born and bred in North London and had come to Chad from Iraq. Other than explaining the provenance of his taken name, he told Yaroslav nothing more that might yield a clue as to why he was being held.

For the first few days he had exercised, using various Pilates moves to stretch and maintain his muscle tone. As the heat, physical weakness, depression and the hopelessness of captivity descended on him, this had ceased to be of interest and, despite his efforts, the lethargy of confinement had taken over. He had been at a low point when, three weeks in, Raheem had entered with a younger man and, instead of leaving some flat bread and a bowl of lentils, his companion started fiddling with the locks on the shackle and the hasp.

He beckoned Yaroslav to his feet and placed an oily black hood over his head. He was too weak to cause any trouble, but saw Raheem was holding a semi-automatic rifle. He also noticed he stood far enough away to avoid any sudden lunges.

"Come," Raheem said, "they want to speak to you."

"Who do? What for?"

"Just come. There is no problem."

Yaroslav was no coward, but his throat was dry and his knees were shaking as he shuffled out, cringing away from the full glare of the sunlight that penetrated the hessian hood. He walked maybe one hundred metres and caught the smells of cooking; the harsh guttural tones of the Arab tongue; the sounds of large diesel engines ticking over. He concluded it was a sizeable camp but, by sound alone, could only guess at the numbers of men present.

Eventually, he felt a coolness on his neck and head as he entered deep shade. He was pushed into a structure and the hood removed. He was in a large tan-coloured tent of heavy-duty vinyl. Where the window covers had been rolled back, he could see a further black coating, designed to frustrate heat-sensitive surveillance. To his surprise, he realised the coolness had not come from entering the shade of the tent, but from air-conditioning units attached to the rear fabric wall. He smelled cigarettes, sweat and his own fear.

The command centre was three large integrated tent units. A sophisticated communication setup occupied one corner. Yaroslav quickly assessed the level of organisation and resources. This was no squalid temporary camp.

A small, plump, middle-aged man in camo fatigues got up from a folding chair and walked over to Yaroslav. He had a long grey beard, but no moustache; the left side of his beard was stained yellow from years of heavy smoking. There were half a dozen others in the tent: some working on laptops, others lounging in camping chairs, weapons at their side. A tall, thin man in baggy grey trousers, sandals and a long sleeveless quilted jacket stood up and came across to join them. He had a long, greying beard, but his black eyes remained hard and the intensity of his stare told Yaroslav it was he who shouldered the responsibility for whatever was going on here.

The shorter man pointed to a cluster of chairs in the corner of the adjacent tent. He shouted something in Arabic and a youngster appeared with a bottle of ice-cold water, which he gave to Yaroslav. He greedily opened it and poured a huge measure of the icy liquid into his mouth, immediately causing every nerve in his jaw and forehead to jangle in pain. He gasped.

"Slowly, friend. I have seen horses become ill drinking cold water that way." The plump man laughed. "You can call me Faysal."

Yaroslav sat and breathed out heavily. The pain subsided.

"So, you are a Russian Volunteer? Arrived in this faraway country to help Boutros in his good works?" Faysal smiled.

"I am a Russian civilian, here to survey oil fields."

"Then it was not you in the convoy of armed Russians? It was not you who attacked our comrades on the desert road and gunned down six men while they fled? And I suppose it was not you who paid us in weapons to attack the Italians at the Marsabar gas terminal, so you could take it for yourselves?"

The tall man with the black eyes, who sprawled, long-limbed, across a flimsy canvas chair, turned to Faysal and said: "Well, you have got the wrong man. We must let him go."

Faysal looked at him and said in a mocking tone: "Abu Muhammad, please forgive the mistake. It was honestly made."

Abu Muhammad gazed at Yaroslav, his dark eyes and fixed expression giving no clue to his deliberations. Nevertheless, Yaroslav knew his life hung by a thread.

"You would be dead, Russian, if I did not have need of you. I will know what you know, about the oil fields and how they can be used. I need to get the crude refined at the wellheads or send it to refineries on the coast or else Egypt. I need to avoid Boutros in Benghazi and the thieves in Tripoli. I have road transport. I need you to show us the best sites for this and help us make arrangements. I want all your ideas. If you mislead or trick me, there is only one outcome."

Yaroslav understood.

"So, you know I am oil man and not soldier?"

Abu Muhammad was impassive.

"I know you are a Russian and no friend of mine."

"What will you do with me?"

"I will free you from the chain. For thirty minutes in the morning and in the evening, you may leave the house to exercise. If you wander into the desert, we will see which way you choose. Likely, we would let you go, because there is nothing around for a hundred kilometres and you will soon die. If you take a vehicle, I will launch a drone. My men will fight for the pleasure of hunting you down.

"You will work with Faysal and Raheem. When we are happy, we will exchange you for money or for prisoners. If your Volunteers will not trade you, we will kill you. I will decide.

"You can say now that you do not want this work and Faysal will take you outside and it can all be over. No more heat, no more cold, and no more hunger or thirst. Is that what you want?"

Yaroslav looked into the face of the tall man with the black eyes and realised there was only one answer.

"I work."

He racked his brain for what he knew of Abu Muhammad. He knew the name and that he led an IS-affiliated group in Libya. They usually operated further to the west, near to the Sharara oil field and had bases around Marsabar, where they had control of the refinery and port. That was why the Russians had paid them for the raid to scare off the Italians.

After the meeting, things improved dramatically. He was given a camp bed with a fitted mattress and blankets to keep him warm at night. He had a bucket of water every morning, as well as a supply of cold bottled water. He even had a daily allowance of fruit, to help relieve the skin complaint he had developed during his weeks of confinement.

He received a wooden table and a couple of chairs. In the morning and late afternoons, they would work. He told Raheem what he needed.

"I need, how is this called, 'exploration software' to tell me where are good deposits. If deposits are good and well is working, we make arrangements for photographs to see site layout and security.

"I need all geological maps of Sirte Basin. You buy online from Centre of Industrial Studies in Tripoli. They are old maps, from nineteen sixties surveys, when times were good. Things are different now. This is a shit country.

"I want all maps you find. Economic maps, population, transport, climate maps, all maps."

Raheem had a degree in Applied Science from London Metropolitan University and proved able to access a lot of the technical information Yaroslav needed from various commercial sources.

He did not see Abu Muhammad again for some time, but Faysal, his number two, and Raheem busied themselves, ferrying information and instructions to him. Faysal was less forthcoming about his technical background, but Yaroslav soon guessed he must have been involved in the oil and gas sector during his time in Iraq.

Yaroslav learned the group had originally come from their base near Marsabar to reconnoitre the south-west. They wanted to assess the oil fields, to explore what might be extracted from them by way of revenue. It was clear they lacked Yaroslav's practical experience and that was why he had been taken. Since Syria and northern Iraq had fallen, they had lost access to the oil revenues they needed to fight their battles and develop their Caliphate. Abu Muhammad's militia had been instructed to seek out revenue from the more remote deserts of Southern Libya.

They had a small drone they used to deliver photographs of sites Yaroslav had previously visited. The photographs reminded him of each location, its capabilities and his conclusions when he had been there.

He sent them out to reconnoitre and photograph certain wells to help assess whether they were working; how well they were defended, the size of the workforce and where they came from. Yaroslav was in his element. They were producing a plan to become an oil business in their own right – just stealing the crude for their own purposes. He found himself becoming more and more enthusiastic about the project and started to amuse himself, modelling likely outputs and constructing a rough financial forecast. He knew the harder he worked, the better his chances were of staying alive. He had seen how little this group valued human life.

At some of the northern wells, he proposed a plan to load the crude into a fleet of tankers, which could shuttle to the coast and back, taking the crude to refineries. There, they would either sell it, via intermediaries, or have it converted into petrol and smuggle it into Egypt or Sudan, for the black market. In Libya, they would just sell it at the pumps, through independent garages that did not care who they bought from.

He had even identified a small primitive refinery, built by smugglers, which produced *mazout*, the heavy oil commonly used to fuel domestic generators. He told Faysal they should just use their muscle and take it. There was good money to be made.

In addition, ISIL had started 'taxing' the production of crude at certain well heads. Faysal told him that, in Iraq, ISIL had controlled the oil fields in the north of the country, producing thousands of barrels of heavy crude oil a day. They had been able to recruit engineers and expert personnel to manage over 200 wells. Yaroslav was impressed, but he thought this opportunity wasted in the hands of a bunch of barbarians. There were times when he had to remind himself who he was and what he was doing. He was a prisoner held in a concrete box, in the eastern deserts of the Sahara.

One night everything suddenly changed. For a day or so beforehand, Yaroslav had been aware of an increase in the level of activity around the camp. There seemed to be a lot of new faces he had not seen before. The technicals were being checked over and large metal boxes of cannon shells, petrol and machine gun ammo were being strapped onto the rear decks. They were preparing to move out.

The morning after, Faysal failed to appear and Raheem was tense. He refused to be drawn about what was happening, but said Yaroslav was to stay in the camp and continue his work. The Russian put the move out of his mind and continued concentrating on the task in hand. Raheem was forever looking out of the doorway, smoking and watching what proved to be the final stages of the preparations.

That night, almost immediately after the sun fell, there was a big commotion lasting for several hours as the fighters started to form up the convoy. Engines fired and there were raised voices, instructions being shouted and the nervous laughter of excited men. Yaroslav could not see anything, but suddenly the engines stopped and the fighters fell silent. He heard a gentle wind rippling the canvas tenting and rustling through the low scrub. He could almost hear the breathing of the large crowd of men, waiting, anticipating. Then he heard the distorted tones of Abu Muhammad ringing around the camp. He had a microphone and some type of portable speaker. The tinny sound echoed around the desert as he led what Yaroslav assumed was the prayer before battle.

"Merciful Father, I have squandered my days with plans of many things ... For all we ought to have thought and have not thought, all we ought to have said and have not said, all we ought to have done and have not done, I pray thee, Allah, for forgiveness

"For Your sake, I go forth, and for Your sake I advance, and for Your sake ... I fight!"

A loud throaty cheer was followed by the sound of engines and the shouting of commands.

CHAPTER 29
NATASHA BONNICI
SAVIOUR AZZOPARDI'S HOUSE, SOUTH MALTA

NATASHA'S DATE had gone well. As arranged, she had found Savi sitting on the blue bench outside Mario's Café on the promenade at Pretty Bay, a nondescript coastal resort on the south side of the island. Its name was a misnomer, given it was overshadowed by Freeport Malta, the big commercial freight terminal, with its travelling cranes and mountainous piles of stacked containers only an icecream cone's throw from the public beach.

She had to smile when she first saw him. He was sitting on the back of the bench, with his feet on the seat, engrossed in something on his phone. He either had no decent clothes in his wardrobe or had made no effort whatsoever to dress up for the occasion. He wore battered, dirty old jeans, a white T-shirt with some sporting logo and a pair of trainers that must have cost some money when he had bought them, several years earlier.

He was skinny and had shoulder-length, lank, mousy hair that hung limp against the residual acne on his pitted cheeks. Natasha was surprised. He looked very young, though his profile had said he was thirty. She doubted he was any more than twenty-five.

She had sat down next to him on the bench and looked straight ahead, out over the beach towards the fleet of small, multi-coloured fishing boats that gently rocked in the waters of the bay. It was some minutes before he was even aware of her presence. She could sense him looking at her and glancing back to his phone, checking her profile picture on the dating app.

"So, when you've finished playing with your phone, are you going to buy me this ice cream, Savi?"

"Er, yeah, sure. Hi!"

He stepped off the bench, smiled at her and gave a little wave.

"So, you want the ice cream now? This minute?"

"That's what you offered." She smiled sweetly.

"OK. It's yours."

He thrust his hands in his pockets, turned his back on her and shuffled off towards the café.

Natasha shook her head and went after him, walking alongside.

"D'you treat all your girlfriends like this?"

"Like what?"

"Like you don't give a shit about them? I suppose you're shy." She wrinkled her nose as she said it.

"I'm not shy. It just takes me a while to loosen up, that's all."

"Fair enough. OK, so, here it is. I don't really want a bloody ice cream. Do you live nearby?"

"Sure."

"Let's cut the crap and go to your place then."

Natasha smiled at him and put one hand on his shoulder, looking him straight in the eye.

"Do you have clean sheets?"

He stared at her, speechless, his mouth open. She pressed herself lightly against him. They were the same height. Savi took a small step back in surprise.

"Well? Have you got clean sheets?"

"Yeah, sure. What for?"

"For God's sake, I'm not looking for a husband! I use the app for casual sex. Still interested?"

A faint smile crossed his face.

"Yeah, of course!"

"Good. Where's your car then?"

"I've got a scooter."

"A scooter – really? Well, I'm not riding on that. I've got a car, I'll follow. Off you go now."

He started off then turned back, looking at her askance.

"Are you being serious or are you just taking the piss?"

"D'you want to take a chance or should I just leave now and find someone else? Come on, I'm really in the mood."

"OK, let's go. The scooter's parked over there."

He pointed to the end of the promenade.

She watched the boy go to his scooter and then walked back to the BMW SUV, where Simon was sitting in the driver's seat, smiling.

"Not a fucking word!" she warned.

He burst out laughing. Simon looked after security for Marco and her. He was a large Polish man, who spent a lot of time lifting weights, as well as running up and down the long steep hill that climbed to the *castello* from St Paul's. He had messed up badly when chasing Nick Walker across the Mediterranean, during the oil-smuggling fiasco, and had succeeded in losing Marco's million-euro yacht from a marina in Tunis. Ultimately, Marco had forgiven and reinstated him. After all, he trusted the bodyguard with his life – what was the loss of a boat? Natasha knew this man was a total professional and would help her in anything she needed to do.

"Quite a catch, Miss Natasha. Not sure how he'll fit into life at the *castello*!"

She punched him on the arm, hard.

"I said, not a word! Listen, get in the back and keep your head down. I don't want him seeing you."

They followed Savi out of town, Natasha keeping well back just in case she had to stop for traffic lights or at junctions. She need not have worried. The scooter had no mirrors and, as far as she could tell, Savi never turned his head once.

After ten minutes, the scooter pulled up a narrow dirt track and Natasha followed. She nearly swerved off the road when a jet thundered over the car before bouncing down onto the airport runway, only metres ahead of them. It gave her some satisfaction to realise he lived in such an isolated spot.

She said to Simon: "What a convenient place to live! OK, I'll go in first. You wait right outside the door. When I shout, you come in – and make sure you do!"

"How do I know I won't be interrupting anything?" he asked tongue in cheek.

"This is getting really tiresome. We need to ask this boy some questions and, if we don't get the answers I want, we need to persuade him to talk, OK? We don't need to get too rough – just scare him a bit. I can't imagine he's going to be too much of a problem."

"I get it."

"Good. We're here."

Natasha watched Savi park the scooter, remove his helmet and turn to beckon her in. She followed on his heels and drew in her breath sharply as she entered. Then regretted it instantly. Savi lived by himself and he lived in filth. There were flies in his kitchen and open takeaway cartons of food on the unit tops. Juice bottles and beer cans were piled in the sink, alongside stacks of unwashed dishes. His lounge was even worse. The windows had been painted shut and there was no ventilation. Pizza boxes and kebab wrappers had been routinely stuffed under the couch and ashtrays were filled with cigarette butts. Natasha had a thing about cockroaches – they terrified her. With a shudder, she tried to put the thought of them roaming through the filth out of her mind.

The shock must have registered on her face, as he said over his shoulder, "Yeah, it's a bit of a mess – I usually clean on a Friday. Sorry about that.

"My God, Savi, how can you live like this? It's a shithouse. Do you never get ill?"

"Look, I've only got one set of sheets, but I've got a clean sleeping bag. Shall I go and get it?"

He looked at her hopefully.

"No, I'll tell you what, let's talk first. There are some questions I'd like to ask."

"Yeah, cool."

She shouted loudly: "Simon, come in here, please."

The back door opened and the big man walked in, grinning.

"Hi, Savi!" he said. "Good to meet you. Oh, Jesus, it smells in here!"

Natasha wrinkled her nose, this time in disgust.

"It's making me gag."

Savi watched the big Pole as he slipped off his black jacket and started to work his large hands into some tight black leather gloves.

"Who the fuck are you? What are you doing here?"

Natasha sighed and went up close to Savi.

"OK, you disgusting little dirt bag, fun's over. I need to know what you've told the Americans about jacking a container. It's simple – tell me and they'll never know you've talked. Stay schtum and Simon will beat the shit out of you. Then, I'll tell the Americans you told us everything and they'll be pissed off and *they* will beat the shit out of you. Got it, Savi?"

His eyes opened wide, pupils dilated.

"Americans? What Americans?"

Natasha looked at Simon, and pointed at Savi. Simon stepped forward and cuffed him hard across the ear. Savi cringed and wrapped his arms around his head.

Natasha continued.

"Do I really have to spell it out for you? Because I can go away if you want and leave you with Simon for thirty minutes. I'll bet you'll be ready to talk when I come back!"

He did not respond. Natasha picked up her bag and turned as if to leave.

"Wait, I can't tell you what they're up to, they'll kill me! It's the CIA, for fuck's sake."

Natasha turned to look at him.

"If you're clever they'll never even know. Remember who you're stealing from. Make it look like an inside job. Russians stealing from Russians. That happens, doesn't it?"

"What d'you want to know?" he whined. "I'm not saying I've got the answers."

"I want to know all about the ship and its cargo. Its name, when it leaves, and I need to know when it reaches a certain position in the Black Sea. I need to make sure our container is on the top of the stack on that ship and I need it unloading on a certain date, at Constanta, Romania. I need the port authorities there to release the container to our carrier. Oh, and I need some software in place, to remotely open a set of battery-powered actuated valves.

"All stuff you'd be doing for the Americans, if you were going to steal the container in Istanbul – true?"

"No, not true. I won't be able to do all that. I need the shipper's details from the Americans. I need to get hold of a copy of the Bill of Lading and do a switch, then a change of destination. So, I need to get a copy of the email from the shipper of the goods, releasing the Bill of Lading. It's not that easy. And I need to know a lot more about all this."

"OK, good, you're talking. That's a start. There's work to do, we understand that. Get a few things together. You'll be away for about a week, I'd guess. Pack your laptop and anything you need to work."

"Why, what's happening?"

"You're coming with us until this is all done. It'll keep you out of the hands of Mike Lloyd. Yeah, I know who you're dealing with. Go on, get your stuff together and give your passport and ID card to Simon."

The bodyguard followed Savi around the house as he picked up bits of clothing from the floor, several remote hard drives and some notebooks. All he needed went into a rucksack and two carrier bags.

"I don't understand why you're taking me. And where to?"

"Listen, you dolt. I don't want you running off to Mike Lloyd, or whoever else will have you. So, for the time being, you're staying with us. We have a nice place with a TV and some old school DVDs. The WiFi gets turned on when you're working and not when we can't watch you. Now, give me your phone."

As with all younger people, that was like demanding the sacrifice of a limb and his hand instinctively went to his rear pocket. Simon's meaty hand fastened itself to Savi's wrist and Natasha gingerly slid two fingers inside the pocket to retrieve the phone.

"There. Are we all ready? Let's go and see your new home." Casting her eyes around, she said: "It can't be any worse than this shithouse. When it's done, we'll pay you ten thousand euros. That's a lot of money. You could get a cleaner."

She fixed him with a cold stare and waved his passport in front of him.

"If you try and fuck off or screw this up, we'll kill you – you can be sure of that! It's a small island and you're going nowhere, so just bear it in mind."

Savi was cowering. Natasha thought he was about to cry.

"Who are you anyway?" he muttered.

Simon grabbed him by the collar and pulled him towards the door, saying, "Shut up and get in the car."

He bundled Savi into the back of the SUV and then sat next to him. Natasha activated the child locks and drove.

When they reached the entrance to the *castello*'s estate, Natasha drove past the main gate until she found a small farm track that dropped down onto the valley floor. There another rutted, orange-clay track weaved its way westward, through tall clumps of bamboo, towards the coast. Finally, they reached a three-metre palisade fence with a padlocked gate. Behind the fence was an old chapel, dating back to the seventeenth century, set high on the cliff top. It had spectacular views over the ocean, where a blazing pink sun was rapidly falling below the horizon.

"This is it, our family chapel. It's called Our Lady of the Abandoned! Quite apt, in your case.

Savi looked at the building suspiciously.

"There's food, a basic kitchen, water, sanitation, and Simon will come twice a day to let you get some sun and have a wander around. There's just the one stained-glass window and just a single door to the outside, which makes it perfect. But please don't think you can take advantage of that because it also has some underground stone caves, which used to be catacombs. One has an old wooden door and I've fitted it with a very modern lock. Any messing around and we'll keep you down there. You won't like that, I guarantee it!"

"What about Mike Lloyd, won't he want to know where I am?"

"Of course. We'll WhatsApp him and tell him you don't trust him and you're staying someplace safe until this is over. He needs to know you'll still do what he asks and we'll give him your bank account details, so he can pay you too. You could score big time here!"

Savi stared at Natasha imploringly.

"OK, listen, I'll do what you want, no problem. There are no guarantees, though. It's not like boosting credit card data. But, please, I'll go loony in that place." He pointed to the chapel. "At least get me an X-Box, I'll use it off-line, and the latest *Fifa* and *Civilisation VI*. That should keep me sane for a week."

"Oh," said Natasha, "and one more thing … can you remotely access a network and disable the security cameras? I've got the password."

"How come? Is it your house or do you work there or something?"

Natasha just looked at him.

"OK, don't tell me, I don't care. Give me your email address and write down the network password and the date and time you want the cameras disabled. Consider it done. Do you want me to turn them back on again?"

"Yes, forty-five minutes later."

"OK, piece of cake, and I'll fix it so no one can trace the hack back to you or me. Just get me the games."

Natasha looked at Simon, who gave a curt nod.

With that, they locked Savi in the chapel and made their way back to the car. After a minute or so, they saw a glow at the back of the building as the lights came on and illuminated the old stained glass.

Simon smiled: "Looks like the genius found the light switch. Let's hope he's as good at hacking as the Americans think."

"Better," she replied, "because he'll need to keep them convinced he's following through on their plan at the same time as he dismantles it. And if he messes up …"

She glanced over to the cliff edge. Simon stared back at her.

Natasha tilted her head to one side, thinking.

"I haven't decided yet. Maybe he'll turn out to have other uses. Let's see."

Simon raised his eyebrows and she punched him painfully on the arm.

"Definitely not that!"

CHAPTER 30
MIKE LLOYD

EXECUTIVE LOUNGE, ZURICH INTERNATIONAL AIRPORT

MIKE LLOYD and Mary-Ann Baker were sitting in the executive lounge of Zurich Airport, waiting for the Aeroflot flight from Moscow to land. Mike was a negotiator at heart and achieved more through his address book than the pen-pushers in Langley ever knew.

He was passing the time by fiddling with his phone.

"I'm telling you, Mary-Ann, turn off your data roaming. This place is the biggest rip off I know. Last time I was here, I got a bill for data for two hundred euros just for downloading a couple of sports pages." Mike nodded to himself. "Yeah, it's true."

Mary-Ann sighed. "Come on, Uncle Sam won't begrudge us a few euros."

"Don't you believe it. The American taxpayer likes to know his dollar is being well spent."

Mike Lloyd was known for being tight with money; his and the taxpayer's.

"So how do you know Petrov?"

"I don't. I know someone who does."

"You've never met him or spoken to him?"

"Nope."

"This should be interesting then. He's not gonna be pleased with us."

"He certainly won't be!"

Mary-Ann Baker had been a little concerned about this off-the-books meeting. She found that a lot of what Mike did was off-the-books and worried that one day it could come back to bite him – or, more importantly, her. She was totally unprepared for the meeting and worried that Mike was too. She had no idea what might happen when they met the Russian.

"You don't seem very certain about the play here?"

Mike was reading the sports section of one of the free American newspapers he had picked up at lounge reception.

"I'm not! I'm just reaching out to see what we can do, before the Pentagon and the Russian Ministry of Defence start throwing rocks at each other. Maybe nothing. Could all be a waste of air fare."

He returned to the report on the Virginia Cavaliers' latest basketball game, but noticed the minute Valentin Petrov entered the lounge.

"Game time," he muttered, without looking up from the paper.

Mary-Ann tried not to swivel her head.

"Where?"

Mike turned a page and shuffled in his seat, recrossing his legs to face away from the counter.

"The older, big guy with the silver hair, in the fifty-bucks suit and brown shoes."

Valentin Petrov entered the executive lounge and stood by the reception desk. He spotted Mike Lloyd at a table on the far side, reading the paper. Mike crossed his legs and then uncrossed them again – a signal to show he had been recognised.

Petrov was a commercially minded man at heart, but politics and Russian pride could not be ignored when dealing with the Americans. Lloyd had suggested the meeting, let him make the play.

After the niceties, Lloyd asked about the missing gas specialist.

"So, where's your boy Yaroslav? Careless of him, getting picked up like that."

Petrov smiled and grimaced.

"Yes, poor Yaroslav. Islamic State have him in Chadian desert. There is no recent contact. When we hear, we pay or we exchange for him. He is worth much to them. They are clever – they know his price will be good."

"So why did they grab him anyway?"

"They tell me they drive him around the desert and Yaroslav looks at oil fields for them. Which field is good, which not so good. If you have intel on him, in spirit of co-operation, a call would be appreciated."

"Hmm. That's a reasonable request. I'll bear it in mind."

Petrov leaned back in his chair and crossed his legs. He unbuttoned the jacket of his bird's-eye weave, steel grey business suit. Mike found the cut a bit too aggressive for the Western taste, but he noticed it perfectly matched the colour of the Russian's swept-back hair.

"So, Mr Lloyd, what are you doing in Libya? I am very interested to hear."

"Well, after the bomb in Malta, you basically gave us no choice but to get involved. That was a mistake on your part."

Petrov moved to speak. Mike held up his hand to silence him and continued.

"We won't let Boutros take Tripoli and we're not going to let Libya end up as a satellite state of the Kremlin, on Europe's doorstep. It's only three hundred kilometres from Sicily, for Christ's sake. We're talking Cuba here. Not going to happen. Not on."

Petrov considered this opening gambit.

"So, you are ready for another Iraq, another Afghanistan? How long you plan to stay for this time … ten years … twenty? I do not think we see American boots on ground."

"No, Valentin. This is different. The Libyan people are sick of militias, sick of foreign fighters, sick of ISIL, sick of their country, which should be one of the richest in Africa, getting messed about by foreign interests."

Petrov laughed.

"Sounds same as Iraq to me. Great thinking, Mr Lloyd! So, you will go in, give everyone democracy and sort out all problems?"

"Yeah, we'll do it differently this time. Project Democracy! Quite a good ring to it, hasn't it? Remember, there's no Muammar Gaddafi or Sadam Hussein this time, no figurehead. It'd be low key, apart from taking out Boutros and maybe ISIL. That'll be a big bang! But afterwards, it'll be easier. There's no Sunni and Shia conflict in Libya. One Sunni government, for a Sunni people. We'd tolerate a moderate Islamic government, just a few Muslim Brotherhood, we can live with that. Iraq was Sunni government for Shia people, with Iran shit-stirring on the sidelines."

"OK, all very interesting worldview and I am sure someone has gamed this back in Moscow, so it will be no surprise to Kremlin. Say it all happens this way. What about our pipeline?"

"We'll buy it."

"You can license it."

"No, that means you retain control. We'll buy it."

"What about lifting threat of sanctions on NordStream2 and TurkStream?"

Mike Lloyd glanced up at Petrov, rather too quickly, and mentally kicked himself. So that was what the Russian was after.

"Now *that's* interesting. You hope maybe someone in the US can take the heat off the Europeans, so they can finish their end of the project and grant you the licences?"

Petrov gazed steadily at Mike, as he thought for a few seconds.

"I can see you'd like to get those lovely pipes ashore. How

about that? Not much point having them all under the Baltic and the Black Sea, if they lead nowhere!"

The pipelines from Russia, under the Black Sea to Turkey and under the Baltic into Germany, were designed to supply gas to replace the declining North Sea output and fuel Europe's growing economies. Following the invasion of Ukraine in 2014, and Russia's aggression in the Balkans, the US had threatened European contractors with sanctions preventing the completion of the projects. It was a threat the Russians needed removed, so they could get the pipelines finished and start getting a return on their considerable investment.

"Yes, Mike ... I call you Mike, yes? Nearly as useless as having a pipeline on edge of European territorial waters, from big unexploited African fields, with no gas flowing!"

"You've got a point there, Valentin."

They talked for another three hours, neither man taking notes. It became apparent that Petrov's main goal was to secure the supply through NordStream2 and TurkStream, the two new routes that avoided crossing Ukraine. In principle, he thought a sale of the VertWay Libyan-Malta pipeline infrastructure could be arranged, if Mike could put a buyer forward.

Mike was surprised the Russian seemed to be prepared to drop the Libyan project, without much argument, prompting him to wonder whether the whole thing had been designed to bring about this very scenario. If so, it was an extremely expensive geopolitical gamble, but one that seemed to be about to pay off. By threatening to construct a supply route from Libya, the Russians had created another bargaining chip, one they were willing to surrender to secure their real goal – security of supply for their other trans-European pipelines.

Mike was a chess player and Valentin had seized the initiative. Mike did not like that. It left the US with a big job to do in Libya; one that could be seen as an escalation of their involvement in another Islamic, oil-rich nation, which would not play well globally. The VertWay supply had all sorts of benefits for

Libya, Malta and Europe, while pushing the Russians away from the Libyan oil fields. So, it kind of worked all round.

As they boarded the direct flight back to Malta, Mary-Ann noticed Mike was in a contemplative mood and was curious.

"So, talk about putting the world to rights! What are you going to do now?"

"I'm gonna go back to Langley. There are people there I've got to talk to. I also need to speak to some people in the government, plus oil industry players, and I need to know what's happening on the ground in Libya. Can you get me an update on that?"

On the plane, he quickly turned on his phone to check for messages. He was surprised to see one from Savi Azzopardi, under the alias 'Snakehead'. They used an encryption app, so it took a little time before he could read it.

Gone dark until this is all over. Nervous about it. Will work from somewhere I feel safe. Send info when you need action.

Lloyd was surprised, because he did not think Saviour Azzopardi had enough wit to do something like that. It did not seem like him.

CHAPTER 31
GEORGE ZAMMIT
UBARI AIRPORT, LIBYA

THEY HAD ARRIVED in Ubari during the early hours of the morning and the contractors were already busy preparing defensive positions around the airport. Their base was in the terminal building. A long line of Hesco gabions formed a perimeter wall across the main car park to the front and there were protected positions on the apron, to the rear of the terminal building.

George had been nabbed by Sam as he tried to take a nap inside the departure lounge on the first floor of the terminal.

"Hey, soldier, come here. Time to meet your squad leader and get to work."

He had changed out of the *bubus* robe into his camo cargo pants, but had kept the *cheche* around his head, for practical reasons. It kept the dust and sand out of his face and protected him from the worst of the sun. He had acquired a sand-coloured military jacket and, with his growing black beard, was looking more and more like one of the Tuareg fighters. The only problem was that the Tuaregs were used to going a long way on very little fuel, so George's portly physique did not quite complement the look. But with no fridge on hand to snack from and only eating occasional sparse meals, he noticed he had begun to pull his belt tighter and tighter.

Sam marched him out onto the edge of the apron, to a Hesco wall that ran thirty metres and ended in a block structure, to protect those inside from mortar blasts. There was a platform made of wooden pallets, with firing slits for observation and defence.

"OK, we're out on the west flank here, so you've got eyes over a ninety-degree field, from that yellow directional sign on the taxiway over to the beginning of the turn into the apron. That field is your responsibility. Got it?"

George peered nervously out over the runway. Beyond the scrubland, there were some low buildings that he thought might enable would-be attackers to get within a few hundred metres of their position unobserved.

"Yes, I've got it. *Mela*, don't expect trouble, do we?"

"In this job, we always expect trouble.

"You're an assistant machine gunner. Harley will be along soon and he'll tell you what's what. Basically, you feed him ammo but, if you have to shoot, anything in your field of vision could be a hostile, so shoot the fuck out of it. You're four hours on and four off, 24/7. Put a claim in for your overtime when you get home!"

At that moment, Harley ambled into the block. He was tall, gangly and stick-thin, with long white hair tied into a short pony tail behind his head and a white goatee beard. Like all the contractors, he favoured wrap around Oakleys. The contractors all added their own little embellishments to their corporate clothing, but Harley had excelled himself. He had embroidered Confederate flags, neatly sewn onto his tactical vest, and a strip of denim from an old jacket bearing the words 'Filthy Few Forever' on the back. A red and white arched badge proclaimed 'Sacramento' across his shoulders. Below his battle belt, low on his hip, hung a Wild West holster arrangement with a Smith & Wesson revolver and .357 Magnum ammo studded around the belt.

Sam banged knuckles with Harley and said: "Here's the bad

ass Maltese sharpshooter I was telling you about. He's trained with the Rangers and Green Berets, and has shot up a whole load of Taliban!"

"No way? So you're a bad ass dude? Coulda fooled me." His accent was Texas.

Harley cleared his throat and shot a lump of spit over the Hesco wall.

Sam slapped him on the shoulder and said: "I'll leave you two to get on with it. Things to do."

"So it's you and me against the world?" Harley looked George up and down. "You an A-rab? I don't much like A-rabs."

Harley clearly liked to talk and did not care whether anyone was listening or not. As the afternoon wore on, he told George he had left Texas, after some woman trouble, and became a Hells Angel, out of Sacramento. The words 'Filthy Few' meant he had been an enforcer for them. George nodded his head to show he was impressed, as he did for the rest of the time he listened to Harley's endless stories.

George learned that he had been in the Marines, but those guys apparently had not appreciated his free spirit. He did one tour of Iraq, where he had met Sam. He had been with Sam for nearly ten years and had *'seen the fucking world through the eye of an M16!'*

By the time the four hours was up and the new crew arrived, George knew more about the brotherhood, their runs, scrapes, bike blessings, drug purchases, motorcycle maintenance and punishment beatings, than he would ever have thought possible. He sloped off into the terminal, his head ringing, in search of food and sleep. He found it no surprise that Harley did not have a designated partner!

A row of plastic chairs had just provided the opportunity for a few hours' sleep when Abdullah appeared behind him.

"Hah! The machine gun man! Are you safe to be firing these things?"

"If I have to, I follow your instructions, Abdullah. *'Shut your eyes and pull the trigger!'*"

"I think maybe now they expect you aim first, no? Anyway, listen, we must be parted for a little while. I am going north to meet old friends in the Nafusa Hills and then I go to Marsabar. We take a small plane and there is only room for Edal and me. This time, Goose must stay on the ground. I will be back here in a few days and then maybe we get the chance to fight together, side by side, like before."

George sat bolt upright.

"You can't leave me here! No, I'm coming with you. They're all crazy here!"

"No, it has been decided – only Edal and I must go. When we go to Marsabar, it will be dangerous, so it is best we Arabic speakers go alone. We will be back soon. You are a soldier now, my brother."

George shook his head and lay back down. Even the plastic ridges on the seats, which dug into his back, could not stop him from falling into a deep and dreamless sleep. The blissful state lasted until he was shaken awake by Harley.

"Come on, shithead, time to go!"

Wearily, George followed him out onto the apron. It was late afternoon and the sun hung low in the sky. He had not counted on it being so low in the west, the glare obscuring his view of the other side of the runway.

As they walked to their emplacement, a small Cessna Skyhawk approached, its high wing tipping and rocking as it came in to land, bouncing along the uneven runway. It taxied around and he saw Edal and Abdullah running from the terminal building towards it. It did not stop. Abdullah managed to clamber inside the open passenger door, but had to drag Edal through the cabin door, his *bubus* rucking up to his waist, as his feet kicked and scrambled for purchase. Then the door slammed shut and, with an increasingly intense buzzing from the solitary engine, the Cessna took off. Its wings rocked from side to side as it climbed into the sky, heading north.

George felt very alone, knowing Abdullah had gone. Harley was telling a story about a bad trip he had had after taking a hallucinogenic drug made from a Mexican cactus. George had zoned out but, while Harley smoked and droned on about mescal tequila, something attracted his attention. He did not know what it was he had seen, but there had definitely been movement. He peered through the orange light of the afternoon, his eyes half-closed, squinting, and saw it again. A small object, maybe a head, but definitely something to the side of some bushes, several hundred metres away, right on the edge of the airfield. Then he saw it again, maybe thirty metres to the left.

Harley was droning on.

"Well, the thing is, when ya do lots, and I mean lots, of Mexican drugs, ya get this kinda mind-bend phenomenon, ya know? It's a crazy …"

"Harley, shut up. I can see something moving. Look over there!"

Harley dropped his cigarette and picked up the binoculars. He peered through them.

"To the right of them bushes, ya say? I ain't seein' nuthin'."

He went onto the hand-held radio and started the call protocol.

"Cas 2, Cas 2, this is Cas 6."

"This is Cas 2. What've you got, over?"

"Possible movement, western perimeter. Keep eyes on. Over, out.

"OK, George, so we'll keep a look out. Anyway, where was I … yeah – these Mexican girls, they were hot, you know. I mean, really hot! So they came up to me and I'm thinking, like, wow! But because I was doing all this heavy peyote, it'd given me mind-bend and …"

The first mortar shell struck the apron twenty metres in front of them. The blast sucked the air out of the bunker and made George's ears ring. Bits of shrapnel tinkled on the Hesco.

Harley leaped into action. He screamed: "Ready the SAW!" and grabbed the radio set.

"Cas 2, Cas 2, this is Cas 6."

"Cas 6. All cool, over?"

"All cool. Incoming mortar from boundary, two hundred metres north of runway threshold. Ready to engage, over. Out."

He then threw himself on his stomach and grabbed the M249 machine gun. George was trying to control his shaking hands, so he could loosen the ammunition from the cloth pouch, to ease the feed. After the explosion, all had gone quiet. George was hoping it was all over and that whoever it was had disappeared back to where they had come from.

But before he could wipe the smile of relief off his face, all hell broke loose. Mortar rounds came whistling in. They had adjusted their range and the shells went smack into the gabions. Several burst open, throwing sand and rocks up into the air. George saw a dozen or so fighters rise from the scrub in his sector and start running towards him. They had used the glare of the setting sun to creep on their bellies, through the long wispy grass on the airfield, towards the terminal, ready to launch their attack.

George was lying next to the M249. Harley, for some reason, was sitting back, resting against the rear of the enclosure. George was in a blind panic. He set the gun to fully automatic fire and, lying face down on the floor of the bunker, started randomly spraying fire across the field, without raising his head. The M249 could expel 1,000 rounds a minute, so he could use a vast amount of ammunition very quickly. As he had been taught at Al-Udeid, he pulled the trigger and counted: 'Fire, one, two, three.' Pause. 'Fire, one, two, three.' Pause. 'Fire, one, two, three.' The gun jumped wildly on its rest, twisting his wrist left and right, his one hand exerting just enough pressure to keep the trigger depressed during the firing sequence.

The spent brass cartridge cases were spinning and clattering around, while the noise of the gun in the confined space deafened him. For a moment, he became aware of the acrid smell of the propellant from the bullets, the smoke from the mortar explosions and the smell of dead, damp earth from the damaged Hescos. He did not realise it then, but it would be the smell that would stick in his memory afterwards; not the noise of battle, the fear, or the sight of the fighters advancing on him, wanting to take his life. It would be always the acrid, pungent smell.

He risked a look out of the bunker, but quickly pulled his head back as he saw more figures creeping to within fifty metres of him. He was shaking wildly. He put the spasms down to the recoil from the gun, but was surprised to realise they did not stop once he had ceased firing. More mortar rounds kept landing and, at some point, he realised Harley must be either dead or injured, given he had not moved since the second mortar blast.

After what seemed like hours, but was probably less than a minute, George risked another glance through the firing slit. He saw that he had hit some of the oncoming enemy. Two or three were lying on the scrub, injured but still moving, while one or two more had obviously been shot and were lying very still. But more of them were out there, some crawling through the grass towards him and close enough for him to see the grim intent in their faces.

He took his position behind the gun, but could not bring himself to fire directly at the oncoming fighters, so he sprayed bullets over their heads, in an attempt to scare them off. He counted again. 'Fire, one, two, three.' Pause. 'Fire, one, two, three.' Pause. The attackers lay flat, with their heads down. After a little more time, he realised the belt of shells was coming to an end.

The radio was crackling and alive with shouted messages and commands that George did not understand at first. He started to hear 'pull back, pull back'. Out of the corner of his eye, he was aware of a single fighter running past his enclosure and getting behind him. At this point, there was little else he could do except wait for a hero's death.

He turned to check on Harley, who lay as dead as dead could be, with his chest soaked in blood. Gingerly, George took the Smith & Wesson out of Harley's holster and flicked out some shells from his belt. He loaded the revolver and shoved it into the hip pocket of his cargo pants. Then, crouching, he made his way along the Hesco barriers, back to the door of the terminal.

George rounded the corner at a trot, intending to access the door into the terminal. Three fighters were trying to get in, ramming the glass with a fire extinguisher. George stood, frozen, trying to make himself invisible. One turned and saw him. For a moment, they looked into each other's eyes. The fighter shouted, causing the others to stop battering the door. One dropped the fire extinguisher and picked up a weapon that was propped against the wall beside him. George took Harley's pistol and pointed it at them threateningly, while backing away. When he had turned the corner again, he started to run. He heard a shout above him. It was Sam calling down to him.

"Other way, go through the stairwell!" He gesticulated, pointing to the far side of the terminal building.

George realised the main force of the contractors was inside the terminal building. He and Harley had been out on a limb, at the end of the western flank.

He went as fast as he could, around the side, his feet crunching on broken glass, aware of smoke from burning vehicles set alight by the mortar rounds. Climbing over a baggage cart, he barged open a swing door into the lobby area of the stairwell – and froze.

In the lobby, there was a crowd of a dozen fighters peering up the stairs. Every few seconds, the crack of a shot came from above, keeping them bunched in the well. George had burst through the door, head first, right into the middle of them. For a moment, they did not realise who he was but, as he tried to back out slowly, he was aware of raised voices and hands reaching out for him. Instinctively, he pointed the revolver and fired three shots, in rapid succession, into the mêlée. The sound ricocheted up and down the stairwell. There were screams and shouts and then he heard a fourth shot go off, which flashed through the side of his *cheche*, jolting his head to one side and grazing his scalp. He ended up on the floor, blood running down his face, with a fighter on top of him, pounding his head against the tiles. He felt no pain as he gradually slipped away into unconsciousness.

CHAPTER 32
MARCO BONNICI
ZONA TORTONA, MILAN

It was early August in Milan and the holiday crowds were in evidence across the city. The clouds were hanging low over the Sacred Mountains to the north and the earthy smell of ozone promised unseasonal rain.

Sitting outside a coffee shop in the Zona Tortona, the formerly run-down industrial area revitalised by the fashion houses of Milan, Marco wondered whether he was losing his grip on things. In the past, he'd had Sergio to fall back on, to provide balance, support his ideas, challenge his judgement. He had always felt he and Natasha were on the same page, co-conspirators, a familial double act. Now, she was making power plays behind his back, Sergio was dead and Camilleri seemed to be busy playing with the Americans. And, to cap it all, Simon was never to be found. Every time Marco went looking for him, he was told the bodyguard was out doing some mysterious errands for Miss Natasha! Buying an X-Box?

Salvatore had asked to meet him, to bury the hatchet. Marco, suspecting this was on instructions from the Wise Men, had agreed. He wanted to explain to the younger man that there was no hatchet, but there could never be any burying of the feelings Marco held for him and certainly no forgiveness. He felt the Wise

Men's solution, allowing them to express their views, had freed them from each other. Like much of what the Wise Men decreed, it had a certain elegance to it.

He had decided Natasha should chair MalTech Energy, the new company formed to manage the gas deal in Malta. It was the right choice; she had earned it. He had not told her yet, but he had an appointment, later that day, with Signor Bruno, to seek his blessing. She would need help in running BetHi, but this was an opportunity he could not deny her. Marco did not have the stomach to take on the job himself. It was a long-term appointment and his lack of appetite to make such a commitment to the project told him that this part of his life was coming to a close.

Increasingly, he thought of his estate on the slopes of the western Serbian mountains. He wondered whether the small team of gardeners there were following his instructions on its upkeep, or whether they had retired to the village, to drink *rakija* and their homemade plum brandy.

It was a huge project he had undertaken, a landscape of over seven hectares. He had themed the estate around the surrounding high plateau; his forest walk was lined with beds of high-altitude flowers, sourced from the Dolomites and Swiss alpine areas. He introduced shrub plantations, which gradually faded into the indigenous forest. At the top of the walk, higher up the mountain, he created giant rockeries from the glacial detritus of sedimentary rocks. There, carefully selected mosses and a profusion of further hardy alpines rewarded those who made the climb up the steep slopes. His mood lifted as he considered what he had achieved in the four years of self-imposed exile; he also pictured what else could be achieved if he gave himself another four.

His mellow moment instantly disappeared when he saw Salvatore moving purposefully towards him through the crowds of tourists and shoppers. He wore his trademark black suit, white shirt and a scarlet tie. Marco looked at him more closely; there was something different about him. He was paler and his hair had lost its usual gloss. His face looked waxy and a little thinner. Salvatore looked ill.

Even so, he retained his old composure and confidence. Before he sat down at the table, he caught the eye of a waitress and abruptly signalled for two more coffees. Marco watched this with amusement as the two tables of tourists next to him had been studiously ignored by the same girl for the last ten minutes.

Salvatore sat down and fixed Marco with a stare. The older man was perfectly able to meet this fierce gaze. After a few seconds, he began: "Salvatore. Where do we start?"

"Marco, I've always respected you and I'm upset that there's bad blood between us."

Marco shrugged, maintaining the eye-to-eye contact.

"Straight to the point, Salvatore – let us not waste time, spit it out! What troubles you? Your conscience?"

"It's strange, but one thing does bother me. You've been quick to blame me, but you've never asked me who ordered Sergio's death?"

Marco relaxed a little and thought about this.

"No, because I do not wish to know the answer. And probably because I can guess it anyway."

"That's no longer acceptable, Marco. You can't go round focusing your anger on me, when you know what happened wasn't my decision."

"Come on, Salvatore. That is the Auschwitz guard's argument. 'I was just taking orders.' You have got to do better than that. Sergio's blood is all over your hands. I cannot forgive you, I will not do it."

"True, and I'm sorry, Marco. I should've said no. But I didn't dare. Maybe I was too ambitious. I thought I'd be proving myself by doing the thing nobody else wanted to. The truth is, I hate myself for it.

"I know what it's cost me. Your friendship ... possibly the chance of something with Natasha, who knows? And when I look at myself now, I don't like what I see. I think it's done me more harm than good within the Family too. It wasn't exactly a popular move."

Marco snorted his contempt.

"Well, Salvatore, I am sorry for your pain and your regrets. If Sergio were here, I am sure he would be heartbroken at how it has all worked out for you!

"But I can assure you, that is nothing compared to the loss I feel. So, if this is your apology, I accept it and hope, over time, things will sit easier with you. But do not count on me to help that along."

Marco rose to go but Salvatore got up and put a hand on his wrist.

"You know, it was Signor Bruno who asked me to organise it."

Marco sat back down. He did not know what to feel. He knew the Wise Men; he knew their names, where to find them, who their wives were, but he had also avoided attributing Sergio's death to the decision of any one man in particular. He could not cope with that. He preferred to think that the decision was taken at a higher corporate level, with no one individual leading, or voicing, the instruction. Rather that it had emanated from a collective mind. That was the only way he had been able to continue looking them in the eye. Now, Salvatore had shattered that fragile illusion. To put a face, and a name, to the thing that had hurt him so much, was difficult to bear.

His anger subsided. He felt deflated.

"So, Salvatore, what has this confession achieved? Do you want me to go and kill Signor Bruno now? Have you brought a gun for me to use? Or do you just want more forgiveness, redemption, something to make you hate yourself a little less? What is it?"

Salvatore looked downcast. He took a sip of coffee. Marco was not finished yet.

"You could have had it all, Salvatore. You could have shadowed Sergio for a few years, become a Wise Man, enjoyed friendship, loyalty, respect! Had all the good things that power and money cannot buy. Now, you will always be the boy who killed Sergio Rossi. No one will trust you. You will never sit at the top table because people know you can be turned. You have helped me, Salvatore, you really have. I can stop hating you. From now on, I will pity you instead!"

Salvatore hunched over his coffee cup, head down. The strength he had mustered for the confrontation had dissipated, spilling out of him as he sat there.

Marco threw twenty euros onto the table. Before he left, he said: "Do not try to do this again. You will get no further with me. If we have to do Family business together, I will try. But that is it."

He walked away down the street, hands in the pockets of his baggy corduroy trousers.

He went back to the boutique hotel he was staying at and lay on the bed. Nothing that had been said had changed how he felt about the Family, Salvatore or the direction of his life in general. He had decided he needed to get Natasha established in Malta and complete his legacy by finalising the energy deal. Then, he would sever his ties with the Family and return to Serbia, where a bigger and better project needed his attention.

He felt the tension in his neck and shoulders start to take a grip. He took off his shoes and lay on the bed for an hour, gently dozing, drifting in and out of sleep. At 17:00 the alarm went off on his phone, alerting him to his meeting with Signor Bruno. He was washing his face and generally tidying himself up when he heard the soft buzz of his phone in his jacket pocket.

Marco had a pager app on his phone and it was his emergency red light. When it buzzed, it showed a code, alerting him to ring the sender immediately. Now that Sergio was dead, only four people had the number: Natasha, Simon, his personal lawyer in Valletta and Hugo, who managed the Wise Men's legal affairs.

He wiped the soap from his face and slipped into a shirt, before dialling Hugo's number.

"Mr Bonnici, you are still in Milano? Yes? You are required at Signor Bruno's *palazzo* immediately."

"Hugo, what is this about?"

"Mr Bonnici, Signor Bruno is dead and it's not due to natural causes!"

CHAPTER 33
IVAN KARAVAYEV
GOZNAK PRINTING WORKS, MOSCOW

WHEN A COUNTRY COLLAPSES, people rarely think about the scale of theft that is possible in the aftermath. After Gaddafi was overthrown in 2011, Libya was in a state of complete chaos. In the midst of the vacuum, the Central Bank of Libya struggled to restore the country's crippled banking system. Sanctions and mismanagement of the currency had created their own problems, but the main reason for the crisis was self-evident.

The bank had been robbed of its reserves when Gaddafi's entourage seized between three and four billion dinars in cash and nearly two and a half billion dinars' worth of gold. In addition, the motley crew also plundered two billion US dollars from the sovereign wealth fund, set up from the legitimate proceeds of oil sales. The Panama Papers revealed the whereabouts of only a fraction of this treasure trove.

The only comfort was that the new regime at the bank decided to withdraw the old currency from circulation, making some of the stolen notes worthless. This was not done to frustrate the thieves from the old regime but so as to remove images of Gaddafi, in his trademark sunglasses, and the pre-coup monarchy, from the notes, replacing them with more suitable emblems of the nascent state.

The French printers charged by the Central Bank of Libya with the job of etching the new graphic designs onto copper plates and then printing the bank notes, took over two years to work through the various denominations of bills, finally celebrating the delivery of a stock of new fifty-dinar notes in June of 2013. It was this denomination that Ivan Karavayev was currently watching fly though the old offset printing press at the Goznak high-security printing works, in Moscow.

The paper itself was manufactured at the company's own mills near St Petersburg, where the forests of pine, fir and larch provided plenty of softwood pulp. This was then blended with linen so that the long cellulose fibres would give the finished notes strength. The pulp was then washed, pressed and treated to make top-quality banknote substrate. The large finished sheets were stacked, two thousand sheets high, and taken on pallets to the new print works in central Moscow. The Goznak Print Works were sited behind the original, classically styled, old Mint building, which had been built in 1917. Ivan managed a series of offset presses, each twenty metres long, where thousands of sheets of bank notes rolled by every hour. Multiple processes overprinted colours, embossed and coloured various security features, until the sheets were finished and ready to be guillotined into recognisable individual banknotes.

These were then sorted into stacks of 200 notes and each was bound with a green wrapper and encapsulated in plastic film.

Today, the press was busy with the order for the Eastern branch of the Central Bank of Libya. Ivan Karavayev found nothing strange about a country having a central bank with two branches, each independently operating the same currency. He did not think it odd that one half of the country starved the other half of cash, as an act of war, nor that the Tripoli branch would honour any new notes that Ivan printed on behalf of its adversary in Benghazi. If the government in Tripoli were to dishonour any of these notes, it would ruin the entire national currency and make the ultimate reunification so much more difficult, whichever side won the current tussle.

Ivan saw dozens of different currencies being printed, given the presses also produced notes for countries in Asia, the Middle East and Africa. As long as they met the strict specifications and passed inspection, Ivan was happy to see them bundled into five stacks of one thousand notes and layered into wooden packing cases containing one hundred thousand notes per case. These would then be weighed, securely sealed, stamped with a reference number and barcoded. Each case was fitted with a location transponder, which would reveal its whereabouts, anywhere in the world, at any time.

Final audit checks would be made and the cases would then be taken to the secured despatch bays, to await shipment. Mistakes were seldom made, but were not unknown. A single packing case containing one hundred thousand fifty dinar notes was worth three and a half million US dollars. For this print job there were enough notes to fill two hundred packing cases: seven hundred million US dollars or one billion Libyan dinars!

Ivan did not see the notes in terms of what they might buy. To him, they were either printed in accordance with their specification or they were not.

The transport section of Goznak managed the delivery of the goods. The weight of one billion Libyan dinars was over twenty tonnes, excluding packing materials. Such consignments were routinely packed into a standard container, padded with baffles, sealed, tagged and freighted either by road or rail. On this occasion, the journey started with a short trip by road to the freight terminal at Moscow Station, where it waited to begin the forty-eight-hour transfer to Novorossiysk, on the Black Sea.

Goznak had long accepted that its customers were reluctant to assume risk and ownership of these valuable consignments, until the goods were outside the Soviet Republic. As Goznak was wholly owned by the Russian state, it was reasonable for customers to expect the Russian government to take the risk of transporting the money to the point of exit from the country, which it did. Once it reached the port of Novorossiysk and the export procedures had been completed, a bill of lading was physically handed over to the shipper and the ownership of the goods, and risk of loss, transferred.

As the battered light green container from the Goznak works sat in a loading yard, waiting for the start of its onward journey, a smoky thirty-year-old diesel train from Krasnodar creaked and clanked into the yard, at the end of its three-hour journey. It slowly screeched to a halt, its linkages jangling and the metal-on-metal brakes sounding like fingernails on a blackboard.

Its consignor was a well-known fruit-juice manufacturer, based on the outskirts of Krasnodar, who regularly filled twenty-foot containers with twenty-four thousand litres of fruit juice, for export to Northern Europe and North Africa. The juice was pumped into giant disposable polyethylene bladders, which, as they expanded, nestled securely against the packing and baffles around the side of the containers. Once they were three-quarters full, they could be jumped and bounced on, like giant water beds.

This particular order had attracted some excitement, as it was for a consignment of half a million litres of juice. The order had also specified the shipper to be used and the ship that was to take the cargo. The purchaser had asked for the identifying codes for each of the containers. The juice supplier had been surprised when a large box arrived with a bespoke set of fittings that had to be attached to each of the valves on the bladders. The purchaser required photographic evidence that each bladder had been fitted with the component. Those on the production team recognised the fittings as some sort of actuator, designed to open and close the valves, on a remote control. They were perplexed, but the instructions were very specific and easy enough to implement.

CHAPTER 34
MARCO BONNICI
PALAZZO BRUNO, BRERA, MILAN

MARCO HAILED a taxi and went directly to Brera and Signor Bruno's *palazzo*. The first thing that struck him was the silence. No police cars, no ambulances and no people in uniform managing the scene. He had expected the place to be swarming with Servizio di Pronto Intervento. Yet in the street outside the palazzo, life continued as usual.

He rang the bell and, seconds later, the Sicilian driver, Toni, opened the door, his face looking pale and gaunt. For a horrible moment, it occurred to Marco that Signor Bruno might not have died after all, and that this was some diabolical ruse to bring him to the palazzo. He told himself to get a grip.

Toni took him up to Signor Bruno's study. It was in its usual tidy condition. Marco was a little shocked by what he found, having braced himself to see Signor Bruno's bloodied corpse, his office turned upside down, crowds of investigating police and forensic examiners. Instead, he noticed there was a stuffed bin liner and a janitor's zinc bucket with mop, in one corner of the room. The rug that was usually in front of Signor Bruno's desk had been rolled up and placed upright next to it. The Family's Milanese lawyer, Hugo, stood leaning over the desk where another man sat, examining some papers in front of him.

Marco said to the seated man, "What is going on, Signor De Luca?" He nodded to the lawyer. "Hugo, where is Signor Bruno? You said he was dead."

The seated man looked up and took off his spectacles. He was short and portly, in his later years, with a penchant for suits worn with waistcoats and flamboyant silk pocket handkerchiefs. He had a high forehead, surrounded by close-cropped, snow-white hair that grew over his collar at the back. His salt-and-pepper beard was tightly trimmed and covered several of his chins. Gabriele De Luca was a former chairman of a major Italian car manufacturer, who had found life a little difficult following the scandals surrounding Prime Minister Giulio Andreotti in the early nineteen nineties. He had had the sense to withdraw from public life, moving into the shadows and using his money and influence on behalf of the Family until, eventually, he became a Wise Man some ten years ago.

"Marco, Signor Bruno is indeed dead. He was found two hours ago, shot in the back of the head, execution-style. Most unpleasant!"

"What? Shot? I was due to meet him at six. Where is he? And where are the police?"

"He is being properly looked after and we do not need the police. We can deal with this ourselves."

"You cannot just ignore a murder! What about the legalities?"

Signor De Luca huffed and pulled himself up from his chair.

"We have no intention of ignoring his death. On the contrary, the murder of one of the Family is a most serious issue, but legalities are legalities. We have lawyers who can take care of those. So, please, Marco, we ask for your discretion. And it is not just one death, it is two."

"Two? What on earth has happened?"

"Before we get into that, Hugo needs to ask you some questions. We will also need to talk to Natasha as she was here earlier today for the monthly meeting. I understand she has already boarded her flight. I will telephone her tomorrow. We are in exceptional times."

Hugo then questioned Marco about the reason for his meeting with Signor Bruno. Marco was precise and clear in his answers, with nothing to hide. The next question from Signor De Luca was trickier.

"What have you been doing for the rest of the day? I'm sorry, but I need to ask."

De Luca was rather too quick with this question and the flicker of his narrow eyes put Marco on notice that he had better be careful with his reply.

"I had coffee with Salvatore Randazzo. You will be aware that we have had our differences. We were meeting to try and find a way to set them aside, so we can work together in the future. Signor Bruno was aware of our meeting."

"Ah, yes. And did you resolve your differences?"

"That will never be possible, Signor De Luca, for reasons you well understand, but I am hopeful Salvatore and I can work together, when occasion demands."

"We spoke to Salvatore an hour ago. He told us he informed you that Signor Bruno had given him the order to dispose of Sergio Rossi. He said that you then discussed killing Signor Bruno. Shooting him. Is that true?"

Marco sighed wearily.

"We argued, that is all. He taunted me with a fact that I had already worked out for myself – that Signor Bruno had ordered the killing of Sergio. I asked Salvatore what he wanted me to do with the information he had just given me, whether he expected me to go and kill Signor Bruno – it was a rhetorical question."

"Coincidental, though," Hugo interjected, "given that Signor Bruno was shot not long afterwards."

"Unfortunate timing, certainly. But make of it what you will, my conscience is clear. It is plain to me that Salvatore seeks to take advantage of the situation."

There was an uncomfortable silence in the room. Marco was

determined not to waver and be the first to break it. Finally, Signor De Luca removed his spectacles and rubbed his eyes.

"We do not believe this has anything to do with you, Marco, and neither does Salvatore. But we needed to hear your answer to that question."

Marco slumped back in his chair and sighed, shaking his head in disbelief.

"You said there were two bodies? Who else is involved?"

Hugo glanced at Signor De Luca, who waved his hand at him, indicating he should continue.

"Unfortunately, Signor Bruno was involved in relationships with young men. We know who they are. Toni *facilitated* these friendships, it seems. The boy upstairs was one Alberto Fabbri, whose street name is apparently Tesoro. Mean anything to you?"

"Do you really think it likely I would know a youngster by the nickname of 'Treasure'?"

"Sorry, I have to ask. Fabbri was new on the scene. Met Signor Bruno in the Orto Botanico di Brera. Signor Bruno took a daily stroll through the botanical gardens every afternoon, after lunch. He was regular in all his habits. Alas, it seems someone knew this and capitalised on it."

"Was Tesoro shot too?"

"Yes."

"So – what does this mean?"

"Well, according to Toni, he let Tesoro in through the side door at around 16:00, then he immediately went down to the data room as he realised the CCTV wasn't working. He says he keeps out of the way on Monday and Friday afternoons."

"I can understand that, but hardly a professional approach," said Marco.

"The only other thing we do know is that Signor Bruno had a call arranged with a tax accountant at 15:45, which we have confirmed took place. So, Signor Bruno was in his study when Tesoro arrived and the papers on his desk related to the conversation with the accountant.

"We suspect Tesoro must have waited for Toni to leave, then came back downstairs, opened the backdoor and let in the shooter. The pair of them went upstairs to wait for Signor Bruno, but the gunman had a tidy mind and got rid of Tesoro before coming downstairs to shoot Signor Bruno in his study."

"That assumes the gunman could find his way around the *palazzo*?"

"Yes, it seems so, doesn't it?"

Marco looked around the room.

"There must be security-camera footage available?"

Hugo nodded.

"Yes, you would think so. But the cameras on the main door, the lobby, that stairway and in this office were all disabled, somehow. Someone accessed the network, identified the Mac address of the cameras and then launched multiple 'denial of service' attacks against them. They knew what they were doing. That is why we think this could be an inside job."

Hugo then asked Marco: "What can you tell us about Salvatore's manner this morning?"

Marco locked his fingers together in front of him.

"He was unhappy. He felt he had done the Family a service in following through on the order to kill Sergio. He felt unappreciated and that several Family members, me included, were unfairly hostile to him as a result. He felt that Signor Bruno could have been more supportive of him. He said the episode had cost him dearly."

"What did you say to that?" Hugo asked.

"I said, '*Tough!*'"

De Luca cracked a thin smile.

Hugo went on, "He seemed a little disturbed to us."

"I would not have said that. Salvatore is a proud, even arrogant, man and his ambitions have taken a knock, but I would not say he is *disturbed*."

De Luca shifted his weight in the chair.

"OK, Marco, thank you. Can we change the subject? This situation has consequences for Natasha."

Marco blinked, unsure for a second what that meant.

"We will need her here in Milan more often. Weekly, for two to three days. She knows Signor Bruno's work and is the obvious choice to step in and expand her role. He had great faith in her and intended to talk to her about her long-term prospects.

"She can take the chair of the oil and gas business, but she needs to step away from BetHi. To continue there as well would be too much of a burden. Can you fill her in, after Hugo has spoken to her, and ask her to put arrangements in place to ensure continuity at BetHi?"

Marco got to his feet, nodding agreement.

"Of course. Now, if you do not need me further, I am going to my hotel."

He sat in the back of Signor Bruno's 7 Series BMW, in silence, while the hapless Toni made the fifteen-minute drive to the Tortona Hotel. As he stared idly out of the tinted windows, it occurred to Marco that here was yet another situation where Natasha had benefited from the misfortune of another.

She had been in Milan earlier but had declined his offer of dinner, keen to return to Malta for some reason. He had thought it a little strange at the time, as she would usually grab any opportunity to dress up and step out into one of Milan's finer places. He quickly rebuked himself for these dark thoughts, frightened, as usual, of where such thinking might lead. He turned his mind to more practical problems, such as how they would go about finding a replacement CEO for BetHi.

CHAPTER 35
NATASHA BONNICI
CHAPEL OF OUR LADY OF THE ABANDONED, MALTA

NATASHA HAD RETURNED from her usual monthly meeting with Signor Bruno late the previous night. She knew her father was in Milan but, given their conflicting appointments and Natasha's wish not to be away from the chapel for too long, had left for the airport straight after her visit to the *palazzo*.

She and Simon had settled into an easy rhythm with Savi. He had relaxed into captivity and, when not following their orders, was happy to play endless games of *Fifa* and build his empire in *Civilisation*, on the X-Box. In the early evenings, Simon brought him takeaway food, beer and some weed, and they would sit together until it got dark, watching from their clifftop eyrie, eating, drinking and smoking, as the sun slid down the sky and dipped beneath the darkening sea.

Beyond the chapel, waves pounded against a mass of fallen boulders, sheared from the cliff face over the centuries by the action of wind and rain. The chapel had been built as a place of quiet contemplation. The rumble of the sea and the continuous passing of the wind created a backdrop of white noise which, in time, became its own strange silence.

It seemed Savi had become perfectly at ease with the new

arrangement, where he had no responsibility for anything except the two things he loved most: gaming and hacking computer systems.

Simon had worked out that Savi was awake for most of the night and only rose in the early afternoon. He left boxes of crisps and snacks that seemed to keep the boy happy until his pizza, or kebab, arrived in the evening. In reality, there was not much difference in age between the two of them, but Simon could not help seeing Savi as a useless younger brother and, despite himself, had started to feel a little protective towards him.

Savi had asked Simon to get him some clean clothes. It was true, the jeans and sweatshirts he had brought with him were now filthy and stained with slops from takeaway meals and the dirt and dust of the chapel. Simon had looked him up and down and agreed he could do with some new things. He had asked the boy what he wanted. Savi had thought for a bit and chewed on his bottom lip, then said: "What do you think Natasha would like?"

"Natasha? What's it got to do with her?"

"What do her sort of guys usually wear? She must go out with guys. Well, she's hot, isn't she?

"So?"

"Well, I sort of … like her. She was up for it, you know, with me, until you barged in. So … you know? I need to look my best."

"You're kidding me? You don't think for a minute …" Simon was incredulous. He started laughing.

"You can laugh all you want, but I know when someone's into me. I don't see why you think it's so funny."

Simon's peals of laughter echoed around the deserted countryside.

Savi was hurt by this ridicule.

"I bet you I bang her before this is over!"

Simon spluttered, beer spilling out of his mouth.

"Oh, God, stop it, don't say anymore!" He held his head in his hands. "Fantastic, that's a bet I really want to take. Please, please, promise me one thing? You must tell me when you're going to make your move. I can't wait to see it!"

Savi flicked his greasy hair back and, in all seriousness, preened himself, pouting.

"You wait and see. I know how to get what I want from a woman."

Simon collapsed in fits of laughter again.

Apart from fantasising about what he might get up to with Natasha, Savi was busy using his skills, as a hacker, scammer and internet-nuisance, to phish, hoax and impersonate his way around the Novorossiysk shipping agents. Eventually, he got the information he needed about the carriage of the container from a helpful, but gullible, lady at Krasnodar Krai Freight Forwarding Company.

He then used a mobile WiFi hotspot to connect to the server at his home and set up a VPN link into his EDI terminal. EDI was the electronic tool that enabled all import and export operations and cargo movement at the world's ports.

He logged into the shipper's website, bypassing the firewalls and security features, and inserted a virtual network implant, which allowed him to extract the container-release codes for the container in question. This, in turn, enabled him to access the EDIFACT messaging features.

Savi quickly found the shipping destination fields and changed the container's destination from Istanbul to Constanta. He also added the PIN randomiser that would provide Natasha's haulier with entry to the port of Constanta and trigger release of the container. All of this information was programmed to be released at a future date and time that Natasha had yet to give him.

Savi had asked why Constanta, not Istanbul? Natasha had told him to 'just do it'.

On the shipper's server, Savi had found the load plan for the ship, the *Kapitan Markov,* and the departure date in question. The containers were batched and assembled on the quayside for loading aboard the *Kapitan Markov*, in strict order.

The *Markov* was a small unassuming vessel, with its superstructure rising at the stern of the ship, allowing easier access to its deck hatches. She shuttled containers between the Black Sea ports and Istanbul, where they were transhipped to bigger vessels for the more substantial part of their journeys.

The twenty blue containers of juice sat alongside several hundred others, including the solitary pale green container, stuffed full of Libyan dinars, which Natasha had told Savi should be loaded last.

The large container crane slowly trundled back and forth on rails set into the quayside. Like a giant four-legged spider, it negotiated the piles of containers, dropping its cables and spreader beam, hauling the boxes into the air, before lowering them into the dark holds of the *Kapitan Markov*. It was capable of lifting 400 tonnes, but seldom had to bear that amount. Sitting in the cabin, attached to the trolley, the crane operator loaded the containers, strictly following the load plan that had been worked out by planning software previously hacked by Savi.

The purpose of the load plan was not only to position those containers that needed to be unloaded first, but also to evenly distribute weight, so the *Kapitan Markov* would not become top heavy and start to roll and pitch, once at sea. It was crucial to the ship's safety to ensure a low centre of gravity so as to maintain trim and stability.

The blue containers with their load of juice weighed twenty-four metric tonnes each, so the twenty containers, along with the other heavier ones bound for Istanbul, went on first, deep into the holds, while other lighter loads were stacked on top of them. The *Kapitan Markov* was a small vessel, one hundred metres long and carrying only five hundred containers, three hundred and fifty in the holds and one hundred and fifty stacked above deck, so the 'juice' was a sizeable percentage of its cargo capacity.

Novorossiysk was on the north coast of the Black Sea. The passage to Istanbul involved heading directly south-west, to skirt Sebastopol at the foot of the Crimean Peninsula and then across the centre of the Black Sea, into the mouth of the Bosphorus, the narrow channel that linked Russia to the Mediterranean, at Istanbul. With the *Markov* doing ten knots, the trip usually took about two and half days.

The whole exercise had taken Savi a little under two hours. But he remained puzzled.

"How are you going to divert a ship bound for Istanbul to Constanta in Romania – and why would you want to do that?"

Natasha fixed him with a no-nonsense expression.

"We want a head start on the Russians and the Americans. The Russians own the goods and the Americans think you are going to steal them on their behalf in Istanbul. Once our container is off-loaded in Constanta, I want you to go into the system and reallocate its number to another container, and then set up the heist in the same way, but this time in Istanbul."

"Oh, I get it! You nab the real container in Constanta and the Americans end up stealing the wrong container in Istanbul?" Savi scratched his head. Then his expression became one of concern. "Wait a minute ... no way! That puts me right in the shit!"

"Why would it? The container will still have the same code attached to it. They won't know you switched them. You've done exactly what they asked. And you'll get paid twice!"

"I suppose ... I still don't know how you're going to get the ship to Constanta."

"OK, I'll tell you how. Work out when the ship is at its nearest point to Constanta and then calculate backwards four hours. At that point, send the message to open those actuating valves."

"What the hell for?"

"That gets the ship to Constanta. Trust me! Then, and only

then, activate the EDIFACT message to the *Kapitan Markov* to unload our container at Constanta."

Savi went through the process again and explained to Natasha exactly what he had been doing.

"You're sure everything is going to go through as it should?"

"Yeah, I know my stuff! If you were standing on the dockside at Novorossiysk, you'd see your containers just about to be loaded."

"OK, so in two days' time, it should all be over and you'll have a pocket full of money."

"That's me done? Can I go now?"

"Don't be stupid. I want you here, following what goes on, so if there're any glitches, you can fix them. Two more days, that's all."

"Well, if I've got to stay a bit longer, tell Simon to get me *The Witcher* and *Doom*. I'm sick of winning on *Fifa*."

Simon and Natasha locked Savi back in the chapel and turned the SUV to drive down the track, towards the *castello*. Simon turned to her and asked: "What happens to the little dickhead once we've got the container?"

She thought for a moment and then said brightly, "Throw him off the cliffs. You can do that, can't you?"

Simon looked straight ahead and kept on driving. He was stunned by how casually she could say such a thing. He knew she had a dark side to her character and was fairly sure it had been her who had taken the *castello's* old Land Rover and used it to kill the Albanian in the Aquarium car park. Simon was no angel himself, having served in the Military Gendarmerie, Poland's military police, but he had never murdered somebody in cold blood.

More to the point, the kid did not deserve it. He had done everything he had been asked to. He was no real danger to them, just a stupid boy who liked computers, gaming and smoking dope. He had stumbled into all this and had no idea what he was dealing with.

Well, even if Natasha gave him a direct order, Simon would not do it. Instead, he would try and find a way to get Savi out, so that the boy could make a run for it. If only he knew, his protector thought grimly. While Savi was planning his wardrobe, ready to make an amorous move on Natasha, she was making plans to pitch him into eternity.

CHAPTER 36
GEORGE ZAMMIT
ABU MUHAMMAD'S CAMP, NORTHERN CHAD

THE CONTRACTORS HAD WITHDRAWN to the relative safety of the terminal building almost immediately they realised the scale of the assault. The attackers were lightly armed and Sam had rightly assumed this was a hit-and-run strike, made primarily as a warning to the new arrivals. The machine gun emplacements had served them well and, despite the odds and the loss of Harley, the Maltese policeman had held the western flank, allowing the others time to set up a defence inside the terminal. Sam calculated that they had killed or disabled about thirty fighters, which was about a third of the attacking force. Judging by the position of the bodies, the Maltese policeman was probably responsible for a good number of those downed.

Sam led a party of contractors and Tuareg out to recover Harley's body and generally survey the damage. He had been on the radio and was assured that three platoons of US Rangers would be with them first thing the next day, to resupply them and help strengthen the base's defences. Now their presence was known, there was no secret to protect and it made it easier to fly in materials and supplies.

During the next few days, US Reaper drones from Turkey were due to hit Boutros's airbases in eastern Libya with large and very expensive rockets. It would be the largest drone strike ever mounted and the US intent would be made clear. A-10 Warthog jets had been briefed to hit Boutros's ground forces and part of the 'big bang' Mike Lloyd had alluded to would be provided by four AC-130 gunships, circling over the airfields. These large Hercules planes carried a massive cargo of armaments with huge destructive capabilities. The aim was the complete annihilation of Boutros's airfields and a good percentage of his ground capabilities.

In the meantime, the Maltese policeman was missing. They had searched the terminal building, the scrubland around the runway, the corpses they had piled near the treeline, but the policeman had not been found. The Tuareg had bagged the enemy bodies and loaded them into four trucks, which they took to the mosque in town, laying them in a line in front of a crowd of silent townspeople. An Imam appeared and they handed over to him the responsibility for a respectful Muslim burial. The Americans had learned their lesson in Iraq, where GIs disrespecting the Muslim dead had turned local populations against them and incensed their enemy.

Sam had got a message through to the operational control at Al-Udeid airbase in Qatar. The assumption was that George had been captured and taken hostage. A senior officer had made a call to the Assistant Commissioner of the Maltese police, informing him of the situation, while the Tuareg fighters quickly let Edal Essa and Abdullah know of the attack and George's capture.

George's unconscious body had been dumped into the back of a Kia SUV with additional metal plating welded onto it, making it look like an upside-down bathtub. There were no windows, merely slits in the metal sheeting. They had been driving for over an hour before he regained consciousness. He opened his eyes, or rather one eye, and all he could tell was that the sun had almost set and was casting the last of the day's shadows in their direction of travel. He guessed they were travelling east, then he must have shut his eyes for a moment and fallen asleep or passed out because, when he next woke up, it was totally dark and the vehicle was racing through what felt like empty desert.

He stirred where he lay, the truck still bouncing him along the rough unmetalled road. His body did not hurt, but his head and face were agony. The taste of blood filled his mouth and one of his front teeth was loose. A swelling over one eye hung low, obscuring his vision. There was a driver, and a young boy peering over the front passenger seat and pointing a gun straight into George's face. The way he felt, he wished the kid would just get on with it and pull the trigger.

Sensing his movement, the driver slowed and started to pull over. Once the car had stopped, he jumped out and pulled the rear door open. He roughly yanked George from the car, grabbing his wrists and placing them on the roof. George spat a thick stream of bloody saliva onto the ground and rested his aching head against the roof. The car following them pulled in behind, its full beam forcing them to shield their eyes.

The occupants got out and crossed over to them. A hefty young man in a tan camouflage outfit, with full tactical belt, emerged through the glare. He spoke English with that strange London accent. He took George by the collar and turned him round to face the light. A tall, sour-faced man with a long beard, dressed in a calf-length long black tunic reaching to his knees, followed behind. He approached and looked at George carefully. He had something in his hand that he was studying, looking closely at George and then back at what he was holding.

"Get that stupid turban off him."

The hefty young man pulled the *cheche* from George's head and threw it into the dust. He searched him, going through his pockets and patting down his arms and legs.

The tall man in black came closer and looked again at the card in his hand, then back at George, a smile spreading over his face.

"A day of many blessings! You are the Maltese policeman George Zammit, no? It is hard to be sure, with your face as it is – but I am sure it is you."

The tall man pushed George's Pulizija identity card back into his top pocket.

"We have not met, but I know of you. Where is the *shu hayee*, backstabbing Abdullah Belkacem?"

George did not know who this man was or what he wanted with Abdullah, but he guessed it was not a polite enquiry after a mutual friend.

"At this moment, I don't know. Who are you and how d'you know me?"

"My name is Abu Muhammad. I followed you and Abdullah around Marsabar and I cannot count how many deaths you have caused my people. But now, things are different. I will need to know what you were doing in Ubari, with Tuareg and Americans. You will tell me everything. I will enjoy making you."

George swallowed and his heart sank further as he realised the depth of his predicament.

From nowhere, Muhammad's hand appeared and he swiped the back of it across George's bruised and broken face, a large ring scoring a deep line on his cheek.

"We cannot stay here. *Ant kalbi*, put the dog back in the car. The sky has eyes, even at night."

George slumped in the seat, willing sleep to take him away from this nightmare. Unfortunately, the pain and the trembling in his limbs made that impossible. The long cut from Muhammad's ring caused his cheek to bleed profusely and the blood soaked down through his clothing. It took another ten hours to reach their camp.

It was nearly dawn when Yaroslav heard the trucks arrive back. He got up from his mattress and studied the convoy. There were fewer vehicles and many fewer men than had left. He saw

Raheem, in full battle garb, his head hanging low. The body language was one of defeat. Only Abu Muhammad held his head high, quietly issuing instructions, seemingly unfazed by events. There were several injured men being helped out of the trucks, their wounds still untreated and undressed. Yaroslav could only wonder at the consequences of the inevitable infections that would soon develop.

They had also brought a prisoner with them. Yaroslav watched with interest as the man was led to a small stone hut nearby. He was a middle-aged Arab who had been roughed up, his face badly beaten. Yaroslav noticed the new arrival carried some weight but, he thought grimly, that would soon change.

George was led to a low door and pushed through it, into darkness. He fell onto the damp earth, smelling vegetal rot and animal musk. He lay very still, the cool dirt floor providing some relief for his aching head. Sleep came, as did the searing heat of the Chadian desert morning. When he woke up the pain in his head was soon replaced with a painful thirst. His tongue felt swollen and the perspiration was already soaking through his shirt. The sweat in his hair had loosened the dried blood from the cut on his scalp and cheek. When he rubbed his hands across his face, a red stain spread across his features.

It was several hours before the door was yanked open and the Londoner pulled George to his feet. By then, he was barely semi-conscious and all he could think about was water. He muttered the word time and again to the Londoner.

"Water."

"Later."

"Water."

"Later, I said."

Abu Muhammad sat inside his cool tent, on a canvas director's chair, and smiled when George was dragged in, looking very sorry for himself. He was pushed down onto his knees.

A small, pleasant-looking bespectacled man entered the tent. He was bald, a large shiny forehead emerging beneath the black turban that covered the rest of his head. His long, grey beard reached halfway down his chest. He was smiling and had an affable, gentle manner.

"You may call me Faysal. In this camp, I am the only friend you have. You are surrounded by enemies, only waiting for the word to do terrible things to you."

He smiled cheerfully.

In the background Abu Muhammad sat watching, his expression grim and threatening. Faysal continued, speaking in a quiet, almost apologetic manner.

"We are going to talk and you will tell me what I need to know. If you do, you will drink, we will wash and dress your wounds and we will ransom you. If you do not tell me what I want to know, you will not drink and you will be beaten again, not with fists, but this time with metal and wood. Bones will break. And still you will not drink.

"Now, I must know that you understand? Speak."

George tried to open his swollen and cracked lips and remove his tongue from the back of his mouth. He swallowed, but it was only a reflex movement in his throat. There was no saliva to clear.

"Yes. I understand," he croaked.

Faysal went to the back of the tent and picked up a small bottle of water, placing it next to him, within George's view.

"Where is Abdullah Belkacem?"

Without a second's hesitation, George started speaking.

"He's in Marsabar."

"Who is he with and what are they doing there?"

George did not even try to hide the truth. He told Faysal everything he knew: about their trip to Al-Udeid, the alliance with the Tuareg elders, the contractors and the planned air attack by the Americans on Boutros's forces. All the time, he kept glancing at the water on the table next to Faysal. After ten minutes, he was finished and slumped, his head on his knees, prostrate as if in Muslim prayer. He hated himself for his weakness.

Faysal looked at Abu Muhammad, his eyebrows raised. With a flick of his wrist, Muhammad dismissed George, who was taken back to the heat of the searing stone hut, with his bottle of water.

Abu Muhammad and Faysal sat with glasses of tea. Muhammad had been considering the new information.

"It is a good thing the Americans are attacking Boutros. Let them feel the sting of an American air attack. When they are depleted, we can take advantage. What we know of the Americans is that they never stay anywhere for long. I would rather fight them than other Arabs. Americans you can see and hear, a hundred kilometres away. An Arab, though, he can creep up on you while you sleep."

A little later, the padlock was undone and the door opened, a shaft of light falling across George's red and yellow face. An accented voice said, in English: "Oh, I see they beat you. You are not pretty and you smell bad. My name is Yaroslav, they say I must help you."

George could not make out any face as he peered into the direct sunlight that silhouetted the figure at the door.

"I have bucket of water to wash your hands, face and wounds. There is cloth in bucket. The water is not for drink. It is bad water."

George raised himself and, without speaking to the man, plunged his head into the scummy water and drank deeply. The blood and filth from his hair and face mingled with the scum floating on top of the water.

"Ahhh ... I said, do not do that! Maybe you choose to die with cholera. They can kill in many bad ways, maybe cholera is not most bad. Sleep, and put water on your head to be cool; it helps. Remember, is important: do *not* drink more water! I will come back. Now, sleep."

CHAPTER 37
ABDULLAH BELKACEM
MARSABAR, LIBYA

THE CESSNA that left Ubari had landed near the tiny mountain village of Rehibat, which served as the Nafusa Hills' only airport, thanks to a mile-long stretch of straight road that acted as the landing strip. Abdullah and Edal had been met by Rania's brothers and had returned to their family home, some fifty kilometres away. The next day, as Abdullah had done seven years previously, they started the job of building a local resistance to the Islamic State-in-Libya of Abu Muhammad and Boutros's encroaching militias.

Abdullah had old Berber allies in Nalut, a village in the Nafusa mountain range, just east of the Tunisian border. Its position as a crossing point made it a key town in the area and its Berber inhabitants were among the first to rise in protest against Muammar Gaddafi. Abdullah and Edal spoke to the elders and showed them photographs of the Americans alongside them in Ubari. They promised them protection and freedom to live how they chose; in return, the elders promised Abdullah men to fight alongside him.

The same thing happened in other neighbouring Berber villages such as Ghezaia and Wazzin. There was no love of the 'Beards' there and, since Abdullah had been forced to flee, there had been no protection from Abu Muhammad, who had terrorised the villages, forbidding the speaking of their old Berber language, taking food and supplies, forcing sharia teachings down their throats at the mosque and persecuting their women.

Such was the hostility to the Beards, the clans of Berbers and Arabs set aside their age-old differences and soon Abdullah found himself with a force of nearly 300 men to arm and train.

At that point, he called in the first team of US Rangers, a dozen of whom arrived during the night from Tunisia, in three trucks, bringing weapons and equipment. For the next two weeks, the hills crackled with gunfire and explosions. Those living in Marsabar heard the sound of aircraft and helicopters flying overhead. Word spread that Abdullah Belkacem was back, hiding in the hills, with at least 1,000 American Marines, if not more, just waiting to drive Abu Muhammad back to the wastelands of the south.

Those of the Beards who had for so long terrified and controlled Marsabar stayed in their camp in the middle of the Nafusa Hills, awaiting further instructions. In the Chadian desert, far to the south-west, Abu Muhammad and what was left of his militia, were licking their wounds and listening intently to news of the developments in Marsabar.

Abdullah took to making staged appearances in the streets of the town and found, each time, a crowd would quickly develop to walk alongside him, asking questions and pledging support. He would gather the small groups in a local square or on a street corner and pledge he had come back to fight and free them from life under Islamic State. He explained he would take a share of the wealth generated from the port and the refinery, giving back cash to health centres and schools. He promised them a better life, such as they had before the Beards drove him away and diverted the money to their own causes. They would cheer and shout, and Abdullah would draw on their energy, while one or two of his clan would move amongst the crowd, taking names and phone numbers of the men they knew to be most likely to commit to him. He walked the streets without fear, daring the local Islamic State fighters to challenge him. And still the technicals, with their black flags and bullying zealots, stayed away.

One Friday, shortly after his re-emergence in Marsabar, Abdullah went to pray at the mosque and then travelled a short distance out of town, to a remote farm. There he met with Sheik Ahmed al Habib, a local teacher and religious leader, who directed such opposition as there was to the IS presence.

He told Abdullah: "It was not so bad at first – they were more with the oil and the port. It was money they needed. They did not trouble the townspeople. But now it has become bad. They come into town more often, looking for 'wives' to marry. We know what that means.

"They preach on the streets, urging young boys to join them as fighters in jihad. Now the Imam has problems. They challenge his teaching. They say he is betraying and dishonouring those who pray in his mosque. They have set up two of their own *madrassas* in town and threaten parents that, if the children do not go to them, they will be taken away, to protect them from false teachings. Always the young – they always want the young."

They sat cross-legged on the *mergoum*, a brightly coloured and patterned traditional Berber carpet, woven in the old way, without synthetic materials or machines. The faint chatter of women came from a nearby room and Abdullah could smell *ftat misrati*, Libyan flatbread, cooking on an iron skillet. He shook his head. It sickened him to hear what Abu Muhammad was doing in Allah's name. They talked for several hours and, although the Sheikh was reluctant to fully commit his support, Abdullah felt he was making progress with the man.

"I understand you do not know me well. But you know I have done good things before and will do them again in the future. I ask you to trust me and give me your support."

The Sheikh smiled at him.

"They say that, four years ago, you ran away and did not stay to fight. They say you left your family and your clan. They say the Americans pay for you to have an easy life in Malta; that you are no longer a true Muslim."

Abdullah knew the Arab love of gossip and he could imagine the naysayers in the cafés: the old men sitting by the dried-up fountain outside the mosque, the youth hanging around with their mopeds in the squares. He wanted them to talk about his return. He wanted them to talk about the evil of IS and their hopes for a free and fair Libya. That was why he paraded around the town – to stir the conversation and talk of a better life. It would be naïve to expect that all the talk would be good.

"Yes, yes, I can understand this being said. But now, I am here. Imam Ali, the prophet's son-in-law, said: *'People are of two types in relation to you, either your brother in Islam, or your brother in humanity.'* I am different because I am both and I am here to turn word into deed."

The Sheikh bowed his head, always finding a well-chosen religious quote persuasive. Abdullah continued: "So, I once went to the Islamic State-in-Libya camp, some years ago. We left the road at Al Jawsh and headed south on a rough track, then up an old riverbed for maybe two kilometres. This led us to a cleft in the rock, high above the town. At the bottom, there was a wide flat area that was Abu Muhammad's camp. You cannot see it from the air, they have hung camouflage netting between the two rock faces. Do you know this place?"

The Sheikh nodded, but said nothing.

"I am guessing this is still their camp. Do they have trucks and fighters there?"

"Yes, they have over one hundred men, maybe two hundred, with weapons and vehicles."

"I live by my word and my deeds. Tomorrow, that camp will no longer exist. Tomorrow, at first light, watch the sky. You will see a bright early sunrise, but from the south, not the east."

Abdullah had asked the Americans for a show of strength

and to hit the camp as part of their 'shock and awe' raids. Thermal imaging surveillance had established the camp was still very much active, a base for several hundred fighters. Abdullah wanted a 'big bang' to help his recruitment drive with the Marsabar locals and to tug on Abu Muhammad's tail!

The white-haired US general in Al-Udeid loved 'shock and awe' as a tactic, so he had authorised deploying a Massive Ordnance Air Blast bomb, one of the most intimidating non-nuclear weapons in the American arsenal, to destroy the camp and half the hillside with it. The enormous bomb would be dropped from a C-130 cargo plane and guided to its target by a GPS system. The tight ravine was perfect to concentrate the destructive power of its blast. This was intended as a huge, expensive statement of US intent to discourage the civil war and the ISIL militias, as well as to send a message to other foreign powers that their meddling would no longer be tolerated.

Abdullah was confident that once the local community saw and heard the blast, proof of American support, he would acquire sufficient fighters to establish a camp openly in Marsabar. Then, the job of properly arming and training them could begin. The general could start bringing in weapons, vehicles and advisers. The port of Marsabar would soon be in his hands and would be the gateway for supplies and all the hardware Abdullah's men would need to secure the district and protect Tripoli's western flank.

CHAPTER 38
CAPTAIN ERIC SOBOLEV
ABOARD THE KAPITAN MARKOV, BLACK SEA

THE *KAPITAN MARKOV* had left Novorossiysk and was well into her two-and-a-half-day journey across the Black Sea to the Bosphorus channel and on to Istanbul. Captain Eric Sobolev had sailed the route hundreds of times and knew the seasonal moods and temperament of the waters. In winter, the Black Sea was an evil place, with north-easterly Arctic gales and treacherous winds, which whipped up currents and white-topped waves. In spring and summer it became easier sailing, as the tropical air pushed up from the south, reducing the strength of the wind and calming the sea. It was mid-August, so he was expecting a pleasant crossing and there would be little to do until he reached the narrow, thirty-kilometre channel of the Bosphorus.

After a day and a half's steady cruising at ten knots, the *Kapitan Markov* was to the south-west of Sevastopol and due east of Constanta when, deep down, at the bottom of her hold, the battery-powered valves on the bladders of juice, in their twenty containers, began to turn and a trickle of liquid became a steady stream.

For some hours, this unusual occurrence went unnoticed, other than the occasional waft of a zesty orange scent that floated briefly across the deck and off into the stiff sea breeze. All ships are fitted with automatic bilge pumps that get rid of any water finding its way to the bottom. Be it storm water from the deck, condensation, leakage due to corrosion – all ships take in water and need to get rid of it. The *Kapitan Markov* had two pumps; one fore and one aft. Pipework ran from each area to collect the water and pump it out of the side. The pumps could move hundreds of litres an hour, which was enough to cope with the initial trickle, but, as all twenty containers started to pour juice from their bladders in a steady stream, the five hundred tonnes of liquid quickly overwhelmed the pumps.

This had two effects. First, the juice started to slop around the holds of the ship, becoming 'free water', which was highly dangerous. Secondly, the emptying bladders resulted in a redistribution of the cargo, making the ship top heavy and unbalanced.

Three hours after the valves had first twisted open, the helmsman reported to Captain Sobolev that he thought the ship was becoming heavy to handle. The captain himself had noticed the vessel rolling significantly, from one side to the other, and had started to become concerned. He stayed on the bridge for another ten minutes and felt the situation getting worse. He grabbed the chief officer and told him to take the chief engineer and check out the levels in the bilges and ballast tanks and make sure the cargo was secure.

He was horrified when they reported back that there was a large amount of free water slopping around in the holds and they had no idea where it was coming from. The chief engineer told him that if there was a change in the weather and the seas became rougher, the bilge pumps would not be able to handle this volume of excess water. It was likely the ship would capsize.

The only good news he received was that, strangely, the liquid appeared not to be salt water, but orange juice. Captain Sobolev was relieved in one sense – it was not the case that the ship had sprung a catastrophic leak – but he was annoyed and mystified as to how tonnes of free orange juice had found its way into his holds. Nevertheless, he immediately reduced speed and plotted a course to the nearest decent-sized commercial port, where the cargo could be unloaded and the juice pumped out. That was Constanta, in Romania.

Constanta was three hundred kilometres north of the entry to the Bosphorus Straits and had access to the European hinterland via the Black Sea canal, including the one thousand five hundred kilometre route up the Danube River. Traffic from there could also easily join the Pan European highway and rail system that stretched from Dresden in Northern Germany to Istanbul.

An urgent radio request ensured a berth was quickly organised for the *Kapitan Markov*. As soon as the ship docked, Captain Sobolev and the chief officer began unloading the cargo, while powerful pumps flooded the harbour with gallons of foaming juice.

The Chief was so heavily engrossed in handling these problems, he missed the significance of a strange EDIFACT message, which informed them there was a container that had to be unloaded at Constanta and was cleared for release from the terminal. A similar message had been sent to the port's EDI addresses. The green container, conveniently situated at the top of the first stack, was unloaded and dropped onto a trailer, to be whisked away.

It was all so smooth. The driver, a local smuggler, well versed in stealing from the docks and transporting all manner of cargo, owned a garage some five kilometres outside the port. There, he and his brother, removed the transponders from the body of the container. Then, they broke the seals and locks on the container doors and examined the 200 wooden crates inside, removing more transponders, which they gave to a small boy, along with five Romanian leu to take them to a bridge over the Black Sea canal and cast them into the blue and black, oily waters.

The brothers had been told to wear gloves, face masks and visors, as the cargo was a liquid from a Russian chemical plant, ultimately bound for Syria. Once they were sure the container and its crates were clean, they filled the tractor with diesel and set off on the six hundred kilometre drive to a small village in Western Serbia.

As soon as the EDIFACT system sent a message to Savi's EDI terminal, confirming the release of the container from the Constanta terminal, he immediately set about reallocating the container number, so it appeared that the cargo of Libyan dinars was still sitting on the deck of the *Kapitan Markov*.

Two days later, after a quick clean of its holds, the *Kapitan Markov* left Constanta, cargo restacked, trim adjusted and ballast in order, minus the twenty empty juice containers. Savi had swapped the container numbers and told Mike Lloyd the *Kapitan Markov* had experienced some engineering problems but was now underway, and the release of the container to the haulier in Istanbul had been instructed. It was the same process that had happened earlier in Constanta, except the container in question was now a faded red colour, bearing the logo of a global shipping company.

Angry enquiries were made of the consignor of the twenty juice containers that had caused all the trouble, who reported that all trace of their customer had vanished.

Three days after the switch, Mary-Ann Baker took delivery of the faded red, forty-foot steel box at the US Air Base at Incirlik, in eastern Turkey. She had had several agents tail the container for the twelve-hour eastward journey from the port at Istanbul. It was her first solo mission in the field and she was determined not to be involved in a screw up. Inside the small hangar she had requisitioned, they set about opening the doors and removing the large pallets, stacked with cardboard boxes.

She knew something was wrong as soon as she saw the boxes. She climbed into the container and started squeezing and pushing them. They felt too light and insubstantial. She took a knife to the strapping on the first pallet and threw its contents to the floor below. It weighed less than twenty kilos. She did not even bother to open it.

"Drag the rest of the pallets out!"

Soon the floor was littered with boxes as they ripped the pallets apart, hoping that, somewhere, there would be wooden boxes stacked with green fifty-dinar notes. There were none.

In desperation, Mary-Ann took a knife to one of the boxes. Inside were quilted jackets, packed in cellophane bags and tied into bundles.

"Fuck, fuck and fuck! How's this happened? And what the fuck am I gonna tell Mike Lloyd!"

A week or so later, after an extensive search of the port of Benghazi, an official at the eastern branch of the Central Bank of Libya telephoned the Goznak Printing Works in Moscow to ask what had happened to the delivery of one billion Libyan dinars. The Chief Officer and the Logistics Manager of Goznak were extensively, and unsympathetically, questioned by the Russian state police and the Investigative Committee of Russia (the Russian FBI). It was the FSB who traced the container to Constanta, where the transponders on it, and in the packing cases themselves, had been removed and, presumably, destroyed.

A call was eventually made by the FSB to Valentin Petrov, informing him that the monies bound for eastern Libya had been stolen in transit and enquiries made suggested the theft was organised by security forces of the Government of National Accord in Tripoli. Petrov thought about it and decided that was a highly unlikely explanation.

It was stressed to him that nobody stole that amount of money from the Russian Mint and got away with it. This was a question of national pride. The file on the theft was to remain open and enquiries were to continue, until an accountable person was found and punished. He was ordered to be vigilant and to report any suspicions he might have back to Lubyanka Square. Even someone in Petrov's position shuddered at the mention of Lubyanka Square – a heavy-handed reminder to less diligent citizens of what went on in the basements below.

CHAPTER 39
RANIA BELKACEM
NAFUSA HILLS, LIBYA

IT HAD BEEN VERY EARLY in the morning when Abdullah had woken Rania and they had left her brother's farm, in the dark, to drive the thirty kilometres towards Al Jawsh. The dual carriageway took them east, through the town and up onto the barren sandstone ridge that overlooked the plain running to the coast. Abdullah had chosen the spot carefully. All he had told Rania about the trip was that this day was going to be a new beginning for them. She had begged him to tell her more, but he had tapped his nose, in that annoying way, and said what he always said.

"Allah has a plan for us all! *Inshallah*! Be patient!"

As the sun started to come up in the east, they settled back in the truck and Rania wrapped a blanket around her. She had brought a flask of hot tea that she and Abdullah sipped, to warm them in the chill of the dawn. He had found a patch of flat scrub on the roadside, overlooking the hills to the south, and had used a small compass to take a bearing so he could manoeuvre the truck to point exactly in the direction he required. Rania was puzzled.

"Husband, you have dragged me from my bed before dawn

and brought me to an empty hillside. Now it is time to tell me what is happening. You are scaring me."

"Relax, Rania. Today is the start of a new era. There will be no more hiding. Wait for a few more minutes and you will see something important – no, amazing!"

Rania pulled the blanket up to her chin and snuggled down into it. She felt sleepy and her eyes started to close. Suddenly, Abdullah sat up straight, then leaped out of the car. He pushed his head in through the window and pulled on her shoulder with his hand.

"Get out – come on! There," he pointed skyward, "there, look … listen!"

They could hear the sound of an airplane. It came into sight, emerging from behind the hills to the east, low enough for them to make out its military insignia. It was a lumbering cargo plane, four propellers powering it through the air towards them. Abdullah grabbed some binoculars from the dashboard and trained them upwards. The plane was flying low and seemed to labour noisily over their heads, shattering the peace of the morning. As it did so, Rania could see that the cargo hatch at the rear of the fuselage was open. She was frightened and stood tight against Abdullah, linking his arm.

The plane crossed the valley beneath them. Once it was over the hills to the south, she saw a long cylinder slowly slide out of the rear of the plane. It fell for a few seconds before a parachute opened, silhouetted black against the morning sky. The plane banked to the left and immediately started to gain height. The cylinder swung in the air, suspended by the parachute. It stabilised and hung for a few seconds more. Then, an unseen hand released the cylinder from the chute and it began to fall directly below, gathering speed, ever faster, until it disappeared into the mountains.

A second later, there was an enormous flash of light, as if, through some cosmic miracle, a second sun had instantly been born in the south; then, in a second, it was gone. As sound follows light, there a was low rumble and then a deafening roar as the energy from the explosion ripped its way through every crevice, nook or cave off the ravine where Abu Muhammad had made camp. Anything soft vaporised instantly. The massive force of ten tonnes of explosive material pushed down, deep into the mountainside, heaving the rock, bending the strata and prising open fault lines.

The remnants of the blast wave hit them, even though they were at least ten kilometres from the strike zone. It was a warm wind laden with dust and gravel that flicked at their clothing and lightly scoured their flesh. Rania found herself in pain, but a glance down told her the cause was the ferocious grip Abdullah had on her upper arm.

They stood, transfixed, not sure what to expect next. The earth rumbled and shook beneath them.

Slowly, there was movement on the mountainside, some kilometres away, on the opposite side of the valley. First, a shower of scree rattled down, tinkling in the quiet of the early morning. Then Rania gasped as vertical fissures and cracks seemed to open in the rock face. A slice, maybe several hundred metres wide, peeled away from the mountainside and started to slide smoothly downwards, in one vast piece.

Rania felt that if she could only stand on top of it, she would be lowered gently to the valley floor, where she could hop off in one seamless movement. But then, the huge mass of sliding mountain violently accelerated and smashed against the base of the plain with an angry roar, disintegrating into clouds of dust that mushroomed high into the clear desert sky.

"*Ya 'iilahi*! Oh my God," she muttered, her hands to her face. "What have you done?"

Her husband stood looking at the earth cleaving itself in front of him, a fierce light burning in his eyes. She knew that look, and the fire in his heart that caused it. She had not seen him this way since his return and it frightened her.

"Praise be to Allah, always and eternally. Rania, that was the birth of a new time. This quiet morning, the time of Abu Muhammad is over. That was the first step in our revenge. There is still more to be done, but today is a happy day."

He grabbed her portly frame and held her tight. '*Revenge*,' she thought, '*is that what this is all about?*' But she said nothing.

Abdullah led her back to the truck.

"The explosion has wiped out the valley road!" He laughed manically. "Do not worry, it is not much further to go the longer way."

"Where to now, husband? What further destruction have you planned for us to see? I hope you have prayed hard for guidance on all this. To destroy the world like that is no small thing."

"It is Allah's will, Rania! I know that. I do not need to pray and examine my conscience. By now, the Beards will know if their dreams of *shaheed* have come true – or not! Martyrs? Hah! They are but thieves and murderers. But it is good the roads are clear of their evil and it is safe for us to travel. Now, let us be happy and celebrate!"

They drove back towards Marsabar. The explosion and the shock wave had been clearly heard, and felt, in Al Jawsh and beyond. There was a stream of traffic driving past on the other side of the road, full of people curious to know what had caused the huge vibrations that rattled their china and scared the dogs. Abdullah lapsed into a thoughtful mood and remained quiet until they turned onto the Marsabar road on the coastal plain.

"Where are you taking me?" his wife asked.

"You will see. We will be there shortly."

"You are taking me back to the farm, the homestead? You know it will break my heart. All those memories of the children playing and happy times with Tareq. Abdullah, no. Must we go?"

She risked a glance at him. He had forbidden any mention of Tareq's name. He had said that, until his brother was avenged, he should not be spoken of. Now, Abdullah's eyes remained trained on the road, but there was a faint trace of a smile on his face.

Although she had protested, she did not dare hope it could be true; he was taking her home – back to their farm, destroyed by Abu Muhammad and lying ruined these past four years. No man dared to touch the land that belonged to Abdullah Belkacem.

He had heard the farm had been burned out, but the stone framework of their house was still sound, apart from where the explosions had ripped the side wall down. The blackened shell of his brother's old Mercedes lay in the front yard, stripped back to metal, bare as a picked-clean carcass.

Rania got out of the car and quietly walked about the yard, memories of the past swirling around her. She saw where her mother would sit on an evening; dead now, some three years ago. The scaffold arrangement they had built as a frame for the raised swimming pool, for Jamal's twelfth birthday party, was still there, its planks hanging loose. Remnants of shredded tarpaulin fluttered but were still attached. She heard the cries of the children, playing in the dirt, and the barking of the dogs. The echoes of home sounded powerfully in her ears.

She saw her husband, inside the shell of the house, tearing timber aside and moving rubble.

"Abdullah, why are we here? Do you torture me with these memories?"

"Come here and look."

He stood in what was once the kitchen. There had been looting, but she recognised two of her old saucepans lying amongst the broken tiles and heaps of plaster. She bent to collect them. He was grinning broadly.

"Look at the entrance to the cellar. It is buried and undisturbed! The rear wall has fallen up against the door and buried it. There must be tonnes of stone over the stairway down to the tunnel."

She saw him dare to hope.

They ran back to the truck and he gunned it through the yard, the few hundred metres to the rough shed in the rear field. While they had lived there, Abdullah had wisely built an escape route, through the sandstone, that exited in the old shed. It was through this low, narrow tunnel that Rania and the children had run, terrified and in total darkness, to escape Muhammad's attack, four years previously.

Inside the shed, Abdullah looked around. The door to the rear cupboard hung loose, but the swing panel in the back, that concealed the steps down to the tunnel, was firmly shut. They looked at each other and Abdullah took his cigarette lighter, pulled at the panel to free it, and plunged down the roughly cut stone steps. Rania waited, not knowing what to think. Soon, she heard her husband scrambling back up and then he appeared, cobwebs hanging from his hair and beard, the dust of years over his clothing. He spat some matter from his mouth and then his face cracked into an enormous smile.

"We are truly blessed today, *Allahu Akbar*! The door is locked and has not been opened. If Allah is willing, we will have our gold and money back. We will rebuild the house and we will start again. We will make up for lost years!"

He grabbed Rania, who could not stop herself from sobbing in his arms.

Abdullah had a strong room in his cellars where he had kept gold and bundles of US dollars, earned through migrant trafficking, smuggling and other such enterprises. The door looked like a section of the stone wall and relied for its security on concealment, rather than the strength of its locks.

He rooted around in the shed for plastic fertiliser sacks, emptying the dried pellets onto the floor. From the truck, he took some long, hexagonal-shaped keys for window locks and a torch. There was a pickaxe in the shed which he gave to Rania.

"I cannot use that!"

"I joke, wife, give it to me. Today, I have the strength to dig a hole a kilometre deep."

Abdullah grabbed Rania's hand and guided her down the narrow stone stairs into the cramped, dark passage. She stooped, but Abdullah had to walk bent double. The fear and claustrophobia returned, reminding her of her flight, with the sobbing children, down that passage.

It took thirty minutes for Abdullah to open the door to the small cave he had hacked into the sandstone and fill two heavy-duty fertiliser sacks with gold bars, sovereigns, kruger rands and rolls of dollars, euros and dinars. They dragged the heavy sacks along the tunnel and up the steps, carefully placing them in the back of the truck where they lay in full view. He had scooped handfuls of fertiliser pellets from the floor of the shed to fill the gaps between the tubes of gold coins and rolls of currency and tied the tops of the sacks, tightly, with blue nylon twine.

"If we are stopped, there are only two old plastic sacks of fertiliser in our truck. They will not look further."

"Will we really rebuild our home? Tell me that is true?"

"It is true, Rania, and our happiness will be part of my revenge!"

"But you will leave to find Muhammad?"

"I must leave – I still have work to do. I have promised the Americans. That bomb this morning? It cost a fortune in US dollars. They have kept their promise to me. There is a good chance, by Allah's will, we can live in peace. But first, I must go and find Abu Muhammad: not for me, but for Tareq. When I come back, this house will be rebuilt and you will make it a home I can return to!

"All is well, is it not?"

Rania looked at him and said: "*Mashallah*, thanks be to Allah! Do not fail Him, or me, Abdullah."

CHAPTER 40
GEORGE ZAMMIT
ABU MUHAMMAD'S CAMP, CHADIAN DESERT

GRADUALLY, the effects of the beating started to subside and the swelling on George's cheek and above his eye turned from red to blue to yellow. The terrible bouts of stomach cramps, diarrhoea and vomiting brought on by the filthy water he had so readily drunk, finally stopped. The effects of the sickness left him exhausted, sore and dehydrated. He slept for most of the day, only to wake at night shivering and trembling under the thin, ragged blanket Yaroslav had thrown into the hut.

George had lain semi-conscious, in his own filth, for four days. His clothing was sodden and soiled, flies and mosquitoes swarming around him. By the third day, he was barely conscious, gripped by fever. He had dreamed of Marianna at the door, shouting at him to come for dinner, kindness in her voice. He had tried to answer, but could not get his words out. Another time, he was back home, at Gina's party, in full dress uniform. Camilleri was sitting in the armchair in the corner of the lounge, with his service medals pinned on his chest, running his white-gloved hands up the leg of Madam President, who sat on his knee like an oversized cat, her skirt pulled up high.

On the fifth day, Yaroslav found George awake. He was naked, covered in his own excrement, his skin red and scabbed where he had scratched at the mosquito bites that tormented him. He was crouching in the corner of the hut, his beard now fully grown and his hair matted, wild and starting to knot. He looked as though he had just spent the last year as a castaway on some faraway island.

At first Yaroslav thought George had lost his mind but, after speaking softly to him and establishing his sanity, he had gone to fetch him a bucket of water, some new clothes and a shovel. Once George had rinsed the worst off himself and put on the T-shirt and loose black cotton trousers, he took the shovel and slowly scraped the top layer of earth out of the hut and relaid the floor with fresh dirt from outside.

The pain in his face was now equal to the pain in his stomach, as his abdominal muscles ached from the vomiting and retching. Little by little, he started to eat, the meagre ration of lentils and bread more than satisfying his appetite. He was weak and miserable, but marvelled at the reduced size of his paunch and the sagging skin that hung from under his jaw.

At least he was receiving a plentiful supply of clean water, in unopened plastic bottles. During the daylight hours, his door was left open and he was free to sit outside the hut. The first day he sat and watched the September clouds start to build – plump white pillows in the clear blue sky. Back home they called them the 'back to school' clouds, as they appeared every year, before the start of the new school year, causing every child's heart to sink.

On the evening of the fifth day, he sat with his back resting against the still-warm blockwork, talking to Yaroslav and thanking him for his care.

The Russian laughed and said: "I am not becoming nurse after that. So, now you better, *da*? How come you get into this mess?"

"Oh, I don't know. I'm a policeman and I've got a damn' fool boss who sent me here to babysit my crazy Libyan friend." George shook his head, asking himself the same question. "My friend has dreams of raising a private militia to settle old scores against IS-in-Libya and stir up trouble for Boutros. I shouldn't say too much."

"So where were you captured?"

"We were digging in at the airfield in Ubari when they hit us. We weren't quite ready for them. One more day and it would have been different."

"I hear you are machine gunner. Ubari, is that south of the Sharara oil fields?"

"*Mela*, for God's sake. I'm a policeman, not a soldier. They gave me the gun but I was terrified, even though I did stop a few. The people I was with are interested in the oil fields, sure."

"In this country that is true of everybody! So, how is it you need airfield?"

"We're working with the Americans and they're airlifting supplies in for us."

Yaroslav's head flicked towards him and his expression told George he had just done what he had decided he would not do – revealed too much. He hastily tried to move the conversation away from what he was doing in the deserts of Libya.

"So, anyway, tell me, who did you meet when you were in Malta? Cheer me up, let's talk about home!"

They talked about his island and Yaroslav told George he had been sent to explore some business opportunities there, but nothing much had come of them. He then went through a list of names – government officials, politicians – while George told stories and made derogatory remarks about each and every one of them. Yaroslav decided not to mention the fact that he had had lunch and several meetings with Assistant Commissioner Gerald Camilleri.

Yaroslav was thinking aloud.

"So, who else I know in Malta? Oh, *da!* There is family – they have *palazzo* up on hill, the Bonnicis. The old man is Marco and the daughter – oooh, a beauty! – is Natasha. For one night, I would pay everything I have. Everything!

George laughed.

"I know her. She's a looker alright!"

Interesting, he thought, the old policeman's instinct returning to him; he knows the Bonnicis.

"I thought Marco Bonnici had left the country and was living in the Balkans somewhere?"

"Maybe. Now he come back. I met the two, the father and the daughter. Nice people. Especially the daughter … oomph!"

George got up and started to walk the stony ground in front of his hut, stretching his limbs and looking around the camp. He smelled earth, diesel and, from somewhere, the faint aroma of spice. Little pleasures were important. Yaroslav looked around and checked him.

"Hey, stay close, two metres! Or they will shoot you!"

The English jihadi, Raheem, had already told George to stay within two metres of the hut, otherwise the guards had permission to fire on him.

"Why would they do that?"

"Because some do not like you! You machine gun their relatives and friends at Ubari! Because Raheem, he say, Americans drop a 'Mother of All Bombs' on their camp in the Nafusa Hills. Everyone there is killed. Many men, their comrades. Someone makes a lot of trouble and we make sure, not trouble for us. *Da?*"

"How many were killed?"

"They say, everybody in camp. Plus, all transport and many weapons destroyed. What you see," Yaroslav looked around him, "is all of Islamic State-in-Libya! Good job done, I say."

"Oh! Was it the Americans? Are Abu Muhammad and Faysal angry?"

"Oh, yes, and they are shocked. It is only Americans have bombs so big. That is why they locked us up. They have been thinking on other things and that is dangerous for us. So, you stay two metres of your hut, because ground is hard and to dig two-metre-deep hole for you is much work."

Yaroslav looked around, to make sure they were not being

watched.

"Listen, big English guy – Raheem – he says they move out soon. He says they will move us to a safe base in Sudan. I beg cigarettes and he talks to me."

"Is that good news?"

"Every day we are alive is good news! Do not think they will not kill us. That would be very stupid."

Yaroslav pulled half a cigarette from his top pocket and lit it. He muttered to George: "Be quiet, here comes Faysal."

Muhammad's deputy walked with a slight waddle and was rocking his way across the rough ground of the camp towards them. He usually had a smile on his face although this evening his expression was anything but friendly. George noticed the change of demeanour and kept his eyes on the ground. Faysal squatted on his haunches in front of them.

"You're both lucky. It's Allah's will that you're not to be killed. I would've shot you both. It'd be a fitting response for what you've done in Nafusa. But others persuaded me to exchange you for prisoners held by Boutros in Benghazi."

Yaroslav scrutinised Faysal as he spoke.

"Tomorrow we'll give you some water, food and a tarpaulin for shelter. We'll drive you into the desert and take co-ordinates, to give to the Russians. They can come and collect you. So, when you're dropped, don't move from there. The desert's a big place and a man could easily get lost and die."

Yaroslav was uneasy.

"Where is this drop?"

"Half a day's drive away from the Sirte Basin, where your Volunteers work security at some of the wells."

"What if they think it is trap? What if they do not come for us? I am not a Volunteer and he is not Russian! Why would they come?"

"That's between you and your countrymen. Or would you rather have the bullet?"

George thought about all the possible downsides: what if

Faysal did not ring or got the coordinates wrong or some idiot threw them out at the wrong place? What if there was a sandstorm, or if their truck broke down? He liked the plan as little as Yaroslav did, but a quick exchange of glances between them showed they both understood there was no choice.

The next morning, they were given rucksacks and climbed into the back of the faded green Patriot SUV that Raheem and his jihadis had stolen after they had killed Lev and his Volunteers all those weeks ago. Abu Muhammad and Faysal came outside the command tent to watch their departure. Faysal nodded to them while Abu Muhammad glowered, hand on the pistol at his hip.

Raheem was driving. George watched him strap two jerry cans of fuel onto the rear deck. Seeing that partly reassured him they were going to be taken a decent distance north and not just shot once they were out of camp.

Raheem and a second man, wearing a long red-and-white-checked *keffiyeh* slung loosely round his neck, climbed into the two front seats, while Yaroslav and George slid into the back. Yaroslav was quiet and did not say a word after getting into the vehicle. Instead, he crossed his arms, rested his head against the door post, shut his eyes and fell asleep.

George watched and listened to Raheem and his partner, chatting and laughing. After a couple of hours, the guy in the passenger seat started to nod his head as Raheem drove the SUV down a never-ending red, hard-packed desert road that went straight as an arrow towards the horizon.

George was daydreaming, looking out of the window, when he sensed, rather than saw, Yaroslav suddenly lunge forward and grab Raheem under his chin and put his other arm across his forehead, pulling his head back and to the side, with one sharp movement. George heard Raheem's neck snap and he immediately went limp.

Yaroslav then lunged over the front seat, pushing the dead Raheem to one side and grabbing the wheel. The sleeping man, woken by the commotion, leaned over to stop the Russian, who yelled at George: "Pull on his *keffiyeh*!"

George grabbed the ends of the red-and-white-checked scarf and pulled it hard and tight around the man's throat. He leaned back as far as he could, choking him. The man's hands grabbed at the scarf, but he started to kick and twist in his seat, his flailing feet knocking Yaroslav's arms off the steering wheel.

George's eyes were wide with terror. He pushed himself even further away, to avoid the clutching arms of the man in the front seat. The more he leaned back, the tighter the cloth bound itself to the throat of the blue-faced man.

The truck veered off the road and, as it went onto the scrub, there was a jolt causing George inadvertently to release the *keffiyeh*, causing the other man to lurch forward and put his head deep into the front windscreen.

As the truck ground to a stop and stalled, Yaroslav leaped out and went round to the other side, to pull the dazed passenger out through the door. George watched, mesmerised, as Yaroslav grabbed a rock that was lying beside the vehicle and repeatedly beat the jihadi's head. People do not die easily and George had to turn away while Yaroslav hit the man hard, several times.

Finally the Russian lay panting on the sand, laughing.

"*Bot te ha!* I need gym! When I get back, I must exercise." He paused, breathing heavily. "You did good, letting him go like that. Head through window, it is neat trick!"

"Really? It just slipped out of my hands. I didn't mean to kill him, that's for sure. And you didn't need to do that."

George pointed to the mess that had been a man's head. He felt sick and a heave from deep in his gut made him belch.

"We could've tied him up or something."

Yaroslav looked down.

"What? And when he wake up, we keep looking back to see who chase us? No, this way is better."

He put a gratuitous kick into the side of the bloodied corpse to make his point.

George folded his arms onto the scorching roof of the car and buried his head in them for a moment. A wave of dread gripped him and he fought to control his rising panic. It was good, he told himself, it was all good. They had escaped captivity. He promised himself this was the first step to getting home. He was on his way. He had to be.

The truck was fine, apart from the egg-shaped bulge and dense latticework of cracks in the windscreen that was going to make driving tricky. George suggested punching it out, but Yaroslav said hours of driving with the sand blowing in their faces would be worse than peering through the web of glass.

They dragged the bodies away from the road to a small depression and took their cigarettes, money and the passenger's bloodied *keffiyeh*. Yaroslav wrapped this around his fair hair and white brow, leaving only his eyes unveiled. These he covered with Raheem's sunglasses.

"You already look like Arab. Me, I must try harder."

Together, driving their battered truck, they could easily have passed for a pair of Libyan labourers.

The drive was a torture. Yaroslav had to keep his head about half a metre to the left, to see the road round the enormous dent in the screen. By the time they had driven into Bayda, many hours later, he was sure his spine was permanently deformed. They turned up at the Volunteers' compound, exhausted, hungry and feeling terrible. There was no one there that Yaroslav knew; his people were all out driving around the desert, with fifteen IS prisoners, trying to find him and his companion. The exchange had been for real.

What came as more of a surprise to them was when they were immediately grabbed by a couple of Volunteers and thrown in a locked room, apparently for screwing up the prisoner exchange!

They had clean mattresses to sleep on, a tepid shower, a hot meal of chicken sausage and grain, and even a good measure of vodka from a more understanding Volunteer, who had heard what had happened. George's head swam with the alcohol and sleep came quickly; as did their release, early the next morning.

He rose to find Yaroslav arguing with a group of Volunteers in the large dining hall of the makeshift barracks. They were planning to pull out of Libya as soon as they could. Boutros's air support had taken a beating from the American airstrikes. The US planes and Reaper drones had destroyed the UAE-supplied fleet of ten Chinese Wing Loon drones and six ancient MiG jets – which was Boutros's entire air force. Word had it that he had also run out of cash and promised wages were not being paid. The militias were thinning out as fighters drifted off home with empty pockets.

On top of all that, the Americans had also hit an IS base in the Nafusa Hills and totally demolished an area the size of Gorky Park. With one blow, they had wiped out Islamic State-in-Libya! It was time to leave – none of them got paid enough to fight such odds.

George had to turn away to hide his triumphant expression. He clenched his fists in excitement at the thought of soon being on his way back to Malta.

Yaroslav looked at him, trying to decide what to do with him. After a moment, he turned and spoke to one of the Volunteers. The man left the room, to return with a bundle of dinars. Yaroslav gave George the money, a 9mm Makarov pistol, and threw him the keys to the Patriot SUV.

"Go, my friend. It is one thousand kilometres to Tripoli. You drive, do not stop, you do it in a day and a half, if militias do not kill you. Good luck!"

George was shocked, but realised it was a better outcome than he could have expected. He reached over and took Raheem's sunglasses off Yaroslav's face and the soiled red and white *keffiyeh* from around his neck.

"I'll need these. I'm punching that windscreen out."

CHAPTER 41
NATASHA BONNICI
OFFICES OF THE DEPARTMENT OF ENERGY, AUBERGE D'ALLEMAGNE, VALLETTA, MALTA

THE KNIGHTS HOSPITALLERS came into being as a medieval Catholic medical order, which later turned into a significant naval power that went marauding across the eastern Mediterranean, to the annoyance of the Ottomans of Istanbul. In the early sixteenth century they had made Malta their home. The island's history is still defined by their presence, in particular the Great Siege, where the heavily outnumbered Knights defeated the Ottomans in 1565. Learning from their near defeat at the hands of the Turks, they built the fortified city of Valletta on the high peninsula that juts out between the Grand Harbour to the south and Marsamxett Harbour to the north.

The Knights themselves lived together, by nationality, in monastic palaces called *auberges*, the most famous being the Auberge de Castille that today houses the offices of the Maltese Prime Minister.

The little-known Auberge d'Allemagne, tucked away on the north side of the narrow peninsula, had been left derelict and ignored for centuries. Its shallow steps, leading to the columns that supported the portico, were originally designed so that knights in full armour could ride their horses into the *piano nobile* – the floor where the knights conducted their business. In the nineties it had been rediscovered and refurbished, and today it was home to the Department of Energy. Natasha had just finished her first formal meeting there as chair of MalTech Energy, the joint venture company in which the Family had invested over two hundred million euros.

It had been agreed that MalTech Energy would buy gas from the Libyan wells and operate the receiving plant in Malta. It would on-sell the gas, via a consumer division, to the entire population of the island. In addition, it would lay the pipeline to Sicily and make further sales of gas to the European transmission companies. It was a bold plan – and Natasha sat at the head of the top table, where she felt she deserved to be.

Once the meeting had finished, she asked for the use of a private office and settled down with her phone. She rang a number with a Gibraltar prefix. The call went unanswered. Not fooled, she sent an SMS.

Pick up Nick.

She rang the number again.

"Natasha. What can I do for you? You want another story planting?"

"Nick, hi. No, not this time. I've got something entirely different to talk about."

BetHi had originally been Nick Walker's brainchild. When Marco and Sergio had bought the company under its original first name of BetSlick, it was with the express intention of funnelling millions of euros of the Family's illicit earnings through the operation.

If Natasha were to fulfil her ambition to rise to the top rank of the Family and get close to the seat of power in Milan, she had to find someone to run BetHi for her. Who better than Nick Walker?

She explained the deal to him.

"Come on, Nick, there's nothing to discuss, surely? The whole operation is almost legitimate these days. Crypto has sorted a lot of the problems and, once we get the cash, we roll it through the gaming systems. If there are winnings, we repay them as clean cash to our accounts, and the losses we keep as profits. It's a lot less risky than it used to be."

Nick had yet to be totally convinced.

"It's not every day someone rings you up and offers you the CEO job at one of the biggest gaming platforms in Europe!"

"I don't know, Natasha …"

"Look, you can keep the Gibraltar operation going as insurance. BetHi is so big it nearly runs itself."

"Well, why do you need me then?"

"Come on, Nick, you know why. We need eyes and ears. We need our person on the inside, we …"

"Exactly! You're asking me to put myself back into an exposed position I've been trying to avoid for the last four years!"

"Look, I know the Gibraltar business hasn't exactly thrived. No fault of yours, but you haven't got the cash for TV and sports advertising. The game has moved on and you can't do it your way anymore. Come on, come back and make some serious money."

There was a short silence while Nick pondered the unpalatable truth of what Natasha had said.

"OK, let's just say I agree to think about it, it has to be strictly business. No wider Family involvement and there's no you and me. That wouldn't be good for either of us. Agreed?"

She was silent for just a second too long.

"Agreed. Absolutely. It didn't exactly end well last time, did it?"

She struggled to control her irritation at his insistence on making the point. Who was he to decide a thing like that? She ran her hand over her head and, through the thick mass of hair, felt the scar on her skull made by the Murano glass vase Nick had used to strike her. Then he had left the island without a further thought. He had been a bastard. No one had ever treated her like that. She conveniently overlooked that she had been carrying a gun at the time. Now he had the cheek to say a thing like 'no you and me'! Who did he think he was? She pulled herself together.

Nick said: "Is Camilleri still onside?"

"Of course. Gerald is part of the furniture."

"Does Marco still hate me?"

Natasha forced a laugh.

"Probably. But you know Dad, he's the forgiving sort. Anyway, he's leaving the Family. He's going back to Serbia, for good."

"No way!"

"Afraid so. Come on … what d'you say?"

"I'll think about it."

"No, I haven't got time for that. I need to know now."

"Patience! Twenty-four hours?"

She sighed.

"OK. Twenty-four hours. I'll ring you."

As she descended the steps from the Auberge de d'Allemagne, swapping her spectacles for sunglasses, her mood changed. She had one more unpleasant job to deal with, which was resolving the problem of the overgrown child currently locked up in the family chapel on the cliff top. On the one hand, Savi had done everything she had asked of him; on the other, he knew far too much about her affairs and that was always a worry. She wondered about retaining him, paying him money to sit in the chapel forever, with unlimited supplies of pizza, beer and computer games. She actually thought he might not even notice that his captivity had been indefinitely extended.

She rang Simon and told him to meet her at the chapel.

CHAPTER 42
MIKE LLOYD
HASTINGS GARDENS, VALLETTA

Hastings Gardens sit on top of St John's Bastion and St Michael's Bastion, formerly the western defences of Valletta. From the gardens, visitors can look out over the four-metre-thick walls to the pointed church spires of Floriana, the contemporary high rises of Sliema and the marinas of Marsamxett Harbour.

The minute Marco saw Mike Lloyd steaming in through the gate, flanked as usual by his security detail of look-alike nightclub doormen, he knew there was something on Lloyd's mind.

"What the fuck, Marco?"

The American's tone was loud and belligerent.

Marco sighed.

"Good morning, Mike, how are things?"

"I was expecting three-quarters of a billion US dollars and ended up with some fucking jackets! I look like a major dick, that's how things are!"

"What, you stole the wrong container?"

Marco did not understand what had happened.

"No, we got the container alright – the right container – but it was full of jackets – dick-licker puffer jackets! This was supposed to be an off the books job, but now it's all round the Firm and I'm a laughing stock!"

Marco felt on safe ground as he had genuinely had no idea of the particulars of the American plan to steal the notes.

"You must have got the wrong container. Anyway, what has this to do with me? I did not even know for sure you were going to steal it."

"Listen, Marco, you tipped me off about the notes, yeah? Someone has been fishing upstream. You're the only other people who knew about it. We had it all sorted. We wait in line and the system magically delivers a container, out the air, like the stork, dumps it on our trailer and, if everything matches, the port gates swing open and we drive out. Well, it's the right container – except it's full of fucking jackets!"

Marco was speechless. He had no answer and could not begin to work out what had happened.

He shrugged and held up his arms in surrender.

"Nothing I can say. I honestly know nothing. You have the Russians involved; the Libyans knew the cash was coming – could have been anybody. I do not know why you are pointing the finger at me. Maybe the Russians have the cash and you messed up?"

"Well, we won't know that until the damn' boat arrives at Benghazi. Then Petrov might be good enough to tell us he's been shafted too.

"OK, Marco, here's how it is. I'll level with you. I was using this guy, IT contractor, skateboarder-hacker type, to pull off the heist. He went dark on me. Not like him. He's as dumb as shit, would never think of doing something like that. So, I set the technicians onto him – they monitor internet traffic and all that clever stuff. They get a ping. A faint ping and only the once, but it's enough. And guess what? It came from right on your doorstep, near some closed-up chapel. So, I'll ask you once more. What the fuck?

"If you're pissing with me, Marco, I'll make sure there're consequences. I'll screw your pipeline deal and to hell with the blow back. This is personal. I can't stand being made to look like a turkey."

It took a few seconds for what had been said to register with Marco. Then, as the possibilities dawned on him, he tried desperately to hide his shock. He did not blink or change his facial expression but, involuntarily, put a hand to his head and ran it through his hair. He should not have done that.

Calmly, he said, "Mike, this one is down to you. I do not have a clue what went wrong with your operation."

Once Lloyd had calmed down, he returned to sit next to Marco and they talked about the purchase of the VertWay pipeline from the Russians by an American consortium, and the gas supply contract to MalTech Energy. The London and New York lawyers seemed to be producing thousands of pages of incomprehensible documents which, Mike complained, he was actually expected to read!

"OK, let's leave that to one side. You probably heard – the military side is going like a dream. We hit the rebels and IS with some big airstrikes and, man, was there some damage! If our boys and the militia guys on the ground can follow through, we'll have made significant progress on the mission soon.

"But once we get control of the western desert and the Marsabar and Az-Zawiyah refineries, you've got to be certain you've the muscle to keep those assets safe."

Marco nodded in agreement.

"My daughter has spent a lot of time working on that side of things and she says she has a plan to tie things up. I will keep you in the loop," he promised.

"Hmmm. That should be interesting. And, by the way …"

"Yes?"

"If I ever catch you, or any of your crew, with bundles of Libyan dinars sticking out of your pockets, I promise you, you'll learn the meaning of US black ops!"

"Charming!"

"See you, Marco."

Mike Lloyd strode away, his black-suited bodyguards to left and right of him, the three of them swaggering off through the tranquil gardens.

Marco smiled to himself, watching their departure. The smile soon faded as his thoughts returned to the missing money and Mike Lloyd's reference to the chapel on the cliffs. He thought about the young hacker and then Simon, with his recent out of character errands to purchase computer games. He considered the theft of the dinars and Natasha's cryptic comment about tying things up in Libya. His heart sank and he walked wearily back to his car.

He had not really felt in control here since his return. It was as if he only ever knew a piece of what was going on, never the whole picture. He wondered whether it was him. Had he lost his edge during the time he had been away? Was he too slow to spot the angles, anticipate events? Or was Natasha pulling his strings? He could not disagree that she was growing into a formidable operator – who would not want that for their son or daughter? But her methods and her ruthlessness both shocked and frightened him. He did not want to find himself unable to trust her, but he feared that was already the case.

He went back to the car park and drove up through the central belt towards the hilltop town of Mdina, the old capital. Behind the Silent City, he joined the maze of rural back roads that crossed the less frequently visited north-west of the island. Leaving the road, he drove the Range Rover along the rutted, unmetalled farmer's track that ran alongside his small vineyards and fields of potatoes, cauliflowers and cereals. He wanted to approach the chapel from the south, to avoid being seen heading down the long track from the *castello*.

He needed to know if there was anything in Mike Lloyd's suggestion that the hacker kid had been held in their family chapel, under Marco's very own nose!

As he turned a blind corner on the track, where a high bamboo thicket blocked the driver's view of oncoming traffic, he nearly collided with his own black SUV, being driven by Simon. Marco had to stare hard through the glare of the windscreen to be sure that it was Natasha sitting alongside the bodyguard. Both vehicles skidded to a halt on the dirt road and Simon got out first.

"Boss, what are you doing here, I nearly hit you?"

"Get in my car, Simon, and take it back to the *castello*. I need to talk to Miss Natasha. I will see you later."

CHAPTER 43
ABDULLAH BELKACEM
THE FARMHOUSE, MARSABAR, LIBYA

THE REPERCUSSIONS of the American bomb on the Islamic State-Libya camp and the destruction of Boutros's air support proved to be a turning point in both conflicts. Not only were the attacks totally unexpected, they also brought a whole new degree of chaos to the east of the country and threw the rebels into disarray. The Russian Volunteers were pulling out and Boutros's long-promised cash had failed to arrive, more or less crippling his progress on Tripoli. The sudden and unexpected involvement of the Americans caused the UAE, Turkey and Egypt all to pause, trying to make sense of the new realpolitik.

Abdullah's militia had taken Marsabar without a bullet being fired, as those few IS fighters still left alive in the Nafusa Hills fled south to try and rejoin Abu Muhammad in Chad or Sudan. The Tuareg had expected this and moved several hundred well-equipped militia men of their own from Ubari to establish roadblocks on the routes to the south and east. Little mercy was shown to the fleeing militia.

As he had expected, Abdullah's reinstatement was cause for great excitement within the town and he was overwhelmed by masses of eager young men, all keen to join him, crush the threat of IS and push back Boutros once and for all. The Americans were as good as their word and material was flown from the Middle East bases into Ubari, which was now a secure location with a series of berms and bunkers for planes, ammunition and other equipment.

The Americans established a one thousand kilometre safe corridor, from Ubari in the south, through the Sharara oil field, to Marsabar on the coast. Their idea was to ensure the safe, uninterrupted supply of oil and gas from the largest Libyan fields to the Marsabar and Az-Zawiyah refineries in the north, which could then be piped or tankered by ship to Europe. Abdullah's idea was to have a local Libyan militia, under his command, large enough and well enough equipped to take over the security of the corridor once the Americans pulled out.

Until they could open the port at Marsabar, daily convoys arrived from Ubari with weapons, ammunition and other equipment. Once Marsabar was secured, the US Navy supply ships would be free to dock and the heavier weapons and supplies could easily be unloaded. US advisers had arrived as well, men with expensive sunglasses and pristine desert camouflage fatigues. Abdullah noticed these were regular US military and not the rough and ready contractors he had experienced at Ubari.

Abdullah had also made good on his promise to Rania, who had persuaded him to start the rebuilding of the farmhouse immediately. Cannily, he had invited the US advisers to join him and use the compound and surrounding area as their base. Lines of large command tents formed accommodation for Abdullah, the advisers and the army of recruits that were to become his militia.

It turned out the Americans had a knack for being able to source almost anything and have it brought into Marsabar. Rania was thrilled by the range of Italian tiles and bathrooms, air-conditioning units and UPVC double-glazed windows that magically appeared, every time a convoy of trucks rolled up the dirt road.

Local builders worked the stone and rebuilt the farmhouse

around the door and window units that arrived from Italy. They installed the new services, while Rania took over the planning and set about modernising the finishes inside.

Abdullah had noticed that the US advisers had learned their lessons from Iraq and Afghanistan. They no longer shouted and screamed at the recruits, like West Point drill sergeants, but embraced the Arab values of respect, honour and reputation. They talked of responsibility, teamwork and accepting the word of a superior. When it was time for prayers, a break was scheduled and the advisers withdrew a respectful distance away. They worked closely with the men, identifying leaders and teaching what had basically been an enthusiastic mob to become a paid, well-organised and equipped battalion-sized combat unit of just under one thousand men. It was a level of organisation the Russian Volunteers had never even tried to achieve with Boutros's ragtag Libyan National Army.

One evening, when peace had descended after another hectic day of training, building, shooting and praying, Abdullah was walking between the lines of tents, when he noticed the most senior of the Rangers, Major Floyd Hamilton, sitting in a khaki canvas chair outside his tent. He was holding a book and had a bottle of Coke by his side.

Abdullah liked Floyd, whom he considered a patient and thoughtful man and, he guessed, probably a religious one as well. Abdullah lit a cigarette and squatted down in front of him.

"So, General Floyd, my brother, what do you read when the work is done and the evening is upon us?"

Floyd smiled and put the book down.

"Hey, Abdullah, don't call me General – you'll put a jinx on my chances! A soldier's work is never done, man, and this is my sort of work." He offered the book to Abdullah. "It's *The Seven Pillars of Wisdom*, by a hero of mine, a Brit called T. E. Lawrence. Have you heard of him?"

"Yeah, I have heard this name. He was a friend of the Arabs in Jordan and is long dead?"

"Yeah, he was a British officer – an adviser – like me, I suppose! He stirred up an army of Arabs to beat the Turks in 1916. He respected the Arab people and tried to live like one of them; no air-con, no Coke, no Land Cruisers. You know, just camels and tents – the real deal!"

Abdullah nodded sagely at the major and waited for him to continue.

"He promised them that after the war there'd be an independent Arab nation. But he got pissed on by the English and French governments. Lawrence wanted a democratic state for the Arabs, on the land that's now Iran and Iraq."

"Aha! So, he wanted what ISIL want … but maybe less Shia! A Caliphate on the old lands. But did he know how much oil there was in the ground there?"

"No, probably not."

"And where were the Americans? If there is only the smell of oil, you appear like cats to a roasting chicken."

Floyd smiled.

"It was before our time. Anyway, Lawrence didn't get what he wanted and he was so ashamed that he'd broken his promise, he went and tried to kill himself!"

"A man of his word! Rare in an Englishman. So, what promises can you give me? The smell of oil in Libya is strong." Abdullah held his head up and breathed in deeply. "You can smell it too, no? You Americans are here so we can be free? Are you men like Lawrence, eh? Or is it because we have the oil?"

Abdullah smiled at Floyd, who took the jibe in good humour.

"That's politics, Abdullah! I am just a soldier, but one day soon you gotta think about these things." Floyd paused and looked at him intently, to let Abdullah know he was being serious. "If the rebel wins, the time comes when he's gotta take control and try to do a better job than the other guys."

"Yes, I have been waiting for someone to tell me what is expected of me, if that time comes."

"Ain't no one going to tell you what to do, you know. You gotta work that out for yourself."

"Easy for you to say. But I can do nothing without this!"

Abdullah gestured to the military set up behind him.

"Well, sure. But you've still got choices. Taking the refinery at Az-Zawiyah shouldn't be a problem. The gas gets pumped up here and down the pipeline to Malta and everyone's happy. I bet you could get very rich, offering protection to politicians and the oil guys on the Sharara."

Abdullah lit another cigarette and listened attentively. He wondered whether this was just a man speaking his thoughts or whether these were the instructions he had been waiting for. Floyd continued.

"Or you could become a politician yourself – move on to Tripoli and take power. That's a possibility, too. The government here's weak, getting weaker by the day. The UN has no love for them." He paused. "And we don't like them much, either. Too friendly with the Muslim Brotherhood.

"Boutros and IS-in-Libya have been hammered. This is a real opportunity for you, especially if we agree to help you. You could unlock its resources and do good for your country. All big questions!"

Abdullah was squatting on his haunches, poking the ground in front of him with a stick, deep in thought.

"I hear all this and I know, in every country the Americans take over, they find someone like me and put me in a businessman's suit. Then you say: *'We did it for the people.'* But it is the oil that is your real interest, no?"

Floyd remained still as Abdullah continued speaking.

"Me? I want my town to be safe and my family to live in peace. I do not give a pickled fig for the rest of it. Allah has a plan for me and it is not to be another Gaddafi! That is not the will of Allah!"

"No, Abdullah, I can't see you becoming another Gaddafi. I wouldn't let you!"

Floyd laughed.

"Still, Mr US Major, I mean no offence and maybe I will read your book. I would like to understand an Englishman who thought he was an Arab!

"So, when will we be ready to leave for Az-Zawiyah?" He gestured to a group of young men, kicking a football, tripods of automatic rifles standing in for goal posts. "They are looking good, no?"

Floyd shook his head.

"I'd like to have them for another six months, if it was up to me. You can't build a soldier overnight. But we need to strike while we've got the advantage. I think we're going to have to move out in about ten days."

"Allah be praised! This is good news."

Abdullah suddenly sensed a change in Floyd Hamilton's demeanour. Looking over Abdullah's shoulder, he had seen something. His body had tensed and he jumped to his feet, his hand unclipping the holster of his side arm. He kicked back the canvas chair and pushed himself in front of Abdullah, raising the gun.

A short but trim figure, with a long straggly beard and a stained red-and-white *keffiyeh* wrapped around his head, was walking directly towards them, at speed. He padded up the dusty white path that had gradually appeared between the tents. Even though it was nearly dark, he wore a pair of wraparound sunglasses, a crumpled collarless shirt that had once been white, and baggy black cotton trousers.

There was a sense of purpose in his approach that Floyd Hamilton did not like.

"Stand back!" he shouted, raising his gun.

Abdullah looked on in shock as he suddenly realised who it was coming towards him. He placed a hand on Floyd's arm and gently pressed it.

"All is well, Mr Major. This man means us no harm."

The man stopped three metres away and put his hands on his hips.

"So, is this the famous Berber welcome I get?"

"*Mashallah*, as Allah has willed it!" Abdullah beamed and rushed to meet the visitor, wrapping his arms tightly around him. Not breaking the embrace, he shouted as loud as he could: "George is back! George has returned! Give thanks!"

CHAPTER 44
MARCO BONNICI

CHAPEL OF OUR LADY OF THE ABANDONED, MALTA

To say Natasha had got a shock when her father's car had appeared around the bamboo was an understatement. There was no chance of fabricating an explanation. She realised the truth had to come out at some point, but the abruptness with which they had been discovered caught her out, making her breathless and momentarily light-headed.

"So, Natasha, you have truly excelled yourself this time. You know that you have crossed the line. You are on your own from now on. I am going back to Serbia, as soon as I can, and I will leave you to finish whatever it is you are up to.

"I will sort things out with the Wise Men and then I am out. I cannot stand what is going on here. You want to make a play in the big game, go ahead, but do not count on me to stand behind you.

"I think now is a good time for you to move back into the apartment at Portomaso. I assume you have kept the lease on?"

Natasha was stunned. She believed some things in life were a given and had thought she could always rely on her father's support. The fact it was conditional and could be withdrawn had never occurred to her.

"Dad, how can …"

"Shut up, Natasha. I fear for you, I really do. If I can see straight through your dealings, so can others. Some ugly things have happened, not just recently but back over the years, and your fingerprints are all over them."

"Dad, I ..."

"I have kept quiet for a long time, about a lot things, but I cannot ignore them any longer, especially as you seem happy to put me at risk, whenever it suits your purposes! I have just been protesting that I knew nothing about the stolen money and listening to Mike Lloyd's threats about what he would do if he found out I was lying."

"Please Dad, let ..."

Marco put up his hand to stop her.

"Be quiet. Now, tell me, where is the kid Mike Lloyd was using? Locked up in the chapel still? You kidnapped him and have been keeping him there, yes? You stole the Libyan dinars from the Russians, under Mike Lloyd's nose, goodness knows how. Where is that money?"

Natasha was shocked that her father knew so much, but did not let her expression betray it.

"Yes, you're right. The money's in Vlado's uncle's woodyard, in Užice."

Užice was the town nearest to Marco's estate in Serbia and Vlado was one of his foresters, who had taken a shine to Natasha when she had visited her father there.

"It'll be perfectly safe until we need to move it. Vlado thinks it's equipment for the next stage of your project. It won't be there for long."

"My God! You are hiding the money in Užice? If the Americans or Russians track it there, they will assume it was I who stole it! Do you not realise that? Or do you just not care?"

"I've just said, it won't be there for long."

"I do not know what you are planning and I do not want to know, but move that money today, or tomorrow at the latest, do you hear me? Do you seriously think you can outsmart both the FSB and the CIA? Who the hell do you think you are?"

"I'll move it. Soon."

"Good to hear! Now, we are going to see this guy back at the chapel and you can explain to me exactly what you did."

"We can't, he's not being co-operative at the moment. In fact, he's not there. It seems he made a run for it this morning. Broke the roof tiles and climbed out."

"Where do you think he is now?"

"We've no idea."

Natasha was unaware when she said this that it was not strictly true.

Simon had gone to the chapel, very early that morning, at first light, and climbed onto the roof with a large hammer and a steel bar. A few hard blows and the thin, brittle stone slabs that rested on wooden corbels, forming the chapel's roof, had easily cracked and broken. It was the only credible way he could think of to fake Savi's breakout.

As chunks of shattered limestone fell to the chapel floor, Savi's frightened face peered up at him from beneath the hole. The kid was dressed in the new gear that Simon had bought him from some crazy shop in Hamrun: voluminous baggy jeans that hung round his hips, branded unlaced trainers and an oversized, brightly coloured hoody that reached to just above his knees.

Simon lowered a wooden ladder that he had taken from the *castello* and shouted down: "OK, let's go. I'm getting you out of here."

"Hey, wait a minute. What for?"

"Savi, don't fuck around, we've got to go – *now*."

"No, no. I'm cool. I'm happy here for a bit longer. It's OK. I haven't had a chance to, you know, show Natasha my new gear?"

"Savi, you fool, she's not going to shag you, she's going to kill you! She wants me to throw you off the cliff."

"Nah! No chance. You're messing with me."

Savi had a stupid half-smile on his face, but suddenly felt his confidence desert him.

"Yes, of course I'm kidding!" Simon told him sarcastically. "Think about it. You're no more use to her and you know too much. You're a dead man if you don't come with me. Now do as I say and climb the fucking ladder!"

Savi reluctantly loaded his laptop and X-Box into his rucksack, put on his new baseball hat and came up the ladder.

"Really? You being serious? She really asked you to do that? I don't get it. You're not going to, are you?"

"I will if you don't hurry."

"Wait a mo'! How am I going to get paid?"

"Money's no good to you if you're dead. Let's go."

Simon had an on–off girlfriend whom he knew from back home and had set up in a flat in Sliema. Given his work at the *castello* he did not see a lot of her, but he figured she owed him a favour or two. He had told her to expect a guest for a couple of days and to make sure he stayed put. Danka was a stocky, well-muscled woman with cropped, dyed-blonde hair and a body adorned with tattoos she had designed herself. Her impressive physique came from her work as a kettlebell fitness coach, at her own studio in a converted garage, just off the Sliema promenade. Simon had also seen her in a boxing ring and was not certain, whether he would be able to get the better of her, if they ever got into a full-on fight. Not that it would ever come to that, he was far too fond of her. But he had no doubt she could handle Savi.

He dropped the boy off and had to hurry straight back to the *castello* to pick up Natasha. Danka, meanwhile, made Savi take a shower and showed him to a small box room that was to be his bedroom. She threw him a can of Coke and locked the door on him. Once he had finished beating on the door and cursing the block of a woman who seemed to be his new gaoler, he reached for his laptop. He might as well finish building the last bit of his empire on *Civilisation*. But, before that, there was something he needed to do ...

In the car with Simon, Savi had been thinking about how to get himself out of this mess. His first step had to be to make peace with Mike Lloyd.

Using a pocket-sized wireless modem and his encrypted email service, he routed his VPN through a series of servers in London, Thailand and Johannesburg. Then he sent an email from his Snakehead account.

Mike,

Sorry about the double, i was made to do it. If i tell who forced me, will we be cool? I have insurance so don't come after me. Snakehead

Mike Lloyd authorised the opening of the strange email and, once he had cleaned up the coffee he had spilled over his desk, screaming and shouting about the treacherous nature of human beings, he realised he had no choice but to reply.

He and the hapless Mary-Ann Baker, who still had not recovered from her own humiliation and the recriminations about what had happened in Turkey, sat down at Mike's screen.

He typed: *Who did it? Tell me and I won't break your skinny neck. Promise.*

The reply was almost instantaneous.

Some woman called Natasha and her security guy Simon. Kept me in an old church place. But Simon's a good guy. He bust me out. Can I get paid money for expenses?

As a matter of professional pride, Mike Lloyd needed to know if he had been lied to.

Ever meet or hear them talk about a guy called Marco?

No. Just the woman.

OK. Turn up at the guardhouse at the embassy. There'll be an envelope with $5000 with your name on it. Keep quiet about this or I'll come for you. I mean it.

Don't get heavy. I get it.

Mary-Ann Baker said to Mike: "You're paying him, after what he's done?"

"If he's stupid enough to turn up, which he is, there'll be a standing order for the marines on the gate to grab him."

"What about the Bonnicis? What's the play there?"

Mike went to the window and looked over the embassy's extensive car park, towards the trees of the Ta'Qali parkland.

"I can wait a couple of weeks. You know what they say about revenge. I'll think of something. They're not getting away with this."

When Mike walked to the coffee machine, he passed the team noticeboard, where some wag had pinned a mocked-up advertisement: *SALE! Guys' Black Puffer Jackets – going cheap. Unwanted stock. Ask Mike.*

CHAPTER 45
GEORGE ZAMMIT
ABDULLAH'S CAMP, MARSABAR, LIBYA

George had let himself be led through the camp by Abdullah, who had one arm around his shoulders, while holding a pistol in the other, which he fired into the air in celebration. This act brought a dozen Rangers rushing towards them, with M-16s pointing directly at their chests!

After the excitement had calmed down a bit, Rania insisted they sit down to eat. Under the awning of their tent, there was a green plastic table and chairs. From the top of a single gas ring, she produced a large tagine of spiced rice and chicken, studded with chickpeas, apricots, crumbled cinnamon and livid green coriander leaf. George took one look at it and said to her: "Tonight I'll eat everything you can spare, then I'll eat your husband's share because it's his fault I am so thin and hungry!"

Rania laughed.

"And eat you will! You have come back half the size of the man who left. You must excuse Abdullah; he is a terrible man. Everywhere he goes there is trouble and suffering! Tonight he will fast until you have eaten your fill. Then we will see what is left for him."

Abdullah slapped the plastic table.

"No, woman! You will feed me so I have the strength to hear

George's story." He turned to his friend. "Now, you start from the moment I left the airfield and you will not miss one moment!"

So George started to tell his story. He told him about Harley and the attack on the Ubari airfield, then his kidnap and time as a hostage with Abu Muhammad. Abdullah laughed and clapped his hands enthusiastically as the tale of the battle unfolded. During George's description of his spell in captivity, Abdullah held his head low and studied the ground beneath his feet. However, when George recounted his escape, Abdullah leaped up and roared in approval.

"Rania, he killed them with his bare hands! No gun, no knife – just his hands. How I wish I had been there! Strangled him with his own *keffiyeh*!"

Abdullah laughed heartily.

"It wasn't funny! I never meant to kill the man, it just happened that way. In fact, I didn't finish him. The Russian did."

George sighed at the memory. He had examined his conscience time and again, to assure himself he did no more than he had to, in order to escape.

Just as George was set to continue, a beaming Sam, the muscle-bound Texan contractor, stuck his head under the awning.

"Excuse me, folks, but I heard he was back and I just had to see for myself. George the Maltese Machine gun, that's what you're called now! You saved our necks, buddy! You saved our necks! I've gotta give you a man hug!"

Sam pulled George out of his chair and dragged him into a tight embrace. He then held him at arms-length and said: "Thanks, man, from all of us."

Sam turned to Abdullah.

"You know what this guy did? He emptied over a thousand rounds into Johnny Jihad, took down twenty or more, gave us a chance to get into defensive position so we could stop them getting into the terminal. Fucking amazing, man!"

Abdullah glared at Sam and Rania lowered her head.

"Sorry, ma'am, language. But the best bit ..."

"Sam, you know that's not quite right."

He grabbed George by the shoulders.

"I couldn't believe it ... the weekend-warrior here, he chases a group of them into a stairwell lobby and unloads a Magnum into them, at point blank!

"Blam! Blam! Blam!" Sam made his hand into the shape of a pistol and mimicked the shots, pointing around the tent. "Takes down six more of them – incredible! That's how he got captured! No shame, man, he fought to the last, and then some!"

Abdullah watched, shaking his head in amazement.

"The Maltese Machine gun! I have seen this man do these things before!" Abdullah pointed two fingers back at himself. *"With these eyes!"*

"Please, come on, Sam, don't make too much of it. I was terrified. I was just trying to get back into the terminal building, so I could hide!"

Abdullah was bursting with pride in his friend and more than willing to believe anything he was told about George's 'heroics'.

"He says he is no hero; he says he is not brave; he says he is just afraid and does not know what he does ... phaa!"

Sam shook his head.

"Oh, no! He knows what he's doing alright!" He turned to address George directly. "Some of the boys want you to come round to the tents tonight. We've a little Jack Daniel's, to show our appreciation."

Abdullah raised his hand.

"No, my friend! I do not like to spoil parties, but you know, we do not have alcohol here. It is *haram* – forbidden – so, I think I have not heard that. Anyway, George must rest, he still has important work to do."

"OK, man, whatever you say. But, George, if you ever want a job, you can come and work for me. It's good money and you see the world and get to die young! See you around."

Sam laughed out loud as he made his way back between the tents. George watched him go, then turned to Abdullah, stony-faced.

"What important work have I got to do?"

"We will speak of it tomorrow. Tonight we eat and talk!"

"Abdullah! What important work do I have to do?"

The arrival of Major Floyd Hamilton saved Abdullah from having to provide an answer. The officer shook George's hand vigorously.

"Well, when I heard you're the Maltese Machine gun, I just had to come round and say hi, apologise for the welcome I gave you! You've made quite a name for yourself. They're talking about you in every US base in the Middle East!"

He looked around at the laden table then pulled a phone from his pocket, saying: "Sorry, folks, I don't mean to disturb dinner, but this is important. It was sent to me a few days ago, in case you showed up here. It's a privilege to be able to play it for you, Superintendent."

He gave George his phone, on which he had a saved video message. An image of Sergeant Mario Barrasso, from the training camp at the US Air Base Al-Udeid, stared out at them. Had George been standing, he would have involuntarily taken a step backwards. The unsmiling man took a sheet of paper from his breast pocket and began to speak.

"Superintendent George Zammit of the Malta Pulizija, it was my honour to conduct your induction training on the Desert Warfare and Survival course at the US Army Al-Udeid training facility. It is with great pride that I can inform you that, following reports of exceptional bravery in the field of battle, you have been recommended for the Army Distinguished Service Cross, the highest military honour that can be awarded to a non-US citizen. Congratulations. We salute you. God bless the United States of America!"

The sergeant briskly saluted and the screen went blank.

The major lead a smattering of applause and said: "They tried to get him to record another version, where he smiled a little, but you know how these hard-ass sergeants can be. Anyway, I'm just glad it will not be awarded posthumously!"

Floyd then told him there was an opportunity to repatriate him to Malta the next day, if that was not too soon.

George said it was not a moment too soon.

After Floyd left them, Rania glanced over at George and said to Abdullah: "He must rest, do not talk of more work. Has he not done enough for us?"

Abdullah threw his napkin onto the table.

"I see we will have no peace until I tell you. I am pleased you can return to Malta and see the lady wife and family. That is the right thing to do. But then your policeman boss, the old policeman, will speak to you and there is something we need from you. It is easy and has no risk, but it is very important. But do not worry now. Eat and tell us more of the story – I am enjoying it very much!"

"I suddenly don't feel hungry. I thought I was finished here and was going home to stay? I've been away for nearly four months. My wife won't ever let me leave again; she'll divorce me if I try!"

"Hah, the lady wife will be very much pleased you are coming back a hero, with more medals. She will have her picture in the paper again and she will like being the wife of the Maltese Machine gun."

Rania looked at her husband disapprovingly.

"What, woman? Why do you look at me like that?"

"George, we will have coffee and then you will rest. Abdullah, George is tired, he has had many troubles. Not like you, who only eat, talk and sleep. George, sleep well tonight and the good news is – tomorrow you go home!"

While Rania made them espressos with a small machine she had been given by the Americans, Abdullah leaned across the table and whispered to George.

"Listen, brother, we are close to finishing our journey. We

have taken our town and the refinery, and the pipeline will make this country rich. Soon, we will move further east and get rid of the corrupt and useless government. By then, there will be no Boutros, no Abu Muhammad and no slippery toads sitting in Tripoli, getting fat on the people's oil money. The Libyan people can return to peaceful living and there will be money to be spent on schools and hospitals and there will be work. To do this, there is one more job I need you to do for me. I can only send someone I would trust with my life."

Abdullah explained what it was he needed. George sighed deeply.

"*Mela*, I'll do it, but then I'm going home and I'm going to stay there. You can continue your revolution without any help from me."

———

George's trip home the next day was direct and very expensive, but the bill was taken care of by the US military. A Super Huey army helicopter landed in the morning, kicking up a storm of dust, and whisked him south to the airbase at Ubari. There he boarded a twin-prop Beechcraft, an executive transport plane. He relaxed into the well-worn but comfortable leather seating, and enjoyed coffee and pastries. It was wonderful to be able to eat, any time he wanted to, an experience he had not enjoyed for many weeks.

Within three hours of leaving Marsabar, George found himself in one of the US Embassy's long sedans with tinted windows, giving the driver directions as it squeezed through the busy streets of Birkirkara.

It occurred to him that, following his arrival at the camp the previous evening, he had not spoken to Marianna to tell her he was coming back. He hoped there was somebody in at home and he would not be left sitting on the doorstep.

Before his departure, Rania had ordered him to the toilet

block to shower and change his clothes. She had given him some of Abdullah's underwear, one of his calf-length, white *djellabas* and a bottle of beard oil, so George could tame the ferocious growth on his jaw that, by now, was nearly touching his chest.

It had been weeks since he had washed properly and the shower tray in the communal toilet block ran brown, black, red and brown again, as the caked filth and blood was loosened. Under the filthy *keffiyeh*, his hair was knotted and wild. After washing, he had used the beard oil to smooth the tangled mass back off his brow and plaster it tight to his head. His hair was long, well over his collar.

He stared at his own image in the mirror and the tanned face that looked back at him was not one he immediately recognised. His cheeks were sunken and his cheekbones more prominent. The oiled mass of hair and beard seemed to make his eyes burn more brightly. There was a long white scar on one cheek, where Abu Muhammad had raked a ring across his face. When he smiled, there was a gap where Muhammad's fighters had pummelled his face and a tooth had fallen out. He looked down at his flat midriff and saw his feet, in plain view – a sight he had not enjoyed for some years.

As the embassy car pulled away, leaving George on the doorstep, his worst fears were realised. The house was empty. He had been dropped with no key, no phone, and no money. All he had were the clothes Rania had given him. His hair she had tied back in a small ponytail that he flicked over his collar.

Rather than bother the neighbours, he sat on the front step that gave directly onto the pavement. He enjoyed watching the local people passing in front of him, going about their business. Some he knew, so he gave them a cheery wave and a smile. But none were returned.

After a few minutes of watching people, he noticed a coldness in their stare. A group of youths he had known since they were children, passed him and stopped their chat to look down with disdainful expressions. An elderly woman, Mrs Gauci, who lived some houses away on George's Street, came past, pulling a shopping trolley. She seemed to cross the road to avoid him, even though George knew her house was on his side of the street. He was musing on the nature of prejudice and exclusion when he heard two familiar voices coming from the top of the street.

He watched Marianna and Gina come into view, shopping bags and packs of bottled water in hand. He had never thought about how his wife, who did not drive, managed the shopping and felt a stab of guilt. Suddenly, Gina saw him sitting on the step and grabbed her mother's arm in alarm. The pair of them stopped and stared at him for a moment before Marianna started walking purposefully in his direction.

Gradually, she realised the disreputable-looking foreigner she was frowning at was actually her husband of twenty-two years!

"George, my God!"

She rushed up to him and dropped her shopping, fumbling in her bag for her keys.

George stood there with an inane smile on his face and his arms wide open. Marianna took him by the upper arm and moved him briskly up onto the front step.

"Gina, quick, help me get your father inside, before somebody sees him looking like this!"

CHAPTER 46
NATASHA BONNICI
PALAZZO BRUNO, BRERA, MILAN

THE EXECUTORS of Signor Bruno's will had told the Wise Men they had no immediate use for the *palazzo* in Brera, although they were quick to have the property valued. More out of sentiment than for any other reason, the Wise Men agreed to pay a commercial rent to Signor Bruno's estate for a lease of the *palazzo*, so as to maintain a working base in Milan. This pleased Natasha, who loved to spend her days in the heart of the bustling city, which was always a welcome change from the small, sometimes claustrophobic, island of Malta.

To the rear of the property there was a self-contained flat that had recently been renovated. Although many original features had been preserved, there was modern recessed lighting, underfloor heating and brand-new bathrooms, as well as a contemporary kitchen. The flat enjoyed its own entrance from the turning circle to the rear of the *palazzo* and had a balcony with views over the enclosed private garden. Natasha was immediately taken with it.

She did not like thinking that it might have been for the use of Tesoro or his friends, but it seemed that no one had been there for some time. She had a quiet word with Hugo, who confirmed it had been prepared for a live-in housekeeper, but nobody had been hired and it had never been occupied since the renovations. Natasha telephoned Signor De Luca and suggested it would make a perfect home for her during her stays in Milan and that she would much prefer it to living in a hotel. Signor De Luca had no objection to the arrangement, so it was agreed.

Her new work was fascinating, not from a technical perspective, but for the window it opened onto the extent and variety of the Family's activities. Running through the accounts and company records, she realised the Family had interests in European commercial property and forestry, Argentinian vineyards, Middle Eastern pharmaceutical companies, hotel chains and franchises, quarries and cement works, waste-disposal businesses, a fleet of Rhine barges, numerous prized works of art and a portfolio of properties in the 6th arrondissement of Paris. That was on top of their interests in banking, oil, energy and i-Gaming, which Natasha already knew about. Putting a value on it all was impossible, but it probably meant the Family was one of the wealthiest groups of individuals on the planet, a thought that made her tingle with excitement.

The beneficial ownership of these assets and interests was carefully concealed through a network of trusts and offshore companies that it would be Natasha's job to manage. She realised, with some satisfaction, that the Wise Men had let Signor Bruno create a web of ownership that, at the time of his death, only she and he understood – a dangerous strategy for a group of octogenarians!

It was on her second trip to Milan in her new role that a meeting appeared in her electronic diary between her, Salvatore and Signor De Luca. Its purpose was an update on the energy deal in Malta and the wider distribution arrangements Salvatore was managing, on mainland Europe.

Since Signor Bruno's death, several weeks previously, she had studiously avoided mentioning the investigation or the friction between her father and Salvatore. She was there solely to do the job she had been recruited for and did not want to be seen using her new position to go fishing for information about things that should not concern her. Obviously, she was acutely interested in both matters, but thought an air of studied indifference would be the fastest way to gain the confidence of Signor De Luca.

It had seemed before this as though there had been some tacit agreement to keep her and Salvatore apart, so this appointment came as a surprise to her. They met in Signor Bruno's old study, with Signor De Luca sitting in the place of honour behind the large, antique Tuscan desk. Natasha was shocked by the change in Salvatore's appearance. Although his clothing was immaculate, as usual, the man inside the suit was a shell of his former self. His face had a sickly pallor to it. He had missed his regular fortnightly haircut. His hair was untidy and looked unwashed. He was anxious and stammered through parts of his presentation to Signor De Luca – even calling him Signor Bruno on one occasion. He never stopped fidgeting and, at times, his foot nervously tapped a beat on the tiled floor.

On the way out of the meeting, he grabbed Natasha by the wrist.

She glared at him, aware that she remembered enough of her judo to break his grip, unbalance him and put him on the tiles in seconds. A few years ago, she would not have hesitated.

He saved himself by releasing her and saying: "Sorry, I didn't mean to alarm you. I'm a bit edgy today."

"I know, I can see. You look like shit, by the way."

"Thanks! I feel like shit. I'm not sleeping, I ache and I've been vomiting for the last two days. I can't stop worrying. Can we get a coffee? I need to talk to you."

They walked out onto the street and crossed over to the Palazzo Citterio, an eighteenth-century gallery with a coffee shop in its central courtyard.

"So, what's turned the handsome, assured, self-confident Salvatore Randazzo into a walking zombie? Tell me."

He stirred his coffee, not making eye contact with her.

"Don't you think it's strange that there's been no mention of

Signor Bruno's death? Not from Hugo, Toni, De Luca? Nobody's saying a word."

"Yes, but I've been ignoring it. They like to keep up appearances. But why's that bugging you?"

"I think I might be next. I think someone's poisoning me, but I don't know how. In fact, they may already have done it – I feel terrible."

He hung his head and cast down his eyes. There was not an ounce of fight left in him. Natasha looked at him and noticed his laboured breathing.

"Why on earth do you think that?"

"I'm being followed, for one thing. If the Family have now started murdering their own – first Sergio, now Signor Bruno – I've offended Marco and a few other people, so maybe I've become more trouble than I'm worth? Nobody's telling me anything and it's driving me mad!"

"Calm down, Sal. Why do you think you're being followed?"

"I've had a feeling, several times, and someone's been in my flat and left me a message. There was a dead rat on top of the kitchen worktop. I took it to a private forensic lab and they said it'd been poisoned. I'm telling you, it's a message."

"Really? Have you been tested?

"No, not yet. Maybe I should. Look, if you knew anything about this, you'd tell me, wouldn't you?"

She looked him straight in the eye.

"Yes, Sal, I would. I can see how upset you are. Have you spoken to the Wise Men?"

"I've spoken to Hugo. He says nothing's going on, that I shouldn't worry. But, listen, I've been down to see Tesoro's friends who hang around the Central Station, to see what they know. Apparently, Hugo and his police connections have been all over them, but one of them did say something interesting. Tesoro had been seen with a short, stocky guy with long grey hair. Might have had a Sicilian accent. His friend said this guy had given Tesoro a lot of money, but he didn't think he was a punter. What do you make of that?"

Natasha stopped stirring her coffee and looked at Salvatore closely.

"You can't be serious! You're asking me to believe in ghosts?"

"No, but you can see why I'm jumpy."

"I'd forget about it, if I were you. But, yeah, I can see that it's got you spooked. If I can help, of course I will. All I can do is keep my ears open."

"One more thing – please don't tell Marco this. I wouldn't like to give him the satisfaction of knowing I am slowly going mad!"

"You can forget about my dad – he's backing out of Family things and will soon be rolling boulders around the estate in Serbia. I'm afraid it's me in charge now."

She smiled and flicked back her hair.

"Come on, relax, it's not as bad as it seems. But you need to see a doctor – you look awful – and, remember, there's no such thing as ghosts! I'll pay for the coffee."

They left. Salvatore barely made it to the end of via Brera before he succumbed to another bout of retching, behind an overflowing green dumpster.

Back in her apartment in the *palazzo*, Natasha went out onto the balcony, taking out a burner phone that she kept at the bottom of her wardrobe.

Her call was answered on the third ring.

"He's on the run and looking shocking. He's suspicious and one of the male hookers ID-ed you to him. I've got to say, the thing with the rat was a bit much! He's had it tested and he knows somebody is onto him. So, if you're going to finish it, now's the time."

There was a deep cackle of laughter from the other end of the call.

"I would've paid serious money to have seen his face! OK, message received."

Before hanging up, Natasha said: "Listen, I'm going to Libya for a bit. I haven't told anyone yet, but I need to get that end of things buttoned down."

"*Sì*. Be careful, it's *una lotta tra cani* over there."

"It's a dog fight everywhere! Why should Libya be any different? But, before I go, I think it would be a good idea for us to wind up our business in Milan. Don't you agree?"

CHAPTER 47
NICK WALKER

LUQA INTERNATIONAL AIRPORT,
MALTA

A WARM, south-easterly wind blew fine red dust across the tarmac. As Nick Walker walked around the wing of the BA aircraft, he felt the familiar, dry salty taste of Malta in his mouth. The airport sat on a plateau at the southerly end of the island and, when the wind blew in the right direction, the fine sands of the Libyan desert were carried to it.

His decision to return had not been taken lightly. Natasha had tried on several occasions over recent years to lure him back to BetHi, but he had always managed to persuade himself that, having escaped his ties to the Family, it would be foolish to offer himself back up. He knew what joining them again would involve and, although he was not averse to cutting corners and a little financial gamesmanship himself, the Family operated in a different league altogether.

If he looked hard enough at himself, Nick had to acknowledge his return was largely due to his enduring fascination with Natasha Bonnici. He had not been able to get her out of his system, even after four years, so he reasoned he probably never would. He had had relationships with women on Gibraltar, but Natasha was always there in the background, whispering in his ear, sowing the seeds of doubt, offering herself in comparison.

Although there were a million reasons to avoid her and the Family, he had accepted he was a moth to her flame.

He had no doubt she could be ruthless in her treatment of anyone who stood between her and her ambitions. Having worked on the pieces of the puzzle many times over the past four years, he was convinced she had engineered his exit from BetHi so she could take the CEO job for herself. Few people knew her as well as he did. She had tried to frame him for theft and, that fateful night, he had caught her stalking him around Villa Bianca, barefoot for silence and with a gun in her hand. He would never know what she was really up to. He had panicked and struck out at her with a nearby glass vase. It was a miracle she had not died. The sickening sound the heavy glass made as it hit her skull, and the feel of it as the impact reverberated against his arm, still resonated in his mind. For a while, he had sought to escape both her and the Family, yet here he was, back on the courtesy bus, heading towards the customs desks. Her last message had said the keys to his old home, Villa Bianca, had been hidden under the potted oleander tree to the left of the front door.

Natasha had told him she would be in Milan when he returned, but someone would meet him in Arrivals to take him to the villa and settle him in. He went from the relative calm of the baggage collection carousels, out through the sliding doors, into the noise and chaos of the Arrivals Hall. Dozens of couriers waved signs with hotel logos. VIP drivers, standing a step or two back, brandished the names of visitors from around the world.

For a moment, he thought he had been forgotten, but then he noticed a familiar figure, hunched over a newspaper, wearing a cardigan and some corduroy trousers despite the thirty-degree heat. At first, Nick thought he would slide past, to avoid any confrontation, then realised this was probably no accident. So he went and stood beside the man, who continued to stare at the newsprint.

After a moment or two, Nick said: "Marco? Hello – it's been a long time."

Marco looked up at him with a half-smile.

"Nick Walker. Well, I never thought I would see the day!"

Marco Bonnnici stood up and they exchanged a brief handshake, for the sake of good manners.

"Yes, Nick, a lot of water has passed under the bridge, but Natasha tells me you are back and all fired up to run BetHi?"

"Yes, that's the plan."

Marco nodded.

"I thought we should meet sooner rather than later. Give ourselves a chance to chat. So, hand me your bag and I will give you a lift to the villa."

They sat in the white Range Rover, the same car Natasha had arrived in when she had returned to the villa after their quarrel, that fateful night, four years ago. Nick looked out of the window, the high plateau giving him a vantage point over the urban sprawl that comprised the south-east of the island. He started counting the number of tower cranes projecting above the skyline, but stopped when he reached thirty.

"I'm surprised there is any land left to build on!"

"The building is relentless. A lot of it is poor-quality apartments for the rental market. There will be a price correction soon, the market is far too hot," Marco replied, "So, how did she convince you to come back? I thought you had fallen out with us?"

"Well, yeah, but let's say time is a great healer. Gibraltar was fine, but the business never really got to the size I wanted. I hadn't the budget to compete with the big players and I didn't want to sacrifice my independence. This way, I can grow the business in Gibraltar with overflow from BetHi and still get the chance to be CEO of one of the biggest i-Gaming platforms in Europe."

"What about Natasha?"

"I'm looking forward to working with her."

"That is not what I meant."

Nick laughed and shook his head.

"Look, Natasha and I have had our chances, but this is just about work, Marco. Nothing else, honestly."

Perhaps it was the corrupting air of the island, but Nick was shocked by how easily the lie came out of his mouth.

"OK. I think that is very wise."

Marco took his eyes off the road for a second to share a smile with his passenger.

"Listen, I'm sorry about selling the *Blue Cascade*; it's just that I was desperate ..." Nick blurted.

"Forget it. That is in the past. None of us behaved well at that time. I should not have deceived you by moving Natasha into the housekeeper's apartment at the villa, to keep an eye on you. I was at fault too.

"How much did you get for the boat by the way?"

"A hundred thousand euro."

Marco laughed.

"Jesus, it was worth ten times that!"

"Not for same-day cash it wasn't – believe me, I tried!"

"Anyway, I have bought a new one. She is a beauty. If you do not steal any money or attempt to kill my daughter, I might take you out in her."

"I promise, none of those things'll happen and I'll look forward to it!"

Nick smiled. He watched the urban landscape flash by as they took the main regional road to the north. The new overpass at Marsa had been completed and it seemed that most of the roads had been resurfaced. A lot had changed in the four years he had been away, yet much of what he saw felt very familiar. He was disappointed Natasha was not going to be there when he arrived at the villa, but checked himself; he had to put those thoughts out of his mind.

"Natasha tells me you're planning to return to Serbia in the near future?" he addressed Marco.

"Yes. Since the death of Sergio, the fun of it all has gone for me. You will find Natasha has her own way of doing things these days. I do not think she needs me around, so I am happy to step back again. I am talking to Milan and completing one or two things here, then that is it, I am done. I will let you young blades take over."

"I've told Natasha, I'm purely here to run BetHi, I've got no interest in any of the other businesses. I'm a civilian. That's our deal."

"Make sure you stick to it – it is a sensible approach. Things are different from how they were four years ago. The game has become a lot rougher than you might imagine."

Nick looked at him, waiting for him to go on, but Marco kept his eyes on the road and his mouth shut. Nick sensed something was not quite right, but did not want to push too hard. Marco seemed absorbed in his own thoughts.

Eventually he said: "You think you know Natasha, but I do not think you do. She has changed – well, maybe not changed, but now she has power, it makes her more ... shall we say, up front. And she can sometimes make decisions that are ill considered. I worry someday she might find herself in serious trouble."

He paused before saying, "After I have left Malta, if ever you need to talk to me, please feel free to do so. I will make sure you have my current number. I suspect you always have her best interests at heart. As do I, of course."

Nick looked at him, trying to understand what had just been said. He was confused by this conversation. He thought Marco was the last person he would ring for advice. Then it occurred to him that was not what Marco had meant. He was asking Nick to keep an eye on Natasha.

The car swung off the coast road and into the drive of Villa Bianca, standing alone on the rocky hillside. In front of them stretched the blue waters of the Mediterranean, a distance of one hundred kilometres to the southern Sicilian coast. Urgent, incoming waves burst on the rocky limestone platform, throwing white plumes of spray high into the air. Nick took a moment to reacquaint himself with the familiar place. The wide deck and pool had been cleaned and the new season's striped cushions put out onto the sun loungers. The polished, stainless-steel banisters and fittings gleamed brightly, yellow and white and hot to the touch in the reflected light. The outdoor kitchen had been swept clear of leaves and the villa's long windows opened, so the salty, iodine-scented sea breeze could run through the rooms, tugging at the voiles and gently shaking the fronds of the potted ferns.

Nick exhaled deeply; he was pleased to be back. He entered the house and, with a smile, went to settle the query that had been on his mind since he had accepted the offer to return to the villa. He opened the light ash door into the lounge and looked towards the console table, positioned against the back wall. There, standing fifty centimetres tall, with the swirling colours of cupric, cobalt and chrome inside its glass body, was the thin-stemmed Murano vase he had used to hit Natasha. He picked it up, to feel its weight and remind himself how well it balanced in his striking hand.

CHAPTER 48
HUGO, TONI AND SIGNOR DE LUCA

LA SCALA, MILAN

MILAN WAS a city familiar with violence. From the mid-nineteen-seventies to the end of the last century, the Red Brigades, Prima Linea, Unità Comuniste Combattenti and other leftists, and Neo-Fascists, had bombed, assassinated and fought each other in the streets of Northern Italy. The last car bomb of the era to explode in Milan was in July 1993. It went off in via Palestro, by the Galleria d'Arte Moderna, some eight hundred metres from Signor Bruno's *palazzo* on via Brera. Whether or not he heard the blast would never now be known.

On that occasion, the bomb was set, not by the warring political extremists of left and right, but by Cosa Nostra as an act of criminal terrorism. It killed three firemen and a security guard who were investigating a Fiat Uno with smoke issuing from under its chassis, prior to it exploding. The fifth death was that of Driss Moussafir, a Moroccan migrant, asleep on a nearby bench, torn in two by a sheet of spinning metal.

Since that time, car bombs had been absent from the city centre, certainly in the vicinity of La Scala, the eighteenth-century opera house, referred to as the heart and soul of Milan. The great and the good of the city gathered there throughout the season, cheering and applauding singers of works by Verdi, Rossini and

Puccini amongst others. Tonight there was to be something different – a performance of Wagner's *Tannhäuser*.

La Scala's *loggione*, the six tiers of boxes above the stalls, were known to seat the most exacting of audiences. For a singer to appear before them for the first time was a baptism of fire. And among that audience, none was more critical than Signor Gabriele De Luca.

He knew opera, meaning – for him – purely Italian opera. In fact, he was of the opinion that any libretto in a language other than Italian did not have the right to call itself opera. He was president of the Amici della Scala, an old-established, elite group of supporters of the opera house. They promoted music, art and culture in Milan and the wider Lombardy region. The Teatro alla Scala was their main and constant point of reference, and he saw himself as the leader of the *loggione*.

It was to him that they would turn after a performance for an indication of whether they should applaud, remain silent or, in extreme cases, boo and catcall. Visitors who attended La Scala in a spirit of reverence, noted that the Milanese treated it as if it were their own private drawing room, where they felt free to behave in any manner they saw fit. It was Signor De Luca who, in 2006, had instigated a show of disapproval so intense that it led tenor Roberto Alagna to flee the stage, in the middle of a performance of Verdi's *Aida*.

That night, the role of Tannhäuser was to be sung by an exceptional young German tenor, who had never before performed at La Scala. Signore De Luca intended to make his debut memorable. He hated Wagner, the Germans, and especially *Tannhäuser*, with its themes of moral laxity and repressed sexuality. He had pleaded with the programme director not to include it in the current season, but without success. So he was now intent on leading the *loggione* in a show of disapproval nobody would forget.

Fortunately, or unfortunately, it was not to be. As usual, Toni was driving the black 7 Series BMW down via Giuseppe Verdi, towards La Scala, where he intended to drop off Signor De Luca and Hugo before returning to the *palazzo*, a few blocks north on via Brera, to wait until the event had finished. At the junction with via Andegari, Toni stopped the car at the pedestrian crossing, blanking the man who tapped on his window, offering flowers for sale.

At that moment, a signal was received that led to a flash of white light, directly underneath the vehicle. It lifted the car vertically, two metres into the air, throwing open its bonnet and blowing its windscreen outwards. With a crash, the car fell back into position in the queue of waiting traffic and bounced on its suspension, onto the bonnet of the car behind it. This coincided with a dull thud as the explosion's sound wave hit the shocked pedestrians, who cowered or lay injured on the pavements.

Then, for the next thirty seconds, onlookers heard the rattle and tinkle of a million pieces of glass falling from the sky in a sparkling shower, as shop windows blown out by the explosion rained back down to earth. Gradually, high-pitched human screams and cries mingled with car and shop alarms that whooped and wailed. Shortly afterwards there was a second explosion, more of a yellow light this time, that engulfed the car in flames, black sooty smoke beginning to plume into the city sky.

As well as the three in the car, later identified as a retired industrialist, his lawyer and driver, seven others were killed, including, ironically, a Moroccan migrant, Saad Kharbouche, a roadside flower seller, plying his trade by the pedestrian crossing.

CHAPTER 49
GEORGE ZAMMIT
GEORGE'S HOUSE, BIRKIRKARA, MALTA

T̲h̲e̲ ̲f̲i̲r̲s̲t̲ ̲t̲h̲r̲e̲e̲ hours after his return home were a blur of chatter, barbering and clothing alterations. While Gina trimmed George's beard and hair, Marianna rummaged through his wardrobe to find clothes that could be cut and cropped to accommodate his considerably slimmer physique. She sliced along seams, took in waistbands and bored new holes in places on his belt that had never been near the buckle.

She watched a new man emerge from this grooming process. As he had to return to Libya, he had decided to keep the beard, now trimmed closer to his face. The desert tan and collection of facial scars from the beatings he had suffered, lent him a rough and rugged look. His hair was brushed back off his forehead and fell over his collar. George sat quietly in a chair, letting his daughter fuss over him. Marianna noticed the new width to his shoulders and the strength in his arms as he sat shirtless at the kitchen table. His flabby pale midriff and pronounced paunch had disappeared and there was now a tanned hardness to his torso. She sensed a new strength and confidence in him, and felt a little flushed around the neck at the thought that they would lie in the same bed together that night.

It did not take long before there was a knock on the front door to disturb the makeover. Gina broke off to answer it. Assistant Commissioner Camilleri popped his face through the kitchen doorway, sporting his best attempt at a sincere smile.

"George, George, how wonderful to see you back! Marianna, I will not disturb the homecoming, but I do need to talk to him for ten minutes. Then, I promise, he is all yours."

George sighed, stood up, grabbed his shirt, brushed the piles of hair off his lap and wiped his face with a towel.

"If we need to talk confidentially, Gerald, we can go outside. Marianna will just listen behind the door if we talk in here."

Outside on the street, Camilleri lit a cigarette.

"So, George, well done! Stories have been getting back to me and some, frankly, I have found hard to believe. The Maltese Machine gun – really?"

"Yes. I've had some astonishing experiences, but don't believe everything you hear. There're some ridiculous exaggerations flying around."

"That is a relief – I was getting quite worried about some of the stories and this 'new' man who was returning to us."

"Listen, I know what you're going to say and I've agreed with Abdullah Belkacem I'll do this one last trip, then I'm out. Finished. I've had enough. I want to go back to real old-fashioned policing. I've done my share of this sort of stuff. From now on, I want a good old boring life, doing the job I enjoy. I know you can fix it and I deserve it after what I've been through."

"George, we can talk about that when we have finished the task in hand and you are well rested. I can understand you are feeling ... well, a bit tetchy at the moment."

"Feeling a bit tetchy! Have you any idea what I've been through? I was held for weeks in a concrete box by crazy Islamic terrorists, in the middle of a desert. Those bastards behead people like me. Look!" George grimaced at Camilleri, to show him the gap in his teeth. He pointed to the white scar running from under his eye across his cheek, and the graze from a bullet on his scalp. "I've been beaten, shot, starved, have lived in fear for weeks on end – all for a policeman's salary! And I bet you didn't turn up for Gina's party!"

"George, George, calm down! We'll talk about this later. I am sorry, I never thought it would turn out like this."

Camilleri glanced nervously up and down the street.

"Look, I need you on the Croatian border with Serbia on the E70 at Batrovci, at 18:00 hours, the day after tomorrow. Fly to Trieste, then the Italian police will lend you an unmarked vehicle to escort a wagon, carrying precious cargo, down through Italy to Malta.

"I do not expect any trouble but, just in case, you will need to be armed. So bring the firearms certificate for your weapon and pack the ammunition separately for the flight. It should be straightforward. There will be about thirty hours' driving back from the border to Malta, so take someone with you. Someone experienced and handy with a gun, not a friend to chat with."

George shook his head and went back into the house. He decided the best way to handle the situation with Marianna was to come straight out with the fact he would be leaving the next day. He explained it was just to finish off what he had started before he was taken hostage, and tempered the blow by telling her and Gina that, once he was back, in a couple of days, they would book a holiday to Spain. He told them to have a look for a nice place and work out all the prices. He knew that would keep them busy for the next week, at least.

As Camilleri had requested, two evenings later, George and Sergeant Major Chris Grima of the Maltese Pulizija, Rapid Intervention Unit, stood on the Croatian side of the border crossing with Serbia. George had picked Grima because he was known as a competent marksman and a fitness fanatic. He had boasted to George he only needed four hours' sleep a night, so George thought he would be the perfect partner. He was a little alarmed, therefore, when Grima slept all the way through the six-hour drive from collecting the car at Trieste's Friuli Venezia Giulia Airport, to arriving at the Batrovci border between Croatia and Serbia.

The E70 on the Croatian side of the crossing cut through wide swathes of arable farmland, which changed to dense undeveloped deciduous forest as soon as they had crossed into Serbia. What was common to both sides was the kilometres-long lines of trucks and private cars, queueing for hours to present papers to get in and out of the European Union. George had fixed the blue light to the roof and cruised past the lines to get to the border terminal buildings.

The allotted time of eighteen hundred hours had come and gone and they still could not see the yellow, curtain-sided, eighteen-tonne *Jami-Volet-* branded wagon that was carrying a load of two hundred wooden packing cases. Grima stood on a viewing platform on the roof of the building and looked down with a pair of high-powered binoculars at the row of trucks inching towards the crossing point. Eventually, he turned to George, who was absently gazing at the landscape, and gave him a thumbs up. The truck was heading towards them.

The rest of the journey down through Italy passed without incident. The speed limit of seventy kilometres-per-hour felt intolerably slow to George, sitting at the wheel of the Italian police Alfa Romeo Giulia, which could easily cruise at three times that speed. They by-passed Rome on the Grande Raccordo Anulare ringroad, just before the early-morning traffic, and hit Naples' infamous Tangenziale by mid-morning. In the late afternoon, they were queueing for the ferry at Reggio Calabria, to cross the narrow Messina Straits into Sicily, and by nine o'clock that evening, they were the last two vehicles to squeeze onto the late sailing of the *St Jean de Valette* hydrofoil to Valletta, Malta.

Once on the island, George phoned Camilleri and was instructed to meet him at the Freeport in the south of the island.

The yellow *Jami-Volet* wagon pulled into the security check at the entrance to the port and George watched, as Camilleri and six heavily armed officers from the Rapid Intervention Unit surrounded it. George turned to see if Grima was inclined to join them, but he had fallen into another of his deep, hours-long sleeps.

The wagon was escorted by the officers into a closed warehouse, a few dozen metres along the dock. George drove the Alfa Romeo into the building and the large sliding doors were closed behind them. Some dock workers appeared with a forklift. They pulled back the curtain sides of the lorry and lifted the cargo of substantial wooden crates, with Cyrillic script down the sides, onto waiting pallets. Other workers set about securing the crates to the pallets with strong nylon banding.

Camilleri raised a hand and halted the work so he could walk round each crate, inspecting seals, and then gave one of the port workers a case of small plastic nodules, which were attached with electric screwdrivers. George assumed these were transponders of some sort.

He stretched and yawned. Then, he casually walked over to Camilleri, who, having finished his inspection, stood a little apart, watching the proceedings.

"What's in the crates, Assistant Commissioner?"

George did not expect to be told, so was surprised when Camilleri said: "Money, George. Lots of it. That is why you and these officers are going to accompany it all the way to your friend Mr Belkacem. You are going to Tripoli, though nobody needs to know that except the skipper and you. I have checked the seals, so you and I can both confirm the money is intact at this point. Please, George, make sure it stays that way."

He looked at Camilleri aghast. Further explanations were curtailed by loud banging on the large metal sliding door to the warehouse. The armed police immediately drew their weapons and fell to their knees, covering the entrance. Grima, who by this time had woken up, walked over to the door and slid it open slightly, peering out.

A shapely leg, in tight jeans, appeared through the gap and its owner squeezed in at the narrow opening. She strode into the unforgiving high-bay lighting that bounced off the blue gloss resin flooring.

George could not believe it was her – Natasha Bonnici, coming towards him. She walked across and stood beside them as the police officers shouldered their weapons and work recommenced on securing the crates to the pallets. Even from two metres away, she seemed to project an allure, a scent, a cloud of pheromones, that woke George from his lethargy and had him stealing glances at the woman standing beside him.

"Well, well! Inspector Zammit – or is it Superintendent Zammit? Whichever, I'm sure this will all be safe in your hands. I hear you are quite the soldier!"

George gaped, but could find no words to reply.

Natasha continued: "I expect I'll see you on the other side of the water. Be vigilant, Superintendent. Libya's full of crooks."

Even Assistant Commissioner Camilleri could not help but raise an eyebrow at that remark. Natasha turned to him.

"And, Gerald, you're certain nobody else knows about this shipment? No Russians or Americans?"

"No, Miss Bonnici, certainly no Russians and I have said nothing to our American allies. George, you had better be aware: the existence of this cargo is known only to the three of us here and to Abdullah Belkacem. It absolutely has to stay that way."

Later that evening, the eighty metre long, one thousand and five hundred tonne general cargo ship *Lorelei* left the Malta Freeport on a charter passage to the Port of Tripoli, Libya. The cargo was a modest load of wooden crates and a passenger manifest of seven heavily armed Maltese policemen. The charter price offered was the equivalent of a full load of general cargo, so the ship's agent had no qualms about accepting the job. There were no customs formalities and no documents or notices to be filed with the port authorities at either end. The trip took thirty-six hours and proved uneventful.

CHAPTER 50
SALVATORE RANDAZZO
ISOLA, MILAN

THE AREA CALLED Isola was in the northern part of Milan and had become one of the city's trendiest neighbourhoods. It had seen the development of a new district, Porta Nuova, that had changed the city's skyline with its avant garde skyscrapers, such as the Bosco Verticale, where Salvatore had his apartment.

The balcony, along with most others in the so-called Vertical Forest, was festooned with climbing plants that draped the sides of the entire building, to form spectacular green walls. The building was an architectural triumph - not that this mattered to Salvatore who lay dead in his austere, unadorned bedroom, on top of a two-metre square bed.

The murderer had injected ricin powder into a number of coffee capsules that stood in a chromium rack next to the espresso machine in the kitchen. While Salvatore sipped coffee and fretted over his declining health, the cup before him held the seeds of his destruction.

It was a sad truth that he had had no family left alive, nor close friends to whom he could turn as his illness progressed. As his condition worsened, Salvatore had called his doctor, who was confused and worried about what he had found. The doctor had, in turn, called an ambulance whose crew was waiting in the entrance foyer of the block at the moment the poison completed its job of destroying the cells that formerly comprised Salvatore Randazzo.

In due course, the Milanese *polizia giudiziaria*, the investigating authority, realised they were managing a murder inquiry and, once they had examined his phone, found a series of unanswered calls to a Maltese number belonging to one Natasha Bonnici. When questions were asked as to what the purpose of the calls might have been, she told the prosecutor, through the office of Assistant Commissioner Camilleri of the Maltese Pulizija, that Randazzo was an old boyfriend who had started pestering her and she had thought the best policy was to ignore the calls that had become increasingly annoying. Other than that, she had nothing to say.

CHAPTER 51
ABDULLAH BELKACEM
MARSABAR, LIBYA

As his militia started to make their way towards Tripoli, in trucks and technicals, Abdullah's thoughts were embroiled in Libya's rancid pit of politics and proxy wars. He dreamed of a free and peaceful Marsabar, without foreign threat or interference. He knew that would never happen while he had the Americans for friends, the Turks on his doorstep and the likes of Abu Muhammad and the southern Islamic militias yearning for their Caliphate. Those seeking power, governance and riches had torn Libya to pieces, and now those pieces were being snatched at and picked over by a pack of vicious street dogs.

On the ground, Abdullah had just over 1,000 men, but in the air he could not be matched. Abdullah's friends had brought the mountain down on the hopes of a Caliphate in Libya and chaos had flowed through the valleys of Nafusa. Boutros's Chinese drones and Russian MiGs were burned shells on their runways and global TV coverage had ensured there could be no pretending otherwise.

The Russians were quietly planning their departure, while the Emiratis kept their money under their long white *dishdashas*. The Sudanese units headed south for home, their pockets empty of the dinars currently sailing across the sea in the general cargo ship *Lorelei*.

At the farm outside Marsabar, the tents had started to come down and the number of advisers and contractors was beginning to thin out. Abdullah knew it was time for them to leave, as it had never been part of the deal for an American army of occupation to remain in Libya. Air support was to be continued and he had now acquired three drones of his own, which gave him sharp eyes and fierce firepower. A small team of specialists, based somewhere in Arizona, were allocated to pilot the lethal machines.

Abdullah had spoken, along with Major Floyd Hamilton, via conference calls, to representatives of the Tripoli government and had agreed to flush out the remnants of Boutros's forces that lurked to the east of Tripoli. As he had done in the past, he would take responsibility for the security of the Coastal Road, from the outskirts of Tripoli to the Tunisian border. The lands to the south of it, including the Nafusa Hills, up to the borders with Algeria and Niger, would also be his to secure. The dispute between Tripoli and the rebels in the east, and the arguments about the type of Islamic government the country should have, was pure politics. Abdullah decided there was nothing he could do about that. It was for others to resolve.

The Americans also agreed to honour his promises to the Tuareg and allow them to create a semi-autonomous province in the south, which they would control, again in exchange for them helping to secure the southern desert borders. That way, the Americans and Europeans hoped to stem the tide of displaced migrants on their way north. Whether they would be able to stop the rising tide of refugees from the Sahel was a question for another day.

Abdullah would retain his base at Ubari and provide security for the oil and gas operations in the Sharara oil and gas fields, as well as the pipelines to the refineries at Az-Zawiya and Marsabar. He could charge the Libyan Resources Corporation, who controlled the sale of all Libya's oil and gas, for protecting their assets, allowing him to collect sufficient money to provide local services to the people – and get rich in the process. In short, he had got just about everything he had wanted when he had set off from Malta all those weeks ago.

Apart from the head of Abu Muhammad.

CHAPTER 52
GEORGE ZAMMIT
FREEPORT MALTA, MALTA

Before the *Lorelei* had set sail from Freeport Malta, Natasha, Camilleri and George gathered in the small office that sat high on a gantry, overlooking the floor of the warehouse. Natasha took the seat behind the desk and was scrutinising George. Without breaking her gaze, she said: "How much does he know?"

Camilleri replied: "Nothing."

Natasha nodded and gave George her most winning smile. He felt himself start to blush.

"OK, George, we've been speaking to your friend Abdullah Belkacem about our business in Libya. Basically, the oil fields and pipelines that're going to deliver the oil and gas to the refineries at Marsabar and Az-Zawiyah need protection and Abdullah and his militia will provide it. The LRC and the government in Tripoli have promised us the earth but, as you know, their promises are worthless. We must look after this ourselves.

"So, in the crates you're carrying, there's a huge amount of money, in Libyan dinars. In fact, one billion dinars. Over six hundred and thirty million euros."

George's eyes grew wider and his mouth opened slightly.

"Yes, it's a lot, isn't it? For that money, we expect our interests to be safe and secure, at least until the oil revenues start to flow and we can replenish the funds. Your warlord friend should be able to buy himself a decent army for that amount of cash. We want you to make sure he doesn't just run off with it."

"Me? How am I going to do that?"

"You'll control the cash. Audits, authorisations, accounting – all that boring stuff. I'll set it up and we'll have accountants to service it here in Malta and in Tripoli. You'll operate the account established by the Central Bank of Libya, in Tripoli, deal with requests for cash and recommend the release of funds. You'll deliver the cash and authorise payment of local expenses. Once money has been released, you'll ensure it is spent correctly and account to me for any discrepancies. More importantly, Belkacem trusts you. He'll do as you say. There's a bond between you. And, even more important, I trust you."

George was confused and worried; he did not like this suggestion at all.

"But … can this be done from Malta?"

"Of course not! We need eyes on the ground, in Libya – we'll build you a nice house somewhere in Marsabar."

"*Mela* … You can't do that! I'm not living in Libya. I'm going on holiday to Spain – I've promised the family! My wife won't agree to move … no, this isn't going to work at all."

Camilleri stood and reached across the cramped office to put his arm around George's shoulder, who flinched and looked imploringly at his boss.

"George, this will make you a rich man. It is a big responsibility and I am sure it carries a big salary. Also, I have authorised a large bonus for you and an enhancement to your pension pot! How about that?"

George was even more confused.

"What d'you mean? Am I being fired?"

"I am sorry, George. There has not been time to talk about this. But, in your absence, there was a small departmental reorganisation and, in the interests of cementing links between the Pulizija and key parts of the Maltese economy, I am seconding you out of the department for a while – national interest and all that. It is splendid news! This is truly an excellent opportunity and has arrived at just the right time for your career development."

"But I don't want to do it. I want to go back to my normal duties!"

"Sorry, not possible just at the moment. The country has greater need of your unique experience and skills. We are all here to serve. You can return to being a policeman once things settle down in Libya and we can find something more suitable and less … stressful for you. In the meantime, you will work for MalTech, as their Libyan Security Liaison Director. I think that is the right title, Ms Bonnici?"

Camilleri smiled triumphantly.

"Oh, I nearly forgot – I have told Marianna you have been unavoidably delayed for a few more days."

Natasha looked across the table at George.

"Welcome aboard, *Mr* Zammit. It's all worked out well for everybody. You come highly recommended. Don't let us down."

She opened her briefcase and gave him an A4 envelope.

"Here are your instructions about what happens when you reach Tripoli and my letter of authority. Don't be bullied into any nonsense by Abdullah. Remember, this is our money and you're responsible for it. If any goes missing, we're not talking about slapped wrists. You understand what I'm saying?"

George swallowed hard and nodded his head.

Once the ship had set sail, he found a spot on the deck of the *Lorelei* and watched the lights of Malta fade to pinpricks, then disappear into the enveloping blackness of the night sea. A warm wind cut through his thin jacket as he huddled up against the steel plating of a hatch cover, his knees drawn up to his chest.

He could not believe he was no longer a policeman, even if

temporarily. The Bonnici woman had called him *Mr* Zammit, not Superintendent; he did not like that one bit. A senior police officer was all he had ever wanted to be. He was proud of his rank, the respect it afforded him. And what would Marianna say? Would there be any more invitations to the senior officers' garden parties and the Commissioner's Christmas drinks? Now he was expected to live in Libya … she would not stand for it.

It seemed that he had already accepted the new job, even if he had not said as much. Natasha Bonnici and Camilleri just assumed he was now working for MalTech Energy, whether he liked it or not. It was all a bitter disappointment.

He did not know what the job was, how much he would be paid or even if there was a uniform. All he knew was that he had a billion dinars to look after. They would be unloading it in twenty-four hours and he had to get it into an account with the Central Bank in Tripoli.

He stayed on deck for an hour, until the weariness of three days of travelling drove him to his narrow bunk. The noise and vibrations of the engines shook the ship from top to bottom, but such things rarely bothered George Zammit, who escaped his troubles by falling into a deep and dreamless sleep.

CHAPTER 53
NATASHA BONNICI
PALAZZO BRUNO, MILAN

Natasha had returned to Milan, having watched the *Lorelei* sail from Malta Freeport, bound for Tripoli. She was in her apartment, applying makeup and preparing for a meeting downstairs in Signor Bruno's office. Following the bombing that had killed Signor De Luca, Toni and Hugo, she had telephoned the third Wise Man, Signor Massaro, asking him to come to the *palazzo*. She could sense his hesitation so deliberately dropped all pretence of deference and framed the invitation almost as an instruction. Signor Massaro had asked if Marco would be attending the meeting and she had told him her father had asked her to confirm his retirement from the Family, with immediate effect, and to thank them for the generous retirement benefits.

There had been a long silence on the other end of the line. Natasha did not push things but gave him time to work out how the chips were falling. Eventually, Signor Massaro had said he too had been thinking of retirement for some time now, as his health had not been the best. In the circumstances, he asked to be excused attending and enquired about the retirement package on offer.

Natasha told him she would send him a proposal for his retirement, so he would not be left wanting any comfort he currently enjoyed. She also said that delivery of the retirement package was conditional on his not contacting Herr Schober who, as Natasha reminded him, was the only other Wise Man still left alive.

If he did all this, Massaro had her assurance that he would live to see out his remaining years as a rich man and leave a sizeable legacy for his family.

Herr Schober was not so easily persuaded and demanded to know what the hell was going on and who she thought she was to be telling him what to do? Natasha calmly replied that she was prepared to explain it all to him in person at the *palazzo*. He huffed and puffed and finally agreed to meet with her.

In good time for the meeting, she went down to the study and arranged the seating. Simon had accompanied her from the *castello*. As Marco was making preparations for his permanent departure, he was happy to surrender the Pole's services and she had now officially appointed him her head of security. She had told him to come well prepared and Simon had packed a heavy-duty handgun. He had also hired extra security in the form of three ex-military bodyguards from a Serbian agency, operating in Belgrade. They would be armed but would stay out of sight, in the small room behind Signore Bruno's former office.

Herr Schober turned up fifteen minutes late to the minute, which made Natasha laugh because it was so obviously calculated. He entered without knocking and was accompanied by three suited men who stood at the back of the room.

Natasha smiled sweetly.

"Herr Schober, please, there is no need for muscle in this room. Kindly ask them to wait outside."

Herr Schober looked at her for a minute and then nodded to one of the men, who left with the other two trailing behind him. Outside, they found Simon and the three security hires, waiting with guns drawn. They were swiftly disarmed and Simon disconnected the earpiece and microphone that kept Herr Schober in touch with his detail.

Natasha watched the immaculately dressed, elderly Austrian financier, sitting erect in his chair, his pale blue eyes unwavering. In the nineteen sixties, he had been asked by his government to lead a commission charged with restoring Jewish assets, looted by the Austrian SS, to their rightful owners. Unfortunately, Herr Schober had taken the view that some priceless pieces of art deserved special care, and these were transferred to the vaults of his ancestral home, amongst the vineyards of Burgenland. There, he held secret viewings for 'specially chosen art aficionados from across Europe. Word got out and his subsequent fall from grace was inevitable. It was then that he rekindled his family's long association with the Family in Milan, bringing a harder edge to their financial and banking activities. He had the reputation of being the hawk amongst the Wise Men and Natasha treated him with caution.

"So, Herr Schober, your colleagues Bruno and De Luca are dead. Hugo and Salvatore as well. My father has retired, along with Signor Massaro. I'd say that leaves an opening for some new blood, wouldn't you?"

"You obviously think you have pulled off some sort of coup – and I am as impressed as I am shocked. What do you intend to do with it all? You obviously know all about our financial arrangements, as Signor Bruno made the mistake of trusting you implicitly. Does your father know you are a serial killer? Marco always struck me as a decent man."

Natasha smiled as she went to the burled walnut credenza and poured two cups of coffee.

"Cream?"

He smiled faintly.

"In the circumstances, I think I will decline, thank you."

She made a show of deliberately drinking her coffee, then said: "Why did you come today? You know you're going to take the money because you know there's no alternative."

"I am curious. I want to know who else is involved. I want to know who killed my friends. Because I know it was not all your doing. You could have made yourself invaluable to Signor Bruno and, in time, would have earned a promotion. But there is somebody else involved, who is taking this very personally and is in a hurry. And I repeat, that is not you."

"Yes, you're right. All of that's true. So, are you going to take the money and leave?"

Herr Schober sat impassively, his hands clasped together in his lap.

"You are asking me to walk away from a lifetime's work without understanding the reason why. So no, not until I know who is behind this."

Natasha leaned forward and pressed a button under the desk and then sat back in her chair, arms folded. A buzzer sounded in the next room and the door behind Natasha swung open. A short, stocky man appeared. He was dressed in a blue-grey suit, with an open-necked white shirt beneath. There was a wide beaming smile on his face.

"Wolfram, *ciao*! *Sorpresa!*"

Herr Schober froze in his seat. It took several seconds for him to process what or who had just appeared.

"Surprise indeed. Now I see … It all makes perfect sense."

Natasha stood up and said: "Well, now you know, I'll leave you two to catch up."

She waited in the next room.

The grey-haired man walked behind Herr Schober and placed his hands on the back of his chair. He brought his mouth close to the old man's ear.

"I know it was you, you old fuck! You never could stand me. Even as a boy, you despised me – I got up your stuck-up nose, didn't I? None of the others would've had the guts to make the call. Even if Bruno passed on the message to Salvatore, it was you behind it. So, well done for that. I'm sorry, Wolfram, but you won't get to enjoy your retirement package!"

Herr Schober tried to swivel in the chair but the wire garotte around his frail, wrinkled neck tightened and cut into his thin white skin, a line of dark blood starting to flow down under his collar and soak into his vest. It took less than two minutes before Herr Schober was limp and lifeless in the chair.

Sergio Rossi looked down at the old man's body in disgust. All Sergio's adult life, Schober had treated him with contempt -- be it for Sergio's lack of sophistication, his Sicilian background or for generally not being 'one of them'. Sergio had qualities Schober never recognised, the strongest being his sense of loyalty to those who trusted him. But equally prominent in his character was the Sicilian need to avenge himself on those who disrespected and betrayed him.

CHAPTER 54
MARCO BONNICI
CASTELLO BONNICI, MALTA

MARCO WAS in the process of getting ready to leave. There was no rush, he was having one or two farewell dinners and putting his affairs in order. He had directorships to resign, financial matters to organise and he had decided to put the *castello* onto the market. His time in Malta was over and he needed to sever all links with the island. For as long as he had the house and, more importantly, the garden, part of him would always be connected to it.

Disposing of valuable artefacts, accumulated over centuries by his family, took time and dealers told him he would swamp the local market if everything arrived in the auction houses all at once. Accordingly, the more valuable pieces and collections went to Rome, Milan and Madrid; the pieces with local appeal to the auction houses in Sliema and Valletta. The books in the library he donated to the Bibliotheca, the National Library of Malta in Republic Square, Valletta.

The farmland he planned to lease on favourable terms to some of the long-serving workers, and he set about establishing cooperatives for the winery and olive presses.

He also needed to find some way of resolving his differences with Natasha. They had not had a meaningful conversation since their falling out. He had no doubt as to the gravity of her behaviour and knew he would never feel the same about her again. Nevertheless, he could not contemplate moving to the Serbian estate without a word of farewell.

However, when news filtered through from Milan about the killings of Salvatore, Signor De Luca and Herr Schober, Marco simply refused to believe it. He thought it was some ridiculous rumour. Only when his phone calls to the Wise Men in Milan were not returned did he start to worry. He phoned Natasha, who said she believed the rumours to be true, but was staying in her flat in Portomaso and waiting to see what the outcome might be.

The news was finally confirmed by Signor Massaro, who had telephoned, weeping, to tell Marco of the murder of his fellow Wise Men, saying they had been cut down in cold blood, in Mafia-style executions. He was seeking help and protection from Marco, saying he feared for his life.

He went on to say he held Natasha responsible for the deaths and that she had more or less demanded his retirement as the price for his life. Marco felt an icy chill run through him, as every fear and doubt he had ever nursed about his daughter came flooding back, to hollow him out. His knees felt weak and he closed his eyes. The room started to sway back and forth. He grabbed a chair with his hand and put the phone down on the table. He tried to steady himself, but sent the chair sliding away from him, while Signore Massaro cried and pleaded from the telephone speaker.

Doing his best to gather himself, Marco told Massaro to stay calm and keep safe. He said he would talk to Natasha and find out from her what was happening.

He was totally adrift; not knowing which way to turn. He felt the panic of a swimmer, way too far from shore, who realises he has neither the strength to return to land, nor the energy to keep his mouth above the waves surging around his face. His hands shaking and his legs unsteady, Marco dialled his daughter's number.

"You'd better tell me what is happening in Milan. What the hell have you done?"

"I've done nothing that didn't need doing, Dad." Natasha's voice was flat and cold. "But there's someone you need to see. He'll arrive in Malta tomorrow and I'll bring him up to the *castello* late morning. We should've had this conversation before now; it would all have made more sense to you then and would probably have saved you a lot of worry. I'm sorry for that."

"Nothing about what I have just heard will ever make any sense to me, if it is your doing. Answer me one question: am I safe?"

"Dad, how could you even ask? I promise it'll all make sense when we meet tomorrow. Please, trust me and don't worry."

The next morning, instead of heading out onto the terrace, Marco took a seat in the formal drawing room, an overly elaborate space that was seldom used, but afforded views down the short drive to the main gate. He sat and looked out of the window. He could not read or work. Instead, he just sat watching the gates, in a semi-trance. Katia, the housekeeper, brought breakfast, then later his coffee, and finally asked him if he wanted his lunch served there as well.

He was about to reply when he saw the three-metre steel-plate gates before the house start to move. He abruptly dismissed Katia and hurried to the front door, to watch Natasha's sports car pull up under the portico. She stepped out, took off her sunglasses and looked at him with a peculiar expression on her face. She did not approach him or come towards the front door, but stepped back and to one side. He saw a figure awkwardly lever itself out of the low seat on the passenger side of the car.

When the figure turned to face him, all the breath left Marco's body. He had expected something out of the ordinary this morning and his imagination had taken him to strange and unlikely places, but never had he contemplated this encounter. It was too much for him to comprehend. He walked towards the man in silence. The visitor had a rueful smile on his face, his eyes glistening with tears. Marco was shaking with emotion; the visitor could see the shock and pain of this unexpected reunion written all over his face. Marco had adopted the gait and posture of someone ten years older. He shuffled his way to the inevitable embrace.

Natasha watched from a distance. She slowly got back into the car and left the two of them together, arms around each other. As she drove away, she saw her father in the side mirror, watching her as the gates swung shut.

The two men automatically walked onto the rear terrace, where they had always sat. Sergio had his arm around Marco's shoulders as he struggled to bring his emotions back under control. They sat down in easy chairs and Katia appeared at the terrace door, tray in hand, her face as white as a sheet.

"Yes, Katia, it is him, Lazarus himself. You had better bring us wine. Let us see if ghosts can drink!

"OK, Sergio." Marco exhaled deeply. "Start at the beginning. I cannot wait to hear this."

"Marco, I'm sorry for the deception but they tried to kill me. I didn't know who to trust and I didn't want them to know I was alive. At least, not until I was ready! I didn't want to drag you or Natasha into this or make it your fight.

"I only just escaped … it was blind luck. There was a limo at the gates when I was released, with two Neapolitans in suits. I thought they were drivers, but they were assassins."

Sergio gulped his wine and sighed, gathering himself to tell the story.

"They gave me champagne and I finished it in the car. Then, I realised what was happening. We were in some woods. They opened the door and I charged at them. I threw the bottle; one of the idiots fired, just as the bottle hit him, and the bullet hit his *amico*. Can you believe it? A million to one chance!

"I knew then I could survive. I got the shooter's gun and

finished him. The second guy had a bullet in the leg, but he spilled the beans. I put the first guy in the car and burned him, taking photos as proof of death. I made the second guy send the photos to Salvatore. Then, we drive in their escape car to Le Vele di Scampia – you know, the big block of flats shaped like sails, on the outskirts of Naples? There, I pay some Camorra youths I know to kill him and get rid of the body and the car.

"Lucky? Yes, very. But after that, it's been purely about patience. Marco, they ruined my life, destroyed my marriage …" Marco raised his eyebrows slightly. "Well, she divorced me when I was in prison, which was no big deal, but that bastard Salvatore was fucking Carlita … now *she* I was fond of!

"Anyway, they left me flat. All those promises about a nest egg waiting for me – lies! They let me rot for four years and had no intention of doing the right thing when I got out. There was never any doubt in my mind, Marco, that they'd pay for what they did. You understand that, don't you?"

"I can see it perfectly, Sergio. And I do not blame you. How did Natasha become involved in all this?"

Now the shock was wearing off, Marco was beginning to recover some of his composure.

"I was watching Signor Bruno's *palazzo* from that café across the road, and she saw me. Simple as that. I told her not to tell you because I didn't want you to try and stop me, or get involved. This wasn't your fight, Marco. I told her my plan; she told me how upset you'd been and how you'd distanced yourself from the Family. She offered her help, I'd be lying if I said otherwise, but I did all the wet work!

"But now," he leaned closer to Marco's chair and grabbed his wrist, "*we* can be the Wise Men working with a Wise Woman! How many times have we dreamed of that? Since we were boys in Bologna … remember those times? The way's wide open – we've destroyed all the others. Think about it. The things we can do, you, me and Natasha! What could be better?"

"To live peacefully and quietly, Sergio. Or should I call you

Signor Rossi? And I do not want Natasha tied up in any of this madness."

"It's a bit late for that now. Signorina Bonnici's officially head of the Family! That was her price for agreeing to help me. I came round to the idea pretty quickly. She's got the brains, you know that. She understands all the financial stuff and she's ruthless." Sergio paused and deliberated for a moment. He continued: "I've known that, ever since she pushed Sophia down the staircase."

There was silence between them until Marco said softly: "You knew?"

"I guessed. It was a long time ago. Natasha was very young, Marco."

"She was five years old and she killed her pregnant mother in a fit of jealousy. I knew she had done it but there was no proof. What was I to do then? Sometimes, you know, it has been hard to love her."

"No, she is what she is. We're not going to change that part of her – ever."

The two men looked at each other.

"Anyway, that's why she needs you. That's why I need you. The three of us – we complement each other. Listen, setting the past aside, I'll take back my old job as head of operations; watch Natasha's back and hold a seat as a Wise Man. I'm happy with that! But we need you, Marco. You'll bring stability and experience. Natasha needs and respects you. She's still young."

"She does not need me. She does not tell me what the hell she is up to. She stole a fortune from the Russians, under the nose of the Americans, and they accused *me* of the theft. She even hid the money near my place in Serbia! She and Simon kidnapped a young guy and held him in the old chapel. I swear to you, she would have killed him if I had not stumbled across them. She has left a trail of wreckage behind her these last few years and I worry about her. She is reckless."

"I knew about some of it. Stealing the Russians' cash was a genius operation!"

"What? You knew about it and did not stop her?"

"Well, I thought it was a good idea. The money always had a purpose, that's why she stole it! She's using it to buy an army in Libya, to secure the oil and gas deal."

"For Christ's sake! Does nobody tell me anything? This is what I mean by reckless!"

"No, it's actually very clever. She's got a ruthless streak, I grant you, but that makes it all the more important that you watch over her, no?"

Marco sighed and decided to change the subject.

"Anyway, where did you get the ricin from? That had me really scared, I had no idea what was going on! And, seriously, giving it to Salvatore like a KGB assassin? Did it really have to be that way?"

Sergio laughed.

"Oh, yes, it absolutely did! You wouldn't believe how that bastard wound me up while I was inside. To her credit, Natasha refused to have anything to do with that side of things. I bought the stuff from Danylo – the Ukrainian, you remember? We washed his money, until there was that incident where it seemed Walker had been on the take. Danylo got it from some Russian ex-military type. We owe him a favour for that, by the way."

"Yes, it figures. But no, Sergio, I owe him nothing. I am out of this. You and Natasha can rule across half of Europe, for all I care. You two have changed the rules by killing your own; you have behaved like the Mafia. I am so glad to see you still alive, Sergio, but I cannot be part of the new regime. Why not get an Uzi and shoot up the next person who upsets you when you're driving? This is not us! It is not what *we* do."

"*Sì, sì, hai ragione*, I know. But I needed to make a statement and clear the way for the future – our future. And it felt good to get those old fuckers back for what they did to me!"

"Not my future, Sergio. Not mine! Come on, drink some of this wine. It is last year's and rather good."

"No!" he howled. "Please, not your wine! Haven't you got

anything better to offer a friend who has just returned from the dead?"

"No! Drink it as punishment then, for all the upset you have caused me." They touched glasses, smiling.

"Good to have you back, my old friend," said Marco.

"It's good to be here again, it's been far too long."

They sat on the terrace together, talking in low voices, while Katia set the table for lunch and then approached them to say it was ready to be served. There were grilled prawns since she knew they were Signor Rossi's favourite. For a few hours it felt almost as though Sergio had never been away in prison or taken his bloody revenge after being released. Almost. But each man privately acknowledged that the repercussions of Sergio's return from the dead were unlikely to end here.

CHAPTER 55
NATASHA BONNICI
OFFICES OF BETHI, PACEVILLE, MALTA

PACEVILLE IS the brash centre of Malta's so-called entertainment district; that is, if your idea of fun centres around gentlemen's clubs, dancing with drunken local teens or squeezing up and down the slimy St Rita Steps, a thoroughfare of greasy, broken tiles onto which the area's bars and fast-food outlets spew spilt liquor, discarded pizza slices, drunken Maltese youths and wasted tourists. The B&Bs, hostels and cheap accommodation house a young crowd of travelling fun and sun seekers, for whom the party never stops. Every day from May to September, the bars pump out music and exhausted clubbers lie on the little patch of man-made beach, like a colony of skinny, multi-coloured seals.

Natasha was oblivious to it all. The offices of BetHi were on the upper floors of a fifteen-storey tower block, which put them out of reach of the smell of fried food and pizza toppings. Driving down from the *castello*, she wished she could have sat in on the two men's reunion. Sergio had promised her he would convince Marco to join them and take the Family through the next stage of its journey. The three of them, working together, an invincible trio, bound by blood loyalty and the fun of the game. She had gone along with him, confident that the last thing her father would do was follow her lead as the new head of the Family, a position she had no intention of relinquishing – not even for him. She had got what she wanted by doing what she had to do. It had taken nerve but, amidst the wreckage Sergio and she had created, she had seized control of one of the most powerful business organisations in Europe.

There were others in the Family, of course, who needed managing; she and Sergio had met or spoken to several of them over the last few days. A mix of fear, bribery and charm had been sufficient to bring them into line. She had convened a wider ten-person council, to sit every other month, to whom she would report. This enfranchisement of the Family's more senior members was well received and lent substance to her claim that this revolution was not a putsch against the Wise Men, but a justified reaction against a small, secretive, self-protective group of octogenarians, who had been reluctant to share power or knowledge in an era that demanded more openness and transparency.

Her long-term strategy was to move the Family away from some of the more troublesome areas of its business, where it bumped up against the traditional organised crime groups, such as waste disposal and construction, and focus more on big ticket, more stable income-generating projects in infrastructure, finance and energy.

Sergio did not really understand the change of strategy, but that did not bother Natasha unduly. He either did or he did not, it did not matter to her. She knew he would always defer to her and be totally loyal; that was just the way he was. Her father was a different matter. She knew he would always doubt her at every turn.

These thoughts ran through her head as the car descended the ramp to the underground parking at the BetHi offices. She had a MalTech appointment that afternoon and, as the new prestigious offices in St Julian's had yet to be opened, had arranged to meet in her old office in Paceville.

The meeting was with the deputy editor of the *Malta Telegraph*. Amy Halliday wanted to do a profile piece on Malta's up and coming new businesswoman. Such PR pieces were usually anathema to Natasha. However, with MalTech being what it was, her new PR agency had told her she needed to start to engage more with the press and develop a personal profile, so, with a resigned sigh, she had agreed to the interview.

The two women met, shook hands and then Natasha directed Amy to the low sofas, set either side of a glass coffee table, from which there were panoramic views over St George's Bay.

They chatted generally about Natasha's background, being brought up in the *castello*, her education on the island and, later, in Italy and in California. Amy pushed her on what it was like to be a woman in the upper echelons of commercial life in Malta and whether she had experienced sexism or unfair treatment at the hands of men. Natasha made some bland statement about the gallantry and good manners of Maltese gentlemen, which she hoped did not sound too patronising.

Then the conversation started to take an awkward turn. It seemed Amy was interested in the origins of the Bonnici family and how it had made its money.

"So, the Bonnicis … it's rumoured you go back a very long way – what can you tell me about that?"

Natasha blagged her way through the family's history, careful to recount how its wealth had all been lost after the First World War, until her grandfather had restored their fortunes in the post-Second World War era of reconstruction.

"Well, yes, but the Bonnicis have invested hundreds of millions of euros in MalTech. Where did that sort of money come from?"

Natasha was ready for the question, but knew she had no convincing answer available.

"Well, we haven't invested quite as much as that – I wish we had!" She laughed. "There's a syndicate of investors, which we're a part of. But, yes, it's a considerable amount of money."

"It's an unprecedentedly large amount for a group of private investors. Don't the Maltese public have a right to know who is behind the supply of their gas?"

"All I can say is, it's a group of private, and I stress *private*, investors. The source of our funds has been checked out by the regulators and the Department of Energy. Everyone's happy with the participating investor group."

"Well, Natasha, that's not true, is it? The investors hide behind a British Virgin Island trust, and those trusts are notorious for their lack of transparency. My research also tells me this company, BetHi, one of Europe's biggest i-Gaming companies, also hides behind a BVI trust. Why is everything around your business so secretive?"

Amy Halliday pushed and probed and Natasha batted away the enquiries. She could see the shape of the piece that would emerge. Eventually, she said: "Can we talk off the record for a minute?"

Amy turned off the digital recorder and smiled sweetly at her.

"Look, I can see where this is going, but the reason our affairs are so complicated is that, after World War One, as I've said, the family were nearly wiped out. My grandfather was determined that would never happen again, so he created a protective structure over the family's assets, which my father continues to use."

Amy nodded along, encouragingly.

"Now, I accept times have changed and so we're looking to move to a more transparent arrangement, but I can't tell you how complicated that is. Don't give me a hard time about it. Malta is a small island and I need friends like you. Can we be friends?"

"I do hope so, Natasha, but I'm going to have to touch on this issue – public interest and all that. Can I say you're looking to simplify …"

Suddenly, Natasha jumped in.

"No! Please, you can't say anything about the money. I don't want you setting hares running, do you understand? You do that and you'll be frozen out of every MalTech press conference, you'll never get a press release and you'll find some new members on your board of directors who won't take kindly to your unsupportive tone. Now do you understand me?"

Gobsmacked, Amy fell back in the sofa.

"Wow! Interesting. You *have* got something to hide!"

Natasha was furious with herself for losing her temper.

At that moment, the door opened and in walked Nick.

He hesitated, hand on the door handle, sensing the atmosphere in the room.

"Natasha, sorry to interrupt. I heard you were in and I thought …"

She stood up, composing herself instantly.

"Nick, nice to see you, come in. This is Amy Halliday from the *Malta Telegraph*, she's here doing a profile piece. Amy, I think you've probably got everything you need?"

Nick smiled at Amy and glanced at Natasha. He had spoken to Amy anonymously, when they were planting stories about the Russians, but they had never met.

Amy started to gather her things. She had been thrown out of better places than this. Interesting, though, how she had touched a raw nerve in Natasha during the interview.

Amy ignored the blatant attempt to get her out of the room and turned to face the newcomer.

"So, Mr Walker, how're you settling in? You were at BetSlick, weren't you? Welcome back. Actually, now I have you, maybe we could arrange to meet up so I can do a profile piece on you, too? New man at the helm of BetHi and so on. I'm sure the gaming community would be really interested. Exciting!"

Nick shrugged.

"Yes, of course, why let Natasha have all the action? It's good to be back, actually, I missed Malta. Gibraltar is small and very parochial – even compared to Malta!"

"Oh, so that's where you've come from, Gibraltar?"

"Yeah, I was there for four years – but anyway, we can talk about that later."

It did not take Amy more than a few seconds to connect his English-accented voice to her tip-off caller. So, Nick Walker was the source behind the leaks about the Russians and the VertWay pipeline. She had noted the Gibraltar international dialling code on one of the incoming calls. And standing behind him, scrutinising her very carefully, was Natasha Bonnici.

Well, these certainly would be interesting profile pieces.

Natasha suddenly walked towards her, arms outstretched, and launched into a display of sisterhood.

"Well, so great of you to come, Amy, many thanks and I can't wait to see the draft!"

Amy hung back, avoiding the attempt at an embrace.

"I'm afraid I don't work like that, Natasha – but I'm sure you'll love the piece once it's in print!"

Natasha dropped her smile.

"I can't wait."

The door shut behind Amy while Nick and Natasha turned to face each other. She was silent, her face fixed, unsmiling.

"She's trouble, that woman. She was fishing."

"She's a journalist, for Christ's sake, that's what they do! Your problem is, you're just too used to ordering people around and getting your own way."

"Maybe, but I lost it with her. I've got to sharpen up. I can't go round being bettered by the likes of Amy bloody Halliday. And you be careful with her, I think she's worked out you were the mystery caller."

"Really? Maybe I shouldn't have mentioned Gib."

"Just avoid her and don't do the profile piece. We don't want the whole oil-smuggling thing being brought up again."

Nick flicked back a lock of his blond hair.

"You're just jealous!"

Natasha smiled at him. Being with Nick always improved her mood.

"Please, she's old enough to be your mother!"

"Yeah, but she's kept herself in good shape. Anyway, come on, welcome me back, have a drink with me. Let's slum it in Paceville!"

"OK. Oh, by the way, I've got news."

"Yes?"

"Sergio's back!"

Nick stopped in his tracks.

"What? You told me he was dead?"

"I know. I was wrong."

As Nick stood there, flummoxed, Natasha grabbed her bag and headed out. Nick's good mood started to ebb away. He saw Sergio as an uncultured, Sicilian Mafia boss and had not been upset when Natasha first told him he was dead. But she had been 'wrong', apparently. Natasha Bonnici, who never made the same screw-ups as ordinary mortals. The first feelings of anxiety about his return to Malta started to pump through Nick's veins.

As Natasha entered the ladies' cloakroom, her phone buzzed in her handbag. It was Camilleri.

"I have some information for you. You asked me to find out the whereabouts of Saviour Azzopardi. I think I have been successful."

"Gerald, how clever of you! And where might I find the little squirt?"

"Well, he's obviously turned over a new leaf. We found him trying to lift kettlebells in a no-nonsense gym off the Sliema promenade. Apparently, he is friendly with the owner, a Polish lady, Danka Bijak, and is tucked up in her flat around the corner. I will text you the address."

She pondered this for a moment, gazing at her phone, then went to her contacts and set up a meeting with *Il-Barri*.

CHAPTER 56
GEORGE ZAMMIT
MARSABAR, LIBYA

GEORGE CLAMBERED down the steep gangway from the *Lorelei* onto the quayside in the Port of Tripoli. The waters of the port were an oily green colour, thick with plastic waste, discarded packaging and, to his disgust, a bloated, dead sheep, its four legs poking upright, the gas in its swollen belly providing buoyancy. The papers Natasha had given him contained a map, which pointed out the silver domes on the top of the brick-red towers of the Central Bank of Libya, visible from the quayside, on the other side of the busy road that ran along the coast.

The sun was up and the heat was already building, lifting the fetid aromas off the greasy dock. He wished he was standing back in Malta's Grand Harbour, which was fresh as a mountain lake by comparison. The port was quiet, with a few small container ships and a bulk carrier moored along the wharfs. Some local fishing boats were unloading the morning's catch. The only other activity centred on the travelling crane that had set about the relatively small job of lifting the pallets of wooden packing crates from the *Lorelei* onto the wharf.

There, a forklift waited to load the crates onto two curtain-sided wagons, their drivers chatting with a security guard and smoking cigarettes. The whole atmosphere was totally relaxed; the only person showing any sign of tension was George.

Natasha Bonnici's instructions clearly said that, on arrival, he had to ring the Central Bank and three armoured trucks would be sent, with an armed escort, to transport the crates the short distance to the bank premises. Only then could unloading from the ship begin. He had made the call, but the crates were already being lifted up and out of the holds and dumped onto the quayside.

The contingent of armed policemen who had accompanied George were watching proceedings from the ship's rail. They had been ordered not to go ashore in Tripoli and to maintain security from the ship.

George was starting to panic when he heard a voice behind him.

"Relax, my brother! You look like you have robbed a bank! Be calm. How are you, my friend? It is always good to see you."

George spun around.

"What are you doing here?"

Nothing in the papers had said Abdullah would meet them on the quayside. His friend wandered over to him, cigarette in hand and looked thoughtfully at the cargo.

"I thought there would be more. Bigger boxes. More boxes. You know? Are you sure that is all there is?"

"No, there was a lot more, but I stopped in Lampedusa and took half for myself. Is it every day somebody gives you a billion dinars?"

"Shhh! Be quiet!" Abdullah pulled a warning expression. "It is a cargo of guns and parts for the Toyotas – that is what I have told them." He nodded towards the drivers. "That is why there will be no worries, no gossip and no trouble!"

"So, you know what we are doing with it? Why are those trucks there?"

"Hah! Now that is a better question!"

"You know we are putting this money in the bank?"

"No, I think not. You remember Gaddafi's family stole billions of dinars from the Central Bank in Tripoli? That bank." Abdullah pointed to the imposing building in the distance. "So I know that place is not safe."

"Then if not the bank, where?"

"Caves!"

"No, no, no! Abdullah, no!" George pulled his friend towards him, by his sleeve, and whispered, "It's a billion dinars – you can't keep it in a cave! I'm responsible for that money. I've got my instructions and that money goes into that bank."

"Yes, that is why it is such a good thing you and I are brothers, because you know I am right about this. Look, if Boutros takes Tripoli, or somebody else, where is the first place they will go, eh?

"Yes, to the bank to steal my money! No, we go to the caves in Nafusa Hills and my brother-in-law will keep it safe."

"It's not your money," George hissed. "It's available to you, but it's not yours. If you like, it's my money – and it's going into the bank. A billion dollars will earn a lot of interest. You can't earn interest in a cave!"

Abdullah was shocked.

"You cannot do that, it is *riba, haram*! Muslims do not do this!"

At that moment, four armoured trucks drove through the port gates and made their way towards the *Lorelei*. George heaved a sigh of relief.

"Take your trucks and go. That money goes to the bank!"

Abdullah cursed and grabbed him by the shirt.

"You are mistaken, my friend. This is not wise. If this money is stolen, then a great opportunity will be lost."

George brushed his hand away.

"There's a bigger chance it'll be lost if you hide it in the hills. It's your job to defend Tripoli. That's how you stop the money being stolen – not by hiding it in a cave!"

Abdullah cursed and glared at him.

"In front of the bank there," he pointed to the left of the bank building, "is the Saraya Lake. It is in a park where you can sit and cool your feet. On the south side, there is an icecream seller. I will meet you there, after you have given my money to General Boutros."

George sighed.

"OK. But it'll take the rest of the day for them to count the money and sign all the papers."

It did take the best part of the day for the thirty tellers at the Central Bank of Libya to run twenty million individual fifty-dinar banknotes through the electronic money detectors and counting machines. Ivan Karavayev of the Goznak Print Works, Moscow, would have been pleased, as all bar two dozen of them were accepted. All twenty million notes, less twenty-four, were rebound in paper wrappers of 1,000 dinars, replaced in their wooden cases and wheeled into the bank's underground vault.

George signed the paperwork and smiled to himself, as he realised he was now the signatory to one of the biggest bank accounts in the world! It did not quite work so simply, of course. There was a complex authentication and second authority process to follow before any money was released, but the thought amused him.

Given it was now evening, he was surprised when he entered the grounds around Saraya Lake, to see Abdullah squatting on his heels, chatting to the icecream vendor.

"Have you been waiting all this time?"

"No, I have just arrived. I have been shopping. There are many exciting shops in Tripoli! I paid a little baksheesh to the bank security guard and he called me when you left. So, we must hurry or we will be late."

"Where're we going?"

"I will tell you on the way! You will be very happy."

Abdullah threw a backpack at George. He looked inside and saw his laundered long blue Tuareg robe, a *cheche* turban and a pair of sandals.

"There is a toilet over by the gate. The floor is swimming, but you can change quickly in there."

"Where're we going, Abdullah? I don't work for the Malta Pulizija anymore – I don't have to take instructions from you, Camilleri or anybody except Signorina Bonnici. So tell me!"

Abdullah looked hurt.

"I have a special trip planned for us both, to be together as brothers – and you say you will not come?"

"Not unless you first tell me where we're going."

"We are going to kill Abu Muhammad! Just you and me. To make things right, *Inshallah*."

George could not believe what he had just heard. They argued and they fought, face to face, showering spittle over each other as they batted words backwards and forwards.

Eventually, after twenty minutes, Abdullah fell silent for a moment, his eyes cast down, before saying, "I will go alone then. Even though, without you, my plan is no good. But if you refuse to help me, I will still go and maybe die trying, because it must be done – finished!

"If I die, then you will have failed me and your people in Malta. Who will protect the oil then, eh? Who do you trust, eh? Who will fight the Beards and look after the people in Marsabar? You?

"You go and tell everyone that now they must trust the government to protect them, *Inshallah*! Please, you leave and tell Rania I have gone and tell her why you are not with me, as I promised her you would be! Go!"

George slumped against the wall of the walkway around the lake. Without looking back, Abdullah started walking down the path to the park exit. George watched him go. With a shake of his head, he set off in the other direction.

CHAPTER 57
ABDULLAH BELKACEM
JEBEL UWEINAT MOUNTAINS,
SOUTH-EAST LIBYA

IT HAD TAKEN Abdullah several days and nights to skirt the northern sands of the Sahara and drive the 2,000 kilometres from Marsabar to the mountains that straddled the border of Libya, Egypt and Sudan. There were easier routes but, in Libya, to head east was to head into trouble, so Abdullah drove south to Ubari, where they rested. Then onwards, west, parallel to the border with Chad. On arriving in the Jebel Uweinat Mountains, he drove through a volcanic landscape with alternating bare rocky plateaux and rolling sandy plains. The land was sparsely populated: harsh, arid and inhospitable.

At times, the Land Cruiser had struggled with the extremes of the journey and George had regretted every minute spent inside it. Back in Tripoli, he had got as far as the park's northern gates, at which point he had turned around and jogged back to find Abdullah. The one thing he had not been able to face was going back to Marsabar and telling Rania he had let her husband go alone to confront Muhammad. He knew Abdullah had pulled a dirty trick, but it had worked.

He hated having allowed himself to be manipulated in this way and thought about his own family. Marianna had been expecting him home days ago, but she had been told George had been asked to stay on to help devise policing strategies in Tripoli. She would have been horrified if she had known half of what was happening.

It seemed to him that what they were doing was pointless. If Abdullah knew where to find Abu Muhammad, why not get the Americans to bomb him in the same way as they had hit the camp in the Nafusa Hills? When asked this, Abdullah had merely said that would be dishonourable and it was better done this way – whatever *this way* turned out to be!

George did not want to think of the treatment they would receive if Muhammad got his hands on him for a second time. He remembered the beatings and the concrete box they had kept him in, to freeze him at night and cook him during the day. He had decided he would rather kill himself than go through that again. This prompted him to ask Abdullah for a side arm, which was kept in the dashboard compartment. In the hours of darkness, when his mood was at its lowest, George wondered if he would have the guts to use it against himself, should the time come.

He had tried to persuade Abdullah to turn back, on several occasions, but was met with a silence as profound as the emptiness of the desert they were driving through. He was scared and exhausted. Jolting over the rough terrain had battered and bruised him, his teeth were on edge, and the few hours of sleep they had snatched had made them both bad-tempered and irritable.

Abdullah had refused to discuss the plan with George, which had wound him up even more and thrown him into a prolonged sulk that had already lasted several days. They spoke little, each passing the indeterminable hours daydreaming and watching the bleak, windswept landscape change from rock to sand and back again.

Abdullah seemed to be following some coordinates on a GPS, not a map, so George did not really know where they were, although he believed they should be somewhere near the

Sudanese and Egyptian border. He was not wrong. When he saw high mountains appear in the distance, he guessed they must be the Uweinat Mountains, which rose to 2,000 metres above the Western Egyptian desert.

That night, they stopped early and Abdullah made them change out of their robes and turbans into desert camouflage jackets and trousers. He threw a brown and tan net over the Land Cruiser and announced there would be no hot food that night as tomorrow they would put the plan into action. He told George they were close to Muhammad's camp and would have to be careful from now on. Abdullah pulled a long rigid metal case from the boot and put it in front of George, who was sitting in the dirt, leaning against a dusty tyre.

"You look inside and do what you have to do."

George watched Abdullah stalk off, then turned his attention to the case.

He opened it and saw that it contained an M24 Army sniper rifle, with hollowed out, large-calibre shells. There was also a small tablet containing a US Army Sniper tutorial, that helped shooters calculate and set up the gun to account for elevation, spindrift, wind speed and air density, to get the perfect shot.

George looked at Abdullah.

"*Mela!* What am I supposed to do with this?"

His friend came over and squatted down in front of him.

"Every morning at daybreak, when the air is still and before the heat builds humidity, Muhammad leaves his tent to pray. He looks north to the *qibla*, towards the city of Mecca. To the northeast of him there is a ridge." He turned and pointed behind them. "From there, it is a clear shot for a man with a good eye and a steady hand.

"It will be your honour to kill him for me and avenge Tareq, *Inshallah*. And I shall be forever grateful to you."

He looked George straight in the eye as he spoke, and George realised this was the plan and Abdullah would not deviate from it.

"You are joking? How far is it from the ridge to the prayer mat?"

"It is less than a thousand metres."

George gasped.

"A thousand metres? I can't do that! Are you crazy?"

Abdullah held his gaze.

"You have the eye. You have the gun. And you have Allah's blessing. You cannot miss!"

"And you, a Muslim, are happy that we shoot a man at prayer? That's the plan?"

"Prayer will not draw Abu Muhammad closer to God. That man lost Allah's love many years ago. I have prayed on it and I am certain."

"If you say so. Seems wrong to me. Say I hit him – which is very unlikely – what happens then? We get chased across the Sahara for a thousand miles by a mob in technicals?"

"No. You kill him then this happens."

From a canvas holdall, he pulled out a short stubby weapon with a shoulder stock.

"It is a laser sighting gun. It paints the target for the Warthogs. They will come immediately and bomb the camp. Tomorrow morning, either way, Muhammad's jihadis will die. But Abu Muhammad himself must die by our hand."

With that, Abdullah got up and walked a little way away, squatting on his heels in the way he did. He lit a cigarette, lost in his own thoughts.

George took the rifle, with its over-long barrel and rest, out of the case. He fitted the scope and spent the rest of the evening reading from the tablet and making necessary adjustments to the scopes and the set up. A ballistic calculator had already prepared the settings for a one thousand-metre shot, in a light northerly wind, medium humidity at an early-morning temperature of ten degrees centigrade. George read from the program that, to compensate for air density, gravity and humidity, he would, in reality, be aiming the shot some ten metres above

Muhammad's head and relying on these calculations to make the bullet's trajectory fall nicely in line with Abu Muhammad's skull.

The bullets were a larger calibre than George had seen before, as a longer shot needed more propellant. He lay on the stony ground, loaded the weapon and checked the balance and the fit of the stock to his shoulder. Then he stripped the rifle down, removed the cartridge, cleaned and oiled the gun and replaced it in the carrying bag.

He walked across to where Abdullah was chewing on a supper of bread and goat's cheese.

"Abdullah, I think it's one chance in a hundred I can hit a man at a thousand metres. You'd better make sure your painting thing has a full charge; we're going to need it. If we're going to do this, we'll need to be there before first light to get set up."

Abdullah smiled grimly. "You hit him first shot; if not, the second or the third, and you will go on until there are no bullets left. It is Allah's will. You will hit him, I am sure of it."

George looked at him doubtfully. Abdullah said: "Listen, the prayers before sunrise are called *Salah*. It starts and Abu Muhammad will stand and bring his hands to the level of his ears. Like this." Abdullah demonstrated the posture. "This is when you get ready. This is the *Takbir* and it lasts maybe five to ten seconds.

"Next, he will recite longer verses and will become more relaxed. This is the *Qayum*. He will cross his arms over his chest and breathe deeply." Again, he demonstrated the position. "This he will hold for forty to sixty seconds, depending on how fast he speaks. This is when you take the shot. After this, there are many ups and downs and it is no good for the shooting.

"So, I will watch through the binoculars and I will say, '*Takbir*', and you will get ready. Then I will say '*Qayum*', and you have thirty seconds to kill him.

"Then I will paint the site with lasers and we will run down the mountain, happy and joyful. *Inshallah!*"

Abdullah smiled widely and grabbed George by the shoulder.

"It is good to be with a brother on this day."

George had to turn away. He had gone pale and felt a little faint. This was cold-blooded murder, even though Abdullah was completely oblivious to the fact. George had no love for Abu Muhammad and had wished him dead many times during his captivity in the Chadian desert, but this – this was too much. He tried to convince himself it was just another competition on the range in Pembroke and that there would not be a man in his sights, only a paper target, but he felt his hands start to shake.

―――

In the early hours, the two men started the scramble up to the ridge. Abdullah had said there were no lookouts at night as the militia relied on the remoteness of their camp. Had it not been for surveillance drones operating out of Ubari, they would probably never have found it.

Abdullah had a thermal imaging monocular that he used to scout ahead of them, but everything was still and calm, apart from the noise of their footsteps sliding on the loose rocks. They climbed slowly for some hours. There was no path and Abdullah stopped frequently to check his GPS then disappear for minutes at a time, to find a way around cliffs and steep ravines.

The first light was only just starting to bring definition to the landscape when Abdullah turned and beckoned George to get down. He checked the GPS for the hundredth time and, after moving some metres to the west, nodded to his friend and shed his pack. George looked down over the top of the ridge and into the valley, where he could just make out the shape of a dozen tents shrouded in darkness, nestling in the ravine like small black boxes.

He felt calm and steady of hand as he opened the bag containing the long-barrelled rifle and assembled the firing system. He fitted the ten times magnification scope, set up the tripod and ensured the gun was correctly levelled and balanced. There was a grey foam mat to lie on and a desert-coloured camouflage net to put over himself and Abdullah, to break their outline and prevent sudden reflections from the metal objects they were assembling around them.

As the light of morning intensified, shapes started to emerge from the gloom. Black mounds became low-lying bushes and deep wedges of shadow morphed into rocky outcrops. George kept an eye on the shrubs and thin reedy grasses, to watch for any sign of an early-morning breeze but, as the instructions had assumed, everything was still.

There was no sign of his nerves of the previous day. He had settled into a comfortable position and surveyed the camp through the scope. Abdullah was lying next to him with his eyes pressed to the binoculars. He was mumbling to himself.

"What are you saying?"

"Hush! I am doing *Salah*, it is sunrise, I am praying."

"We are about to commit murder and you think that will do you any good?"

"The best revenge is to improve yourself. That I have done, then we will kill him. It is allowed. Now let me finish my prayers."

George shook his head.

"If you're sure."

It was only a few minutes later that the tents started to empty and Muhammad's men drifted out into an empty space in front of them. Some urinated against the nearby rocks, others lit cigarettes and talked in small groups. The tall, rangy figure of Muhammad was clearly recognisable in his long waistcoat, baggy white cotton trousers and pakol Afghan hat. Over the waistcoat, he wore a quilted jacket, to protect him from the morning chill.

They lay very still, facing to the south-west. Down below, the men formed up in lines, looking north-east, towards them and the *qibla*, the sacred building at Mecca, to which Muslims turn at prayer. Muhammad stood in the first line, giving a line of sight and a clear shot. Not for the first time, George realised a lot of thought had gone into this strike. He saw the fingerprints of Major Floyd Hamilton all over it.

George quickly settled down and adjusted his breathing. Abdullah whispered, "They will start soon."

George had checked his set up a dozen times and knew there was no more to be done and no time to do it anyway. It was down to him: his eye, his ability to control his heartbeat and his breathing.

He did not take his eye off the scope for over five minutes and was in an almost serene state of mind. He had decided his strategy last night and had come to terms with his decision. His conscience was clear.

Muhammad started the prayers. His voice was faint, but they could hear the rise and fall of his intonations. Given how few of them there were, he was not using a microphone and speaker.

George watched Muhammad raise his hands to either side of his head.

Abdullah whispered: "*Takbir!*"

George did not move, but kept his eye looking down the scope. Muhammad's voice continued until George saw him pause and drop his arms and fold them over his chest.

"*Qayum!*"

He watched, saw Muhammad bow his head and the top of his pakol fell into the crosshairs of the scope. The adjustments had been made for the bullet drop, for a shot of 1,000 metres. George took a last short breath through his mouth, held it and squeezed the trigger. As he did so, the first finger of his left hand twitched ever so slightly, enough, he hoped, to send the shot over the head of Muhammad and out of harm's way. He could not commit cold-blooded murder. Let the Warthogs flatten the place, Abu Muhammad deserved that, but not to die at George's hand while he was at prayer. He could not do it.

A bullet from an M24 travels at a supersonic speed, even after racing 1,000 metres through the atmosphere. This means it arrives at its destination before the sound of the shot is heard.

Muhammad heard nothing as the bullet ripped through his pakol and spun into his brain. Those behind him would not even have realised what had happened, until the crack of the shot echoed around the stillness of the valley. George looked up, shocked and open-mouthed. He lay frozen, watching while a crowd gathered around Abu Muhammad's prone body. Abdullah, a satisfied smile on his face, dropped his binoculars and coldly pointed the laser at the camp, dispersing the red dots around the tents.

Then he turned to face George.

"My brother, this is a wonderful moment and I am in your debt forever. It was the will of Allah, but it was by your hand!"

George was speechless as Abdullah shouldered the M24 rifle and pushed a pistol into his friend's hand.

"Now we must move quickly or this happy day could end badly!"

Above them, they heard the distant sound of aircraft approaching. They leaped to their feet and George followed Abdullah, who was scampering down the rocky ridge back towards the Land Cruiser. They had not gone far before the first explosion sent vibrations up through their feet and loosened a rockslide behind them. More explosions followed. Behind the ridge, smoke and dust started to rise as the two Warthogs screamed away into the distance.

Abdullah whooped and laughed, jumping from rock to rock. George was leaner and fitter than he had ever been, but this was a descent for youths and goats, not forty-five-year-old policemen. After thirty minutes, they rested and Abdullah scoured the mountainside through his binoculars for any sign of pursuit. Satisfied they were not being followed, he fell to his knees and prayed again, in thanks for their good fortune.

The first shock of seeing Muhammad hit was over. George

had tried to pull the shot, but the twitch of his finger against the barrel had just served to correct some miscalculation in the targeting. Knowing he was relieved of responsibility for the hit, he should have been pleased with himself, but could not shrug off the fact that he had just gunned down a man at prayer.

Abdullah, on the other hand, was euphoric, but in a world of his own. He prayed, he ran around like a child, he hugged George, he shouted into the sky, and then sat smiling, reliving the moment when a wait of four years had finally ended and he could begin to be at peace with himself.

CHAPTER 58
NATASHA BONNICI
INTERNATIONAL GARDEN HOTEL, TRIPOLI, LIBYA

As GEORGE and Abdullah were racing back along the southern Libyan border with Chad, chased only by the cloud of dust and the hail of stones the Land Cruiser was throwing high into the air, the great and the good of Libya's new energy sector were meeting in the banqueting suite of one of Tripoli's five-star hotels.

A host of lawyers from London and New York had prepared a dozen trestle tables, piled high with documents dealing with all the legal elements of the transactions. Many long days and nights had been spent bringing the parties to this point but, finally, the completion meeting was underway. There was a strict timetable for when each of the parties had to present themselves and the agenda for the meeting ran to thirty-five pages.

The Russians, represented by Valentin Petrov, were selling the assets of the companies that owned VertWay to a syndicate of American oil companies, funded by a host of international banks. Mike Lloyd was supervising some US Federal officials who were there to sign papers, waiving sanction regulations.

The Libyan Resources Corporation was signing supply agreements with the American energy companies and MalTech Energy. The bankers and the financiers, who represented the investors, were there to ensure the creation of legal securities and to organise the transfer of funds. The Maltese government were represented and formally delivered the permits and agreements to enable MalTech to bring the gas onshore.

Various accountants presented sets of numbers and financial documents that people signed, initialled, verified and authenticated. Gradually, the assembled parties worked their way through the paperwork.

Natasha sat to one side, having finished a mammoth signing session, speaking to no one but her British lawyer or else looking at her phone. Once Mike Lloyd had put his pen down and pushed a pile of twenty documents back to his attorneys, Petrov had sidled across to him and the pair of them walked to a corner of the banqueting suite, Mike rubbing his aching wrist.

He spoke first.

"I hate Tripoli, it's a shit house."

"Then you have never done business in Baku, Iraq or Syria. I tell you, here is like paradise!"

"You've got me there. Maybe someday I'll have the pleasure. So, I hear you've lost a lot of money recently."

Petrov looked around the busy room, avoiding eye contact with him.

"Do you have it?"

"No, money is one thing we're never short of. But I know who does."

"Really? You surprise me. That would be a very interesting thing to know, but why would you tell me?"

"I'm just that sort of guy. And d'you know what? I want nothing for the information, except your future goodwill."

"Well, the future depends on what you do today. So, you should tell me: who would steal money from Mother Russia's Mint? Who would risk her anger?"

Mike turned to look at Natasha, dressed in a white pant suit, with black patent heels, sitting quietly in a corner, avoiding all eye contact behind her large sunglasses.

Valentin Petrov said nothing for a while.

"Hmm. Her? I will consider this allegation and see if I believe it to be true. You know, if I think you are right, someone will learn a hard lesson."

"Don't upset the apple cart, Valentin. Remember, we're all gonna leave here as winners. And that's the sign of a good deal all round. No need for nastiness."

"Maybe, but this is not up to me. For me, the price has been too high. First, we are thrown overboard as partners, then they steal money from our Mint, taking us for fools. I cannot let us be treated in this way, no? I also think that you, too, want to see me make a punishment. Because, if not, why are you so helpful? Are we such good friends? I think not."

Mike Lloyd smiled, turned and casually walked over to where Natasha was sitting. She watched his approach from behind her sunglasses. Mike sat down on a chair next to her. Her lawyer discreetly rose and moved to another part of the room.

"Well, Ms Bonnici, you've done well for yourself. Congratulations! In the next year or so, I'll be seeing you in the Forbes Rich List. Camilleri said you were smart, but I don't think you're as clever as you'd like to believe."

Natasha took off her sunglasses and started cleaning them with a white silk handkerchief. She turned to Mike and smiled sweetly, ignoring the insult.

He had not even started.

"So, tell me about your little friend, Saviour Azzopardi?"

Natasha hesitated for a second before resuming the job of cleaning the sunglasses, still saying nothing.

"I can't work out how you found out about him, but I know you did. Your father knew we were going to steal the Russians' cash, so you had Savi hatch a plan to cut in and grab a load of Libyan dinars for yourself, to further your interests here."

Natasha looked at him and said: "I've no idea what you're talking about."

"You took Savi to that little church place, locked him up, fed the dumb fuck pizza and *pastizzi*, and put the squeeze on him. He fed me a load of bullshit, making me look like a jerk, while you diverted the ship to Constanta and grabbed the cash. Savi, God bless him, switched the container codes and, in Istanbul, we picked up a metal box filled with cheap men's coats. I became a laughing stock. So far so good?"

Natasha looked across the room, avoiding eye contact, and remained silent.

"No need to confirm it. I know what you did and I'm pissed. And you know what? I'm not half as mad as my friend Petrov over there."

Mike Lloyd glanced in Valentin Petrov's direction and Natasha saw the Russian acknowledge the look. Petrov then turned towards her and his icy stare made her realise what Mike Lloyd had done.

She could not breathe for a moment and felt herself start to shake.

"You fool, Lloyd! Don't you know what those people are capable of?"

"Sure I do. I see their work on mortuary slabs from time to time."

Natasha jumped up, grabbed her bag and hurried out of the room.

CHAPTER 59
NICK WALKER
OFFICES OF BETHI, PACEVILLE, MALTA

Amy Halliday was an accomplished journalist; in fact, she often thought her forensic approach to her work would have been better suited to the courtroom rather than a newspaper.

She was back in the office where she had interviewed Natasha Bonnici, only a week before. Amy admitted to herself she was excited and onto a good story. She knew there was something about Natasha, or the energy deal, that had spiked American interest. Mike Lloyd, she knew, was far too big a fish to be interested in a petty case of Maltese corruption. What it involved, exactly, she could not quite put her finger on.

Despite Natasha's warning, Nick had agreed to the interview with Amy Halliday, partly due to vanity, partly to raise his business profile – and partly to show Natasha he was his own man and would not be pushed around by her.

Nick had spent an hour talking about BetHi and his CV in the gaming industry. As far as the previous iteration of the business, BetSlick, was concerned, he had brushed aside the subject of its closure, saying he had learned some important lessons in staff supervision and systems of control, but had refused to go further.

Amy braced herself for the next part of the session.

"Who actually owns BetHi? Do you know?"

"No, not in detail, but it's privately owned."

"Do the Bonnicis own it?"

"They've got an interest, which is why Natasha took the CEO role, but I don't know the details."

"It's well known the Bonnicis have far-reaching cash-generative business interests in many parts of Europe. Do you think that's compatible with owning an i-Gaming business, which is an industry closely linked to money laundering?"

Nick laughed and slapped his knees.

"You really expect me to give an answer to that? Come on!"

"No, it's true. The Bonnicis, your friends and employers, are just about to take a huge stake in an international energy deal while, only four years ago, they were implicated in smuggling oil from Libya and your business was closed down as part of an anti-money-laundering operation. So I think I'm entitled to ask you, what's going on now?"

Nick brushed back his hair with his fingers and reclined against the sofa.

"Boy, you've got a head of steam on! I don't really know what you're driving at. I'm the CEO, I operate the day-to-day activities and report to the Board monthly. It's my job to run an efficient and compliant company and that's what I do. I can't help you with the rest of it."

"Hang on, you were the source who phoned and emailed me last year from Gibraltar, giving me information about the Russians' involvement in the Libyan oil and gas deal. Information you received from Natasha Bonnici, who wanted to switch out the Russians and bring in the Americans. I'm guessing you two have a more than a professional relationship. Am I right?"

Nick's expression froze and he felt his mouth dry up, making him incapable of speech. He hesitated for a few seconds, then jumped up and clapped his hands together.

"OK, we're done here, Amy. I've got nothing more for you. Please don't print any of this stuff – it'll only cause big trouble."

He walked to the door and held it open for her, a stiff smile on his face.

Amy gathered her bag and walked to the doorway, where she paused.

"Nick, it's not going to go away. When you're ready, ring me, please. I know I've got a story here. It's in the public interest for people to know what's going on with this gas deal in their own country. You seem like a decent type, don't let Natasha Bonnici drag you down."

After he had taken Amy to the lift and they had said curt goodbyes, Nick retired to his office and closed the door. He leaned back on his chair and put his feet on the edge of the desk, closing his eyes. He was not dozing, he was trying to decide what he should do next. His heart was beating quickly and his shirt was damp with sweat. It was only a matter of a week or two since his arrival back in Malta and already he could feel a steel trap closing in around him.

CHAPTER 60
NATASHA BONNICI
MARSABAR OIL AND GAS INDUSTRIAL COMPLEX, MARSABAR, LIBYA

THE IMPLIED THREAT from Petrov had badly scared Natasha. She went back to her room at the hotel, as quickly as she could, alert to possible threats around every corner. Her imagination ran riot. She feared poisoned umbrellas, toxin-coated door handles, lethal coffee capsules and much worse. She knew how easy it had been for Sergio to get the toxins that had killed Salvatore. It had taken only a matter of days to arrange for a local hoodlum to plant the bomb in Signore De Luca's car. These people were very security conscious and, still, they died.

Her first call was to Sergio, who tried to calm her down. He said he would speak to Petrov and offer some form of compensation. He assured her that if it was a question of an insult, that could always be sorted with money. It would be very expensive, but perhaps a cut of the profits from the gas sales into the EU system might do it. It would have to be more than a gesture, but he agreed it had to be done and quickly.

He suggested returning the dinars, but Natasha refused. She was adamant the cash was central to making their security arrangements in Libya work.

She said Sergio should make contact through Yaroslav, now he was back in Malta from Libya, and persuade him to take a longer-term view of things. He was a negotiator by nature and the obvious intermediary to placate Petrov and his damaged pride.

Natasha fell back onto the bed, relieved that there might yet be some way out of the mess she had created. Her next call was to Assistant Commissioner Camilleri, asking him to keep a special eye on Marco. She told him that she had received some serious threats from a Russian organised crime group and feared her father might be at risk. She asked him to place security at the *castello* and to suggest a replacement for Simon, who was now working exclusively with her. The Assistant Commissioner made all the right noises, but spent some time wondering how all this could have come about without him even being aware of it.

Natasha also wondered what she could do to teach Mike Lloyd that she was not a person to be messed with. The more she thought about Lloyd, the angrier she got, until the fury became unmanageable. She had to do some exercise, shower and force herself to calm down. There were still things to do that day.

A few hours later, in the middle of the afternoon, Simon came to get her for the trip to Marsabar. She had insisted that she wanted to see the oil and gas facility and meet the people in whom she had invested so much money. She had dressed in a two-piece, full-length, embroidered black kaftan, secured at the waist by a broad silk belt. She wore a black headscarf, wrapped loosely around her head and shoulders.

Simon raised an eyebrow when she left her room and joined him in the hotel corridor. She saw him looking her up and down as he took her luggage.

"Like it?"

"Yes, very suitable. Should be interesting to see what the helicopter downdraft does to it!"

"OK. I hadn't thought of that."

The black government limousine bullied its way through the chaotic afternoon traffic on the Second Ring Road to the Tripoli National Football stadium, that doubled as the government's heliport. Simon ensured the pilot did not start the engines until Natasha was onboard and then, with an unbelievable racket, the machine rose over the port and the old town, before turning west, into the sun, towards Marsabar.

Within twenty minutes, it was touching down at the Marsabar Industrial Complex, where she was met by the Chief Executive Officer, Adel Abu Khader, who ushered her and Simon into a freezing cold, brand new Mercedes SUV for a tour of the complex.

The process was complicated and Natasha did her best to follow the workflow and ask intelligent questions. Adel Abu Khader had little idea who she was or why she was visiting. He had received a message from the Libyan Resources Corporation with instructions to host a VIP visit, but that was all. He was perplexed about why she would even be interested in the facility, but did his patronising best to push on through the tour, without so much as stopping the Mercedes.

After fifteen minutes, Natasha asked the driver to pull up and go with Simon for a walk down the two-kilometre loading jetty. Khader was taken aback, not used to being ordered about in his own facility, especially by a woman.

"So, Mr Khader, is production running smoothly now?" she asked.

"Yes." He smiled broadly. "Many thousand barrels of oil and gas. Good production numbers."

"Well, just so you know, that's because my company, MalTech Energy, pay Abdullah Belkacem to protect your oil fields and your distribution pipelines. I've bought the rights to transport my product through the VertWay pipeline and the Malta Spur. I now buy all your gas and want to buy more.

"How has it been for the last four years, with IS in Marsabar interfering in the oil fields? How were production numbers then?"

He turned to look at her, any trace of a smile gone. The hardened face of an experienced oil man showed itself.

"Not good. In fact, very bad!" He shook his head. "Very bad! Why do you come here? You know the numbers; you know what we do, you know the problems. So, you think you and Abdullah Belkacem can fix Libyan problems?"

"No, not Libyan problems, but we can fix Marsabar problems and the problems of this complex and the Waha and Sharara oil fields. We want the same thing, Mr Khader. We want the gas to flow north through VertWay. I'm paying you and Abdullah Belkacem to make sure it does."

"You're paying me?"

"Yes, I know who you are. I know about your successes in the Niger Delta and in Venezuela. You're not some lazy government lackey; you can make this complex very successful, if the politics and security issues are managed. Leave those matters to me and Abdullah Belkacem. You concentrate on pumping oil and gas, lots of it. Someone will come to see you shortly and make sure you have enough money to forget about even receiving your government salary. Forget the local bribes and dealing with the oil smugglers. It's a new world, Mr Khader. I'll send people in to help you. If you need anything, you tell me. But you won't remain in post if the numbers fall or even stay the same – then, Libyan Resources Corporation or not, you'll be out. Work hard and enjoy it. Cheat me, Mr Khader, and you'll only ever do it once. This is to say hello!"

She handed over an envelope containing fifty thousand dinars in brand new, green fifty-dinar notes.

"Now, ask your driver to take me to the American camp. There'll be some security vehicles waiting for us at the gate."

CHAPTER 61
YAROSLAV BUKOV

BUTTIGIEG GARAGE, HAMRUN,
MALTA

Hamrun was a crowded inner-city suburb of Malta, just west of Valletta. Its narrow streets were a mix of two- and three-storey housing, food and clothing shops, hairdressers, florists and motor repair shops. In short, everything you could possibly want was tucked away in those congested back streets. If a business needed more space, or a larger access, then the front of a house was demolished and the dining room became, say, a butcher's shop or, in the case of Charles Buttigieg, a garage for the repair of marine outboard motors and mopeds.

What Buttigieg did not realise was that the competent and industrious Syrian who worked for him in the afternoons, while he rested upstairs, Jehad Al-Hafez, also used the space, and Buttigieg's tools, for the assembly of bombs. It was not a high-volume enterprise but, occasionally, local criminals or Italian Mafia types needed to settle scores and Jehad was the man to go to.

His time with the Syrian Army, in bomb disposal, had not only taught him how to clear vacated rebel towns of booby traps and roadside explosive devices, but had also given him valuable insight on how to construct the things in the first place.

It had been his handiwork that had scattered the body parts

of the US Chargé d'Affaires over St Julian's. Yaroslav had come across him through a Russian military acquaintance who knew Jehad to be a competent and discreet explosives man. The Russian had been impressed with his work in St Julian's and had no hesitation in using him again.

Yaroslav had no intention of handling the package personally, but had to visit the shop to pass on two envelopes. One contained money, the other a set of instructions and a photograph of Marco Bonnici.

Petrov did not intend to harm Natasha, as she could be valuable in the future, but Yaroslav had confirmed her father was less of a player these days and of little use, other than acting as the vehicle of their displeasure.

Once Jehad Al-Hafez had finished his shift with Charles Buttigieg, he waved a cheery good night and drove his scooter the short distance to an area of the Grand Harbour, near the defunct Marsa power station, called the South West Extension. Here disused, rusted iron structures and dilapidated buildings sat alongside moribund barges, tugs and small rusted tankers, awaiting the scrapman's blowtorch.

Across the wharf, a set of roller-shutter doors concealed a stainless-steel fabricator and pipe fitting shop, that was set into the limestone cliff face. Two old school friends had run the business for years, but were happy to undertake additional work, including the placing and detonation of explosive devices. Jehad Al-Hafez banged on the pressed aluminium slats of the roller door and, once it had squeaked and creaked upwards, handed over the envelope containing their instructions, together with half of the cash, to one of the brothers. He put the envelope with the remaining cash back into his pocket.

Having done that, he mounted the scooter and drove off to have his dinner in a small Lebanese café he knew in Hamrun.

CHAPTER 62
GEORGE ZAMMIT

THE AMERICAN CAMP, MARSABAR, LIBYA

Following the shooting of Abu Muhammad, it had taken George and Abdullah four long days to travel west along the back roads and tracks of southern Libya, before they felt safe enough to find tarmac and turn directly north. Abdullah was in a good mood throughout the journey, telling stories of his childhood and great Berber heroes of the past. He promised that, one day, children would talk of the great Maltese hero who had helped liberate Libya and how Allah himself had taken his hand and guided the shot that miraculously destroyed the face of evil itself!

"It is true, my friend, I saw it with my own eyes! I will fight anyone who says it is not true. The shot was over two thousand metres – never has there been such a shot! And there was wind, I felt it. The air was like molasses – thick with dew – slowing the bullet, but still it flew, fast and true, then dropped like a stone, into his head. I saw it myself!"

As they drove through the desert, the distance of the shot increased, the conditions worsened, the light dimmed and the hand of Allah became ever larger. George told Abdullah the death of anybody was no laughing matter and begged him to keep this between themselves. Abdullah swore at him, saying great stories such as this had to be told and the only way to silence him would be to rip out his tongue. By the time they drove into the camp, exhausted, filthy and hungry, a crowd was awaiting their return.

Abdullah went to Floyd Hamilton and embraced him, grinning from ear to ear.

"Thank you for the planes. The sound of the bombs falling on Muhammad's camp echoed around the mountains. I will never forget it. For me, it was a beautiful moment! It made everything perfect. Now we can get to work, making Marsabar a better place."

Floyd Hamilton turned to George, who was standing next to Rania.

"So you got him? With one shot? Hell, the Maltese Machine gun goes sniper! Amazing."

George said: "He was at prayer, Floyd. I shot a man at prayer. I can't say I'm proud of it and would prefer for it not to be mentioned too widely."

"Don't worry, George. I thought about that as well when we put the plan together. I know you had right on your side, and think of the lives you've saved. I'm thinking how many American lives you've probably saved. Good shot – that's what I say!"

Then Abdullah began telling a group of sceptical US Rangers his embellished version of events, until the major called a halt.

"OK, guys, I get it! I get it! Listen, you better go clean up. You've got a private visitor tonight. We thought you'd be back sooner, so I'm sorry it's a bit of a rush. Some Maltese VIP is calling in. Mrs Belkacem is making dinner and a chopper is coming to take her back to Tripoli at 22:00 hours."

"Her? A private visitor, to see us? Who is she?" asked George.

"Ms Bonnici. You know her, don't ya? She seems like a big deal."

George sighed.

"*Mela*, she is a big deal. And coming here? She's my new boss."

George and Abdullah went down to the shower block to

clean up. George decided to put on a clean robe and cloth turban and continue dressing in the local style. His dark beard was now thick and trimmed evenly across his face. He belted the robe with a canvas web military belt on which he hung his side arm. He remembered Harley telling him that army-issue nylon belts made you sweat. George had not been on a set of scales for some months, but he could tell he had lost even more weight and was not displeased at the tanned, scarred, chiselled face that stared back at him from the showerblock mirror.

It was dark as the Mercedes and the SUVs moved down the track between the tents. The Rangers stuck their heads out of the flaps to see who the VIP might be. Abdullah and Rania went to the awning of their tent, ready to greet the arrival.

The Mercedes stopped and Natasha stepped out into the dim lighting of the camp. George hung back, letting Abdullah take centre-stage and formally welcome his guest.

Natasha looked a million dollars in her black kaftan, but later Rania whispered to George: "She looked like a wanton widow at a funeral feast!"

Abdullah stepped forward and offered his hand in greeting.

"*Salam alaikum.*"

And she responded in Arabic.

"*Wa-alaikum salam.*"

Even though they were in a military tent in the middle of hectares of rough scrub, Natasha took off her shoes before stepping onto the ground sheet.

George watched Abdullah and Rania warm to her respectful manner. Abdullah's youngest son appeared with a bowl of water and a towel over his arm. They stood in silence as Natasha rolled up her sleeves, revealing bare arms devoid of her usual expensive watch and gold jewellery, and carefully rinsed the water over both hands and wrists. She took the towel and dabbed her hands and arms dry, returning the towel to the boy with a smile.

Only after completing the ritual did she sit on the canvas chair at the flimsy folding table, buckling under a huge bowl of couscous and diced vegetables. George appeared from the shadows and she flashed him a smile and a nod. He briefly plunged his fingers into the bowl of water and shook the drops onto the floor.

Natasha enquired about Abdullah and Rania's family, their children's health and education. Rania spoke at length, in good English, something George had not heard her do before in these situations. Abdullah was happy to allow it and smiled along, interjecting to keep the conversation going.

Natasha ate the couscous with a spoon, avoiding the high-risk alternative that Abdullah employed, of scooping up the grains with bread. She waited until everybody had finished before accepting the meat in gravy. It had taken George some time to learn Berber manners for family meals, but Natasha had taken care to come well prepared.

They spoke about the shop in Birkirkara, which Natasha knew, and they joked about how a shopkeeper could suddenly become such an important person! Abdullah replied that being a shopkeeper was an important job and that, without him, no houses in Malta would ever have been built and then where would all the children have lived? The meal had been a great success. When nobody could manage any further food, Rania left a bowl of fruit on the table and took the dishes back to the cook house, to wash up, leaving Natasha with the men. Abdullah lit a cigarette and watched her through a cloud of exhaled smoke.

"So, I thank you for your visit and your respect. It is good to know we work with someone who understands our ways. I know what it is you expect of me and I will act wisely for the people I have to serve, to make sure the oil and gas goes into the refinery and under the sea to Malta. You will not be disappointed in me."

"I do hope not. George is your friend, but you must listen to him because he'll be my voice. The money for the protection of the gas is safe and George controls it. It's not your money -- do you understand that? There'll be an office in Tripoli to help us look after our financial affairs. You must respect their instructions. When you need money, you ask, you don't just take. That's how you show respect to me.

"At any time, if you decide you don't like it, you can always go back to selling brushes in Birkirkara and your family can go back to hiding in the hills. I'll find somebody else to help me and you might not like who that is. Am I clear?"

Abdullah had the fierce pride of a Berber clan leader and was not used to being spoken to like that, especially by a woman. It was his country, his people, his fight. He lit another cigarette and glared at Natasha. George looked at him and caught his eye. The questioning look on George's face told him a response was required.

Abdullah made an effort, calmed himself and visibly relaxed in his chair.

"Yes, I understand, and I thank you for the chance to right the many wrongs that have happened here. I can do that, and I can get you your oil and gas as well. George will make sure everything is good!"

Natasha heard the helicopter chattering in the distance and rose, extending her hand to Abdullah.

"*Mashallah*," he told her. "Do you know what that means? It translates as 'what Allah has willed has happened'. Every time I pray, I thank him. And now, I thank you."

Natasha smiled.

"I'm so glad we got the chance to meet and that we now understand each other. Please, have your son fetch Rania. I can't leave without thanking her for the wonderful meal."

Abdullah shouted for the boy, who flew off down the track to fetch his mother.

Natasha took George by the arm and made it look as if he was leading her out of the tent. She spoke quietly in his ear.

"Desert life seems to be suiting you, George. You look like a different man, if I may say so! But, please don't get used to this and go native on me. Remember who you work for and what's at stake. I expect to see you back in Malta next week. Please wear a suit."

With that, Natasha walked off after saying a brief farewell to Rania, who had hurried back to the tent. The whole camp heard the sound of the chopper landing, its red flashing strobe and landing lights silhouetting the small group of people waiting in the scrub. Natasha met Simon at the stairs of the helicopter to help her aboard, holding her scarf and the back of her kaftan to avoid any embarrassing moments.

Abdullah watched the helicopter go. After the downdraft had calmed and the dust settled, he turned to George.

"So, she is not married?"

"No, she's not."

"That does not surprise me. She is a mantis; she would pull the head off a husband after mating."

CHAPTER 63
MARCO BONNICI
CASTELLO BONNICI, MALTA

MARCO HAD BEEN busy with the team from the auction house, sorting and packing items from the library to go to the Bibliotheca. The dust from age-old books and the smell of leather and tobacco had irritated his airways, making him sneeze and cough. The afternoon was hot and humid. Usually, the heat did not bother him, but the library was full of still air and his long-sleeved cotton shirt was damp with sweat.

He found it hard to believe that not only would he be leaving the *castello*, but the building itself was to be sold. It looked like a consortium of hoteliers would go ahead with the purchase, and the estate, as well as the castle itself, would be changed for ever. The building would be released from its role as an ancestral family home and freed to adopt a showier, more contemporary style.

He needed some air and walked out onto the terrace, to take in the view over St Paul's and beyond the escarpments, to the island of Gozo. As the time for his departure drew nearer, he was conscious of putting together a bank of memories: of the *castello*, of Malta and the people who had been around him here for so many years. It was something he could draw on in the future, when the *castello* was a hotel, spa and nine-hole golf course, and his terrace was littered with cheap metal tables, sporting branded parasols.

Sergio had been staying for over a week now, and was sitting on the terrace, working on his laptop, a neglected beer beside him. The pair had reconciled and enjoyed a few evenings to themselves, bringing each other up to date on what had been happening in their respective lives. It had not taken them long to re-establish the friendship that had endured for so many years.

Eventually, Sergio announced he needed cigarettes and rose from his chair, cracking his knuckles and stretching his arms high above his head.

"I do enjoy it here. I can't bear to think of this place not being yours! I'll miss it. I suppose I'll have to go back to Milan in a day or so, but thank you, as always, for your hospitality."

He looked at Marco.

"You know I think of us as brothers? We were twenty years old when we first met. D'you remember that day on Zio Nico's terrace? It's good to be back with you. You and I being apart was one of the hardest things about the last few years."

Marco laughed.

"Stop it, Sergio, or next you will start weeping. Go, get some cigarettes."

Marco reached into his pocket and threw him the keys to the white Range Rover. "If you are passing the garage, do me a favour and put some petrol in it, will you? It's running on fumes."

Sergio nodded and went out to the garages to find his friend's white Range Rover, whistling to himself as he went.

Marco went back to the library and found himself browsing through an original 1796 manuscript of the first ever Maltese-Latin-Italian dictionary, written by the father of the Maltese language, Mikiel Anton Vassalli.

He was soon immersed in the book, but raised his head when he heard a dull crump from outside on the road. He thought little of it and resumed his reading until Katia came dashing in, white-faced. The fact she said nothing but stood staring at him, speechless, told him something terrible had happened.

Marco dropped the priceless manuscript, ran out of the front door and through the open gates. In the ditch on the left-hand side of the road, totally engulfed in flames and blazing furiously, was the Range Rover. Marco went round to the driver's side of the vehicle, feeling the intense heat. He raised his arms to protect his face, but the hairs on his arms singed and he drew back a step or two, realising going any nearer to the inferno was futile. To his horror, he saw a blackened shape, slumped over the wheel, rocking gently back and forth as the flames sucked out whatever combustible fuel there was left in Sergio's body.

Still shaking, Marco pulled out his phone and rang Camilleri. He asked for help in finding Natasha, as soon as possible. Camilleri told him that he was on his way, but Natasha was in Libya, in the middle of the desert somewhere. He would contact her later, at her hotel.

Eventually, the Civil Protection teams extinguished the flames, took the shell of the car away. But not before the paramedics had gingerly removed what was left of Sergio's body. Camilleri supervised the process and, once the ambulance had disappeared down the hill, went into the *castello* to find Marco, who was sitting in the study with a brandy in his hand. Camilleri found the decanter and poured himself a drink.

"I have never seen you drink before," said Marco.

"I have never had a day like this before. I am sorry, Marco. This is a terrible thing. Especially cruel after his recent reappearance.

"I do not wish to state the obvious, but you do realise that little present was meant for you? Natasha rang me only hours ago. She said there was trouble brewing with our Russian friends. She asked me to put a guard on the *castello* and find you a new head of security. I am sorry, the warning came too late. Do you know what this is all about?"

Marco was slumped in his chair, the balloon of brandy cradled in both hands.

"I can guess. She stole the Russians' money, double crossed the Americans and got to their asset, Saviour Azzopardi. Somehow, the Russians have discovered her involvement."

"Yes, so I gathered. I assume she was also involved in the reorganisation of affairs in Milan?"

"I think that was mostly Sergio, but she was involved, yes."

"I cannot protect her if she carries on like this, Marco. She tells me nothing and then expects me to clean up her messes. She is out of control. She needs speaking to."

"Then you will have to redefine your relationship with her, Gerald. She does not listen to me anymore."

Gerald Camilleri did not do full on anger. He did not shout and rage, but developed deep and visceral hatreds that smouldered with all the intensity of hot coals. At that moment, this was the feeling he felt for Petrov, Yaroslav, and all things Russian. In fact, he could easily have let it spread to the ill-mannered Mike Lloyd, but subconsciously he realised he had to contain the parameters of his anger, to concentrate it, focusing it on the people who deserved to feel it the most.

Camilleri telephoned his office and the Pulizija posts at the airport and ferry terminals. He knew Valentin Petrov was in Libya, Natasha had told him as much. That left Yaroslav Bukov. This had to be his work. Malta was a small island, with complex webs of loyalties, stretching across families and communities. This could make police work infuriatingly difficult but, on this occasion, it could work to his benefit; there would be no vows of silence to protect a murdering Russian FSB officer.

He ordered calls to be made to the hotels, the casinos and the better restaurants. He wanted forty-eight hours of total dedication to finding Yaroslav Bukov. Nothing less. Every hooligan, miscreant, career criminal, was to be bullied and harangued. They were to be beaten, bribed, granted favours ... whatever they wanted. Camilleri wanted Yaroslav Bukov and he gave himself just forty-eight hours to find him.

There were not many people in Malta who knew how to put a car bomb together and the name of Jehad Al-Hafez was soon mentioned. The Rapid Intervention Squad blocked both ends of the street where Buttigieg's Garage was situated. They entered, crashing back the doors, wearing full riot gear, guns pointing. Jehad was changing the fuel pump on a Honda outboard engine.

He was promised immunity and freedom from arrest, in exchange for information. He quickly told them what he knew and mentally started planning to leave the island as soon as he could. They demanded to see the papers and the cash Yaroslav had left in payment. Jehad had handed the instruction papers over to the brothers at the docks, but gave the Pulizija what little there was left of the cash in the second envelope.

Yaroslav's one mistake had been to use an envelope from the stock of stationery left on the dresser in his hotel room. How such an experienced professional failed to notice the name of the hotel on the back of the envelope was a mystery Camilleri could not fathom.

CHAPTER 64
DANKA BIJAK'S APARTMENT
SLIEMA, MALTA

SAVI AND DANKA were in the middle of a two-player mission on the latest *Call of Duty* game, enjoying a couple of cans of lager and the excitement of the action. It was mid-afternoon and Danka was relaxing before the after-work crowd arrived for the early-evening sessions at the gym. She still had her training gear on from the morning sessions and her tattooed arms rippled with muscle from six hours a day of strenuous upper-body exercise.

Savi had been staying with her for the last few weeks and the pair had started to enjoy each other's company. Danka saw Savi as an overgrown child, the antithesis of the muscle-bound, macho types she worked with at the gym. He sometimes joined her classes in the studio and greatly amused Danka with his half-hearted attempts at working out. He always chose the heaviest kettlebells and desperately tried to follow the exercises, his face twisted in pain as his skinny white arms strained and heaved, while Danka shouted instructions and counted repetitions. She noted he had showed no sign of making any moves to leave so far and Simon had merely shrugged his shoulders when she asked him what plans he had for the boy.

Savi suddenly paused the computer game and turned on the

sofa to look at the door, listening intently. He put his finger to his lips.

"Did you hear that? There's someone shuffling around outside."

The pair of them stopped and listened. There was nothing audible, until somebody tapped lightly on the door. They glanced at each other and Danka said, "Go see who it is."

She picked up a three-kilogram dumbbell that lay next to her on the sofa and absent-mindedly began doing some bicep curls.

Savi had barely turned the latch when *Il-Barri* shoulder-charged through the doorway and stumbled into the room, knocking Savi backwards off his feet. The smell of gutted fish and sweat followed him. He snorted at Danka and grunted "Stay!" while pulling a short knife from the back of his jeans. Savi scurried across the floor towards Danka, on his hands and feet, like an upside-down crab, as *Il-Barri* lumbered towards him, holding the knife dagger-style.

What the hitman had not taken into account was that Danka was not the sort of woman to shy away from a fight. With a roar, she leaped up from the sofa and collided with the brute, swinging the weighty dumbbell against the side of his head. Dazed and semi-conscious, he lay on the floor, wondering what had hit him.

Danka stood over him, dumbbell raised, daring him to make another move.

Gathering such courage as he had, Savi approached and gave *Il-Barri* a tentative kick in the pelvis then quickly stepped back. Danka took two handfuls of *Il-Barri*'s denim jacket and heaved him to his feet, putting one hand tight to his throat. He did not look at her but stared beyond her, off into the middle distance. She noticed, with disgust, the glistening fish scales in his short, sweat-plastered hair.

She said to him: "You get out of here, now! If you think I'm tough, you wait till you see my boyfriend. You're lucky he's not here, he would've killed you! Now go. And if I see you here again, I'll make an even bigger fool out of you."

Savi added from a fair distance away: "Yeah, you go. Fuck off or there'll be more trouble."

Danka bundled him out of the door and double locked it, propping a dining chair against the handle.

Savi sat back down on the sofa and picked up the X-Box controller, saying: "Phew, what the hell did he want? We showed him – yeah? So, what's his problem? You owe him some money or something?"

Danka replied, "Fun's over, Savi. You'd better think about finding somewhere safe to hide. That guy was serious and it was you he was after."

He paused the game and looked at her.

"Shit, you think so? What've I done?" He ran his fingers through his lank, stringy hair. "I suppose I do know what it's all about. There was this woman … we had a bit of a thing. She's just mad I skipped off and left her without a goodbye or anything. Are all women like that?"

Danka looked at him for a moment, in disbelief.

"You can't be serious?"

Savi played his game for a few seconds, then hit pause again.

"You know, I've been giving the future a lot of thought. It's time for me to make some big moves. I've been thinking about a university in England. There's a computer-science course that looks kinda cool. I've got money put by and the CIA guy promised me five grand. It's waiting for me at the embassy and now, I suppose, all this trouble should give me the motivation."

"Savi, you don't really think they're going to hand over five thousand dollars to you, after what you did to them, do you?"

He looked at her for a moment and shrugged.

"Yeah, suppose you're right, they're probably pissed off with me. Just hoped he might … you know? Anyway, I can always make some cash online. I'll get my shit together and move out. I don't want to be a hassle to you guys – and I definitely don't want to be here by myself, in case he comes back, you know? Next time, I might not be able to hold back and someone could get hurt.

"Can you ask Simon to come down? I'd like to say thanks to him as well, for sorting me out. I think it's going to be all good from now on."

It was a great plan, but there was a problem with it. In fact, there were quite a few problems with it. Savi had left school when he was sixteen. In the May he was due to sit his 'O' levels, Rockstar Games were stupid enough to release *Red Dead Redemption*. What could he do? It took him the full two weeks of the exam timetable to complete the game. He never did return to school and had no qualifications. Still, he would work something out.

Danka went across the room to a drawer in a sideboard and took out a white A5 envelope.

"Before you go, Simon said you might find this useful."

"What's that?"

"Your passport, your ID card and two grand of Simon's own money, to help you on your way."

"Oh, yeah! Cool. Thanks a lot. No hurry though, is there?"

CHAPTER 65
MIKE LLOYD
EMBASSY OF THE UNITED STATES, MALTA

TWO MONTHS LATER

It was just into the New Year and unseasonably warm when, for the second time in his life, George found himself being honoured with a medal for his courage and bravery. George, Marianna, Denzel and Gina, plus her fiancé Giorgio, were seated in the front row of the huge Reception Room of the purpose-built US Embassy, on land adjacent to the old World War II airfield at Ta'Qali. George was to be formally presented with the Army Distinguished Service Cross, the highest honour awarded to a non-US Citizen.

The event was not as grand as the presentation in the Throne Room of the Grandmaster's Palace in Valletta, where he had received his first medal, four years ago, but Marianna and Gina had behaved as if they were guests of honour at a White House reception. The purchase of new hats, shoes and handbags had been endlessly debated, and finally, the ladies had decided they needed to visit the outlets of Catania, in Sicily, to find suitable outfits. Denzel, meanwhile, looked smart in his Pulizija dress uniform.

The top people from the Embassy were present and they had

brought in Major Floyd Hamilton and, for some reason, Sergeant Mike Barrasso, from the Al-Udeid desert training camp. The sergeant looked over at George, all buffed up with his new suit and shiny beard. He caught George's eye and, while his poker face remained unchanged, gave him the slightest of winks.

The Maltese government was represented by the Deputy Prime Minister, the defence minister and numerous other officials, enough to fill one side of the hall. American diplomats in suits, led by Mike Lloyd, and military representatives in uniform, took up the other side of the aisle. The new Chargé d'Affaires conducted the ceremony and started by praising George's work, as a former police officer, in responding to the bomb attack on his predecessor.

The story of Abu Muhammad's IS assault on the airfield was recounted, as was George's heroic one-man defence of the terminal, a selfless stand that put his life in mortal danger but saved many Americans. At that point, the Chargé d'Affaires handed the podium over to an unsmiling Sergeant Barrasso who explained that George had been a successful candidate on his Desert Warfare and Survival course. His performance on the shooting range had been exceptional and he had acquired all the skills necessary to execute missions in a hostile desert environment.

George could not help but lower his head to hide a smile as he remembered the disastrous weeks he had spent being shouted at and abused by this man. When the sergeant stiffly left the podium, face expressionless, to come and shake George's hand, he smiled broadly while Barrasso's mouth twitched.

George was now a civilian and Head of Libyan Relations for MalTech Energy, so he wore his new blue business suit, with his police medals pinned to his left breast. He sported a brilliant white new tooth, to replace the one lost in the beating at the air terminal, implanted at the cost of the Maltese government. His beard and hair were trimmed and oiled, in the style Abdullah favoured. Rania and Marianna had both told him, in no uncertain terms, it would be a shame if his waistline went back to how it had been before his desert adventures.

On his return to Malta, he and Marianna had cleared out his old clothes and George had joined her and Gina on the shopping trip to Catania, where they had fussed around him, putting together a new wardrobe of slim-fitting suits and on-trend casual clothes. When Denzel saw the purchases, he told his father that he looked like a nineteen nineties golfer!

Once the ceremony had finished and an excited Marianna had sat down to fan her flushed face, the first people to approach him were Barrasso and Floyd Hamilton, the pair laughing with each other. Barrasso, still grinning, came up close and looked around to make sure nobody was listening.

"Zammit, you're a piece of work! I was telling the major here what a useless piece of crap you were and how I wanted to send you home! Then, I get this call about you getting the ADSC and I had to do that video. You know, that medal says 'For Valour'! I say, no way, he's a pussy! Now, the major tells me, not only are you the Maltese Machine gun," he wrapped the phrase in inverted commas by flicking the first two fingers of each hand in front of him, "but you took out a Mooj at one thousand metres. That true? That's some shot!"

George shuffled uncomfortably.

"I can't deny I did it, but I never thought it would happen. I'm not sure I could do it again!"

The sergeant grinned and offered his hand.

"Well, you did it when it counted, buddy. Put it there, Zammit! But," he put his face close to George's ear and glanced around again, to make sure they could not be overheard, "I'll tell you now, if I ever see you lining up for one of my courses again, I swear, I'll fucking kill you myself!"

Barrasso and the major giggled like schoolboys.

George joined in the laughter, but his attention was diverted. He looked over towards the buffet table, where Marianna and Gina were enthusiastically engaged in conversation with the

Chargé d'Affaires and some Maltese government ministers. He realised he had better check to make sure his wife was not getting too carried away by the occasion.

As he approached, he heard her saying: "I just love America – all that countryside. It's very like Malta, from what I've seen, which is only on the television, of course."

The group laughed kindly and the Chargé d'Affaires said: "Well, when you come to visit, and I hope you do, you'll find America a whole lot bigger than Malta, that I guarantee."

George arrived just in time to divert the chat and steer Marianna and Gina away from the buffet table. Gina took her father's arm.

"Dad, he's very nice, the man in 'charge of the affairs'. He told us we should look him up when we visit. Do you think we can go to America? Do you know where he lives?"

"Let's start with Spain and we'll take it from there, don't you think?"

Marianna and Gina were glowing from all the attention, the occasion and the chance to parade in their new outfits. George smiled to see them so happy. He had been away for a long time and, now that he was making regular trips to Libya, it felt good to be home and see them happy, all together as a family.

In the corner, Mike Lloyd was talking quietly and earnestly to Gerald Camilleri, who subtly beckoned George over. George sighed.

"I was talking to Mike about that very unfortunate car bomb that killed your new employer's associate."

"*Mela*, but it wasn't unfortunate, was it? It was murder."

Mike Lloyd glared at George.

"Precipitated by the theft of a shit load of money by your new boss!"

Camilleri sighed and shook his head.

"Nothing to be gained by going down that road again, Mike."

"Well, how about my new posting then? Lima! What a shithouse! To avoid me 'rubbing certain people up the wrong way', I was told. That your doing, Gerald? Or maybe Lady Natasha whispered in the State Department's ear? Langley think it's hilarious. Serves me right for doing an off the books mission. Doesn't look good on my record, boys. Thanks!"

George could not help himself from replying.

"We all know who goes round whispering in people's ears, don't we, Mr Lloyd? That was what got Sergio Rossi killed, and remember who the actual target was! So, no, as far as my employer is concerned, Lima isn't far enough away for you. It's just a shame we couldn't get you to Lagos!"

Camilleri glared at George.

"That is enough!"

George reined himself in.

"Oh, I'm sorry, Gerald. Tell me, when did I start working for you again?"

Satisfied the point had been made and feeling pleased with himself, George turned and walked off to round up the family. He had booked a table for a late lunch at a restaurant overlooking Spinola Bay and his rumbling stomach told him to get out quickly, otherwise he would be at the buffet table and his new waistline would be under serious threat!

Camilleri had picked up Yaroslav Bukov at his hotel in St George's Bay, just as he was checking out. Moments later he would have been whisked off to the protection of the Russian Embassy, to await a flight back to Moscow, via Vienna.

As Yaroslav languished in Corradino Correctional Facility, a Victorian hell-hole of a jail, near the docks, Camilleri had telephoned Valentin Petrov, who took the call whilst at the prestigious White Rabbit restaurant, on the sixteenth floor of the Smolensky Passazh, in central Moscow. Petrov was being entertained by visitors from Baku and the conversation was just getting interesting, so he wanted to wrap things up quickly and get back to the table.

"Make it quick, Assistant Commissioner, it's not every day a humble government servant gets to take lunch at the White Rabbit."

"A deal, Mr Petrov, one in everybody's interest. Leave the Bonnicis alone. You have spilled blood, that is enough. This needs to end. If you agree, I will put Mr Bukov back on the next plane and relations between Malta and Moscow can continue as before while you can get back to your lunch.

"Say 'no' and I will bring Mr Bukov to trial and drag out the whole sorry mess, for the delight of the international press. I have nothing to lose. I can also inform you the government of the Republic of Malta will, as a matter of course, refuse permission for any of your naval vessels to refuel in Maltese territorial waters and we will embargo any bunkering vessels from refuelling on the Hurds Bank shallows."

That was a real threat. There were limited places the Russian Navy could refuel in the Mediterranean and, as Malta was a non-aligned country and not a member of NATO, it had, on occasion been able to help them out discreetly.

There was a pause as Petrov lit a cigarette and inhaled deeply. Camilleri could almost hear his thought processes at work and smiled to himself. There was only one sensible answer.

"Put him on a plane. You have your deal. Tell the Bonnicis never to visit Moscow."

"I doubt it is in their plans, but thank you. And enjoy your lunch."

CHAPTER 66
NATASHA BONNICI
ABOARD THE DASSAULT FALCON

TWELVE MONTHS LATER

NATASHA BONNICI WAS TIRED. It had been a long and difficult year, during which she had achieved all her goals and more besides. She was still young, fabulously successful, publicly feted and potentially richer than Forbes, or any of the other wealth lists, could ever guess. She had become the face of the European business world and it was only shortage of time that stopped her from capitalising on all the opportunities presented to her.

MalTech Energy was going from strength to strength and, soon, the VertWay spur would trigger the start of a five-year project to convert every home in Malta to natural gas. The Family's acquisitions in the Maltese construction sector meant there were few infrastructure projects in which they did not have a direct interest.

The on-sale of gas to the European distributors had been negotiated by Salvatore before his death, and revenues would soon start to flow. The fact that the Family had acquired large stakes in the distributors themselves meant that they had a double benefit from the arrangements!

The situation in western Libya was stable and Abdullah

Belkacem had proved to be a reliable partner, securing the supply from the on-shore oil and gas fields, whilst ensuring political stability through his control of the southern borders by a well-funded militia that maintained order. The port of Marsabar had been expanded and oil was being tankered out of the refinery in unprecedented volumes.

The success of the Tuareg in policing Libya's southern borders had led to a decrease in the numbers of migrants making the perilous journey through Libya to Europe. But, just as water finds its own course, so the traffic from Tunisia and Morocco had increased and the spotlight had now fallen on Spain, rather than Malta or Italy.

Adel Abu Khader, at the Marsabar Industrial Complex, had proved himself to be an astute operator and, as promised, had improved production markedly and made himself rich in the process. In a country, and an industry, renowned for corruption, Khader had told Natasha she could count on his honesty, if she gave him what he asked for. She had recognised that he was as good as his word and, on several occasions, George had been required to authorise the transfer of large amounts of money to Khader's new account with Antalya Bank's branch in Cyprus. It did not take the Family long to make the Libyan Resources Corporation an offer that they could not refuse for the whole of the Marsabar refinery and industrial complex

She was returning from Milan to Malta, after a meeting with the new Family Council, on the Dassault Falcon jet, a luxury, but one she thought she deserved. As with all new groupings, there had been arguments and egotistical tantrums from some members, so Natasha had had to stamp her authority on proceedings,

She often wondered why men – it was always men – had to be so difficult. She had never expected to find friends or allies on the Council and had understood it would take time to build trust and for everybody to take the measure of her. Sergio was dead and Marco had been as good as his word, formally retiring from the Family. She spent a lot of time alone or travelling these days.

In Malta, there was Refalo who, in fairness, helped manage the rat's nest that was the MalTech Energy Board, while in Milan, strictly behind her back, she was called the 'Black Spinster' who, they said, had single-handedly wiped out the Wise Men, bombed her uncle's car and exiled her father, to complete her rise to absolute power. If that was how they saw it, then Natasha was happy to let them believe it.

The only person she had in her life, with whom she could relax and be herself, was Nick, and even he kept her at a distance. She had only managed to lure him to a hotel room once, since his arrival back on the island. Even then, she had to break down his resistance with expensive champagne and Jack Daniel's. It did not matter; the sex had not been great, as he had been too drunk. She had stayed awake and watched him sleep, stroking his head, while he snored gently into his pillow.

Simon, Natasha's head of security, had hated Nick Walker since he had tricked him at the Gammarth Marina in Tunis, while on the run in Marco's stolen boat several years earlier. He was aware that Natasha was still fond of the man, so it had given him some satisfaction to mention casually to her that her reluctant beau had been seen having dinner with Amy Halliday, at the Waterfront in Valletta. He had added that he had been told they seemed very cosy together.

Natasha had thought nothing of it at first, but like all worms, it started to grow and grow, twisting itself around inside her stomach. She could not help herself; she had never known jealousy before and, over the course of a week, it had begun to consume her. She found herself dwelling on why Nick would prefer a saggy-breasted older woman, like Amy Halliday, to her.

Eventually, she could stand it no longer and asked Simon to follow Nick, to see if there was anything in the relationship. Simon had gone to the basement of the BetSlick offices and it had been easy enough to put a tracker on Nick's car. He did not go to

Amy's apartment and she did not go to his. He had told Natasha, in passing, that Amy was divorced and lived by herself in a new-build apartment, overlooking the entrance to Marsamxett Harbour. That should have satisfied her, but the poisonous thoughts continued.

When she was alone in the apartment in Milan, or at her flat in Portomaso, she would torture herself with visions of Nick and Amy in a hotel somewhere, in each other's arms, making love, holding one another, night after night. She imagined Amy stroking his smooth pale body and running her fingers through his fine blond hair. It was ridiculous, Natasha knew, but she could not stop the thoughts and it was driving her mad.

She started to think how easy it would be to get rid of Amy, how Nick would turn to Natasha for comfort as he mourned her passing. Natasha even went as far as finding Danylo's phone number and ringing him. He was the Ukrainian who had supplied the ricin that had killed Salvatore. He knew exactly who Natasha was and assured her, if she wanted to do business, he was happy to help. It was only Nick calling, to arrange to meet with her, that saved Natasha from ordering the poison.

Nick had invited her to a small underground bar in Valletta, famous for its cocktails and whisky collection. She was nervous and dreaded what he might say to her. She fussed with her hair, her outfit, her makeup and, at one point, was horrified to realise she might actually be late! What if she turned up and he had been and gone?

She need not have worried. As usual, when she had a meeting, she was punctual. Within minutes, Nick started telling her about Amy and relief flooded through Natasha, to the extent that she was nearly tearful.

"Listen, I've had a couple of dinners with that journalist over the last few months, Amy Halliday – you remember her?"

Natasha remembered her. She had thought of nobody else for weeks.

"It's pretty clear she's out to get you. She's digging around for information and has somehow found out about what happened between us in the villa."

"What? When you brained me with that vase and stole my jewellery and Dad's boat?"

"Oh, please, let's not go through all that again."

She laughed and reached across the table, taking his hand.

"I said there was nothing to it – but she's onto you. She says there's something 'off' about you popping up from nowhere to become one of the richest people in Malta, if not Europe, when a few months ago, nobody outside the gaming industry had even heard of you.

"She also thinks it's weird that BetSlick was closed down due to allegations of money laundering, with the Bonnici name being mentioned, then, weeks later, BetHi pops up with a Bonnici sitting in the big chair! She asked me how I felt about it?"

"She's still banging on about that? What did you say?"

"I said I needed a new challenge; the time was right for me to leave Malta, so I took an opportunity offered to me in Gib.

"Anyway what do you want me to do about Amy now? Keep having the occasional meet, to see where she's at, or just drop it?"

Natasha pulled on his arm, dragging him across the table towards her.

"I don't care either way, Nick. I don't want to have to get you drunk, every time I want to go to bed with you. So forget that old bitch -- I need you to come with me, now."

Nick was bemused.

"I thought we said ..."

"Right now, I don't care what we said. Just come with me!"

CHAPTER 67
MARCO BONNICI
ZLATIBOR ESTATE, UŽICE, WESTERN SERBIA

To the west of the market town of Užice, held tight in the valley of the Đetinja river, are the hills of Zlatibor. The region has high mountains, pine forests and alpine meadows that extend westward, all the way to the border of Bosnia and Herzegovina. The sub-alpine climate and the fact it is only a five-hour drive from Belgrade, mean visitors arrive here each summer, to escape the hot, muggy air of the capital.

After treeless Malta, Marco revelled in the cool, minty-smelling coniferous forests that covered the one thousand metre high plateau. There were a hundred days a year here when the high ground was covered in snow, which provided a new aspect to his life. His wardrobe was now filled with fleeces, expensive overcoats of breathable fabrics, as well as technical boots with high ankles and fancy lacing.

The land's limestone base was familiar to him but, rather than the stripped, pitted rock surfaces of Malta, here there was topsoil, foliage and water courses. He had caves, ravines and underground rivers that ran across his estate. During the winter months, he had set himself the task of designing a detailed tourist map of the area, to help visitors navigate and fully appreciate the landscaped features. He had become engrossed in the project; a seemingly simple ambition that had become a major undertaking.

He had a basic plan of the estate, but needed to develop the way the elevations, gradients and depressions were portrayed. He used an engraver's pen to draw the hachures, the parallel lines used in hill-shading on maps, their closeness indicating the steepness of gradients. He carefully washed areas of the map different shades of green or brown, to represent lower- and higher-lying ground. Benchmarks and features were identified and marked. His plantings were also identified and an index, written in a calligraphy font on a side box, described the most notable features. He realised that, given the size of the estate and the variety of the landscape, he had enough work ahead of him to see him through to the spring.

He had tried to fill his time, to be busy and not to brood. His departure from Malta had been a rushed and unpleasant affair. Camilleri had assured him an accommodation had been reached with Petrov so he no longer needed to be looking over his shoulder. He had met once more with Nick and reminded him to keep an eye on Natasha and ring him if he ever felt she was in trouble. Nick had wisely said that Natasha would probably always be on the margin of trouble, but never in it. Marco had only met with her once since the bombing, at Sergio's funeral. She had phoned him after the bomb and Marco, in a state of shock, had assured her he was all right. In fact, as he recovered his senses, he had realised he was very far from being all right.

Sergio's ex-wife had been indifferent to the news of his death. As far as she was concerned, he was already dead to her. The funeral they had endured, six months ago, was quite enough for a man such as him. She did politely enquire whether anything of value had been found that properly belonged in his estate.

Sergio Rossi's second burial was held on a stinking hot morning at the Neo-Gothic Santa Maria Addolorata Cemetery, on the outskirts of Valletta. Monumental tombs and family crypts lined the hillside as far as the chapel at the top of the hill. Addolorata was a true Gothic city of the dead. Marco had bought a suitably large and extravagant tombstone, surrounded by statues of angels, in bronze and marble. Natasha thought the flashy Sicilian would have appreciated the memorial. It had occurred to her that there could not have been too many people at rest in Addolorata who also had a similarly ornate tomb in the Cimitero Monumentale, in Milan!

Marco, Natasha, Camilleri, Nick, Katia and some of the *castello* staff had attended the funeral and there was no reception afterwards. To Marco's surprise, Sergio's daughter had turned up; a plump, busty young woman, with heavy eye makeup, tight black clothing and an air of confidence beyond her eighteen years. Natasha had spoken to her, but Marco only had the chance for the briefest of words, before she told him she did not blame him for what had happened and that she hoped this was the last funeral she would have to attend for her father – two were sufficient for anybody. She had then closed down the conversation, climbed into a waiting car and mysteriously disappeared. Marco had stayed behind at the grave and, as the others drifted off, removing their jackets and fanning themselves in the noon heat, Natasha chose that moment to approach her father.

"When do you go?"

"Soon."

"I'm sorry for this. I never …"

"No, you did not think, did you?" Marco snapped. "You can add Sergio Rossi to the list of people who have died as a result of your behaviour. I never thought I would have a murderer for a daughter."

He looked at her with resignation in his eyes.

"You have what you want now, all of it. It should have been me in that hole, not him. How would you feel then? Probably no different to how you feel now. You are cold and calculating. I am sorry for you. Now, go away and leave me alone. You have broken my heart too many times."

Natasha left Addolorata without another word, her face white and pinched.

Simon had found out the times of the two-hour flight from Malta to Belgrade and told her the date on which Marco had reserved a seat. On the morning of his departure, she had driven to the viewing layby on the road that ran around the airport perimeter, and had sat in her car, watching, as Marco's plane slowly processed from the apron to the end of the runway and then, its engines racing, accelerated until it rose and swept away, over her head.

She had briefly felt a sense of loss, but it was a shallow emotion, not one that burned away inside her, like the jealousy she had felt for Amy Halliday. She wondered if she would ever see her father again, whether he would someday return to Malta. The sale of the *castello* had gone through and Marco had been pleased at the speed with which the transaction had completed and at the price that had been achieved. He had also been surprised that the purchaser had offered to buy the entire contents apart from the valuable antiques he had already sold.

The eventual purchaser turned out not to be the consortium of hoteliers he had expected.

Natasha had set up a company, owned by an offshore trust, to buy it. She could not let part of her past disappear. It was the only remaining link she had to her father and her childhood. The plans to lease the estate lands to the farmers and establish co-operatives went ahead and Natasha retained Katia. The *castello* remained cared for, ready for Marco's return, should he ever choose to come home.

CHAPTER 68
GEORGE ZAMMIT
ABDULLAH'S FARMHOUSE, MARSABAR, LIBYA

IT HAD TAKEN A LITTLE TIME, but the farmhouse was eventually finished and it was beautiful beyond Rania's wildest dreams. Not only was there air conditioning in some of the rooms and a small pool for the children, but the tiled Italian showers and modern fitted kitchen were of a style and quality rarely seen outside the cities. Abdullah had urged caution.

"We do not want to make the family jealous and the neighbours covetous!"

But it was too late for that!

Abdullah had insisted on full terraces around the outside of the house, so they could move their seats around to enjoy the morning, afternoon and evening, while keeping a watchful eye on anyone who came within two kilometres. The building had a full range of security features and stood inside a secure perimeter, with a gate house and twenty-four-hour guards.

Abdullah had never forgotten the view from the hill to the south, over five years ago now, when he had seen the smoke rising from his brother's burning Mercedes and had to stand by and watch his home being violated by Abu Muhammad, while Rania and the children had scurried like rats through the escape tunnel. He would do everything he could to ensure nothing like that ever happened again. But he also understood that in this life there are no guarantees; Allah had a plan for everybody.

He and George were lounging in two deep wicker armchairs, on the western side of the house, watching the sun set while they drank tea. The children were enjoying the last of the evening. Abdullah's eldest son, Jamal, was kicking a football around with a group of local kids, who arrived every day, after school to swim in the pool and play football on the small Astroturf pitch Abdullah had laid behind the house, for exactly one hour and thirty minutes. At the end of the allotted time, the minibus that had, in earlier years, transported sub-Saharan migrants across Libya's deserts to Abdullah's compounds by the coast, collected the children and took them home. Jamal then had to do schoolwork. Abdullah amused George with his lectures on the virtues of education.

George came to Libya every two weeks and spent at least two days with Abdullah and two days in Tripoli, at the MalTech Energy offices. The minute he arrived in Tripoli he would change into a long, cotton, hooded *djellaba* and open-toed sandals. In town, he would wear the traditional Berber flat cap, the *shashiyah*, but when he went into the country, he would bind his head in a Tuareg *cheche*.

Abdullah was looking at George and examining his dress. He could not fault it – he did not look like a tourist or a European in fancy dress – but he did wonder why his friend bothered.

"Well, of course, it's more comfortable and when I come here, I prefer to look like a Libyan and think like a Berber. If people see me in a Western business suit, will I see all I need to see, or will they hide things from me? Looking like this, they'll think I am just another Berber!"

"No, my brother, you are wrong. Everybody knows who you are. You see nothing unless I want you to see it! Everything else, I tell them to hide!"

They laughed.

"There's something about wearing these clothes that makes

me feel as though I belong here. I'm not just George Zammit, former policeman, but George Zammit, Berber. Is that possible? Can I be Maltese and also come here, put on a *djellaba* and become a different man?"

"Yes, it is possible. Because I know this man! In Malta, the lady wife is the boss and he must do her bidding and speak only when spoken to. The old policeman, Camilleri, tricks and deceives him. Now, he is slave to the Lady Mantis and must be watchful, otherwise she will pull off his head!"

"Don't call her that! She's my boss," George laughed.

"Ah! But, here, he is different. He is brave and courageous; he can shoot a man at three thousand metres. He can tear a militia of Beards to pieces with any weapon you give him – a technical with cannon or a pistol. He is a soldier, with many medals for his bravery!"

Abdullah tapped his nose with his forefinger.

"I have seen this man do all this, with these eyes!"

George smiled at his antics.

"Be quiet! You don't know what you're saying."

Abdullah pointed two fingers towards his eyes.

"These eyes do not lie!"

"Drink your tea."

Abdullah laughed along with him.

"At least the lady wife is kind, forgiving and is a good cook. Unlike the Lady Natasha. So how long will you work for the mantis?"

"Hmm. I don't know. Until you've spent all the money, I suppose."

"So that could be a long time? That is good. Maverick needs his Goose." Abdullah looked at George, slyly.

"So does the Lady Mantis make you rich? You have to look after yourself. The Prophet said it is a duty to seek lawful earnings. He is never wrong. May peace be upon Him."

George looked across the coastal plain, towards the refinery some ten kilometres away. The flare stack glowed with an orange corona from the burning gases and the waste white steam rose vertically into the still evening sky.

"*Mela*, I'm as rich as a policeman could ever be, which is good, and despite your efforts to put me in an early grave, I'm still alive, which is even better. I take every day as it comes. Marianna is content, for the time being, and the children are healthy and happy. Who could wish for more?"

"My friend is always wise. May Allah always bless you with health and happiness."

Abdullah poured more green tea into the glasses and heaped his with three spoons of sugar. George smiled, refusing the sugar, patting his newly flat stomach.

He did not know how being with MalTech Energy would work out for him in the long term; at the moment, he was happy to be helping Abdullah. In addition to his substantial salary, Natasha had promised him a large bonus, conditional on him staying for two years, to see the 'project' established. George planned to put the cash to one side and make sure Marianna did not find it! When the time was right, it would be enough to buy a good-sized apartment for Denzel and one for Gina.

Evening was coming and the sparse fields were lit ßby a low sun. In the distance, Marsabar's dogs barked and howled the news of the day to each other.

George had been called upon to endure the privations of captivity. He had suffered beatings and illness. There had been no choice but to be subjected to periods of fear and panic. He had lost the security and comfort of his home and family. Out of it all, the loneliness had been the hardest thing to bear. None of what had happened to him was his choice or by his design.

At home, he was sent out for shopping. Marianna and Gina chided him and complained endlessly at his lack of practical skills, his inability to cook a meal, operate a washing machine, and the way his dinner always ended up on his shirt. Denzel humiliated him on the *bocci* pitch and called him 'old and square'.

By choosing to wear the *djellaba* and the *shashiyah* beret and oil his long beard, George felt he was taking back some control of who he was and how others saw him. He ceased to be George, the Maltese ex-policeman, husband and father, becoming Juriege the Berber, wingman of Maverick, eyes and ears of Lady Mantis, doer of daring deeds in the deserts of Libya!

There, he was respected. Doors were held open for him; cars waited, engines running, ready for his instructions. His best friend was one of the most powerful people in the country. His immediate boss was another. He had authority over enormous sums of money, he signed contracts, dispensed cash and, when his trips were urgent, was allowed to commandeer the Dassault Falcon – the private jet!

He would never choose one over the other, but to be able to be both was indeed a blessing! *Inshallah*!

EPILOGUE

AMY HALLIDAY, OFFICES OF THE MALTA TELEGRAPH

AMY HALLIDAY SAT SLUMPED, looking at the screen in front of her. Today, she had received another fifteen emails from the lawyers concerning the thirteen different cases, currently running against her and the *Malta Telegraph*, in the Maltese courts. That was not an unusual number. In fact, it was lower than she normally had to deal with. The subject of the legal actions were her articles and investigations into BetHi, MalTech Energy and the Bonnici family.

It seemed that every legal office on the island had been instructed by someone connected with Natasha Bonnici to bring a claim designed to censor, intimidate, or silence her and the paper, by burying them in a morass of legal proceedings, claiming criminal defamation, libel and actions to protect reputation.

In fact, there were so many firms of lawyers working for the Bonnicis and their companies that the *Telegraph* found it hard to engage anyone with any specialist knowledge in that area of law to act in their defence. She was told those doing the suing never expected to win the cases, but the so-called 'strategic lawsuits against public participation' – SLAPP actions – involved so much work and expense that most defendants found it impossible to contest them and inevitably sought terms of settlement.

The *Telegraph's* board of directors had already told Amy to back off the stories, to give them space, so they could try to get an agreement to withdraw the raft of frivolous claims that had been brought against them.

At first, she argued that the SLAPP lawsuits proved she was onto something important. Then she argued that the newspaper's duty to its readers was to refuse to be intimidated. Finally, she tried to defend the proceedings herself, acting without a lawyer. The harder she tried, the more applications, petitions and requests for further information piled up in her in-tray. Papers arrived by email and by post to her home. She was served notices and requests for information in person, in restaurants and in shops. It was so intense, she could almost believe there was a personal motive behind it all. She found most of her days consumed in pointless legal process which, of course, was the sole aim of SLAPP proceedings.

She was scared, exhausted and financially ruined. At the request of MalTech Energy, the courts had issued precautionary warrants, freezing the forty thousand euros savings in her bank accounts, as potential damages in defamation actions brought against her. Eventually, the *Telegraph* had washed its hands of her and formally warned her that, if she insisted on stirring up any more trouble, they were going to have to ask her to leave.

Her profile pieces on Natasha Bonnici and Nick Walker had been the first to attract legal proceedings. Attempts by her to name Nick as the whistle-blower on the Russian energy deal, were met with similar SLAPP proceedings. Her investigations into the source of monies used by MalTech Energy and its investor group to establish itself, met with more proceedings. An exposé centred on the Bonnicis' involvement with the oil-smuggling case of four years ago prompted a similar response.

None of the stories had ever appeared in print, but one or two blogs had started to circulate, suggesting that Natasha Bonnici was being heavy-handed in her attempts to silence the print media. Those journalists, too, had found themselves dragged into the courts and, despite their protests, their days became filled with endless legal work and their purses were emptied by the lawyers.

It had been a long day. At seven in the evening, Amy walked down to the badly lit underground car park, alone and despondent. Her white Nissan stood alone in a corner. She looked around and noticed there were no other cars on this level. It was getting late. Somewhere, she heard the echo of a loud metallic bang, as a steel fire door slammed shut on an upper floor of the car park. She opened the door with her remote and threw her bag, stuffed full of the day's legal papers, onto the back seat.

Wearily, she slumped into the driver's seat, checked her hair in the mirror, put one arm onto the top of the passenger seat to prepare to reverse and turned the key in the ignition.

ABOUT THE AUTHOR

AJ Aberford is a former corporate lawyer who moved to Malta several years ago. He is enthralled by the culture and history of the island that acts as a bridge between Europe and North Africa. Its position at the sharp end of the migrant crisis and the rapid growth of its tourist and commercial sectors provide a rich backdrop to the Inspector George Zammit series.

To keep up to date on AJ Aberford's fiction writing please subscribe to his website: **www.ajaberford.com**.

Reviews help authors more than you might think. If you enjoyed *Bullets in the Sand*, please consider leaving a review.

You can connect with AJ Aberford and find out more about the upcoming adventures of George and Abdullah, by following him on Facebook or, better still, subscribing to his mailing list.

When you join the mailing list you will get a link to download a novella, *Meeting in Milan*, a prequel to the Inspector George Zammit series.

ACKNOWLEDGMENTS

The Inspector George Zammit series is my debut work and I have too often been blind to my many mistakes. I thank my wife, Janet, for gently pointing them out, the time she has spent working on the various drafts and for her encouragement and support. I also thank my editor, Lynn Curtis, who has worked patiently with me, giving sage advice, steering the plots and refining the prose.

THE GEORGE ZAMMIT CRIME SERIES

Meeting in Milan (short-story prequel)

Bodies in the Water
Bullets in the Sand
Hawk at the Crossroads

MEETING IN MILAN

Short-story prequel available for free: www.ajaberford.com.

What is a family?

Two very different cousins, one from Malta and one from Sicily, are brought together to embark on their university studies in Bologna.

While spending time with their uncle and dying aunt in Milan, they learn some truths about themselves and realise that family is not what it seems.

In the space of a few short weeks, they have a decision to make. It is a choice that could change their lives forever and, once made, there will be no going back …

HAWK AT THE CROSSROADS

George Zammit returns in *Hawk at the Crossroads*

Pre-order now.

Turkey is the new powerbroker in the eastern Mediterranean and The Hawk sits in Istanbul, pulling the strings. But why should any of this concern a Maltese policeman?

Inspector George Zammit, of the Maltese *Pulizija*, receives a phone call from an old friend in need, the Libyan militia leader, Abdullah Belkacem. As a result, George and Abdullah are catapulted into an adventure, taking them from disputed Greek Islands to war-torn Libya, in a journey that tests their friendship to the limit.

As an arch manipulator and power broker, The Hawk plays his cards close to his chest. But, with one daring move, he turns the politics of the eastern Mediterranean upside down, making a powerful enemy.

Natasha Bonnici is now the head of a mysterious organised crime family, based in Milan. She and The Hawk circle each other, as the biggest game of all plays out.

Can lowly Inspector George Zammit face these forces and restore order, before the s slips into chaos?

If you like Henning Mankell's *Wallander* books, or those of Michael Dibden's *Aurelio Zen*, you will love *Hawk at the Crossroads*, with its unique blend of humour, drama and adventure. George Zammit is to Malta, what 'Montalbano' is to Sicily or Donna Leon's 'Commissario Guido Brunetti' is to Venice.

Here follows a taster ...

CHAPTER 1
O. R. TAMBO INTERNATIONAL AIRPORT – JOHANNESBURG

SANT'AGATA PRISON, AVELLINO, ITALY

South African diamonds are legally exported in secure containers with specifically numbered and government-validated certificates. This regulates the trade in stones mined in the warzones of Africa that have caused misery to so many, for so long. It's for good reason that such stones are often referred to as 'blood diamonds'.

Christina Cassar had passed through the security scanner of O. R. Tambo International Airport, overseen by a lethargic, slack-jawed woman whose glazed eyes only occasionally drifted towards the screen in front of her. Christina gathered her blue cabin bag, cosmetics, jacket, and slipped her feet into her expensive sandals. She took the soiled grey plastic tray and headed towards the stainless-steel packing table. They were in no hurry, having plenty of time left before their fifteen-hour flight back to Malta, via Amsterdam. She and her boyfriend, Nick Walker, had spent the last week at an industry conference at Sun City, the large resort 140 kilometres to the north-west of Johannesburg.

There, Nick had attended a relaxed programme of presentations and workshops, meeting colleagues and friends from the world of online gaming. During the day Christina read at the poolside, and when Nick was free, they had visited the Madikwe

Game Reserve, played golf and enjoyed the resort's spas and pools. At night, they dined, took in shows in the big hotels, and Nick took Christina onto the gaming floors of the casinos, explaining why it was odds-on she would never get her money back once she had converted it into chips.

He was at an adjacent security scanner, putting his belt back through his trouser loops and re-packing his laptop, when he noticed a group of four Hawks walking slowly down the security hall. South Africa's Priority Crime Investigation brigade, the Hawks were a much-feared branch of the police and their appearance usually meant trouble for somebody. They wore black berets, short-sleeved blue shirts, stab jackets, and their trouser legs tucked down inside high, black lace-up boots.,

Christina's cabin bag had glided through the scanner. She hadn't noticed the security woman, apparently watching the endless parade of personal items passing before her, signal to a colleague with a nod. He had helpfully corrected the position of the blue cabin bag on the conveyor belt and, in doing so, deftly slipped a paper envelope into one of its external pockets.

When diamonds are traded in Amsterdam, Surat in India or even Kinshasa, it is traditional to package them in a small paper envelope with a waxy blue interior finish. *Briefke* is the Flemish word for this envelope, and it is used by everybody in the diamond trade. Christina didn't realise it, but the *briefke* inside the front pocket of her cabin bag held about 1,000 carats of diamonds, or 240 grams, with a retail value of over $1 million US for accredited stones.

Nick saw the Hawks looking over at the scanner where Christina was fussing, repacking her cosmetics. He zipped up his briefcase and noticed one of the policemen tap a colleague on the arm and point in Christina's direction. Two of them walked slowly towards her, their thumbs tucked under the shoulder straps of their stab jackets. One was smiling and started engaging her in conversation. He watched as she produced her passport and boarding pass, which the Hawk took from her and inspected. Nick smiled to himself. He knew Christina had nothing to fear, but she would be petrified by the big, intimidating police officers in their military-style uniform.

Nick was walking towards her when the second officer started gathering her things from the packing area. He took her cabin bag, her purse and her jacket, while the first man laid his hand on her arm. Nick was becoming concerned. He arrived in time to hear his agitated girlfriend saying: "What are you doing? Those are my things."

The first officer put her passport and boarding pass into the pocket of his stab jacket, then looked at her with an expression that had curdled.

"You must come with us."

Christina saw Nick approach and stepped towards him, fear on her face.

"Nick, they want to take me with them. They've got my things."

Confused, he spoke to the officer who seemed to be in charge, noticing the sergeant's stripes on his epaulettes.

"Hey, what's going on? You can't take her away, she's done nothing wrong."

He'd made to take her hand and pull her towards him when the two Hawks who had initially stood back quickly moved in and grabbed his arms, roughly pulling them behind him. The man with the sergeant's stripes spoke loudly in his ear.

"Who are you to her? Are you two travelling together?"

"Yes, we live together. Now let us go! Get off me!"

There was a brief scuffle as he tried to shake himself free, until he realised he was making things worse for both of them. He forced himself to relax and turned to Christina, saying, "Let's go with them and get this sorted out – whatever they think it is."

Turning to the sergeant who was holding him, he said: "It's OK, we're coming with you."

The police officer relaxed his grip and said: "Sensible of you. We go this way."

He nodded to his colleagues and they set off. Christina grabbed Nick's hand and the pair of them were marched, closely surrounded by the four Hawks, through the endless corridors of the airport. Heads turned and people sidestepped as the Hawks paraded the couple through the terminal to the airport police station. There they were split up and held in separate, stifling interview rooms.

The sergeant interviewed Christina first, after placing her cabin bag at his feet. He looked at her for a while then said: "Is there anything you want to tell me?"

"No. I don't understand what this is all about."

With a shrug, he reached down to her bag and slipped his hand into the front pocket.

Christina gasped in horror and put her hand to her mouth when he produced the white *briefke* and let a small stream of glittering stones tinkle onto the metal table between them. His gaze met hers as, without a word, he slowly gathered up the stones and put them back into the envelope.

The sergeant sighed deeply and closely studied the shocked and tearful young woman, sitting shaking on a wooden chair bolted to the floor. She was a pretty, slightly built woman, with short, pixie-cut blonde hair, clusters of freckles on her cheeks and piercing blue eyes. Tears had smudged her mascara and reddened her lids. Her tip-tilted nose was running slightly. She looked and felt very small in the presence of the bulky law-enforcement officer across the table from her.

Sergeant Enzokuhle Lubanzi was not a man given to pity. He had seen too many tears and heard too many cries of innocence. If he had any sympathy, it was for those who were forced into wrongdoing by threats from organised-crime gangs or else by desperate poverty. He'd seen plenty of that, but here sat a well-dressed white woman, returning from a week in Sun City, with a business-class ticket to a destination half-way across the world, smuggling what could be a million dollars' worth of blood diamonds. If compassion had been in his makeup, he wouldn't be wasting it on a person such as this.

He said: "You won't know this, but the nickname for the Women's Correctional Facility in Johannesburg is also Sun City. Ironic, hey? You won't see much sun, but there is gambling and the inmates are very like the wild animals on the Madikwe Reserve.

HOBECK BOOKS – THE HOME OF GREAT STORIES

We hope you've enjoyed reading this novel by AJ Aberford. To keep up to date on AJ Aberford's fiction writing please subscribe to his website: **www.ajaberford.com** and you will also be able to download the free novella *Meeting in Milan*.

Hobeck Books also offers a number of short stories and novellas, free for subscribers in the compilation *Crime Bites*.

- *Echo Rock* by Robert Daws
- *Old Dogs, Old Tricks* by A B Morgan
- *The Silence of the Rabbit* by Wendy Turbin
- *Never Mind the Baubles: An Anthology of Twisted Winter Tales* by the Hobeck Team (including many of the Hobeck authors and Hobeck's two publishers)
- *The Clarice Cliff Vase* by Linda Huber
- *Here She Lies* by Kerena Swan
- *The Macnab Principle* by R.D. Nixon
- *Fatal Beginnings* by Brian Price
- *A Defining Moment* by Lin Le Versha
- *Saviour* by Jennie Ensor
- *You Can't Trust Anyone These Days* by Maureen Myant

Also please visit the Hobeck Books website for details of our other superb authors and their books, and if you would like to get in touch, we would love to hear from you.

Hobeck Books also presents a weekly podcast, the Hobcast Book Show, where founders Adrian Hobart and Rebecca Collins discuss all things book related, key issues from each week, including the ups and downs of running a creative business. Each episode includes an interview with one of the people who make Hobeck possible: the editors, the authors, the cover designers. These are the people who help Hobeck bring great stories to life. Without them, Hobeck wouldn't exist. The Hobcast can be listened to from all the usual platforms but it can also be found on the Hobeck website: **www.hobeck.net/hobcast**.

OTHER HOBECK BOOKS TO EXPLORE

The Rock Crime Series by Robert Daws

The magnificent Rock crime series from acclaimed British actor Robert Daws – includes free bonus story *Echo Rock*.

'An exciting 21st-century crime writer.'
Peter James

'A top crime thriller.'
Adam Croft, crime writer

Detective Sergeant Tamara Sullivan approaches her secondment to the sun-soaked streets of Gibraltar with mixed feelings. Desperate to prove herself following a career-threatening decision during a dangerous incident serving with London's Metropolitan Police, Sullivan is pitched into a series of life-and-death cases in partnership with her new boss, Detective Chief Inspector Gus Broderick. An old-school cop, Broderick is himself haunted by personal demons following the unexplained disappearance of his wife some years earlier. The two detectives form an uneasy alliance and friendship in the face of a series of murders that challenge Sullivan and Broderick to their limits and beyond.

The Rock crime series transports readers to the ancient streets of the British Overseas Territory of Gibraltar, sat precariously at the western entrance to the Mediterranean and subject to the jealous attention of neighbouring Spain. Robert Daws shows his mastery of the classic whodunnit with three novels rich in great characters, tense plotting full of twists and turns and breath-taking set-piece action.